Death's I ...

Patricia Dixon

To

My dear friend
Jo

with love
from

Trish
x

Also By Patricia Dixon

Over My Shoulder
They Don't Know

Praise For Patricia Dixon

It is truly a gripping and shocking story from start to finish and just shows how easy it is to fall in with thewrongpeople. This book covers lots of issues which might shock some readers, so be warned there is some violence and domestic abuse. Patricia Dixon has written sympathetically and emotionally about some very difficult issues and I think she's done a great job of giving realism to a fictional story. **Rose – Top 500 Amazon Reviewer**

Well done, Patricia – you not only hooked me, but you didn't let me go until the very last word. I am spent! **Helen Laycock – Amazon Reviewer**

Patricia Dixon has written with incredible insight in to the horror that is domestic abuse. She writes with authority but also sensitivity and realism. The setting of the scenes and the language used are so realistic and evocative of the time. Sometimes difficult and harrowing to read it covers a subject which blighted our society. An incredible book. I'm going to read it again and would recommend it to everyone. Bring on the next one. **Jelibebe – Amazon Reviewer**

The pace and suspense ramps up as the story unfolds to a point you feel like you are holding your breath. This was in no way an easy read, but it isn't meant to be easy. It's dark undertones really make for a Gripping Compulsive page turner. A dark Pyschological Thriller that will get under your skin! **Dash Fan – Goodreads Review**

Over My Shoulder is a captivating novel and one that I would highly recommend to all fans of psychological and domestic noir thrillers. (less) **Neats – Goodreads Review**

For Pearl

I wanted to write your name, for others to know it,
and say the words out loud,
And when the ink has dried it will be etched on paper forever,
Just as the memory of you is engraved on our hearts,
and will be for all time,
We miss you every day.
Love you always.

Prologue

Tenley House

I am woken once again from my fitful slumbers and as always, rather than alert anyone to the fact that I have survived a few more hours, I listen. They say that hearing is the last sense to go and my ears, unlike the rest of my body, have not yet failed me. Once I have ascertained that I am alone, grateful for the absence of heavy breathing, a sure sign my dark angel is by my side, I am forced to accept the fact that death has not kindly released me. At this, I am immediately overwhelmed by disappointment which is accompanied by its familiar friend, resignation.

While my reluctant eyelids lift, railing against instructions from my brain, I note that darkness is about to fall and my room is illuminated by the glow from the lamp. I tilt my head to the side and welcome a sense of relief. My pleasures are few these days and I take comfort from the strangest of things, like the sight of an empty armchair. I am glad to be alone and not in the company of my frequent and unwelcome guest, she who insists on keeping vigil, talking incessantly of the past, stroking my forehead with clumsy, clammy hands, constantly asking if there's anything I need. I don't. Not from her, not anymore.

On this occasion I am disturbed by pain, the back of my hand throbs and stings so. The source of my metacarpal discomfort is that dreadful canula which they changed earlier, inserting a sliver of stainless steel through my skin, piercing liver-spotted flesh no thicker than tissue and scraping over bone, causing me to wince. I imagine my hands are covered with plum and wine-coloured bruises and should I be brave enough to look upon myself in a mirror, I would pronounce that I've been in wars. But at least my minor injuries serve another purpose. They prevent handholding. This and my frailty is a useful barrier because I cannot bear for her to touch or caress me. It causes my skin to crawl.

Despite my frequent protestations, they insist on pumping a concoction of liquids into ever narrowing veins that are just about wide enough to allow passage of blood, let alone medicine. I am restless. My bedsores irritate but I do not call for assistance. Instead I try to shift beneath the counterpane but alleviating my discomfort, caused by my bony bottom and skeletal frame as they chafe against the linens, is too great an effort. No matter how many times they turn me from this side to the next hoping to avoid bedsores, the routine causes more agony than relief, forcing me to cry out and beg them to desist. And that is not the only indignity I am forced to endure. There's the washing and feeding. I hate it. Every flannel bath, nappy change, and spoonful of mashed up food which they cajole me into eating is degrading. Ha, just like my body I suppose.

Why, oh why do they bother? If I could move my arms sufficiently I'd tear out that damn canula and allow my life and the saline to dribble away, fluids soiling the floor and mattress. You will never know what a blessed relief my demise would be. I've even considered death by obstinacy. Surely they can't force-feed me. They only do that in prisons, don't they, or to suffragettes? No matter, because I expect the two who care for me on a rota system, my busy little hamsters who perform the same demeaning tasks day in day out would find some way of injecting or infusing nutrition.

In any other circumstance, during those young and carefree years when my purpose in life was to live happily and pain free, for as long as possible, I'd be counting my blessings and grateful for their help. I would have convinced myself that it was a vocational act of compassion, attention given kindly to a patient in need. This is nothing of the sort and merely a chore to be sighed through, food scraped then spoon-fed. Their impatience is a default setting, heads turned in disgust as another grim task is ticked off the list. Perhaps I'm just being tetchy and a tad ungrateful because the hamsters are efficient and to others, appear dedicated to tending my every need, however, one might attribute their devotion more to the fees they charge for private nursing. It pays to keep me alive, even for one more daily rate.

I wish they'd just leave me to die. Seventy-two years on this earth is quite enough and I would like to go now. I've asked them many times but they simply smile and shush me, announcing that I'm confused. But I'm not. I am all there, or here! I'm not loopy or gaga, even though I do wonder if it would be a blessed release to be so. As it is, I remain trapped within a forlorn body and have no other option than to languish at the mercy of my memories, clear and crisp as if they happened yesterday. The past refuses to fade away and only serves to haunt me. I am prisoner of both and this wretched house. And her.

It is her selfishness which suspends me, refusing me leave, conniving and wilful as ever. Dear God, how did such subservience infest me? It is like a disease but not the kind that ultimately sets one free, this pathetic state has me trapped.

I wish I didn't have to die here, in this decrepit place of death and sadness where every room is thick with dust and wicked secrets, but needs must. It serves a purpose, and once I have made my peace, I will be free. I long to go, even if it means joining my ghostly companions. They appeared soon after we arrived, an unwelcoming committee. At first I did think I was losing my mind or the drugs pumped into me were poisoning my brain. But I've got used to my spirit visitors and although I'd prefer they stayed away, I am sure they mean me no harm. They are just waiting, that's all. And they are angry.

Of course I understand why, so I've tried to make amends, whispering apologies for my own weakness and perceived avarice, begging them to listen. Surely they can see my sorrow and just as they, there have been moments when I have known fear, so much fear. But it seems my penitence and suffering is not enough. They want more. To be precise, my impatient guests seek revenge but then again so do I.

They haven't arrived yet, tending to keep their distance during daylight hours so I attempt to stay awake. A few moments of respite from their constant haranguing is all I ask because when night falls and shadows fill the room, they gather in the corner over there, just by the armoire. One perches on the fauteuil chair, one paces the floor, one wrings her hands while the other who holds the baby, she just stands and stares.

Black crows, that's what they are, emerging from the grey mist that seeps from the cracks in the warped floorboards, chilling the air. That's how I know they are here. It reminds me of stepping into the cold store down in the cellar where if you tarry too long, the ice freezes your marrow. And although I have resolved to keep my eyes closed for as long as I can, I still feel their presence.

Their images are as real and defined as the last time I saw them in the flesh whereas now, they greet me from the periphery of another dimension, just out of reach. Dressed in the deepest black of mourning, it is the women who disconcert me most. I recognise them all from their stature and demeanour, just able to distinguish their features. Their respectful garb is macabre and causes me to shudder. It always did. Each woman is wrapped in death's dark veil, watching me from behind a gossamer sheath yet I know them still, despite such theatrical concealment.

The one who wrings her hands stands obediently at the side of the chair where is seated The Crone. She has reverted to type. Even Holy Communion hasn't softened her and she irritates me still with the tap tap tapping of her dratted cane, sardonically marking whatever time I have left. And then I see him, pacing the floor, the only one for whom I feel deep sorrow and longing. I did love him, you know? We loved each other so much, in our own way. He hasn't changed a bit, in manner or devilishly handsome looks. His eyes won't meet that of the woman who confers with The Crone, and I know why. He cannot bear his deceit of her, agitated further by the threat of confrontation so he remains weak, even in death.

But it is she, the one holding the baby, who I cannot bear to look upon for she has been wronged the most, and so cruelly. She stands to the rear of the group, still an outsider, looking in, and this belated observance makes me want to weep. Yet amidst my sadness and regret for this woman, I am grateful too for the care she gives the baby who belongs not to her. From the first time the visions appeared, I watched her soothe the crying infant, rocking it to and fro and it occurred to me that she might be claiming her pound of flesh. In truth this supposition does not vex, if anything it makes me hopeful, absolved even. The soul liveth on. If it makes her happy or recompensed, then so be it.

The bedside clock chimes six and I know that the light of this spring day will soon fade and despite my insistence that the lamps are left on, my attempt to ward off the visitors is, I accept, feeble and futile. They will return again tonight more so because the end is near. I know this. The clearer they become the closer I am to death. I sense it. Perhaps they are draining my life source and if so they can take it, be my guests. But before I am allowed to depart I have to keep my whispered promise to them. I must make things right. They crave reparation in this mortal life before the judgement of the next so I shall set things in motion and then destiny can choose its own course. Even the smallest reprisal might be all that is needed to allow them rest, so we all can rest.

I have thought it through, spent hours going over it all, right back to the beginning in order to make sense of events. Lord knows I have carried this burden for long enough but finally I can place my load, this guilt, onto the shoulders of another. Confession they say is good for the soul and over the years I have contemplated the weakness of mine. Finally, at the end, I find some comfort in the notion that I am being given one more chance and there is hope yet for my own élan vital.

Footsteps in the corridor, swift and light, which tell me it's the nurse. Good. She can finish her duties then once I am calm and prepared I shall have *her* summoned. Then I will make my peace in the company of the ghostly tormentors. When it is done, after the words I have waited to say are spoken, I will leave this world, one way or another. Be it peacefully or at the hands of a monster. Either way I will be free.

Part I

Chapter 1

Georgie

As the train trundled southwards, Georgie's body rocked gently, the motion of the train slightly soothing, lulling her into a thoughtful state. Maybe it was time to take stock of her life so far, think seriously about how she had ended up like this – perishing to death in a second-class carriage. Whilst being well aware of her own failings which she placed to one side, after piecing snippets of Nibley family history and salacious gossip together, Georgie was sure that most of the blame lay with others.

At birth, despite being the most perfect and golden-haired first grandchild, she had been unimaginatively named Winifred in honour of her departed and much-revered great-grandmother. However, according to family folklore, the moment she learned to express an opinion the tiny tot with an endearing lisp announced that she preferred Georgie, derived from her second name, Georgina.

Georgie smiled at the conjured image of her younger self and those early years in the small south Oxfordshire town of Harlbury where after her birth in late 1945, she was glad to have remained the only child of Clifford Nibley. On being discharged from the army, her father had embarked on a summer dalliance with the first willing young lady to cross his path, or in this case, seated opposite during a hot and bumpy bus journey.

During Boxing Day tea, Georgie sat beside her Aunty Mae, who told you all sorts of naughtiness after a couple of sherries, and on this occasion had been happy to explain how Georgie was conceived. According to her, it occurred during a fumble in the back of a hay cart when Mavis, weary of wartime rationing that included all manner of things, unleashed Clifford's similarly pent-up emotions. Two months later, randy Clifford was forced to do the honourable thing and marry Mavis, the shame-faced, deflowered and disgraced third daughter of the town butcher and sister of gossipy Mae.

"If you ask me, our Mavis thought she'd struck gold when she met your dad and I wouldn't put it past her to have planned it all. She was always a conniving minx and thought she was better than us, even when we were kids. You mark my words, all that snivelling when she found out she was up the tub was just an act. Our Mave can't fool me." Mae gave Georgie a knowing look, her raised, pencilled eyebrows rising at least an inch higher than normal.

"I can't believe Mummy would do such a thing... surely they were just madly in love and had a little accident." At fourteen Georgie was already wise to the ways of the world, albeit second-hand via her giggly school friends, but at the time, still believed in true love.

"In my book, accidents occur randomly and I'll tell you this for nothing, our Mave couldn't wait to get out of the shop and up that lane to meet your dad. At it like rabbits they were, every night of the week and you, my love, are certainly not an accident. Still, she got her comeuppance because them Nibley's acted like they'd trod in a pile of smelly dung when they found out and let's face it, your mam isn't exactly brimming with happiness, is she?" Mae's eyebrows raised once more, her eyes rolling in the direction of her sister who was seated alone in the corner, a plate of uneaten sandwiches on her knee while she sipped her drink and gazed off into space.

Georgie followed her aunt's direction. "Yes, I must say she does look rather glum but I thought it was down to these awful fish paste sarnies, not because she's been a naughty girl." While she and Mae tittered, a voice in Georgie's head told her to take note and remember that actions, no matter how thrilling, have consequences. The last thing Georgie wanted was to end up like her soggy sandwich mother, stuck in a corner like a dollop of dismal cow poo.

The paternal family mole came in the form of Great Uncle Albert. While he sometimes lost the plot during his ramblings, he usually came up with the goods in between slurping one or three double scotch on the rocks. Whilst despairing of the unfortunate match and henceforth enduring the hastily arranged wedding, it seemed that Georgie's grandparents could only pray 'The Situation' wouldn't affect Clifford's job at the bank *or* sully their reputation.

Great Uncle Albert had a way with words, perhaps his salty old sea-dog past was to blame but his hushed sharing of the family indiscretions still made Georgie smile, even on a hellish train journey suffering from a runny nose and goose pimples.

It was during Grandfather Nibley's birthday celebrations that fifteen-year-old Georgie took the opportunity to interrogate her half-pickled great uncle. All she had to do was ask him about the good old days and what her daddy was like when he was a boy. After enduring The Great War and Oxbridge days, Georgie was relieved when Albert finally got around to Clifford.

"Oh aye, he's a randy old bugger your father… runs in the family don't you know. We've all got plenty of lead in our pencils. That's for sure. I could tell you a tale or two about my navy days and what I got up to when we reached port." Albert winked at Georgie, his whisky breath settled on her cheek like mist yet rather than recoil, she leaned in, not too close though, eager to hear more.

"That's good to know, Uncle, but I don't think Grandmother would be too pleased about you telling me saucy tales… on the other hand, I am curious to know about Daddy. I always had him down as a bit of a bore." Georgie kept her cheek turned, she knew that Uncle Albert was fond of sneaking a peck or two, and trying not to smirk, she also kept her eyes focused on her father rather than the bulge that had appeared in her uncle's trousers.

"Like I say, he's a bit of a cad and has an eye for the ladies… but there's nothing wrong with having a dabble and dipping your wick. Kept my dead-in-the water marriage alive for years and your father is no different. But that's all hush-hush, strictly off the record, if you know what I mean?" Albert tapped the side of his nose and had a sneaky peak down Georgie's top.

Trying to hide her excitement at being told such salacious facts, Georgie feigned concern. "But does Grandmother know about Daddy? Surely she would have a blue-fit if she knew and Mummy would divorce him, I'm sure of it."

"Of course she does, your grandmother knows everything that goes on in this family. Blasted Mata Hari's got nothing on her. She's a wily old devil and gives her men folk a long leash, as long as the mud doesn't stick."

"But what about Mummy, do you think she knows? And why is Grandmother so mean to her?" Georgie had a feeling she already knew the answer to that.

"Because Mata Hari over there wanted better for her son than a shop girl, it's as simple as that. And as for your mother, who appears to be permanently sucking lemons, I surmise she is fully aware of your father's indiscretions. Everyone else is."

"And what about me… why is Grandmother so kind and generous when it comes to the unwanted child of a shop-girl?" Georgie sounded indignant rather than sorry for herself.

"Mata Hari likes a project and I think she was sick to the back teeth of Nibley men cocking things up so she's set her sights on you. Just make sure you're a good girl and all will be well. As long as you don't get caught with your knickers round your ankles you'll be fine. Now bring me a refill, all this gassing has given me a thirst."

Georgie stood and took his glass. After the knicker comment, she steadfastly avoided looking at Albert's groin and grimaced as his hand patted her bottom. Pushing certain nauseating thoughts to one side, Georgie concentrated on her new-found nugget of information and as she topped up her uncle's glass, resolved to keep a very close eye on dirty Daddy Clifford. After all, knowledge was power.

Despite being the fruit of disappointment, and whilst fully aware of her family's many failings, golden-haired Georgie made the most of being adored by the Nibleys. She was happy to be cosseted and indulged, doted on yet carefully managed by those who aspired to greater things and at all costs, avoided another entrapment of their clan.

Georgie did have the grace and intelligence to notice that whilst she rested on a pedestal, her mother remained on the periphery, looked down upon and frequently disregarded, as were her maternal kinfolk, referred to generally as 'The Butchers'. And while it sometimes saddened her, Georgie felt it wasn't her place to comment and after all, Mother was a grown woman and could fight her own battles, or should at least have tried. Anyway, Georgie knew by whom her bread was buttered and she preferred it on both sides.

The train stopped at some rural back of beyond, and while passengers swapped places and thankfully the chap with the roving eye had buggered off, Georgie ruminated. Perhaps she was in fact the arch manipulator of the family and the others merely pawns in a game. It was a pleasing notion that caused her to smile, that and the irony of being taught well.

In the company of those who took points from all manner of things, Georgie feigned reluctance at spending time with her maternal grandparents when in truth, she enjoyed immensely her once-monthly visits to the home of the Butchers because there too she was treated like royalty. Georgie was their curiosity. She spoke so beautifully and her school photograph, the one wearing a straw boater and blazer, was dusted with pride and shown to the customers with regularity. But whilst her relationship with the Nibleys was superficial and artificial, Georgie's feelings for 'The Butchers' were genuine.

Georgie always loved that cosy feeling when they sat around the kitchen table for tea, eating chunks of thickly sliced bread and golden brown chips cooked in a huge frying pan, with your fingers and not a knife and fork. At Christmas she would receive a stocking, identical to her cousins and stuffed with penny treats and knick-knacks from Woolworths, nothing fancy but given with genuine love. In between special occasions, her nan knitted lovely jumpers, a scarf, woolly hats and mittens in winter, but best of all, the thing Georgie looked forward to on the bus journey into town were the squashy hugs.

Nan had bestowed these upon Georgie for no particular reason other than that she loved her, the scent of talcum powder and baking enveloping her as soon as she walked through the door and when she said goodbye. At home they didn't hug, just a peck on the cheek at bedtime or after a story from whichever parent was on duty. The Nibleys appeared to frown upon shows of affection. Georgie suspected they thought it common.

Hugs and chips aside, Georgie was ever curious as to how the other half lived and her large extended family, whose lack of social grace was a constant source of entertainment, became the most practical form of education. The Butchers served as a warning, a reminder and testament to many things, and during each visit Georgie would watch intently. Human interaction, especially that between her mother and grandparents, was utterly fascinating.

When the train pulled out of the station, the image in her head caused Georgie to smirk. Perhaps her parents should have done the same during their fated fumble because the treatment of Mummy Mavis was so unlike that of Daddy Clifford, the other guilty party in what everyone considered to be a consensual coupling. As she matured it had occurred to Georgie that unlike her mother, her father had simply pulled up his zip and got on with life. Somehow, Mavis had been rendered disjointed. Not fully welcome or accepted by her snobbish in-laws she was then silently punished by her family, perhaps for being too much of a stranger, changing sides, looking down or becoming subservient and not fighting back. Whatever it was, Mavis remained on the edge of both worlds.

The notion of Georgie's mother's predicament was accompanied by a tingling of fear. Being cast adrift, rejected even, was something to be avoided at all costs. Her father was an only child and his singularity had presumably been his saving grace whereas her mother was one of many and surplus to requirements. Georgie, however, had her feet firmly in both camps and had endeavoured to reap the advantages so worked hard at fitting in, wherever and whatever the situation. Faking it was easy once you knew how.

Like the fact she hated going through to the shop where the smell of meat and sawdust made her retch, as did the carcasses of disembowelled rabbits that hung in the windows and the swollen ox tongues that were laid in trays beneath them. But Georgie never let it show, seeing it as a test, presenting another face to the world, one which also hid her growing disdain for those around her. Not for the Butchers, but for the Nibleys. Georgie didn't wish to upset her maternal grandparents in any way so her resilience served her well whereas in the case of the others, Georgie played the game for entirely different reasons.

Apart from the necessary rudiments of life that so far hadn't challenged her to any great extent, Georgie had found it all far too easy. Beauty was just something she was born with and if she hadn't been a clever clogs, would have had to rely more on being sweet and demure, kind and loving, because that was a sure-fire way to get what you wanted. As it happened, most things were given to her on a fine china plate, right from the beginning.

Georgie had lapped it up and loved taking piano and ballet, deportment and elocution lessons, along with how to ride, play tennis and croquet. She had been dressed as any good upper-middle-class young lady should be, in the very best that her paternal grandmother could buy with her husband's substantial savings. Georgie was also popular at school, and until recently admired by the brothers of girls in her group and more than likely still lusted after by those who should know better. With no clear destination in mind, apart from someday making a good match of her own choice, not forced down the aisle with a bouquet hiding her belly, Georgie accepted she had merely jogged through life, untroubled by what the future held.

The motion of the train was making Georgie sleepy, causing her to yawn, bored also by the relentless tableau of fields and backwater stations so giving in, she closed her eyes and focused on the past, the best bits. Her epiphany occurred quite out of the blue during a sixteenth birthday treat when everything became so wonderfully clear. She could picture it all, her parents and grandparents dressed to the nines; the women swaddled in fur, red lipped and smothered in scent; the men in dark suits, smelling of cigars and brandy. They had all driven down to London for dinner and an evening at the theatre and there, in the darkness of the front row, lower circle, Georgie became struck by stars. Mesmerised by the other-worldly thespians that glided across the stage, enunciating words of great playwrights, educing gasps from balcony to stalls, basking in the glow of stage lights to the rapturous applause of an adoring audience, Georgie knew she had found her place.

Later, during the drive home squashed between a grizzly bear and a snow leopard, Georgie had announced to her family that the theatre was where her destiny lay.

Georgie clapped her hands, jolting her grandmother from a brandy-induced nap and drawing the attention of the remaining passengers.

"I have a rather exciting announcement to make on my very special birthday. Daddy are you listening because when I am famous I want you to remember this important moment." Georgie watched her father's eyes through the rear-view mirror and waited for him to reply.

"Of course I'm listening, my angel, although I do need to keep one eye on the road otherwise you'll never get to be famous if we are all wrapped around a tree." Clifford smiled and took the opportunity to take a puff of his cigar whilst by his side, Nibley senior obeyed and turned to face his demanding granddaughter.

"Ta da… I would like to announce that I am going to be an actress of film and stage. You all know how wonderful I was playing Dorothy in *The Wizard of Oz*, and Miss Cartwright who teaches drama always says I'm a natural born star, and she should know because she once acted alongside Lawrence Olivier at the National Theatre." Georgie waited for the news to sink in, remembering that for thespians, timing is key.

"I intend to enrol at drama school at the earliest opportunity but in the meantime perhaps I should have private lessons. I will make enquiries with Miss Cartwright when I go back to school." Georgie paused once again for dramatic effect. She was so good at this.

Mavis was the first to speak. "Well that's wonderful, darling, but I wouldn't take too much notice of Miss Cartwright because rumour has it she was just an extra and dines out on that rather tiresome story whenever she can."

Mrs Nibley senior was having none of it and where Georgie was concerned, always took great pleasure in usurping Mavis. "Whether Miss Cartwright is a fantasist or not, I am sure Georgie will make a fine actress and I for one thought she did a sterling job when she played Dorothy. And wouldn't it be marvellous to have an Elizabeth Taylor in the family or perhaps a Grace Kelly because we all know how wonderfully that turned out. Maybe a future Princess Georgina is sitting right by my side, who knows."

"Exactly, the world is my oyster and I think today is just the perfect way to begin the rest of my life… it's all so thrilling, don't you think?" Georgie settled against the leather of the car seats, snuggled between the smug bear and the resigned leopard she closed her eyes and smiled.

The other passengers turned to look out of the window and concentrated on the road. Whether all three of them secretly presumed it was just a passing fancy, Georgie on the other had spent the rest of the journey lost in the theatre of her own mind, receiving Oscars and reading next-day reviews in *The Stage*.

Ignoring the reticence of her mother and aware of the pre-occupations of her father, Georgie focused her energy on the Nibleys, who up to that point still believed they were in control. After realising that darling Georgie was actually quite serious, she was immediately indulged and swiftly enrolled with the local acting teacher who had close connections with the Theatre of Amateur Dramatics in the next town.

Whilst happy to encourage their golden grandchild, Georgie could tell they merely saw her thespian aspirations as an artistic string to her bow, a quirky accompaniment to her love of painting and melodic tinkling of ivory. Georgie admired them in a way; they had resolve and had strived to produce the whole package, paying close attention to aesthetic and cultural details, wrapping it up in beautiful clothes, waiting and hoping for the perfect suitor to come along and redress the balance. Thus erasing the stain left by inferior genes.

Letting out a sigh that briefly caught the attention of the woman opposite, Georgie felt a smidgen of regret, for herself, not the Nibleys. It had all been for nothing, their grand plans and careful engineering. Georgie did cringe slightly when she thought about her falling from grace. It was a schoolgirl error and she should have locked the door instead of being caught with her knickers down, quite literally when the theatre manager's wife and teenage sons popped into his office during a trip into town. Georgie could hear it now, the piercing sound of the wife who screeched far louder than Eliza Doolittle ever could, while her prophecies of ruin and castration would have made Macbeth's witches proud. And thanks to the wide open door, said scene was played out for free, in full view and within earshot of any amused theatre staff that happened to be passing through the lobby.

Georgie shuddered at the memory. News travelled fast in a small town, and within days, golden Georgie found herself wrapped in shame, hiding in her room beneath a stiff layer of plain brown paper, like the last pork chop in the tray, reduced in price and on offer to whoever would take it off their hands.

After a dreadfully dull Christmas and even drearier New Year of social exclusion, it had been decided that Georgie would be sent away, the sooner the better for all concerned. After realising that their investment wasn't going to pay dividends, the Nibleys were adamant that not one more penny was to be wasted on indulging their embarrassment, not even in the form of a train ticket. According to Great Uncle Albert, repeating her grandmother verbatim, Georgie could walk to London for all she cared.

Uncle Albert had called in to rub salt in the wounds and his body up against that of his nubile great niece, for the last time. "I have to say, my girl, that your lineage is in no doubt and I had to chuckle when I heard about your shenanigans. My my, you certainly put me to shame, I can tell you. Thought your grandmother was going to keel over from the shock of it all, you cheeky minx. Now come here and give me a farewell hug."

On this occasion, Georgie was in no mood for indulging her pervy uncle, his bulging trousers or tiresome tales. In fact she was sick of the lot of them and their misogynistic hypocrisy.

"Actually, Uncle Albert, I have a vat of acid I need to stick my head into so if you don't mind I'll pass. Go rub your tiny cock on Grandmother's dog, or Grandmother, either way I really don't care." And with that she turned and made her way upstairs, smirking as she listened to her mother apologise to a flabbergasted Albert.

But Georgie remembered some kindness. Just across town, those who were somewhat used to their women folk causing a stir felt less inclined to shun but agreed it would do their granddaughter good, living in the real world. Aunty Mae had called round to deliver their verdict and assured Georgie that when she returned and all the fuss had died down, a secure and sensible job would be waiting for her at the butcher's shop.

Startled from her musings by the sound of the train's whistle as it entered a tunnel, Georgie's tired eyes focused on her reflection in the window, her image slightly distorted by the juddering carriage.

It occurred to her then that perhaps the ghostly figure in the glass represented another world, her old life or the one she was about to begin. Earlier, as she loaded her suitcases onto the train and her departure drew near, Georgie was already resigned to her fate, and also accepted that it was too late to turn back the clock. Not on her dalliance with the theatre manager, which after all was merely a means to an end, or more pointedly, the lead in the next production. What she regretted most was saying goodbye to the Butchers and the disregard she had shown her own mother, understanding the pain of rejection and perhaps the solace one might find in an embrace, some compassion even.

While other travellers hugged and kissed goodbye, Georgie had received neither before being waved off by Mavis who, without a tear in her eye and betraying a hint of a smile, turned and walked swiftly towards the exit long before the train had moved off from the platform. And that was how they had left it on a chilly February morning. As the steamer chugged out of the station, direction London, inside the second-class carriage sat Georgie, en route to the home of Evelyn, her maternal second-cousin, the landlady of a three-star boarding house on the Gloucester Road.

Another large sigh escaped Georgie's lips, this time unheard by her dozing, dribbling fellow passenger. Evelyn was a woman who, by every account, had seen it all during her years running the well-respected establishment but nevertheless, still lived by certain high standards. Having great sympathy for the predicament of her cousin, and according to Mavis, less so for the errant Georgie, Evelyn had agreed to take in her wayward relative and thus ensure she behaved *and* found gainful employment quickly. After all, Georgie would need to pay her way. Dragging her thoughts from whatever fate awaited her, Georgie turned her attention to the tea trolley that was rattling along the aisle. Taking out her purse she counted the loose change and despite a rumbling tummy, knew she would have to make do with just a cup of tea. Forbidding tears, Georgie plastered on a smile and placed her order, requesting two big sugars from the trolley-dolly, it would be her only sweet treat that day.

Back in Harlbury, after exiting the train station, Mavis concentrated on making it to the haberdashers before lunchtime. She was in need of more angora so returned to the car where her puffed-up, eternally angry husband waited, tapping impatient fingers on the steering wheel. Mavis cared not about the weight of shame that hung heavy on his shoulders. She was adept at closing her ears as he remonstrated over and over, bemoaning not only their child's sordid behaviour but his own life. It was Clifford's favourite subject.

During the drive, Clifford fumed as Mavis turned her head sideways, looking out of the window, silently forbidding discussion on any matter. Georgie's shame was another burden for him to bear – as if his life wasn't difficult enough. He had a bank to run for heaven's sake, not to mention enduring life with his halfwit, dreary wife. Much worse was being suffocated by his overbearing parents who, mortified by the disgraceful behaviour of their ungrateful and sullied grandchild, were more insufferable and vindictive than ever.

Throughout the short journey home, the interminable silence was broken by deep sighs from Mavis who, due to her husband's dithering at the traffic lights and snail-like pace, had missed the haberdashers.

To add to his angst, Clifford's thoughts were peppered by snippets of a conversation with his mother who, still reeling from shame and wallowing in self-pity had managed to salvage some hint of hope from the wreckage. In her opinion, once dust and divorce matters had been settled the theatre wife and their gossip-thirsty community would tire of the sordid tale. All being well, they could put 'the situation' behind them, especially if Georgie remained in London, out of sight and mind.

"Mother, don't you think you are being a tad dramatic? Georgie is in London now so just move on. Quite frankly I'm bloody sick of hearing about it." Clifford was staring out across the lawn, losing the will to live with every word his mother spoke.

"Dramatic! How dare you, and mind your language. This whole disgraceful affair has made me ill and your poor father has had to endure all manner of jibes at the club, not to mention from Uncle Albert who seems to find it amusing. I wish I could pack him off to London too, or the South China Sea, anywhere will do. As God is my witness, I shall never forgive that girl and mark my words she won't be getting a penny in our will. I'd rather leave the lot to the Conservative Party, which brings me on to your marital state of affairs."

"What on earth have I got to do with all this, or the Conservative Party for that matter? Just because Georgie has put you in an eternally foul mood, don't take it out on me." Clifford had had enough but knew better than to leave before his mother had finished her tirade.

"Don't be facetious or play the innocent, Clifford, it doesn't suit you. I know all about your bit on the side, and as much as your dreary wife drives me to distraction I think it's about time you put in a bit of effort where Mavis is concerned. Perhaps you should book a holiday and in the meantime attempt to rekindle the flame before it goes out forever and she has you in the divorce court. Do I make myself clear?"

Sighing, Clifford attempted to reply in a voice that belied both exasperation and resignation. "Crystal, Mother."

After being reminded that he was the last bastion of family respectability, Clifford realised his mother's comments were akin to a death knell. Any hope that he had of extracting himself from his unhappy marriage and perhaps taking up with his buxom secretary immediately withered and died, just like the poinsettia on the sideboard. It was abundantly clear that their family couldn't, wouldn't, tolerate or survive one more scandal. Clifford's zip would have to remain in the up position and his stockroom fumbling with Sylvia curtailed. His fate was sealed.

As the car turned into the drive, Mavis muttered her unenthusiastic intention to make some lunch as she searched her bag for the door key, lost in a fantasy world that didn't include the man sitting beside her or a selfish spoilt child heading southwards on a train. As far as she was concerned if her toady red-faced husband dropped dead, right there and then, turning blue at the wheel she would leave him where he sat to dribble, leak and decompose. And similarly, if her vain, self-obsessed daughter, the beautiful child she'd hoped to love but never got the chance, who had pushed her away and treated her like a drudge, never came back again, not one tear would be shed. In fact, the absence of both husband and child would not perturb Mavis. Yes, her life would be empty and incomplete, lacking love and warmth but she had become accustomed to that, therefore she would survive.

The sixty-mile journey to London took long enough for Georgie to recover from her rejection and in fact, derive some admiration for her mother who had successfully taught her one more valuable life lesson. As much as it had hurt, for just a moment, when Mavis turned her back and walked away, Georgie knew her punishment was warranted and what's more, served cold. She would remember it always. For now, she had more important issues to occupy her mind and as the train rattled along and she avoided eye contact with the suited gentleman opposite who had got on at the last station, Georgie used her time wisely.

It was necessary to re-evaluate, re-align loyalties and change opinions, calculating also the true cost of persuading the theatre manager to coerce Freddie, the director, into giving her the part of Desdemona. A task she would have happily taken on herself had he not been gay as a lord.

On reflection, Georgie thought she would miss her beautiful bedroom, some of her friends, and definitely the rough hands and many talents of the groom at the stables. But the worst part of leaving home by far had to be the four pairs of shoes and two handbags she was unable to cram into her suitcases. And she couldn't even bear to think of her hats. The choice of which to take had been so desperately hard. Maybe she could ask for them to be sent on with her summer things. As for her cat and cold-fish parents, she would just learn to live without them.

Mother was a drudge who deserved to be treated with disdain by her in-laws, too cold and closed to give her own child a farewell hug, a lost chance that Georgie hoped would haunt Mavis's dreams for the rest of her life. Father was weak, cowed by his parents, and wore their disappointment like a badge. It should have been tattooed onto his perspiring forehead.

And as for them, the unbloodied grandparents with lily-white hands, how Georgie despised them for their shallow souls, their pursuit of excellence in others that was so failed in themselves. They'd been like putty in her hands, so desperate to please whilst in pursuance of their own goals, living vicariously through her. That was their truth and she had spotted the lie long ago, even as a small child. Of all her family, they were the most pathetic and Georgie despised them the most.

But there was one thing she had left behind for which she felt sorrow and pain – the Butchers. Georgie had to dig her nails into the palm of her hand, forcing back tears, blanking from her mind and heart the love she felt for them. Mercifully it dissipated quickly because it was not the time for sentiment, and no more looking back, the future was just ahead.

By the time Georgie had drank the last drop of tea, she had cleared her mind and like the fields of Hampshire, left the past and her family behind her. The world had said goodbye to 1963, a year of scandal and horror and her sins were nothing compared to Mr Profumo and Miss Keeler. If Jackie could survive the assassination of President Kennedy and the Russians could send a woman into space then Georgie would be just fine by herself. It was 1964, a new year had begun and like Steve McQueen she had made her great escape. Georgie had a life to live.

Yes, being caught in a less than ladylike position underneath a man old enough to be her father was rather unfortunate, but the worst that had come out of that situation was a bruised bottom and a bad case of chaffing. She had endured similar liaisons and later suffered mild irritations in the past, after a jaunt in a Rolls Royce with the uncle of her best friend and following a vigorous session with her tennis coach. The first instance rewarded her with a delightful Biba handbag and the clap. The second turned out to be an invaluable and memorable karmic experience of the sutric kind. Georgie learned much from both experiences.

As she disembarked the train at Paddington, the hubbub surrounding her failed to demoralise, in fact it had the opposite effect and after thanking the kind guard who helped her with her luggage, Georgie stepped confidently onto the platform.

She'd only taken a few paces when one of her bulging suitcases popped open, the steel clasps allowing the contents to spill onto the platform, exposing the very best of her underwear to one and all. As she hastily gathered her frillies, squashing them back inside, she became aware of being watched, a plain pinched face observed her from the platform bench. Finding a pair of red knickers on her shoe, the woman bent down and removed them before passing the offending article to Georgie, holding them between finger and thumb as if they carried disease, a hint of disdain held in dark pigeon eyes. As Georgie stood, the discomfort caused by the woman was swiftly erased by that from the smart gentleman seated at the other end. Raising an eyebrow, he seemed amused and rather appreciative of the little display, giving her a cheeky wink as she sauntered off, a smile playing on her lips, hips swaying.

On the busy street outside, Georgie steeled herself, determined not to be intimidated by the noise or bustle, confidently hailing a taxi like she'd done it a hundred times before. From inside the black cab that scurried through the city streets, Georgie took in her surroundings, curious and already enamoured but always keeping one eye on the meter, fearful of being unable to pay the fare.

Passing young women just like her who strode purposefully along, going off to exciting jobs or to meet fabulous people, or to lunch with some handsome chap in a swanky restaurant, Georgie felt a thrill, a sense of expectancy. She was going to be one of these city dwellers. Soon she would inhabit their world, wear clothes just like them, and perhaps even speak as they did. She had arrived and who knew what the future would hold.

But one thing Georgie did know for sure was that as she had been rejected, cast out and looked down upon, no matter how they begged, because one day they would, of this she was certain, she was never going back. Ever.

Chapter 2

Ivy

Ivy was cold and couldn't feel her toes which no matter how much she wiggled them, just wouldn't warm up. Not only was she perished, she was hungry and rather lost, not in the logistical sense, more in her heart. Perhaps it was the waiting that had allowed a touch of melancholy to creep in, or maybe she was tired as it had been a long day preceded by a sleepless night and a very early start. No matter how she tried, she couldn't shake off murmurings from the past, mainly because they had such great bearing on her present chilly predicament. As she waited for her connecting train, her brain insisted on setting itself straight, dissecting the past no doubt in an attempt to bolster her wavering resolve, the ebbing of her desire to flee.

***

Ivy Elizabeth Emsworth was born in 1944 in the market village of Tabberton, ten miles north of Worcester. On the eve of her birth and whilst most inhabitants slept, her mother, Betty, had screamed her way through the delivery, distressed more by the indignity and mess than the pain which tore apart her body. At the same time, across the Channel, her twenty-three-year-old husband Ronald was fighting with the 33rd Armoured Brigade and was witnessing first-hand horrors of a different kind.

Many weeks later, just before Christmas, Betty's letter announcing the birth of their daughter managed to get through the lines and accompanying it was a crumpled photo of a baby her husband never got to meet. Sadly, Ronald's delight at being a father was snuffed out during the Battle of the Bulge. His body was never returned to Betty as along with the photograph, it was scattered far and wide, ashes to dust and snow.

Once the war was over, life for Betty ground on in Tabberton where decent full-bodied men remained in short supply which was the reason she accepted the proposal of the first decent chap to come her way. Her suitor was a kindly gentleman named Geoffrey, the eligible headmaster of the local school. His six-foot-two square framed bulk belied his polite manner and shy nature, bachelorhood being previously blamed on his disability whereas, compared to others who returned, Geoffrey was somewhat regarded as a good catch. Being more or less physically intact and mentally unscarred by war, educated, baggage free and employed it was no wonder that where the headmaster was concerned, Betty was eager to be at the front of a very long queue.

During the war, Geoffrey had skirted danger due to his affliction – a shortened withered leg had deemed him unsuitable for the front line, so he did his bit in The Home Guard, along with educating the next generation of free British children. During his courtship chats with Betty, he omitted to mention that the school environment also provided a fine place from which to observe, casting his benevolent eyes upon those who waited patiently for their loved ones to return. Geoffrey's attention was particularly drawn to widowed women with young fatherless girls and amongst the inhabitants of Tabberton, Geoffrey had the pick of the crop at his disposal. He bided his time and waited to see who came back and in what state. The wives of the men whose names were engraved upon the cenotaph in the square interested him the most. After a respectful amount of time had passed, he picked from those desperate not to be left on the shelf but most importantly with hungry mouths to feed. Geoffrey chose Betty.

Following a brief courtship then a timely and respectful proposal, Betty and her daughter moved up and in to Geoffrey's home where she resumed married life, but desperate or not, this time it was on her own terms. To Betty's mind, their union was one borne more from convenience and the desire for financial stability. The other stuff, her conjugal duties, she endeavoured to reduce to the minimum and if possible avoid completely.

Geoffrey seemed content with their arrangement, acquiescing immediately when Betty laid down her terms, minutes after his proposal and prior to her acceptance.

"Dearest Geoffrey, I would be most honoured to accept your proposal but there are areas of married life that women of a certain age feel less inclined to, shall we say, partake in. That said, I am also a woman of the world and respectful of the fact that a husband expects his conjugal rights to be upheld. With this in mind, I am prepared to accommodate you once a month but in return I request that for the remainder we sleep in separate beds. Would this be agreeable?"

Rejoicing in his wonderful luck at the unexpected gift of a wife and stepdaughter, Geoffrey accepted the conditions and was emphatic in the conviction that his ready-made family was a dream come true. Geoffrey swore to provide for them always and should he ever stray from this or his earlier promise, would pray to God for forgiveness and the strength to crush his selfish desires.

Consequently, Betty was quite happy with her lot. The role of part-time postmistress already afforded her some standing in the community so being the wife of the well respected headmaster boosted her up the ranks. Having a mild-mannered obedient child who studied hard was also a cause for quiet celebration and an easy, crinkle-free life so when Geoffrey decided which path Ivy's life would take, Betty was in full agreement.

Following in his footsteps and under his devoted guidance, Ivy was to become a teacher, a noble profession to which everyone thought she was well suited. Geoffrey had assured his wife that it was the perfect way to keep their daughter close and safe, whereas secretly, Betty rather hoped that once the time came, Ivy would stand on her own two feet and bugger off. Then her burdensome contract as Mother would finally be fulfilled.

For all intents, home life was ordered and calm thanks to the smooth running of the house by Betty who took her practical duties as wife and mother seriously, respecting the contribution her husband made to their lives both financially and socially. Her parental role was more of a necessity than an act of love, and she often reminded Ivy of how lucky they were. For this reason and others, Betty strove to keep every aspect of their lives under control, just how she liked it. To her mind, Geoffrey's benevolence was amply repaid in the deliverance of housewifely comforts, needs of a more personal nature were attended to just once a month. Here, Betty's show of gratitude lasted no more than a few minutes, barely rumpling the starched bed sheets. During the ordeal, she found that counting rose petals on the wallpaper helped to endure what was happening on top, unless she scrunched her eyes which was sometimes necessary.

It wasn't that she didn't love Geoffrey because she did, in a respectful and mutually beneficial way, but the horrors of bloodied sheets covered in the contents of her bowels and bladder continued to haunt her. Betty was therefore avowed to preventing a repeat performance of the sordid event that was a direct result of another. To her, the whole business of reproduction was abhorrent, none of it pleasurable in the slightest, even with Ronald. In her opinion, to endure such a base activity followed nine months later by another round of indignity and pain was sheer foolishness. To then be forced to care for the unwanted culprit of said plight was simply cruel and unfair.

Still, apart from her monthly chore, life was bearable, good even. And Geoffrey had kept his promise although there had been occasions at Sunday service when Betty would glance sideways and observe her husband. His fists would be clenched tightly in prayer, full lips conducting a private conversation with God, causing her to wonder at the content of his communion. And then she would smile, confident that her dear husband was not in battle with lascivious demons but instead congratulating the angels, thanking them and the almighty for his good fortune.

To her left would sit Ivy, also deep in thought and prayer. How ironic it was that on both sides, Betty was deceived and unaware, oblivious to secrets and truths. Little did she know that her auburn-haired daughter, a mere slip of a girl who looked and behaved much younger than her years was in battle with a real-life demon. The one seated next to her mother.

Betty's more benevolent thoughts were that Ivy was a funny little thing, with her dark button eyes that erred on the side of beady, far too gangly, sharp boned, nervy and always pale. Still, Ivy didn't cause Betty any bother and was unlikely to, some comfort after all her discomfort.

***

Obviously, as Ivy waited on a chilly Platform 9 that cold February morning, she was oblivious to the inner workings of her mother's mind along with the finer details of her marriage, and thankfully unaware of her mother's disingenuous thoughts. Had she known, Ivy could have dissuaded her mother of many things, starting with the fact that whilst in church she never actually prayed, but she did listen. You see, Ivy didn't believe in God. In fact she hated church. She had hated school more. There were many reasons for this.

The other girls were wary of being friends or talking to the headmaster's stepdaughter because she might be a snitch. Nobody wanted to come to tea, not even the other outcasts because Ivy's mum was a drag and a snob, so naturally her school-hate extended to the dispiriting home in which she lived.

As she grew older, Ivy's cup of festering resentment and hatred began to overflow especially for *him*, her stepfather, the raven-haired, clumpy-footed ogre who stalked every waking moment and invaded her dreams as she slept. For this and so much more, Ivy also hated her mother for allowing this predicament as well as being a cold fish, a snobbish prude, the withholder of warmth and caresses, praise or comfort.

It wasn't her imagination either. Ivy felt *him* watching her at school, in assembly or the playground, the guise of proud parent and vigilant schoolmaster merely a mask hiding what lay beneath. The stench from his pipe clung to the hairs inside her nostrils, the odour of him crawling upwards to her brain. Even her earliest memories were diseased and poisoned by *him*, and there were stains on her skin, imprints of his touch that couldn't be erased.

Like helping her up the stairs as a small child, too close, too near. A cold clammy palm holding hers, the other supposedly guiding, placed upon her bottom, squeezing as they climbed. Swimming in the sea, clumsy touches in private places and while Mother read he would dry Ivy with the towel, stroking, lingering. Later, she felt his eyes as they bore through the layers of her clothes, resting on budding breasts, causing her skin to crawl and prickle. He stood too close when they dried the dishes as Mother put her feet up and listened to the radio, something hard against her hip as he brushed by.

Ivy had always known it was coming, but *it* was something she had no words for and couldn't even describe or even picture in her head. Maybe that was a good thing, not to be able to see or understand this thing she was afraid of. Or did that make it worse, the fear of the unknown? That she hated *him* already was perhaps useful and this single emotion made her braver and provided a shield to hide behind. But there were so many other feelings to accompany hate, like rage.

He'd soiled her childhood memories and replaced them with confusion. Misremembering a blue-sky, sunny day, unsure why amongst the ice-cream cones and sandcastles, donkey rides and chips in newspaper, she could feel the heat of tears, the sea and sand blurring from view. And balled up nice and tight, deep inside a heart full of enmity was a core of bitterness and loathing that gilded the shield and sharpened her sword. Somehow she had known that one day she would need both.

That's why Ivy didn't believe. Not anymore. She had asked so many times for God to intervene, to somehow remove her from the situation, anything would do. Had she been given a choice, Ivy would have picked death. Not hers, his.

As soon as she left school, the beast began closing in. Ivy could feel 'it'. The oppressive force field that radiated from *him*, even as he chewed his food at dinner, read from behind *The Times* at breakfast, stopped outside her door after supper where the creaky floorboard betrayed his presence, whatever it was, it was getting stronger. A few days after she'd celebrated her eighteenth birthday, the time finally came for Ivy to meet her fears; one April afternoon just before Easter. While Betty embellished her bonnet at the Women's Institute, back at home, her daughter's ordeal turned out to be much less horrific than whatever Ivy hadn't been able to imagine.

Ivy was due to meet her college friends at the cinema and was so looking forward to watching *Cleopatra* with young women who didn't seem to mind that she was slightly introverted, had never had a boyfriend or experienced a first kiss. That afternoon, as habit dictated, Ivy lingered in her bedroom until she thought the house was empty. She preferred the confines of her four walls and often ate meals alone, feigning study or tiredness. Her bedroom was Ivy's sanctuary until morning came and she could flee her cage.

Whenever Ivy left the house a strange panic would rise in her chest, and such was her eagerness to escape that she had to prevent her legs from sprinting up the path. In the evenings, panic was replaced by a creeping dread and her body became leaden, reluctant to step inside. The stench from his pipe turned her stomach as much as the aroma of the food her mother was about to serve. Looking upon either of them was becoming increasingly hard because she detested *him* and despised her mother, which was why Ivy had made a secret plan. The moment her teaching certificate was in her hand, she'd be off. The manner in which she would extricate herself was a work in progress but just the idea gave her hope. In the end, poor Ivy wasn't even allowed the courtesy of arranging or deciding her own fate because as usual it was decided for her.

She would never know or understand why he chose that precise moment or day, as she made her way quickly from bathroom to bedroom in her slip, presuming he was still at the library. Instead he was at the top of the stairs, standing there, for how long she couldn't tell. But he'd been waiting for years.

Taking one silent step onto the landing, he named her as a temptress. Second step he begged her to desist from such cruel taunting. Third step told of the battle he'd fought, resisting the desire that raged within, and by the fourth he could deny himself no longer, he was hers.

Five steps backwards, recoiling from the threat, had taken Ivy into her bedroom, two steps more she felt the edge of her bed ram against her calves and with a final step he was on her. How strange that Ivy felt not fear, perhaps she was resigned to her unknown fate and to resist the great hulk of a lob-sided man would have been futile. Something inside her head advised that it was far simpler to demure because after all, Mother had always reminded her to be grateful, not to make a fuss.

For years afterwards, either in her dreams or unguarded fuzzy moments, Ivy would feel his stubble on her cheek, the curls of his fringe as it flopped onto her forehead as he bobbed up and down. She would hear the church bells chime two, hate forever The Beatles who were singing 'Please Please Me' from her transistor radio, still feel pity for the neighbour's unloved dog who yapped throughout, and smell the odour of stale breath and as she turned her head in disgust, a hint of burnt toast that lingered from breakfast.

Her enlightenment, the bestowing of carnal knowledge for which she had no desire, whilst uncomfortable, due to an explosion of pent-up perversion, was mercifully swift. After the fact, Ivy was more nauseated by the mess he left behind, the residue of his greed that stuck to her leg.

Later as she bathed and sobbed, Ivy winced as soap studs inflamed those invaded regions of her body, yet still she scrubbed. How lonely she had felt that day, waiting for her mother to come home, then realising that she would be of no use because how could she say it, describe or admit to what he had done? Crying into her pillow, Ivy tried to erase it all but each time she closed her eyes, was even more repulsed by a flaccid image, quickly tucked away before its owner hobbled silently from the room.

By the early hours, after refusing supper and listening to every creak and miniscule sound, something else invaded Ivy's body – shock, which summarily banished fear, coating Ivy in an ironic silver lining. She now realised why Betty slept in a separate bed to her husband, dressed in a manner as not to attract attention or desire and kept shows of affection to the minimum. To encourage intimacy, especially with that cumbersome monster was simply foolish. Perhaps Betty felt repulsion at being subjected to acts of this kind, maybe even with her first husband whose body part had entered, leaving behind his fluid, causing a seed to grow and a baby to be born. This was the cause of Betty's thinly veiled resentment of her only child, the reason she withheld love. Yes, Ivy understood it all.

As she lay beneath the sheets, her hands rested gently on a ribcage still bruised from the weight of an invader, tears pricking her eyes. Amongst the confusion of her own brain, she felt a hint of humility towards the cold unloving fish that was her mother. It lasted only seconds before Ivy was overcome by a wave of rage, washing away any trace of compassion.

If her mother knew all this, then why had she not protected her or taken Ivy to one side and explained, warned of the dangers of men, apologised for her own failings and tried harder to show her child affection? During the coming together of man and woman, an act that preceded her birth and then after, Ivy was innocent. While a monster grunted and dribbled as he pinned her daughter to the bed, Betty was only minutes away sticking paper flowers onto an Easter bonnet. For this and so much more, Ivy decided, she would not forgive her mother and denounced humility as a worthless virtue. Both she and her stepfather were iniquitous in their treatment of her, guilty as charged and no reprieve would be given.

In the days that followed, Ivy noticed something else – the absence of that unknown quantity. It didn't stalk her every move and not only that, since the incident, he had changed. Whatever urges had consumed him appeared to have departed. Geoffrey became a shadow whose lustful eyes were now averted, and the footsteps outside the door ceased. Ivy hoped that shame was ravaging his soul, just like it was poisoning hers.

Had they not listened in church? So many sermons, thousands of hours of prayers and yet still they disobeyed, still they went unpunished. Ivy was confused about many things, apart from one. God had forsaken her, and in return she would forsake him and take matters into her own hands. Ivy vowed to escape and not only that, if the monster dared come near her again, she would rather die before he laid one sweaty, stubby finger on her, or she would kill him instead. In Ivy's mind it was all quite simple. Sadly it wasn't.

***

Five months later, a stern-faced woman drove purposefully down the M1. Betty was going a little too fast, urging the car onwards and away from a nursing home in Yorkshire, a cold and uninviting place in which she had deposited her only child like an unwanted sack in the charity shop door. Betty's thoughts were not of being stopped by a policeman or the fate of Ivy and certainly not of her unborn grandchild. Instead, she focused solely on the avoidance of shame, the true purpose of the trip. Her secondary concern was the appeasement of Geoffrey who had been so rocked and clearly disgusted at the discovery of Ivy's pregnancy that she worried for his mental and physical health.

There had been such a terrible scene and once the words were spoken, it was as though a huge mushroom cloud of panic and anger swelled inside the house, like the images of Hiroshima Betty had seen on television. That day, when Ivy announced she was pregnant, an atom bomb went off and decimated all their lives.

"You're what?"

A whispered response was all that Ivy could manage, even fainter than her original confession. "Pregnant."

"But you can't be. You haven't even got a boyfriend. Are you sure? No, this isn't happening, not to us, to me." Betty was horrified, transfixed, staring at her daughter's bent head and just the sight of her auburn locks, the fiery red of movie stars, seemed to fuel her anger. "Ivy! Look at me right now. I am going to phone the doctor immediately and we can sort out all this nonsense. It will be a mistake, just a silly mistake."

"Mum, please, listen. I've already seen the doctor and he confirmed it. I'm pregnant." No matter how many times Ivy had said the words either to her mother or to herself as she lay in bed, panic stricken and terrified, they still didn't seem real.

"Oh dear God… what have you done, Ivy, who did this to you? Give me the young man's name, tell me who it is and I shall speak with his parents and let them sort this mess out. Is it a boy from college or from here in the village?" For some reason the faces of every single male who had stood at the counter and bought a stamp, flashed before Betty's eyes and none of them were good enough for her daughter who was now soiled, dirty and shamed. They all were, or would be when the news got out. It was at that precise moment that Betty thought of Geoffrey, his job and standing within the community and how he had taken them both in, that caused the mushroom cloud to billow and the flames at its centre glowed angry red.

"I will give you one more chance to tell me who it is… Ivy! Stop snivelling. Right now. I demand you tell me his name." Betty was trembling and had balled her fists in temper, fighting the urge to pummel the bent head of her disgusting daughter who sobbed and hiccupped before her.

"Do you realise what you have done, you dirty little whore? You have thrown away your life for some scabby youth who you allowed to paw and defile your body. You will bring shame on Geoffrey and I, and for what? Your own selfish desires, your depraved wants and needs that came before your family, before me and worse, before God. You have let us all down and I have never been so ashamed in my life." Betty spat the words at her child and as she did so, caught a glimpse of herself in the oval mirror that hung above the fireplace. Instead of seeing a face twisted with rage and eyes that were cold hard balls of rage, Betty saw only a God-fearing woman wearing a pinny covered in flour, an upstanding member of the community who deserved so much better than this, than that which sat before her.

"Get out of my sight, do you hear me, Ivy, get out of my sight. I cannot bear to look at you for a moment longer." Betty tried hard to calm the inferno within, paying heed to the voice in her head that told her not to pick up the poker from the grate and use it to beat her daughter.

When Ivy stood, her slight body visibly shaking, for the first time finding the courage to look her mother in the eye, she reached out her hands in the hope that maybe, now Betty had vented her hurt, she would find it within her to soothe her child's pain.

"Please, Mum, please listen. I'm so sorry, I truly am, but it wasn't my fault, I swear. I wish I could make it go away, I wish it hadn't happened, but I need you to help me. Please help me, Mum. I'm scared."

Betty took a step backwards, recoiling from Ivy's attempt at contact. "Scared. Sorry. Oh you will be, believe me. And when I find out who did this to you, he will rue the day he laid a finger on you. You won't be able to keep it a secret, I will find out who he is and he'd better do the decent thing because I won't keep you or a bastard child, not under this roof. Have you even thought how this will affect your stepfather... what it could do to his career and my marriage? Dear God, Ivy, what will Geoffrey say when he finds out?"

Ivy listened in silence as her mother spoke the name of a rapist. The gap between them had been just a few inches, yet in that instant it became a hundred miles, or a deep river flowing with simmering hate. It occurred to Ivy, as she looked into the eyes of the cold frightened woman who stood on the other bank, that there was no way across. Even if Ivy did reach the other side, the comfort she sought, in a simple hug or a gentle word of reassurance would be denied. In fact her mother was incapable, she had been for a long time and as Ivy realised this, the river froze over and so did her heart.

In the desperate hours since she'd learned of the baby growing inside her, Ivy had toyed with the idea of telling her mum who was responsible. In Ivy's mind the weight she had carried on her shoulders for so long would be lifted, her mum would know what to do, she'd sort it all out, banish the rapist, have him locked up, and then they could care for the baby together. Now she knew for sure that Betty would never believe her, she would side with Geoffrey, the shame of the truth was better buried than faced up to.

Wiping away the tears from her eyes and cheeks before smoothing down her crumpled dress that hung loose on her bony frame, Ivy took a breath and found the courage to reply to her mother.

"I don't care what he says, or thinks. I hate him. I always have and always will. The sight of him repulses me, the stench of him makes me sick, and my skin crawls at the mere mention of his name, which for your information will never again include the word father. My dad is dead and that thing you are married to is an abomination, a fake and a hypocrite. And now you and I have made our feelings clear, I will leave this house as soon as possible and seek shelter elsewhere. I hope that is acceptable. I'll go to my room now. Goodnight."

Ivy didn't wait for a response. Instead she walked across the room, out of the door and then wearily made her way upstairs, leaving the screeching voice of her mother demanding that Ivy return, apologise and explain her comments, behind her.

The night had gone on forever. While Ivy hid upstairs, downstairs her shame was laid bare when Geoffrey returned from a governors meeting. Betty wailed and remonstrated but for once found solace in the strong arms of her dumbstruck husband who in the days that followed, found a hasty solution to their problem, thanks to the discreet intervention of the doctor.

In the meantime, Ivy had come to realise that despite her bold statement, she had nowhere to run to, nobody to turn to and no clue what to do next. So when Betty explained all about the mother and baby nursing home in the north of England, Ivy saw it as a lifeline and packed her case, trusting in the advice of her mother and the integrity of the village doctor.

"I will drive you up there tomorrow. We will tell everyone you are going to stay with Geoffrey's aunt who is sickly and in need of care. Make sure you tell your college friends the same. Now pack a case and I will bring you your supper. I think it is best all round you remain in your room until we set off." Betty turned to leave but was delayed by a question from Ivy.

"But what will I do when the baby is born? Where will we go... will the nursing home help me find somewhere because you said I can't come back here, not that I'd want to?" Ivy may have been unsure of many things but on this she was adamant.

"Yes, the home will arrange everything but for now the most important thing is that we get you away from here and let's not forget, you still have to give birth, and that, my girl, will be your punishment and just desserts. So you just concentrate on packing your things and leave the rest of the arrangements to the home. Now I need to get on." With that, Betty closed the door, betraying not a hint of what she already knew to be Ivy's fate.

Privately, the shock of such deceit coupled with Ivy's refusal to name the father was hard for Betty to associate with their good girl. Even worse, that she had given herself freely without thought for the consequences was both nauseating and incredibly stupid. Not only that, when Betty had sought the counsel of her husband, hoping to diffuse the confusion and hurt, each question was left unanswered and only sent him further into retreat. Left alone to agonise, she saw his actions as both selfish yet understandable. In truth, he simply mimicked her own repulsion at Ivy's falling from grace and given the opportunity, Betty too would have hidden from it all.

***

Ivy shivered, or was it a shudder? Edging further up the bench to avoid contact or discussion with the chap who'd joined her, she also ignored the mother who paraded past with her Silver Cross pram. It was unbearable, as was the ache Ivy still felt inside but then again it had only been three days since she'd given her baby away – no that was wrong, she'd had it stolen.

Six months after she'd arrived in Yorkshire, on a chilly February morning in 1964, Ivy had walked the mile or so into town from where she caught a bus to the train station. Arriving at the home of Betty and Geoffrey just after 6pm, Ivy had eaten dinner in silence. Each mouthful was chewed long enough to ensure that it didn't lodge in her throat and was washed down with just a sip of water. During the meal, Ivy had to fight the urge to spit every single drop in the face of one that couldn't or wouldn't meet her eyes, before smashing the bone china plate over the bent yet unrepentant head of the other.

Such control was hard won but necessary because to survive just a few days in that house was all she'd required. Dining with the devil and his demon was shortened by declining dessert and Ivy's need for an early night, her absence at the table no doubt coming as a blessed relief for the remaining shamefaced diners.

Forty-eight hours later, Ivy had risen early and stepped out into a marginally warmer morning, carrying two cases containing her clothes and personal effects, along with as many items of value that she could squash inside, all of which belonged to others. Within a large Manila envelope was her building society savings book, her birth certificate and premium bonds, all removed from the bureau in the lounge that very morning. Two of Geoffrey's most prized possessions, the first edition Thomas Hardy and miniature watercolour, were afterthoughts that she'd grabbed in haste. The contents of a blue velvet jewellery box, hidden at the back of Betty's wardrobe, along with *his* father's pocket watch were taken whilst they both ate peaches and cream downstairs. For good measure, Ivy had also liberated every last bit of money from the kitchen jar then wallet and purse, both of which were left unguarded on the hall stand.

Between them, they had taken everything of value from her. He took her innocence and she her baby. Ivy accepted that there would be no return to her inviolate state and despite what the good Lord said, forgiveness was impossible, especially since her incarceration. Within the walls of the mother and baby home, she'd been damaged by actions that went even deeper than his, generous helpings of cruelty and betrayal. But that was by the by because in the last two days she had done much to redress the balance, mostly in material form, and all that had remained was to repay their unkindness in the best way she knew how.

Without a backward glance, Ivy had made her previous journey in reverse, walking the mile or so into her hometown from where she caught a bus to the train station. She had a firm idea of where she was headed – Bournemouth by the sea. Somewhere she could gain employment, perhaps in a hotel or restaurant that was busy and full of strangers who would never know her face or past. All she cared was that it was far, far away from *them*.

At the entrance to the station the newspaper headline boards were emblazoned with the sensational news of the Great Train Robbers who were standing trial, the thick black words had caused Ivy to smirk. Soon there would be a scandal on the lips of the residents of sleepy Tabberton, one far more close to home and just as shocking. Stopping at the postbox by the news-stand, Ivy had removed three envelopes from her handbag. One was addressed to the vicar of the parish, the second to the Board of Governors at her former school, and the third to her mother, all written in the early hours and specifically worded, detailed and graphic, shame laid bare.

Thrusting all three inside the letter box, Ivy inhaled then muttered a well-used phrase; her Bible classes not such a waste after all. 'Vengeance is mine, saith the Lord'. And soon it would be delivered, their propriety erased, and in Betty's case, replaced with enough images of debauchery to last her ruined lifetime. Objects that had once given them pleasure or attempted to brighten their cold, miserable house, either precious or held dear, had already been taken away, just as they had taken from her.

Her train was imminent and as she looked along the tracks, Ivy's mind wandered, pondering the scene in her old home. At first they might have been relieved, to realise she had gone and would most likely collude to repeat their previous lie and announce that Ivy had returned to her aunt's in Cornwall. But once her thievery was discovered, oh how she hoped they were distressed. They wouldn't call the police. Of that she was certain.

Next, Ivy imagined Betty receiving her letter and as her pathetic world crumbled with each word, just across town, the school secretary would be opening the one addressed to the board while over breakfast, the vicar's eggs might curdle in his grease-laden stomach. Geoffrey would be brought before the school board and eventually the vicar would come to call and then the implosion of their lives could begin, both suffering their penance. This made Ivy smile.

Abruptly interrupted from her enjoyment of their misery by an exasperated cry, Ivy's eyes were torn away from the imaginary tableau of wretchedness by one of real life – the predicament of another young woman whose suitcase had come unfastened, the contents of which spilled out onto the platform. Ivy watched impassively as the golden-haired floozy bad-temperedly scooped her undergarments inside, their eyes meeting for just a moment. When Ivy noticed a pair of red knickers lying across her shoe she felt nothing but disdain for anyone who wore such items, picking them up before holding them out, her distaste made clear. The woman silently plucked them from Ivy's fingers and after closing her case, stood, smiling flirtatiously at the gentleman seated at the other end of the bench before setting off, hips swaying, confidently striding forth.

Ivy quelled a brief yet surprising moment of envy for someone who appeared carefree and so determined, endowed by beauty and a well-cut dress until she remembered her own uncharacteristic rebellion and liberation. It provided a welcome sedative for any hint of apprehension or low esteem.

Minutes later, from her window seat as the train pulled out of the station, Ivy felt no flicker of excitement, nothing good, her life was a flat line like the track ahead. The only emotions that remained were sour. Sweetness had been permanently expunged from her life. The Lord giveth and the Lord taketh away. But the next day she would begin again, forgetting the past, as much as her aching heart and empty body would allow. Yet amidst such future uncertainty there was one thing of which Ivy was sure. While she had breath in her body and no matter what fate had in store, she would never go back home. Ever.

Chapter 3

Kenneth and Daphne

K enneth was hiding in his study. There had been a god-awful row with his mother who was holed up in her sitting room after venting her disgust at his announcement. All he could do now was hope Phyllis would calm down before Daphne returned from her shopping trip.

When Kenneth thought of his wife's pale and nervous face as she'd left him to break their news, the anger he'd felt towards his mother bubbled inside. They both knew she wouldn't take it well and he was glad poor Daphne wasn't there to hear his mother's cruel words. Placing his head in his hands, Kenneth closed his eyes. Had he once ounce of faith, he would've asked God to get his bloody finger out and claim Phyllis for a moonbeam, or whatever he felt inclined because down here on earth she was of no use whatsoever. The proverbial thorn in everyone's side, always had been, always would be.

He needed a drink and didn't care a jot that it was only 11am so he poured himself a large one. It was a glorious summer day and as Kenneth looked across the beautifully tended lawns and flowerbeds, he felt not a shred of joy at his surroundings. Tenley House was his prison, not a home or sanctuary. Even as a child, it had represented nothing more than a place one had to return to, merely an extension of his harsh and frugal boarding school. Turning from the window, Kenneth cast his eyes over the photographs that adorned the walnut surface of his desk. After pausing over the faces of his brother and father where neither elicited even a flicker of emotion, Kenneth's gaze rested on the one of him and Daphne on their wedding day. Picking it up, he spoke to his lovely wife, whose smile lit up the frame, her eyes so full of love, focused on her new husband. A fickle, deceitful man.

"I'm so sorry, my love. I truly am. I didn't mean for things to turn out this way and if I had one wish it would be for you, that you had met a man more worthy, a decent chap who could love and cherish you the way you desire, they way you deserve. But instead you ended up with me, didn't you. If you ever discover the truth I hope you will find it in your heart to forgive me. I have let you down so badly but promise from this moment on I will do my utmost best to protect you from Mother and her cruel ways and together we will find a way to be happy. I do love you, Daphne, in my own way I really do." Kenneth wasn't prone to crying. It had been beaten out of him at school and home but nevertheless he felt a stray tear leak from the corner of his eye which he flicked away quickly.

Kenneth longed to escape not only Tenley but his life and had long since accepted that neither was going to happen, this was it so he'd better get used to it. Shaking his head and slurping the last of his whisky, Kenneth poured another and after slumping into his armchair, sought to make sense of the past and work out how the hell it had all come to this.

Kenneth Horatio Appleton-Tenley, unfortunately for him, was the only living child of Phyllis Appleton and Captain Henry Tenley. The latter was the son of Edgar, a shrewd city banker who, at the end of the First World War when the landed gentry fell to their knees, not in surrender but under the weight of crippling debts, made many wise and profitable investments. Struggling to make ends meet, the upper classes had been further beleaguered by the sudden lack of able men and the gradual emancipation of womenfolk who were less inclined to a life of service. Maintaining and staffing their stately homes became something of a nightmare. Summarily, the Lords of the Realm sold off chunks of land and property, hoping to cling on awhile longer. Consequently, Edgar

Tenley had wasted no time in purchasing the Dower House and a swathe of farmland and property from one of his chums at the gentlemen's club, swiftly renaming his new family home, Tenley House.

Built in 1705, the Hanoverian manor and grounds were set upon five acres of prime Hampshire countryside and across the boundary lines, tenanted cottages and managed farms dot the rolling hills. Made from local brick, the grand exterior of Tenley House was encompassed on three sides by a slate terrace, the cast stone balustrades separating it from the expanse of tended lawns below. These were divided down the centre by a sweeping driveway coming straight off the narrow private lane where, after alighting from your vehicle onto crunching gravel, stone steps led upwards to the marble pillars and imposing studded oak door, solid and ecclesiastical in style.

Once inside the wide half-panelled hallway, the eye was drawn to a central oak stairway, lined on each side by heavy oak doors to reception rooms, the family lounge, a library cum study and an austere dining room. As the sun orbited the house during the day, vaulted ceilings allowed in welcome light while the leaded windows cast eerie shadows onto corners of empty rooms. At night, unless lit from inside, they became black soulless eyes, peering out into the darkness beyond, sinister and watchful.

There were eight bedrooms, almost identical in size and decoration, jaded and lacking in imagination and as with downstairs, each room had an open fireplace to stave off the winter chill and compensate for an inadequate central heating system. The kitchens and utility areas were housed in the rear right-hand corner of the building and opposite, on the left, stretching out onto the bordered lawn was the orangery which housed the swimming pool, a recent addition. This could only be accessed from inside the house and was afforded privacy on one side by the dense woodland that surrounded the entire property.

The south facing area in between the pool and kitchen wing was terraced on three levels, designed as an extension to the dining room for summer entertaining and al fresco meals but rarely used. During the warmer months, light flooded onto the terrace, gently heating the slate floor and stone walls of the house whereas in winter, the sun rarely peeped above the tips of the highest trees or from behind sullen grey clouds, casting the rooms into gloomy darkness.

The house was maintained by a meagre staff of four. There was Cookie also referred to as Mrs Kinsley, Mrs Coombs who came from the village to clean, aided by her daughter, Shirley, and Ernest the gardener and handyman. The other inhabitants, apart from Kenneth were his wife, Daphne, and his mother Phyllis, and it was to the latter that the less than convivial atmosphere, one that sometimes prevented the house from feeling like a home, could be attributed.

During the early fifties, Kenneth had been rather disconcerted to find himself the owner-by-default of Tenley. He'd been exceedingly happy to remain in London, ensconced in his house just off Kensington High Street, the family bolthole that had allowed him to live life quietly and just the way he pleased. Dabbling in the stock market provided a comfortable living and when he wasn't at his desk in the city, he was either at the club, the toilets at Liverpool Street Station or in his study, collating his stamp collection. When Gus, Kenneth's older brother was killed in a gruesome hunting accident in which his torso became separated from his head, the role of looking after the estate fell immediately to the spare son. Once the funeral was over it became necessary for Kenneth to return to Tenley and his grieving mother, leaving London and his secret life behind.

Having to live with his domineering mother had done nothing whatsoever to sweeten the bitter pill he'd been forced to swallow, however, in erudite moments Kenneth did accept that his predicament might also have saved him from himself. He'd been sailing far too close to the wind of late and was fearful, no, terrified of being exposed and, God forbid, arrested for a crime he'd tried so hard not to commit, time and time again. Therefore enforced celibacy was perhaps a good thing because country life gave him no place to hide, or for that matter, an opportunity to indulge in his private fantasies every now and then.

At Tenley, things were expected of him, decisions had to be made, appearances kept up. But after only twelve months on the job, learning the ropes and being a good chap, he had been summoned for a rather uncomfortable and forthright audience with his mother. It seemed an heir was required otherwise those blasted cousins would get their hands on everything and in order to acquire one, Phyllis told Kenneth he would have to take a wife.

"There is no point in beating about the bush, Kenneth. It is high time we found you a suitable filly because Tenley needs an heir and the clock is ticking. You're not getting any younger and if you don't make a match soon you will be left with the rotten apples from the bottom of the barrel and as much as I despair, I wouldn't wish that on you. Now, have you anyone in mind, has anything caught your eye when you've been up to London?" Phyllis tapped her stick impatiently as she observed her son, noting he had paled slightly.

"Mother, I do wish you wouldn't refer to people as objects and for the record, no, I haven't met anyone who I feel attracted to or for that matter, feel inclined to marry." Kenneth knew he'd told a lie because there were plenty of handsome young men who had caught his eye, not that he could ever admit that to his inquisitor.

Phyllis tutted and sighed. "Then it looks like I will have to step into the breach, as usual. If you are incapable of finding a suitable woman then I shall do it for you so don't come crying to me if you end up with some desperate hag whose been left on the shelf. Now jog along and get back to the office. I'll let you know when I have found someone, leave it with me." Phyllis glared at her son and waited for him to take the hint, a twitch of a smile playing on her lips as he silently turned to leave.

In the hallway, Kenneth leant against the wall and sucked in air. He felt rather odd, like he'd just been handed down a death sentence and all he could hope for now was a last-minute pardon, and that every single desperate hag in the county was spoken for.

Before long, he'd been introduced to Daphne and it became clear that his watchful wily mother hoped to match them. After resigning himself to his fate, along with giving the matter due consideration, rather than being repulsed by the idea, Kenneth welcomed it with open arms. Poor old Daphers wasn't such a bad catch and she certainly wasn't a hag. In fact she was rather pretty, an English rose with pale brown eyes and although Phyllis had described her hair as mousey, Kenneth felt Daphne was natural, homely yet somewhat jolly with a bit of a spark. He also felt quite sorry for her, living in the shadow of her reverent parents and now caught in his mother's spotlight. With an ulterior motive and covert agenda, Kenneth embarked on a tentative courtship during which, to both their surprise, they got on remarkably well. Quite soon he became very fond of Daphne, and she him.

Away from others, Daphers, Kenneth's pet name and one that irritated Phyllis in the extreme, was rather sweet, chaste, refreshingly innocent and undemanding. They had mutual hobbyist tendencies and were genuinely interested in the other's collection. Over afternoon tea on the day of his proposal, they had discussed the possibility of embarking on a joint project, Egyptian antiquities perhaps. It was at this juncture, Kenneth decided to lay his cards on the table, some of them.

After over-rehearsing his little speech and then becoming tongue-tied, particularly at the part he made reference to his mother's meddling, Daphne smiled and gently placed her hand over his.

"Oh Kenneth, please don't get into such a flap. You really are a sweetheart and I do hate it when you get all flustered over your mother's domineering ways. It's fine and I understand, I really do." Daphne smiled reassuringly and waited for Kenneth to gather his wits.

It was their first intimate contact and something that Kenneth found both reassuring and surprisingly pleasant. Genuine human warmth was something he'd lacked since childhood days, frequently left in the care of his rather scary nanny. Kenneth's only other experiences of bodily contact had occurred at boarding school in a deserted dorm or in later years during hurried moments, in seedy surroundings and paid for in advance. On this occasion, he relished the softness of Daphne's pale skin, as her fingers gently stroked and soothed, she laid the whole matter very simply and politely to rest.

"Now listen to me, Kenneth. I have enjoyed every moment since we met and these past few months have been the happiest of my life. Now you drink your tea and I shall attempt to set your mind at rest." Daphne watched as Kenneth nodded, her heart skipping a beat as he picked up his cup but kept hold of her hand with his spare one.

It seemed that Daphne was aware of, yet untroubled by, parental manipulation on both sides and instead of being irritated by it, rather welcomed the opportunity the parental plot had granted. She was ready and willing to fly the nest, even if her new one was inhabited by the Queen of Cuckoos. More so, she had confessed to feeling a great fondness for Kenneth and was sanguine in her assessment of her own predicament – spinsterhood was almost a foregone conclusion. Therefore, should he wish to pop the question, right there and then, Daphne said she would be happy, no, delighted to say yes.

Without hesitation, Kenneth replaced his teacup which in his haste, clattered on the saucer and after fumbling inside his breast pocket before remembering the ring was actually hidden in his overcoat, he got down on one knee before a pink cheeked Daphne.

"Dear Daphne, would you do me the great honour of becoming my wife?" In that moment, amid polite clapping from the other diners and waiters as Daphne accepted, Kenneth felt genuine joy, banishing any niggling notion of shame that his forthcoming marriage would be one huge lie.

Ironically in 1957, the very year that the Government announced that homosexuality would no longer be an offence, Kenneth entered into the union of holy matrimony. The knot was tied in the chapel on the estate grounds during a jolly affair, well attended by those necessary to spread the word amongst social circles that the Tenley line was almost secure.

Ever thankful for 1950s' social proprietary and Daphne's patience, Kenneth had been able to prolong the inevitable until their wedding night where their polite union took place beneath the sheets in a darkened room. The groom, whilst considerate and gentle, in order to perform the task in hand was somewhat lost in an imaginary world, one in which Daphne did not feature.

The bride, having been previously warned not to expect too much on her wedding night, for once saw wisdom in some of her mother's words. The rest she chose to ignore, such as rationing the subsequent frequency of marital intimacy. While Daphne was rather deflated by the initial experience, she secretly hoped that next time Kenneth might put in a tad more effort on her behalf. Perhaps he might show some stamina and therefore prolong the duration and quality of their lovemaking.

Sadly, it was not to be, and rather than Daphne curtailing their conjugal rights, it was actually Kenneth who took charge of rationing. Whilst he was affectionate and attentive during daylight hours, holding hands as they strolled through the grounds and bestowing a morning and bedtime kiss on her cheek with regimental efficiency, he rarely instigated intimate contact. Daphne badly wanted to summon the courage to make the first move but she was sure that good girls didn't. Curiously, when Kenneth did finally become aroused and amorous, she soon realised it occurred when he was pickled, relaxed and uninhibited by copious amounts of alcohol.

And there was something else. Knowing little of the male physiology or more to the point the way they ticked, and having nobody in her circle she felt able to confide in, Daphne was increasingly confounded by Kenneth's explosion of desire when he gave in to his needs. Oh how she longed for him to make love to her that way each and every night, touching and caressing, breathlessly exploring, turning her this way and that, and once, almost pushing decency to the limits.

In her solitary moments, Daphne scrabbled for answers and the only one she came up with involved Phyllis and her indomitable and unyielding interference in all departments of Kenneth's life. No wonder he escaped to London half-yearly, insisting that his investments and the London house needed attention. And as much as Daphne was happy to tag along, she demurred to his assurances that he'd be far too busy to gad about while she was left interminably bored. That said, his three-day jaunt did seem to revive him spiritually but sadly not in the bedroom where despite missing her madly, Kenneth was too exhausted for any naughtiness.

***

They had been married for three years and not for want of praying on Daphne's part, even being so bold as to hint at an extension to their once-fortnightly intimacy, it was therefore unsurprising she failed to conceive. And it didn't help that Phyllis was ever willing to add her two-penneth worth. The bitter old woman waited impatiently, tapping her blasted cane as if she were marking the time of Daphne's body clock, falling short of announcing the cessation of her monthly cycle and hinting when it was time to get back on the horse. The woman was becoming insufferable, openly obsessed with thwarting 'The Cousins' and hell bent on securing the bloodline of her family. No wonder Kenneth was uptight and couldn't perform.

And it wasn't just that. Phyllis controlled everything, even the household which by rights should be Daphne's role. *She* was the lady of the house now but felt usurped at every turn. Tenley was tatty and dreary and Daphne longed to redecorate, nothing dramatic, perhaps just a lick of paint and some new wallpaper. But Phyllis liked her home just as it was and wouldn't hear of it being disfigured or what remained of her memories of a dear husband, painted over or stripped away. Not that she or Kenneth would ever put up a fight over such things, it wasn't worth it. In the end, Daphne chose her battles wisely, those she was sure to win and would cause the least disruption to their lives and that of the household in general.

Her victories came in the form of a brand new bedroom suite and the services of a team of decorators who brought their three private upstairs rooms into the present century. The rest Daphne left to peel and rot, just like Phyllis.

Immediately off the master bedroom was a modern bathroom and dressing room, a space that Daphne prized, not only as a place to hang her clothes but one she refused to give over to Kenneth. He'd hinted that perhaps it would be useful to have a spare bed, for those nights he stayed up late – he so hated to disturb her. Daphne stood firm, mindful of an even greater chasm opening between them.

Her greatest triumph was the swimming pool which Kenneth had installed for her birthday. It was housed in the defunct orangery that held only a few benches of jaded plants and was too much for Ernest to maintain, he had plenty to do in the grounds. Daphne loved to swim and so did Kenneth. The pool was heated and perfect all year round and in summer, the orangery doors were flung wide to allow the sun to stream in.

Travel was another joy the newlyweds shared and following their honeymoon on the Adriatic, once a year they ventured further afield to Egypt and then on to safari in Africa. However, on their return, the holiday blues were deepened by derision from Phyllis who no doubt expected an announcement, not an effigy of Nefertiti. By their fifth year of marriage and after bowing under pressure from The Cuckoo, Daphne and Kenneth sought the opinion of the medical profession and after being prodded and poked, left the Harley Street clinic downcast and despondent.

Whilst awaiting the results of tests, they remained in London at the Kensington house, both grateful for some time away from Phyllis. The sixties were in full swing and once they'd got over their ordeal, Kenneth suggested they ventured out and had some fun, dinner and the theatre perhaps. The evening was wonderful and as they strolled home, arm in arm, Daphne felt such love for her husband that it almost broke her, right there on the pavement, just beside The Albert Hall. Perhaps it was the champagne and the effects of oysters and caviar, but Daphne was suddenly overwhelmed by so many things, uppermost in her mind was blame. Her desire for a baby was secondary to her hope that their failure to achieve, something Phyllis considered a simple act of nature, was not rested at the feet of Kenneth. Whilst she knew that the alternative would result in the hard-hearted hag making her life a misery, Daphne would choose that, rather than her poor husband be further emasculated by his own mother.

With age, Phyllis was becoming ever more cutting and obtuse, cantankerous and offensive and Daphne knew her cup would runneth over and spill its vile contents onto whoever was deemed inferior, infertile. As it happened, according to the doctor, neither was at fault and as he tactfully explained, all of the required departments were in full working order. Perhaps patience and a few tweaks here and there would be the ticket. A change in diet, careful monitoring of the monthlies and the avoidance of stress – something they both admitted to experiencing, might be a factor. The consultant did, however, counsel that in some cases these things took time and a certain amount of luck but with lots of practice, he was confident that before long, they would produce a healthy bouncing baby.

Once back at Tenley, Kenneth sometimes likened himself to the train robbers. While they were being hunted down and captured one by one, and likely to do a very long stretch in prison, his sentence seemed more like eternity. He too had been hunted down by Phyllis and was now locked in a marriage where he was under constant pressure to perform, trapped in a house with his bloody annoying mother and it was driving him mad.

Practice sessions were scheduled to coincide with Daphne's optimum bodily cycles while confounding the advice from the quack, Kenneth suggested that to store everything up was far better than diluting his efforts, thus reducing the frequency but improving the quality. Daphne as usual demurred, silently likening her love life to blood and a stone. With every passing month and each distressing visit to the lavatory where she would discover her dismay, Daphne began to lose hope while her yearning almost ate her alive, tension and disappointment conspiring against her.

To make things a million times worse, the tapping irritable Cuckoo oozed disapproval and disdain from every pore which is why, when Daphne could take it no more, Kenneth came up with a solution. It was one he hoped would complete his wife and silence his mother while at the same time allow him respite from conjugal expectations.

Daphne was at first cautious, unwilling to give up on her dream to bear a child of her own, but soon agreed it would be a perfect solution, to give love and a home to a baby in need of adoption. And who knew, one day God might bestow upon them the gift of a natural child, as a reward for their goodness. Kenneth was eager to set the wheels in motion once Daphne was on board and all that needed to be done was announce their decision and joy to The Cuckoo. Daphne was enveloped in a haze of expectancy as motherhood beckoned, while Kenneth felt rather smug after solving two problems at once. Phyllis on the other hand was furious.

Chapter 4

Phyllis

D own the hall, the matriarch of the family, Phyllis, was locked in her room dissecting every morsel of the conversation she'd had with her son. Never in her life had she been so dismayed, incredulous or disapproving than at that moment. To think that everything she had strived for, the indignities and constraints she had endured, would be for nothing. The Tenley line was about to end, sullied. Did Kenneth think that she had brought him into this world for this, and how dare he be so blasé about something so monumentally wrong? She had given her life to this family and expected, no deserved, respect.

Phyllis had remained at Tenley once Daphne and Kenneth were married, a union which she orchestrated from the outset, as with their meeting and courtship. Suitability of personality or otherwise had not been a consideration in her meddling. Phyllis had only one desire – to offload her remaining child onto whoever would have him. The subsequent production of an heir was imperative and overrode any kindlier thought processes. Lord knows she'd done her bit for the family and this was to be her final hurrah after living life dutifully, as she and society saw fit.

Her own marriage had been arranged yet acceptable to both parties. It was a union in which Phyllis observed the rules laid down by those who had gone before and then, once she'd produced an heir and spare, altered things to suit herself. Phyllis was content with her life at the manor, especially when the boys went off to school and her husband buggered off to London to visit his mistress. Happily resigning all that bedroom nonsense to another more suited to the role, Phyllis preferred the glory of being a wonderful hostess to their friends, along with frequent sojourns to the continent and the south coast with her loyal chaperones.

Phyllis was extremely wealthy in her own right and a stalwart of not only the local community but was still in the loop with the London Crowd. She had been on the lookout for an unsuspecting daughter-in-law ever since her peculiar second son was dragged back from whatever he got up to in London. Biting her stiff upper lip, Phyllis resolved that the best way to overcome Gus's death, her precious and delightfully roguish, normal son, was to focus her attention on the disappointing one.

Kenneth was decent enough to look at. Tall and broad shouldered with a fine head of pale brown hair, his spectacles distinguished his scholarly way of dress, perhaps one could describe him as Oxford don but less shabby. But there was a stumbling block. In Phyllis's opinion, Kenneth lacked in many areas – personality, ambition, *joie de vivre*, and on occasions she was horrified to detect just a hint of the nancy boy in him. This characteristic had been swiftly brushed aside, and Phyllis assured herself it was just Kenneth's artistic tendencies and sensitive manner. After all it was impossible. The Appleton-Tenleys bred men, not poofters!

Therefore, to avoid the shame and embarrassment of a shelved or rejected son, Phyllis had taken matters into her own hands and became hell bent on selecting a woman from a decent gene pool, perhaps a religious, military or banking background to match with her leftover son. The notice in *The Times* would be seen by many and Phyllis had a reputation to keep and standards maintained. To ensure a coupling – because the good Lord had not made her task easy, the candidate in question would be in need of a companion, not necessarily the love of their life and one who would appreciate a step up the ladder. The family from which she hailed had to be solvent, and the candidate had to show child-bearing potential but not be seen as desperate or previously cast aside. It was also imperative that they were manageable because Phyllis was not about to lose control, especially of her daughter-in-law. In a nutshell, no-hopers need not apply.

Phyllis was a pragmatist and as the years passed, knew time was running out and in her opinion, the chance of anyone taking a liking to her son, apart from his bank balance, was becoming a huge stretch of the imagination. After compiling a mental list of 'potentials', Phyllis eventually settled on the perfect victim, the daughter of one of her bridge partners and a well-respected canon. And to add value, the young lady named Daphne had recently returned from finishing school. She was perfect.

On first inspection, Phyllis determined that Daphne wasn't ugly – she had her down as plain. And this simplicity could also be appropriated to her personality because while intelligent, Daphne was neither funny nor interesting, or interested in anything other than literature and embroidery, and butterflies. She was mild-mannered, lacking in opinion and never impertinent, easily subjugated, in fact. Since childhood, Daphne had allowed her parents to take full control of her life. Now it was Phyllis's turn.

And whilst Daphne being Daphne might have otherwise hindered her chances of wedded union, Phyllis saw Daphne's marriage to Kenneth as a mutually beneficial situation. Phyllis could not bear to end her days living in some home for gentlefolk or a dismal property on the estate with only servants and memories for company. So gaining a dutiful and grateful daughter-in-law meant that she would never be cast out to pasture by a wicked, wilful wife. Daphne didn't have it in her. The plan had been sound and Phyllis considered her future at Tenley to be secure. Either way, she intended to remain in her rightful place, by her son's side and holding tightly to the reins.

***

The clock struck one and Phyllis rang the bell for tea. Thanks to Kenneth, luncheon had been ruined by his announcement, just as Cookie brought in the main course and Phyllis was feeling peckish.

She was still livid but would have to admit defeat, however, all was not lost. The blasted illegitimate that was soon to poison their line had not yet been found and even when they did bring it home, Phyllis was determined to make life hell, not just for Kenneth and Daphne, but for the thing itself.

Part II

Chapter 5

Vanessa

Chubby hands pounded on the door while the drawing that she'd made especially for Mummy was crumpled and sodden, the colourful stick figures blurred and almost indecipherable. Earlier confusion had been replaced by hysteria which had taken a firm grip as Vanessa cried and begged for someone to come.

Why couldn't they hear? Where was Daddy? She'd looked for him before she came downstairs but he wasn't in bed so perhaps he was still cross and hadn't come home. After searching for him in the study and the kitchen, where she helped herself to one of the morning rolls that Cookie had left out, Vanessa decided to give up looking for Daddy and find Mummy instead.

***

Vanessa had known exactly where she would be, in the pool taking her morning swim so that's where she had headed. In her hand she held her drawing; the one that she hoped would make up for her bad behaviour the evening before. The door to the swimming pool had to remain closed and Vanessa was forbidden to go there without a grown up. She loved her lessons with Mummy who would teach her how to doggy paddle and splash about with the float, but best of all was when they pretended to be mermaids. It was their special time together, just the two of them. The door was quite heavy and to get it to open you had to pull hard on the handle which was high up. It took two or three big jumps before Vanessa managed to grip on and push in unison but eventually it swung open. It was dreary outside so the lights were on, and the rain battered the orangery roof as windblown trees tapped on the glass. As the door slammed shut behind her, Vanessa's eyes searched the pool for her mother, clasping her picture and reciting her apology.

Vanessa hadn't meant to snap Mummy's pearls, not really. It was all Granny's fault for saying those horrid things. Vanessa wasn't sure what all of the words meant but she knew they were bad because they made her feel angry inside and made Mummy cry. She hated already the baby that Mummy had in her tummy but she hated her nasty granny so much more. She made everyone in the house so miserable all of the time.

***

Exhausted from crying and screaming and banging, Vanessa hiccupped and caught her breath before wiping tears and goo from her eyes and face. Her nightie was soggy, a mixture of blood and water after kneeling by the poolside where she had begged Mummy to wake up. Why didn't Mummy wake up? She had to see her drawing and the word saying sorry. Vanessa had written it in her favourite colour, pink, and was sure that once Mummy saw it she would feel bad for smacking her legs and refusing to buy her a pony. Vanessa wanted to be forgiven and then they could be friends again because Mummy had said horrible things too. Vanessa wasn't wicked and jealous. She was frightened that once the new baby came, they would obey Granny and send her away because everyone would like the real baby more than her.

It was very cold in the pool room and the tiles on the floor were beginning to numb Vanessa's bare feet that were streaked with blood and had left tiny footprints leading back to the cause of her distress. Shivering, her plump body slumped to the floor as Vanessa sobbed in between crying out for help, her eyes steadfastly averted from the pool and her mother's floating body. Still, no matter how much noise she made, nobody came. Her tummy rumbled and her teeth chattered while the cruel words of a spiteful old woman rang in her ears.

The previous evening, before Vanessa cried herself to sleep she had gone over and over what Granny had said as she listened at the door of the sitting room, her dark eyes wide with horror and a heart filled with hurt. And then later, Mummy lost her temper and then Daddy shouted at everyone before marching off and shooting down the drive in his car. What if Mummy never woke up and Daddy didn't come home? Granny didn't love Vanessa and would have her sent away forever. Vanessa knew that for sure.

***

Vanessa's parents had been out for the afternoon and on their return, the six-year-old noticed that her mummy's face was flushed and they both seemed excited and full of joy. It was a hot, sunny July day so when Daddy rang the bell and asked Cookie to prepare a special celebration tea, he suggested it should be served outside on the terrace. Here, over jammy wheels and crumpets they told their much loved adopted daughter that soon she would be receiving a wonderful surprise – the gift of a baby brother or sister who she would have to take very good care of. Apparently it was a special job that only Vanessa could be trusted with. She would be seven when it arrived and therefore could help Mummy with lots and lots of things.

Daphne could barely contain herself as she gently pushed a lock of curly raven hair from Vanessa's forehead. "So, darling, are you excited? The four of us are going to have so much fun together. We will be a proper little family. Tell me, what would you prefer, a baby brother or sister? It's going to be such a surprise when they arrive, don't you think?"

There were so many questions, far too many for a child to process. Are you happy, excited, brother, sister, what would you like? Despite her parents' glee, Vanessa felt rather disappointed so instead decided to tell the truth, just as she had been taught. She knew the answer straight away so before biting into a cream bun, her face brightened and she replied with enthusiasm.

"I don't really care for babies, Mummy. Mabel from school has one and she says it cries all the time and smells terribly so if you don't mind, could we swap it for a pony?" Vanessa smiled hopefully, relieved to have delivered a nice simple answer that should keep them happy while she ate up.

Kenneth laughed nervously and ruffled Vanessa's hair, rolling his eyes at Daphne who was doing her best to recover from disappointment but once she'd gathered her wits, ploughed courageously on.

"Now, now, Vanessa, you don't mean that. Everyone longs for a brother or sister. I know I did when I was your age. I grew up quite alone so I don't wish that for you. I understand this is a big change but please don't feel jealous because Mummy and Daddy have lots and lots of love to go around. You are always our special big girl." On realising what she'd said, Daphne caught her breath slightly, the faux pas causing both Vanessa and Kenneth to widen their eyes.

Kenneth interjected before a tantrum occurred. "What Mummy means is that even when the baby comes we will love you both, do you understand, sweetpea?" Kenneth was becoming impatient, spotting the tears welling in Daphne's eyes and disconcerted by the unenthusiastic response from their daughter. They thought she'd be so pleased and mirror their own excitement at such unexpected news.

"Yes, Daddy, I understand but I really would like a pony, a Welsh, just like Jemima's, and I'm going to call it Twinkle Feet." Vanessa was used to making demands so waited for her wish to be granted, filling the silence with another jammy wheel.

Daphne blinked back tears and took a deep breath. "Well, darling, we have oodles of time before your brother or sister arrives so perhaps we can talk about ponies and the new baby tomorrow, when we've all got over the surprise and had a nice sleep. Now, go upstairs and wash your hands while we speak with Granny, and no more buns, I think you've had quite enough. Daddy can tell Cookie to come and clear away." Daphne, struggling to keep her temper, stood, smoothed down her skirt, and almost ran from the terrace, leaving Kenneth to kiss their daughter on the head before following his wife.

Unperturbed by their departure or the fact that her mother sounded cross, Vanessa took the last bun from the plate along with two jammy wheels and placed them in the pocket of her pinny. She would hide them in her bedside drawer before obediently heading to the bathroom to wash her sticky hands.

Inside their bedroom with the door firmly shut, Daphne wrung her hands as she stared out of the window, tears coursing down her cheeks, the day ruined already. Dark storm clouds were coming in from the east and the dulling of such a bright and glorious day did nothing to help her plummeting mood. Vanessa's reaction had rocked her, naively expecting their daughter to feel the same as she, as them. When Kenneth entered the room, he wrapped her in comforting arms, making shushing noises and promises that Vanessa would come round eventually. Surely she wasn't the first child to behave this way and after all, perhaps they should make allowances, take circumstances into consideration before they judged her harshly.

After Daphne announced she was far too overwrought to face Phyllis, Kenneth suggested she had a lie down before dinner where they would announce their news once they were fresh and rested. Brightening somewhat at the thought of finally pleasing The Cuckoo, Daphne agreed and kissed her wise and wonderful husband on the cheek, stroking his hair fondly before moving away, pulling back the sheets and laying her weary body on the bed.

While Kenneth read the paper that was full of the Apollo 11 landings and the mounting unrest in Northern Ireland, he kept an eye on Daphne who fell quickly into an exhausted sleep. She was a dear, sweet thing and he hoped that the birth of their child would be a reward for both her patience and unwitting collusion in his lie. He owed her this, a chance to feel fulfilled if only in motherhood.

On waking, Daphne did appear somewhat brighter as she dressed for dinner, wearing her favourite dress and a splash of lipstick. After kissing Vanessa goodnight and with a spring in their step, hand in hand they headed downstairs for an audience with Phyllis.

Kenneth knocked back the triple whisky in his tumbler and tried to ignore the grating voice of his mother who was having a field day, somehow managing to heap further misery on what should have been such a happy day. Poor Daphne was at the end of her tether and his heart felt sad for her and ashamed at his own impotence, not in the physical sense as he had since proved himself a man. But in the face of his mother, he remained characteristically weak. The thing was, once Phyllis was in full swing there was just no stopping her.

"So you finally managed it! Bravo. I must say, Kenneth, I really didn't think you had it in you. Maybe you're not the gaylord of the parish after all." Phyllis sipped her sherry through pursed lips, her eyes revealing a hint of pleasure, her voice laced with sarcasm.

Daphne sighed, exasperated. "Phyllis, please. Can we not have one moment of happiness? We so wanted to share our joy with you on this very special day and now you are ruining everything with your habitual nasty comments. Kenneth is your son and sometimes I cannot believe how cruel you can be towards him." Daphne, who had been seated on the sofa opposite Phyllis, stood, her hands grasped tightly together to prevent them shaking or, as she had been told by The Cuckoo so many times, wringing them in such a pathetic and irritating manner.

Kenneth, both surprised by Daphne's uncharacteristic outburst and admiring of her defence of him, came swiftly to her aid and placed a comforting arm around her shoulder. He was concerned for their unborn child and his wife who, if he knew anything about his mother, was due for a dressing down. Nobody ever stood up to Phyllis. Kenneth's fears were well founded when in an imperious tone, his mother responded.

"How dare you speak to me in that manner in my own home? What I say to my son has nothing to do with you so I would remind you to know your place and refrain from making such piteous observations." Phyllis would not tolerate being spoken to in that way, especially by Daphne. It irked Phyllis greatly to accept that the vicar's daughter had been a poor choice where matters of procreation were concerned but until recently and for the most part, Daphne had remained manageable and servile.

Daphne, in the meantime, felt slightly unhinged. The contrast of emotions she had experienced since their appointment with the doctor were beginning to take their toll, and after almost ten years of tiptoeing around Phyllis, Daphne's brain, quite frankly had had enough.

"And I would remind you, Phyllis, that contrary to your belief, Kenneth is master of this house and I demand that from now on, especially in front of our children, you show him respect and gratitude because if it were not for him you would be living alone on the edge of the estate or if I had my way, the edge of the county." On saying the words, Daphne gasped, quite shocked by her own admission and that her silent thoughts had escaped.

As one shaking hand flew upwards and covered her lips, Daphne's high-pitched and almost hysterical voice was accompanied by shushing noises from Kenneth as his arm tightened around her shoulder. Daphne was unsure if this gesture was giving or receiving comfort but one thing she did know was that rather than silencing Phyllis, she had simply enraged her.

The Cuckoo didn't speak immediately. Daphne noted the draining of colour from the old woman's pinched and lined face, the white-grey pallor of shock quickly replaced by two spots of red hot anger.

Phyllis observed the two contemptible specimens before her, tapping her cane rhythmically, marking time with the beat of her raging heart. When she deigned to reply, her voice scathing, a look of pure disgust etched upon her face, cruel words cut through the air like a knife, piercing the panelled oak door and reaching the little ears listening attentively on the other side.

"*Our* children? You may refer to that worthless creature you saddled us with in any manner you so wish, however, *I* will never accept the monstrous lump of sullied flesh as my own, now or ever. You infested this house with a rejected abomination that you found in a home for whores and for that reason alone, I refuse to acknowledge her, do you understand?" Phyllis looked from one to the other and once she was satisfied both were sufficiently silenced, continued, pointing her bony finger at Daphne's stomach but addressing her horrified son.

"And as for the one you have miraculously conceived, had it not been for the fact that no other man would look twice at Daphne, I can only presume its parentage is assured. Therefore I suggest we rid ourselves of that which is rendered unnecessary and pack Vanessa off to boarding school the minute she turns seven. The sooner she is gone the better, and I for one can forget she ever existed, a notion I am sure appealed to others before me."

The silence in the room enveloped all of them. It was as though time stood still, suspended in a ball of pure shock once the words impacted. Only the ticking clock could be heard.

Before the sob escaped, it appeared to catch in Daphne's throat causing her to choke somewhat before the full force of her anguish was unleashed upon the room. Her once-nervous hands had ceased their wringing and were now clutched to neck and mouth as she fled. It was as Daphne reached the door that something stirred within her. Rage, repugnance, wretchedness, but whatever it was spilled forth and somehow, through eyes awash with tears and with a body trembling so badly she required the support of the wall, she managed to reply.

"You wicked, wicked woman. Never in my life have I heard something so abjectly offensive. You are poisonous and despicable and I refuse to bring our children up in the company of someone so callous. We will relocate to the London house immediately and before you make one of your manipulative threats, be assured that I would rather live in poverty than spend one more second with you, so do your worst. Mark my words, Phyllis, I would rather die than ever have to look upon your spiteful face or hear your heartless words again. Goodbye."

As Daphne stormed from the room and slammed the door shut behind her, little feet raced ahead, taking the stairs two at a time, horrified and frightened by the commotion yet filled with hate for her horrid, horrid Granny.

Vanessa ran through the first door she came to, her parents' suite, and then into the dressing room where she jumped upon the Queen Anne chair that her mummy used when she made herself look pretty. Hidden from view, crunched into a ball, Vanessa heard Daphne enter the room, sobbing loudly, followed shortly after by Kenneth who did his best to soothe his disconsolate wife.

Trapped inside the dressing room, Vanessa listened as Kenneth reminded Daphne of his responsibilities at Tenley. She in turn reminded him of his duty to her and their children. He counselled against drastic decisions while she warned of the consequences of remaining under the same roof as Phyllis. Daphne was adamant that they would all be on the first London train the very next day, Kenneth said he thought it best to wait until they all calmed down.

Vanessa heard the familiar clink of glass on glass as her father poured himself a shot of gumption and her mother simply sobbed into her pillow. Leaning forward, Vanessa deftly opened the lid of her mother's jewellery box and took out the pearls, her mummy's favourites. She wasn't supposed to touch any of the treasures or play with the lipstick and make-up inside the drawers, but Vanessa couldn't resist. Slipping the necklace over her head before applying a wobbly layer of coral pink lipstick, clumsy fingers then began to count each bead which lay cool against her warm skin. For a while, it occupied tired eyes as sharp ears listened to every word spoken on the other side of the door.

When Daphne eventually stopped crying, Kenneth suggested she drank some sweet tea, that always made one feel so much better then after a good night's sleep they could perhaps approach Mother again and smooth over any discord between them. Vanessa had reached pearl number sixty-two when Daphne screamed in temper, causing her to jump. Next she heard her mother's footsteps on the polished floorboards, coming her way. She was about to be discovered. As the dressing room door swung open, Vanessa pulled hard at the necklace in an attempt to replace the pearls before Mummy saw. Under such panicked force, the string snapped and as the tiny beads strewed onto the dresser and floor, both mother and daughter stared at one another, eyes wide with shock.

"Vanessa… what on earth are you doing? And look what you have done. My pearls, my beautiful pearls…"

"I'm sorry, Mummy, I really didn't mean to, it was an accident."

"No it was not an accident, you did it on purpose didn't you? And you know very well you are not allowed to touch my things… you have been such a naughty spiteful little girl today and I am so disappointed, now go to your room at once." Daphne was furious. Her last remaining straw had been snapped, just like her mother's pearls so when Vanessa petulantly answered back, Daphne simply lost control.

"But Mummy, I said I didn't do it on purpose. You must say you are sorry for shouting, Daddy, tell Mummy to stop being grumpy." Vanessa petulantly folded her arms and refused to budge. That was until Daphne lunged forward and grabbed her daughter by the arm and with her other hand, slapped the back of Vanessa's legs hard, the crack of skin on skin as audible as the wail of pain and Kenneth's horrified voice.

"Dear God, Daphne, stop. What's wrong with you? Vanessa come with me, come along dear, Mummy didn't mean it, let's get you into bed." As his daughter and wife sobbed in unison, Kenneth ushered the child away, leaving the adult, who should have known better, to compose herself.

Over an hour later, Vanessa listened in the dark as the argument between her parents raged on. Glass smashed and doors slammed, then her father's car engine revved before it raced down the drive and into the distance. In their respective beds, Kenneth's wife and daughter cried themselves to sleep and outside, the summer storm raged, forks of lightning as sharp as an old woman's tongue.

Further along the corridor, from her room with a view, Kenneth's mother watched from the window as her son ran away, and at this Phyllis smiled.

***

Vanessa could hear footsteps, at last. Standing, she hammered on the door and cried for help. Overcome by a mixture of hysteria and fatigue, she relieved herself, warm liquid running down her cold legs, flooding the floor and her beating heart with shame. When the door burst open, sending Vanessa hurtling backwards, landing in her own urine, she was discovered by Cookie and Mrs Coombs the cleaner.

Before reaching out to comfort the poor mite, both women recoiled at the sight of the terrified child whose hands were smeared in blood, her face ashen and covered in tears while behind her, Daphne Tenley's body floated serenely across the pool.

Chapter 6

Sandy

Sandy ran through the woodland, rain lashing her body and soaking her hair as spindly branches whipped her face. Her breath rasped, the exertion of her pounding heart as it pumped blood fast enough to keep her legs moving caused a sharp pain in her side, causing Sandy to hold her ribs as she ran. As her chest constricted and her lungs desperately sucked in air, terror prevailed so the only option was to run off the stitch, like the stupid PE teachers used to tell you at school. Despite fatigue and pain, Sandy kept going, fear of being spotted somehow propelling her forwards. Mud splashed up her legs and water seeped into her shoes as she raced towards the lay-by where she had parked her car, desperately hoping nobody had spotted it there, frantic in her desire to speed away from the scene.

As she barrelled through the thicket and into the clearing, Sandy allowed a momentary sigh of relief. The dreadful storm had obviously deterred morning hikers and no other cars were parked beside hers. The coast was clear. All she had to do was get inside unnoticed and then head back into town, away from the horror, fleeing the guilt.

On reaching her lodgings, thus far undetected by early risers, Sandy parked her car on the side street and while the other residents of the flats still slept, removed her ruined footwear before letting herself inside, then crept stealth like along the hall. Once inside her ground floor room, after hanging her sodden coat on the hook and throwing her shoes into the sink of the tiny kitchenette, Sandy stripped off her tights and dress then climbed into bed wearing just her slip, too exhausted to find alternative bedwear. Pulling open the drawer of her bedside cabinet she removed a glass and a half empty bottle of gin, pouring a healthy measure, swigging it back in one go before pouring another. As the clear liquid began to take effect, Sandy slipped further beneath the eiderdown, eyes closed trying to block out the image of Daphne. Every moment haunted her.

***

It began with Daphne's startled face, eyes wide with shock, locked on to Sandy's, mirroring that of being spotted like a creepy snooper, freezing them both to the spot. Daphne recovered first and then shot off in the grip of panic, slipping on the wet tiles before falling in slow motion, unable to prevent what came next, her head whacking against the steel handrail that led to the steps. Even though Sandy couldn't hear the thud, she imagined the dull sound, and then a crack as Daphne's skull split open allowing blood to spray out.

From behind closed eyes, gripping the glass of gin with trembling hands, Sandy replayed the final moments of the scene and as much as she wanted to forget it, was at the same time morbidly fascinated by Daphne's head which seemed to bounce on impact with the steel before slamming onto the slippery tiles below, her cheek squashed flat onto a sea of chlorinated blood.

Seeing Daphne lying motionless on the tiles had broken the spell and forced Sandy into action, running further along the side of the orangery to get a closer look. Using her cuff, she wiped the window which was smeared with rain. Directly in front of Daphne, whose eyes were closed, Sandy noticed that her fingers moved slightly, still signs of life despite evidence to the contrary. Blood had splattered across the floor and a dark, oozing trickle of red escaped from her skull.

Sandy didn't know what to do, should she raise the alarm? But then the police would be called and she would be arrested for trespassing and despite changing her name they might still discover her true identity, reveal her secret. Nobody could know that she was formerly Ivy Emsworth, the real and rightful mother of Vanessa, the baby Daphne stole from her, six long years earlier.

No, doing the right thing simply wasn't an option and she had to flee before someone discovered Daphne, who would say she'd spotted someone in the woods. Sandy told herself that Daphne would be alright, she was still breathing, life not yet extinct. Sandy hadn't come all this way to be discovered. That would be too cruel. There was nothing for it, she had to run because soon the house would awake and realise Daphne was missing. Without a backward glance, Sandy took off, climbing back over the wooden picket fence that bordered the property, racing back towards the public footpath.

***

Sandy's eyes were beginning to close and hopefully she would nod off before her brain could dredge up more disturbing images. The gin would aid a deep and untroubled sleep, it always did. Oblivion kept the nightmares at bay. It was her day off and she deserved a break from being tormented by the past.

By the time only a third of the bottle remained, Sandy had fallen into a deep pool of intoxication, but on this occasion, no matter how much gin swam through her veins, her brain allowed no respite. Instead it insisted on going back, reliving it all, the most painful time in her life. The day they took her baby.

***

The word 'institution' would forever strike fear into Ivy's heart. It was the word used by the matron, however, the sign outside, just by the iron gates, announced to passers-by it was a nursing home. Whenever one of the young mothers-to-be committed a sin, other than having sexual intercourse, Matron would remind them of the rules and what the institution expected.

It took exactly nine days for Ivy to realise the dreadful truth of her situation. She was not residing in a cosy nursing home where she would learn the skill of mothercraft. This was an institution for fallen women who were best removed from society until their baby could be removed from them. And there were further shocking and brutal truths to be learned, like when the first of the girls in her dormitory gave birth. The screams of agony which echoed down the grey corridors and bounced off the concrete floors froze Ivy's heart, her head returning to that familiar state of being afraid of something she did not yet understand.

In truth, Ivy did not fret as some did about the separation from their family, she was glad to be away and at first, despite the unfamiliar surroundings, accepted the mundane regime, clean sheets and even the three bland and unimaginative meals a day and for the most part, the company of the other girls. They were all in exactly the same boat yet some more worldly wise than others, and it was from these that Ivy discovered her true fate, and that of her baby.

When her mother announced she would have to go away and for why, Ivy accepted that it would be for the best because she had no desire to live under the same roof as *him*. What she hadn't fully comprehended at the time was that her mother had no intention whatsoever of assisting Ivy financially or otherwise, therefore the dream of keeping her baby was merely a fantasy. The letters she received from Betty confirming this came as more of a shock than anything else she had suffered, childbirth included.

The birth, on the 22nd November 1963, coincided with the assassination of JFK and due to the furore and the night staff being glued to the television screen, Ivy found childbirth agonising and prolonged, and at times terrifying and solitary. The deliverance of an eight-pound thirteen-ounce bundle of screeching joy was no mean feat for a slip of a girl but she survived. As Ivy held her baby for the first time, she felt not a shred of bitterness or regret for the pain she had endured during conception or birth. Instead she felt an all-consuming love, along with the urge to nurture, care for and protect her auburn-haired, rosebud pink baby girl.

Ivy made the most of every second with her daughter, still convinced that she would get an eleventh hour reprieve, unable to comprehend that she would only spend one Christmas with her baby. Cruelty comes in many forms, none more so than being encouraged to knit an outfit for your child, bathe and dress her and then kiss them goodbye. Despite her previous and desperate attempts to convince the unhearing social worker that somehow she would be able to fend for herself and her baby, nobody listened. The nurses and whatever official she begged to give her a chance were well practiced in their techniques, committed in their belief that they knew best and were acting in the interests of both mother and child.

The day she handed over her precious daughter, a rainy February morning in 1964, Ivy's body was a quivering wreck of despair and disbelief. Her brain somehow transmitted messages to external body parts and allowed them to function as the horror of her situation finally sunk in. The stoical social worker took away the sleeping bundle, moving swiftly through the door held open by a stern-faced nurse, who then slammed it firmly shut. In that moment Ivy's heart froze and anything of any virtue that rested within simply withered and died.

The nurse, after taking Ivy brusquely by the arm, led her through an adjoining door and into another room where she was told to sit at the table and wait. Unable to speak, Ivy watched the nurse leave and heard the click of the lock behind her, blocking the way to her stolen baby. There was another door directly in front and on the other side she could hear footsteps, voices of the other girls, life carrying on, whilst for Ivy, hers had just ended.

Panic and bile rose in her chest, the acid forcing its way upwards, burning her throat before it was unleashed, splattering the carpet and her shoes. When the door opposite opened and a different nurse walked in, noticing instantly the mess, her nose twitched in disgust before ordering Ivy from the room and straight back to her dormitory. Hearing the words but unwilling to follow the instructions, once out of view, Ivy carried on walking. She had to get away from the chatter of voices and the stench of food as they prepared lunch in the canteen.

Ivy couldn't breathe. The panic she felt earlier was building to hysteria as invisible hands gripped her neck, squeezing tightly, restricting the flow of air. The walls were closing in and the ceiling pressed down above her head. Ivy's swirling tunnel of vision began to diminish and consciousness ebbed but she managed to focus on two words, 'Fire Exit', as she staggered towards the steel bar that straddled the doors. With her last remaining ounce of strength she gripped them, as much for support than anything, and then pushed hard. The second they flung open, Ivy ran into the fresh air and driving rain, moving as fast as her shaking legs would carry her.

There were two entrances to the nursing home, one at the front, accessed from the main road. The reception was hidden from view by high brick walls, a private place in which you deposit your shame. At the rear, an even more discreet single-car track led to a secluded by-road, perfect for new mummies and daddies to make their getaway. Bordered by trees and a hedge of coarse privets, the track was out of bounds to those persons institutionalised and was precisely where Ivy headed once she got her breath and her bearings.

Reaching the row of privets, drenched to the bone and missing a shoe, Ivy scrambled along the edge desperately searching for an opening, a way through and onto the track. Her immediate intention was to escape, she had no idea where to or how, all she knew was that she had to get away. It was as she frantically pushed and parted the foliage, sobbing and begging someone, anyone, to help her find a way through, Ivy heard the sound of an engine. In that fragmented second, as the noise pinged back and forth from ear to brain, the message was decoded and understood.

Through the hail and tears, Ivy stood frozen, watching as the car came into view, dark green, moving swiftly but with care, gliding smoothly over the tarmac and only feet away. They came close enough to see inside. A man was driving, wearing a trilby, with a woman seated in the back; her hair in a chignon, head bent downwards gazing at something in her arms, Ivy's baby girl. It had to be.

The occupants of the car didn't hear the anguished screams of the young woman as they drove through the gates, or see her valiant but failed attempt to scale the hedge, ignoring the pain as pruned branches tore her arms and legs, ripping through her tights and skin. It was nothing compared to the damage done to her heart, despair the sharpest knife in the box. In the second before the car vanished from sight, as she felt rough hands grip her ankles and the full force of being pulled backwards, and while angry voices ordered her to stop, Ivy took a photograph of the mind. Its title was *Loss*. The image remained with her always, a piteously poignant moment captured in time and ingrained upon what remained of her soul, forever.

Chapter 7

Georgie

Georgie firmly believed there was a first time for everything although in her experience, some were more pleasurable than others. This 'first' was one she would rather have passed on. Being chased along the Kings Road by an unusually attentive shop assistant who had challenged her as she left the swanky boutique, a pair of gorgeous pink silk pumps hidden inside her shiny Harrods holdall, was no fun at all. Nevertheless, Georgie was far more spritely and wily, darting between bemused afternoon shoppers who might presume the smashing-looking blonde was merely running late, the males amongst them admiring her long legs and a flash of bottom cheek from beneath her mini skirt.

After scooting down a narrow alleyway that led to the back of Sloane Square, Georgie emerged into the crowd, somewhat perspiring and tousled but still at liberty and in possession of her darling pumps. Confident that her pursuer had given up the chase, Georgie made her way towards the tube and after descending into the depths of the underground, became lost amongst the other commuters.

More disgruntled at the thought of having to 'shop' elsewhere for her bits and bobs than the rather hair-raising chase, Georgie cheered herself by peeping into her various bags and admired her hoard of goodies. After treating herself to a new dress from Peter Jones, one of her favourite Kings Road department stores, and a matching purse, obviously, Georgie had set off in search of footwear and here, she'd unfortunately met her match. Still, all was well so she turned her attention to even more exciting things.

That evening she would be dining at The Criterion with Laurie, her bestie, an up and coming actor who had just bagged himself a role on a television hospital drama. Who knew who they might bump into so Georgie had to look better than her best which necessitated a spot of shoplifting.

The desire for and appreciation of the finer things in life had never left Georgie despite her somewhat meagre financial state but minor details such as this didn't hinder or deter, in fact it made her even more determined and resourceful. As much as she despised them, the Nibleys had provided her with most of the tools she needed to survive: social skills, good manners, excellent deportment, a rather nice accent. They had also shown her the true meaning of shallow, the art of manipulation, what snobs look and sound like and how disdain for those less well off made you bitter and cruel. Georgie put each and every one of them to good use.

*****

After the hideousness of lodging with Evelyn finally became too much to bear, Georgie set upon a plan to leave Old Prune Face well and truly behind her. Her job in Whiteley's department store in Bayswater gave Georgie not only a wage but the opportunity to learn many things. Accents were her speciality. She listened to and mimicked the customers, perfecting their little affectations, those subtle hints that gave away their breeding and backgrounds. Imperious looks, tinkling laughs, the way they stood and walked, held their handbags and pulled off their gloves, finger by finger, slowly and gracefully like they had all the time in the world, which they probably did. These cosseted creatures who lunched with friends while nanny cared for their offspring were priceless specimens that Georgie studied in great detail.

She could swing from snob to shop girl in a heartbeat. Georgie was one of the gang and laughed like a drain at whatever fruity titbit everyone was sharing in the stockroom or the pub after work. Everyone loved mischievous Georgie who was full of life and fun. She cheered a dreary day and brightened the lives of whoever she linked arms with, shared a cigarette or sat next to on the bus. And then there were her other chums, a bright array of actors and musicians, artists and photographers in whose world she was immersed, running with the pack, frequenting the most exciting venues and staying out till dawn. They loved her too.

Settled in London, Georgie embarked on fulfilling her ambition to become an actress and in her spare time attended auditions for anything and everything. Being bright and somewhat sensible, it soon became apparent that she was flogging a dead horse, and besides, the whole process was becoming tiresome. It was during one of these that she met Laurie, who did actually get a part in the soap powder advert. That was possibly due to him being drop-dead gorgeous, even more gorgeous than Georgie, and flirting outrageously with the producer. After laughing hysterically in the queue, they hooked up afterwards and headed to the pub, then later into the West End. They had been inseparable ever since and now that Laurie's star was in the ascendant, Georgie abandoned any notion of making it big and instead decided to accompany her bestie on the ride, holding firmly on to his arm, coat-tails, every word, whatever it took.

The thing was, her shop girl wages didn't provide the necessary accoutrements that went hand in hand with her social life. Her style icon was the glorious and fascinating Jackie Onassis, and Georgie aspired to being like her in every way. The problem was, she had the stunning good looks and a fun and rather endearing personality, but not the clothes, handbags and shoes. That didn't stop Georgie.

The only time she stole from Whiteley's was a means to an end. She needed an outfit that said wealth and class, that way nobody would look twice at the fetching young woman perusing the racks of dresses or casually examining the expensive handbags on display and trying on the latest shoes, hot in from Italy. On her day off, Georgie would head to Sloane Square, the Kings Road and sometimes Oxford Street where she would treat herself to whatever she needed to embellish her glamorous lifestyle.

Life was such a whirl, and with the dawning of 1970, hearts and minds had been set free, even more liberated than the swinging sixties when John Lennon gave back his MBE. While jumbo jets streaked above their heads, on the ground someone had the audacity to throw an egg at Harold Wilson. Paul had broken hearts and left The Beatles and once the dock strike was over, the riots began in Notting Hill. Georgie could feel revolution in the air and for the brave and the free, nothing was impossible.

Determined to live life to the maximum, in the evenings she and Laurie would meet their friends at their favourite haunts like The Colony Room in Soho, a nightspot where the eccentric and bohemian enjoyed the privacy of their own clandestine club, or perhaps The Flamingo Club where they listened to jazz and rhythm and blues. There were no barriers, no rules, just creative people sharing their love of the arts and here, Georgie could be anyone she wanted to be.

Quite soon though, Evelyn became thoroughly fed up of her cousin, tipping up in the early hours and waking the guests so ultimatums were given. While Georgie wiped away her panda eyes with soggy loo roll, Old Prune Face droned on and on about respectability and reputations. But Georgie cared not, Evelyn's words washed off like rain because by the end of the week she'd be long gone, suitcases packed and away.

On the back of the advert, Laurie bagged a bit part in a police drama meaning they had just enough money between them to rent a bedsit in Earls Court. It was the tiniest place possible with just enough space to swing their hips, never mind a cat, but it was theirs, boiling hot in the summer and like a refrigerator in winter. Georgie and Laurie cared not a jot because it was merely somewhere to rest their heads and drink whisky.

The remainder of the time was spent having fun or on the stage. And that didn't apply just to Laurie. As far as Georgie was concerned, her life was played out each and every day as though she was stepping in front of the spotlights or the lens of a camera. She was amongst crazy people who lived life as though it were the last day on earth, for whom nothing was impossible. They believed that music and words and images could take them anywhere they wanted to go. Georgie had found her place, for now.

***

Emerging into the sunlight and onto Earls Court Road, Georgie passed the shops that lined the pavement and before she reached one in particular, felt inside her handbag and pulled out her purse. They didn't cook in the bedsit. For one, Georgie was able to survive on thin air and ate only morsels, mainly to maintain her figure, and secondly to save money that could be spent better elsewhere. But once a week she bought a small bag of groceries, just a few treats, not for herself but for someone who needed a helping hand.

There was also a more contrived reason for visiting one shop in particular. It reminded her of something she missed, a fact she only admitted to herself. As Georgie stepped inside the butcher's and joined the queue, she inhaled the scent of blood and meat, a whiff of bleach and the unmistakable odour of sawdust. After glancing at the carnivorous offerings on show, she couldn't help but close her eyes and go back in time to her days with the Butchers. Georgie missed them, everything about them. It was as simple as that.

During the six years since being rejected, Georgie had put many things into perspective. Living with Old Prune Face Evelyn had that effect on you. Oh yes, she loved London life, even the dreary hours in Ladieswear had its moments but Georgie knew all this wasn't real, or enough, not forever. Momentum – that was the key. To keep moving forward and upwards was imperative but every now and then, taking note of what was going on around her, she allowed herself to glance sideways, but never down.

It had surprised Georgie to learn that, despite her upbringing, she had empathy, compassion and kindness running through her veins. She imagined these were borne from knowing rejection and seeing disappointment in the eyes of others. It was a slow burn, a gradual awakening, growing up perhaps. Georgie was able to admit her mistakes, be accountable for the hurt she'd caused yet still winced at the whip of revenge. All this had taught her valuable lessons, as had hanging out with her bohemian free-thinking friends which was why Georgie recognised in others so much more than what was on the outside. What happened inside your heart and head was the thing that counted. The past and her new friends had taught her valuable lessons and as a consequence, Georgie was able to look deeper.

She could see loneliness in your eyes, its weight on your shoulders. Georgie was aware of fear in all its forms, like the fear of others, failure or speaking out. Shame was an easy spot, as was jealousy, and Georgie knew a fake a mile off. Disingenuous people were her number one pet hate. Yet despite whatever they gave away, Georgie reminded herself never to judge, not straight away, because who knew what circumstances had led someone to act in one way or another, what hand fate had dealt them, or how they had been previously treated or mistreated, manipulated or led astray. It was nobody's business and neither she nor anyone had the right to look down on another human being. Not until you knew the facts.

After paying for the chops, Georgie headed home. Her feet ached and she desperately hoped there would be at least a few inches of hot water left in the tank so she could soak her weary bones, not necessarily all of them, just the lower half would do nicely.

Inside the foyer of the flats, an impressive Georgian building that had once been the home of wealthy Londoners, Georgie placed her bags on the dusty floor and knocked loudly on the first door. On the other side, a radio was turned to full blast and while she waited, Georgie eyed the peeling greyish-white paint on the walls of the corridor and the curl of foot-beaten linoleum that was in need of a mop. When the door finally opened, a pinched face peered out, a good foot below Georgie's eye line and recognising immediately her visitor, the old lady smiled and welcomed her guest inside.

As soon as the door swung shut, Georgie enveloped her friend Dolly in a warm hug, not quite as tight as she would have liked but it would do. As they embraced, she told Georgie off for being a bag of bones, the irony lost as her gravelly voice, the result of far too many fags and post-war smog asked if she'd been eating properly. Georgie simply smiled and let Dolly rattle on, relishing the softness of her cheek, lost in the touch of the woollen cardigan below her hands, inhaling the talcum-powdered scent of the past.

"Anyways, fanks fer popping in darlin'. I only just 'eard yer knockin'. I 'ave to 'ave that bleedin' radio on full these days, now, shall we 'ave a cuppa? An I fink I've got a bit of cake out back, I saved it fer yer special." Dolly was already on her way to the kitchen before Georgie could refuse but she would be staying a while anyway, just to keep the old lady company. A cup of tea would be nice.

Georgie settled herself onto the footstool opposite the armchair by the fire. It was the only other place to sit in the tiny flat that smelt quite badly of damp, mildew spotting the wallpaper which was peeling in places. But Georgie didn't mind. Gone was the girl who turned up her nose, who retched at the stench of real life and closed her eyes to things she had no desire for.

They had met one cold November evening, shortly after Georgie and Laurie moved into the bedsit. Dolly was clearly out of puff and struggling with her key so Georgie helped her inside and noting the old ladies peaky complexion, insisted on settling her in her flat. It was chilly and miserable inside, the old lady's bed in the same room as her armchair and meagre furnishings. The sight left Georgie sad so she stayed a while and made a warm drink, got the fire going and then nipped to the chip shop and bought them both supper. They had been friends ever since, four and half years to be precise.

Dolly was childless and had no family in London. Her first husband was killed at The Somme and her second husband ran off with her cousin. Dolly had worked in munitions during the war and got bombed out twice which was why she ended up there, in a tiny two-roomed flat, one step away from the poorhouse. Georgie warmed to Dolly immediately; drawn to her dry wit and plain speaking observations, the way she'd accepted her lot in life but hadn't let it defeat her. More than anything, Georgie was reminded of her gran and there was something else, in Dolly she had spotted a lost soul, well-hidden but there nonetheless. From that day on, by putting a little bit aside from her wages, Georgie had taken care of Dolly in a subtle way, so as not to offend or demean.

The coal man called regularly in the winter months, as did the milkman, and Georgie brought a few bits and bobs, telling Dolly that the woollen blankets and bedspread were in the sale and with staff discount cost only pennies, just like the thermals and slippers. In the summer, they would wander down to the park and have a picnic and a bottle of pale ale. On Christmas Day, Georgie and Laurie ate lunch in Dolly's flat then took her to the pub on the corner where she got tipsy on port and lemon. Nevertheless, Georgie was careful not enter into a routine or have Dolly rely on her too much, her lifestyle didn't allow it. Still, it gave both of them comfort, a non-binding reciprocal arrangement, perhaps another name for friendship.

An hour later they had shared a packet of ten Park Drive and, through a haze of cigarette smoke, ate stale cake and drank dark brown tea made with sterilised milk, plus two big sugars to put a bit of energy in their blood. Reminded of her evening plans, Georgie handed over the bag of treats and said goodbye to Dolly. It was always painful to witness the look of regret, the sag of the shoulders and the reverse shuffle as she closed the door, but as Georgie kissed Dolly's cheek, she promised to pop in soon. It was one she always kept.

As she made her way up six flights of stairs to the top floor, Georgie forced back the tears. Dolly was her weakness, a drug she had to take because just being in her company transported her back to the Butchers, her real family and the loving arms of her gran. Georgie had severed all ties with the Nibleys but had kept in touch with her gran and granddad, sending postcards now and then, showing London landmarks, filling the space on the back with a snippet of information. Work was going well, she'd been to the cinema, to the top of St Paul's and had spotted Princess Margaret as she hopped into a royal limousine. Georgie didn't show off or allude to her racy lifestyle, instead she provided them with nice safe nuggets of information they could pass on to customers.

She remembered their birthdays and sent gifts at Christmas and every now and then, a surprise, bought with her wages, perhaps a packet of handkerchiefs for her granddad and a nice headscarf for Gran, nothing flashy. In return she received the best gift of all – contact. This came in the form of a loving message inside a card or a chatty letter, keeping her up to date with the goings on within the family. Georgie skimmed the letters, caring not about her cousins and aunts, and definitely not her parents. All she wanted to know was that the selfless honest love they had for her, despite her falling from grace, still remained. The rest of them could rot.

As Georgie climbed the stairs, she managed to shake off her gloom and the images of Dolly frying chops all alone. Georgie was going to have some fun and maybe they'd see the princess again through the smoky haze of the club, or bump into a screen actor or two, maybe even one of the Beatles, who knew? As Georgie reached her door, she stopped to catch her breath, wheezing slightly and ignoring the grumble of her stomach, perhaps the cause of her dizziness. Admonishing herself for smoking far too much and double-ended candle burning, she let herself into the flat and flopped onto her bed. A few winks would set her up nicely for the night ahead, or perhaps a splash of whisky might do the trick.

Ignoring the rattle inside her chest, Georgie closed her eyes. Maybe she'd meet the man of her dreams, whoever he was, if such a person even existed. Little did she know that less than a mile away, sitting alone in his house in Kensington was a man who, whilst not fitting the bill exactly, would soon become the one true love of her life.

Chapter 8

The Surprise

Vanessa was giddy with excitement and had insisted on wearing her best dress for when Daddy arrived with his big surprise. Nanny had suggested she read but Vanessa couldn't concentrate so instead, she had positioned herself at the window and watched for the car coming up the drive, taking great care not to crease her skirt. She had no idea what the surprise was but it was such fun guessing. Perhaps it was the puppy or kitten which she longed for but Granny forbade. It wasn't fair because Granny was allowed a budgerigar that nobody was permitted to touch or even feed. Feeling sad again, Vanessa knew she wouldn't be getting a pet because Daddy was scared of Granny, just like they all were.

Downstairs there was a terrible atmosphere because Granny hated surprises and was furious that Cookie had been asked to prepare a special tea and dinner. This was another reason Vanessa was excited because Cookie made the best high teas ever and had promised to bake some scones, the ones with cherries. Vanessa loved cherries. Thinking of food made her tummy rumble so instead she concentrated on the surprise and all the lovely things that Daddy might be bringing home for her. Not a new bicycle, she didn't like to ride them as last time she wobbled over and hurt her knee on the gravel. She was far too old for dolls and eight was a bit too young for jewellery, so what could it be?

As she wriggled and pulled at the neck of her dress which felt a bit too tight in the heat, movement outside caught Vanessa's eyes and sure enough, her father's Bentley appeared on the drive, gliding towards her. Her heart skipped a beat while a bubble of laughter escaped from her throat as Vanessa slid off the window seat and rushed from her bedroom, eager and almost desperate to see her surprise, and Daddy of course.

Phyllis tapped her cane and watched the ticking clock which was marking time with the nerve at the side of her face. Horace, her budgerigar, was trying to attract her attention by ringing his bell but today she had no time for him. She was so cross, no, livid more like. It was as though they were colluding against her, taking whispered calls from Kenneth who it seemed had no time to speak to his own mother and preferred to relay messages via the staff.

Since his phone call the previous evening, where he told the nanny he would be home the next day, adding no doubt shiftily that he'd be bringing a surprise, Phyllis had descended into a state of cool rage. She rang him back immediately but there was no reply and suspected he had waited until she had retired before making the call. The coward.

The nature of the surprise did not concern her. It would most likely be some hideous Egyptian artefact or a monstrous moth that he would glory over for days. No, Phyllis was more annoyed that he'd been away for weeks and had left that sneaky-looking nanny in charge of the brat who ran rings around everyone. Phyllis simply had to glare in Vanessa's direction to quell the beastly child, the only other person to have any control was Cookie and that was simply because she fed her. Phyllis smirked, the notion of Vanessa stuffing her fat face until she quite literally popped always served to amuse.

Contrary to the proposed afternoon tea, Phyllis had no intention of taking tea with Kenneth or his podgy daughter. To listen to his droning on about whatever he'd glued inside one of his tortuously boring albums was more than one could bear. His return was no call for celebration or squandering, they'd be getting out the bunting next. Perhaps the village band and the pompous mayor might attend. Phyllis shook her head. Disdain for her son oozed, like a festering sore while Vanessa caused further irritation on a daily basis. Just the sight of her was enough to ruin the day and Phyllis did her utmost to remain in her rooms until the nanny had taken her off to school. The child was sullen and spoilt, over-indulged in order to paper over her perceived nervous tendencies. Pah!

As expected, Kenneth had capitulated soon after Vanessa found her mother dead in the pool and this, according to the various doctors was the route of some psychosis or other. They'd been called in following tantrums and hysterics, or screaming her way through the night with tortured dreams, keeping everyone awake then refusing to go to school the next day. Phyllis pronounced the diagnosis as poppycock and firmly believed Vanessa could be cured by a damn good spanking and a strict regime.

No matter, it was high time the brat was sent off to school and if she had her way, Phyllis would choose one as far from Tenley as possible, the Highlands perhaps. The nanny was useless and allowed Vanessa to run free while she watched television and read magazines, or skulked off to the village pub once the coast was clear. Phyllis saw everything from her bedroom window and the days of paying out good money to the likes of that nanny would soon end.

No, it wasn't the surprise that caused Phyllis such great agitation, the problem lay closer to home. Earlier in the year, when she became privy to second-hand rumours about goings on in the London house and the whiff of scandal reached her ears and left a bad smell on her upturned nose, Kenneth was summoned to her rooms and thoroughly interrogated. It wasn't necessarily the rumours of a young woman, his mistress no doubt, that irked Phyllis because she welcomed anything that dispelled her fears that he was inclined elsewhere. No, what unsettled the matriarch was the change in her son.

"Mother I don't know who tells you all this nonsense but I assure you there is nothing untoward going on in Kensington and anyway, I thought you'd approve of me sowing my oats, I am a gentleman farmer after all. Isn't that what chaps like me are supposed to do?" Kenneth lit a cigarette and flopped onto the sofa, without being invited, and then crossed his legs and began tapping his foot impatiently, seeming somewhat amused by his retort.

"Do not be facetious with me, Kenneth. I won't have it. But my sources are reliable and I have been told of late-night parties and music playing at all hours, so I suggest you curtail your louche behaviour forthwith. And look at me when I'm talking to you!" Phyllis was becoming increasingly irritated by her son's attitude and despite summoning him, now wished him gone.

As Kenneth batted away her concerns, lied through his teeth and assured her that there was no necessity for a trip up to London, Phyllis noted the somewhat manly air and knew instantly that trouble was afoot. If a woman really was ensconced at the London house, she would be at the bottom of it all.

But there was a more serious cause for haste that added to Phyllis's agitated state. She had noticed another change, not in her son, in herself. Having witnessed the very same affliction in her own mother, Phyllis feared this curse more than death itself; her demise of far less concern than the manner in which it occurred. To feel that loosening of grip not only on her son but her memory, along with bouts of great confusion had stirred in Phyllis waves of panic and necessitated a plan of action.

To begin with, she took to remaining silent until Cookie confirmed whether she was serving breakfast, lunch or dinner and recently, insisted on a newspaper being delivered to her room each morning, thus ensuring the day and date. Names evaded her, like blank spaces that rested heavily on her tongue and prevented speech, causing that wretched vague look to cross her face. She knew it was there, reflected in the bemused reaction from the staff. The nights were worse. Phyllis had such terrible dreams… or were they visions? Creatures would enter her room and crawl along the counterpane, clawing at the bedcovers while their eyes glowed in the dark, red or green, evil and menacing. Many times lately she had called out but nobody came so she waited for the morning, determined to stay awake until it was light.

Phyllis was left exhausted and terrified of what might become of her, so had to secure her position at Tenley, keep control of Kenneth and her estate otherwise she might be carted off to the asylum, just like her grandmother before her.

Footsteps on the stairs alerted Phyllis to the presence of Vanessa who shot past the drawing room door, no doubt to greet her father and his stuffed tiger, or whatever ridiculous relic he'd uncovered in London.

As the large front door was pulled open and she heard Vanessa cry out 'Daddy', Phyllis remained seated, determined not to welcome home her ineffective son. Her face was set like alabaster while ice cold eyes watched the door, poker straight and proud, each breath measured to blanket her rage. Phyllis listened to the commotion outside and waited patiently in her lair for Kenneth and his surprise to come to her.

Chapter 9

Georgie and Kenneth

Georgie leant across and took Kenneth's hand in hers. He was nervous, betrayed mostly by his pallor and clammy palm which he repeatedly wiped on his trouser leg. They had laughed and joked for most of the journey down from London but as they neared Tenley, she had sensed his mood change. Her heart hurt for Kenneth, her shy husband and wonderful friend.

"Darling, please try to relax, everything is going to be fine, I promise. I've told you, we are a team now, you and I, and an indomitable one at that. Just leave everything and everyone to me. I know what I'm doing." Georgie brushed a fallen lock of hair from Kenneth's face and when he turned, she smiled and saw from his eyes that he desperately hoped this was true.

"I wish I had your confidence and bravery, my love, I really do. Even though I've painted a brutally accurate and honest picture of my mother, you haven't met her in the flesh and that is precisely what is worrying me, that and how Vanessa is going to react to having a stepmother… she's so unpredictable and–"

Georgie shushed him mid sentence. "Stop this at once… We've been through this a hundred times and getting yourself into a state won't help. Now relax and concentrate on the road. I will be by your side every step of the way, I promise. And I know I've asked a hundred times but are we nearly there because I cannot wait to see my new home." Georgie adopted her firm but kind tone, one that worked well whenever Kenneth began to flounder and especially when he mentioned his mother.

"I'm sorry, my love, and yes, we are almost there in fact, this is it… just ahead is Tenley House, your new home, our new home." There was no need for Kenneth to point ahead because it was impossible to miss it.

As they swung onto the drive and passed through the ornate iron gates that held the Tenley crest, Georgie couldn't help but smile as her eyes settled on the manor house in the foreground. It was even more impressive than the photos Kenneth had shown her. Set against a crisp blue sky, surrounded by verdant pastures and woodland, it dominated the scene and soon, she would dominate it. After such a long time waiting and much to her surprise, in her darling Kenneth, Georgie had finally found what she was looking for – respectability and belonging. She had arrived.

***

When Georgie had first set eyes on Kenneth, a forlorn-looking figure seated on a park bench, she hadn't intended stopping to chat, or stopping at all for that matter. But when the heel of her boot snapped, mid-strut, causing her to lose balance and then hobble in an ungainly manner, he came to her aid, offering a gentlemanly hand as he guided her to the seat.

On hearing his cut-glass accent, Georgie immediately moderated hers and was thankful she'd left shop-girl Georgie at Whitley's, swallowing down the expletives that had lingered on the tip of her tongue. Once they were seated, Georgie slipped off her broken boot as she thanked her rather tatty-looking knight who had clearly left his armour at home.

"Thanks so much for helping. These blasted boots cost a fortune… I wonder if they can be repaired." Georgie held up boot and heel and gave Kenneth her best sad look.

"I really have no idea. I imagine so, but how are you going to walk with one leg longer than the other?" Kenneth imagined her limping home, lob-sided and looking rather foolish.

Georgie sighed and pretended to think, all the time weighing up her knight, trying to fathom the gorgeous chap by her side.

She had him down as a writer. Yes, he fitted that bill. Rather tight for money but with a burning passion, raging within, or perhaps a boffin from the university with his tweedy jacket and crumpled shirt that was rather tired around the collar. Whatever he was, Georgie thought he was cute.

"I know. What if we snapped off the other heel then they would match." Without waiting for an answer, Georgie whipped off her other boot. "Go on, have a go, I'll hold it still while you yank it off."

Her big blue eyes looked hopefully at Kenneth, and for a second he was entranced, quite fascinated by the thick layer of kohl that lined them, slightly smudged as though applied by a child. He had never been so close to a woman like this. She wasn't like anyone he'd ever met, not personally, but there was something about her voice, it was soft and soothing yet with a hint of fun and mischief. And she smelled divine.

"Alright, if you're sure, but that means you'll have to get two heels repaired, not one."

"Honestly it's fine, let's do this." Georgie didn't care about the boots. She would throw them away when she got home and pick up another pair on her next shopping spree. What she did care about was securing a date with the hot chap who was tugging at the heel of her boot with all his might.

When it finally gave way, nobody was more relieved than Kenneth because he didn't want to look like a fool in front of the gorgeous creature, or the tramp and his dog who had settled on the bench opposite. He was perspiring slightly as she slipped her feet inside the boots and zipped them up her long legs.

Once she had made enough of a show, Georgie turned and smiled at Kenneth then held out her hand to introduce herself. "Thank you so much, kind sir. My name is Georgie and to repay you for such chivalry, I would like to take you for a cheeky drink, or perhaps a cup of tea, whichever you prefer."

Kenneth blushed as he held out his hand, so damned grateful that Georgie, as he now knew her to be, had crossed his path. The desolation that swamped him only moments before had simply vanished.

Smiling broadly, he took her hand and replied. "Very pleased to meet you, Georgie. My name is Kenneth and I would be honoured to take tea with you. I suppose it's far too early for a cheeky drink... is three o'clock too early?"

"Kenneth, it is *never* too early and I know just the place. Let's go, and on the way you can tell me all about yourself and why you looked so dreadfully glum as I walked by. I'm a very good listener and we have all evening. I escaped from work after a dreadful migraine came on but it's gone now, and I have nowhere in particular to go so I'm all yours." As they stood, Georgie linked her arm through his and even though she felt him stiffen slightly, hung on tight.

As they walked and Georgie chatted, Kenneth began to relax and by the time they reached the park gates he didn't feel quite so conscious of having a stranger firmly attached to his side, in fact he was rather enjoying it, that and the thought of not spending another evening alone.

They had been inseparable ever since. Over drinks in Georgie's local pub, that was rough and ready, rather loud and smoky but in a strange way relaxing, Kenneth told Georgie all about the death of his wife two years previously and the effect it had on their young daughter who had since seen off three nannies and from what he could tell, the fourth was fast losing her patience. It wasn't all down to Vanessa though. His pious outspoken interfering mother was impossible to live with and he was convinced her meddling and vicious tongue had much to do with the miserable atmosphere and subsequent resignations. Kenneth suspected her intention was to force his hand and have Vanessa sent away to school and while he accepted this might be a simple solution all round, he had to uphold his wife's wishes. Daphne had been firmly against the banishment of their daughter.

Strains of another life and meddling grandparents came back to haunt Georgie and as she listened, felt empathy for the little girl who was at the centre of a broken family. Kenneth didn't expand on his home life other than to say he had taken the coward's way out and hotfooted it to London, seeking refuge in his town house. Soon he would have to face the music and head south and his responsibilities on the estate. On this note, Georgie suggested that if he only had a few days left in London then he should make the most of it – which he did.

They had three wonderful crazy days together where Georgie introduced him to her gaggle of arty bohemian friends who cared not who he was or where he was from. Kenneth was reborn. Never in his life had he met or mixed with such exotic creatures who danced and drank the night away, listened to jazz in smoky basements. Or ran through the streets in the rain and ate breakfast at six in the morning in greasy spoons, then slept it all off before dressing for dinner to do it all again.

During every moment, Georgie was by his side, waving at celebrities as they passed their table, holding his hand, pulling him onto the dance floor or introducing him to such-a-body, telling them he was the cleverest chap who knew everything about oodles of things. She made him feel like a king, a professor of dusty objects, a gentleman farmer and local philanthropist, a wonderful father and her own very dear friend.

Soon, all Kenneth could think about was Georgie and escaping to London. He spent far too long on the phone, laughing at her wild stories which kept him going while they were apart. The train journey took forever and the taxi always became stuck in traffic, causing a surge of panic to rise in his chest, forcing him to pay the driver and continue on foot, such was Kenneth's urge to get to her.

And in return, all Georgie could think about was Kenneth. Not in a romantic way because she had realised on that very first day as she watched him at the club, blushing when she introduced him to Laurie and the others, that Kenneth was gay. Normally, she would have moved on but there was something endearing about him. He touched her heart. From his confessionals, Georgie had gleaned much about his cold upbringing and the dreadful time he had at boarding school, living constantly in the shadow of his all-rounder brother and under the withering scrutiny of his heartless mother. Eventually and without being pressured, he had been honest about his marriage to Daphne and Georgie could see he was wracked with guilt over her death and the strain of living a lie. But what brought tears to her eyes was the moment he told her all about his secret shame.

It was during his third visit to London and they had just returned from the club. It was 2am and both were exhausted and rather full of gin. As he lay on Laurie's empty bed, just a few feet from Georgie, Kenneth told her of his loneliness, trapped in a world that would never accept him for what he was. He could never ever have a relationship with another man, not openly, not where he came from.

"I don't want to feel that shame anymore, Georgie, or smell the urine as I descend the stairs to the lavatory at Liverpool Street and wait inside a cubicle for a stranger. Do you know how low that makes me feel, how debase?"

"But it's 1971, it's not illegal to love another man, not anymore and anyway, there are men all over this city doing similar things with women in dingy alleys or the back seat of their car. And let's not forget while the hoi polloi are slumming it, the gentry are off with their mistresses or being entertained in some private club or other. I know what goes on, Kenneth, so don't dare feel ashamed, of any of it. You are what you are and I really don't care."

"Honestly… you really don't judge me?"

"Not one bit. But I do think you should curtail your visits to the loos. I don't want to be catching anything and anyway, I can introduce you to lots of lovely chaps so there's no need."

"Yes, perhaps you're right. Meeting you has shown me another world. I love it here, you know, being in this room with you and spending time with your friends. I've wasted so much of my life but from now on I'm going to live it to the full."

"That's the spirit. Bugger the lot of them… if you see what I mean." Georgie laughed and heard Kenneth chuckle. "Now try to sleep, stop tormenting yourself." She looked over and saw his eyes were closed so she returned to her own thoughts.

Georgie had only ever been to the Kensington House the once and they stayed for minutes. It was no wonder as the place was rather depressing, a bachelor's home that gave the impression of servitude, chilly rooms with empty cupboards, well kept and clean but faded, dull really. Georgie understood why Kenneth was eager to escape and it also brought her up short when she realised that if this was what he escaped to, whatever he was running from must be far worse. She could tell that Kenneth really didn't mind the climb to the meagre room she squashed into with Laurie. He seemed quite content there, with her.

The rain pounded on the attic window and the drip of water as it splashed into the bucket under the leaky ceiling prevented any rest. Turning on her side, Georgie noticed tears streaming down Kenneth's cheeks and she knew that his complicated soul needed more than kind words. Perhaps a diversion was required. Or some form of kinship, a deeper understanding of what made people tick to prove to him that everyone had flaws, which is why Georgie laid herself bare and told him her secrets, exposed her life of crime and admitted to being a fake and a reject.

"Shall I tell you my secret, Kenneth? It might make you run for the hills or the night train from Paddington, but I have grown so very fond of you and I cannot bear you feeling this way. You see, we are very alike you and I, so very similar."

Kenneth wiped his eyes and cheeks before turning on his side to face Georgie and once they were eye to eye, she told him her truth.

"My parents aren't dead, they are alive and well and living in Oxfordshire, as are most of my family including my grandparents on both sides. One set I absolutely adore, the other I detest. You see they used me as their puppet, to wipe away the stain of shame when my father impregnated someone they deemed sub-standard. I was their golden child and while they treated my mother, who I shall come to later, with disdain, and looked down on my lovely maternal grandparents, I could do no wrong. And then, just like that," Georgie clicked her fingers, "I ruined it all when I was caught with my knickers down and subsequently, they banished me to London. I was discarded like a bag of rubbish. Since then I have invented a life for myself, one where I can be who I want to be, whenever I choose."

Kenneth's eyes widened. "But you told me they were…"

"Dead? Yes I did because to me they are. Like I said, I live in a fantasy world and most days I act my way through it, depending on how I feel, doing whatever it takes to get through the day. Because believe me, Kenneth, living up here and serving posh bitches all day long isn't exactly my idea of fun. But I get by and I'm free, which is all that matters."

Silence enveloped them for a moment until Kenneth spoke, his voice held a hint of awe.

"I must say that was all rather surprising but thank you for being honest, Georgie, and for the record I really don't care one bit. I love you just the way you are, I really do." Instead of being abashed by his bold statement, Kenneth felt his heart flood with happiness as he realised it was true.

"Do you really love me, Kenneth? Because I truly adore you, in fact I love you too, very much, you funny old thing." Georgie smiled and heard Kenneth laugh.

"But there's more… and because tonight is one for honesty I'm going to tell you how naughty I am and then, if you want to fall right back out of love with me you can."

"Nothing you can say will change my mind so go ahead, do your worst." Kenneth stared, his gaze unwavering, his determination not to be shocked by his wonderful friend and her confessions set in stone.

Pulling the blanket over her shoulders and then lighting a cigarette, Georgie inhaled deeply, forcing the nicotine through her veins, its poison bringing out the devil in her, the one that was setting Kenneth his final challenge. If he ran then she would know he was not her true friend, if he stayed she would love him forever.

Georgie told him she was a thief and why, her story aided by whichever accent gilded the lily best. He listened in stunned silence as she described how she'd bribed the father of her best friend after their tumble in his king-size bed, with photographs taken on the Polaroid camera he and his wife had given to her as a 16th birthday gift. She'd seduced the groom and her tennis coach. Both had been a challenge and a bet between her school friends, one she won hands down. Georgie admitted she never did anything for nothing which was why she encouraged the infatuation of her French teacher. Georgie was terrible at languages but could do a rather good Parisian accent, time well spent in the book cupboard while he whispered sweet nothings in her ear and delved into her knickers. To that day, Georgie remained adamant she'd earned the A+ in her end of year report.

Flinging off the blanket, Georgie stood and paced the room. Kenneth could see the tension in her neck, the stiffness in her back, the veiled temper as she dragged on her cigarette. He wanted her to stop, it was doing her no good, he could see that but she waved off his suggestion and ploughed on, determined, in full flow.

For a while, Georgie had turned a blind eye to her father's rather obvious affair with a bank employee because it served her mother right for being a cold fish. Keeping it in his pants had always been Daddy's downfall, as was failing to forbid her banishment. Georgie's Polaroid camera came in handy again, as did the photos she'd taken after laying in wait on the track behind the old forge, Daddy's favourite place for a Sunday afternoon fumble with Sylvia. Instead of exposing her father to those being cheated on, Georgie sent the photographs to her dear grandmother, letting her deal with her randy disappointing son.

And finally, she told Kenneth all about the married man she was having an affair with, who had come into Whiteley's for a

Patricia Dixon

Christmas gift and left with her phone number. She met him every Wednesday at a hotel on The Strand for an afternoon of sex and champagne, no strings attached.

"So, there you have it. Georgie in a nutshell. Now, do you still adore me? I wouldn't blame you if you didn't, there's really not much to like, is there?" Maybe she'd had too much gin because reliving the past was always a painful mistake, it hurt like hell and was the reason she blocked it out, them out. But as her words caught in her throat and tears leaked from her eyes, Georgie prayed that Kenneth would stay because out of all of it, her fake London life and grimy past, he was real, precious, shiny and new.

When Kenneth saw Georgie slump onto the mattress, tears rolling down her face he sprang into action and was by her side in an instant, holding her while she sobbed, telling her over and over again that he didn't care and he still adored her, every single bit of her. When she finally stopped, hiccupping as she wiped her eyes, Kenneth asked her two questions and although he was quite nervous about the answers, knew they were of the greatest importance.

"Georgie, may I ask you something? Even though you have bared your soul, I am still curious and a little confused as to why, when you had the attention of many that you sought out such unorthodox and rather risqué liaisons, but most of all, why be friends with me? I have to say that this perplexes me the most. You have such a wonderful array of companions surely I am surplus to requirements." Kenneth could feel his cheeks burning and his heart hammered in his chest, unprepared for whatever Georgie would say next.

When Georgie turned to look at him and saw the pools of fear in his eyes her own heart hurt for the pain she may have caused him. Oh how she had wanted to leave him in ignorance of her sins and nature, but he was the one pure thing in her life and she had needed to test him, it had to be done.

"Oh my darling, Kenneth, please don't ever doubt my feelings for you, not for one second. Don't you see, from the moment you came into my life it shifted. I stopped thinking of myself and for the first time wanted to make someone else happy. You know I fancied you rotten when we met but I was barking up the wrong tree. It's happened before but this time I just wanted to keep holding your hand." Georgie smiled when Kenneth laughed at her mistake. "After we chatted and I got to know you more, I saw a lost soul who was so desperately sad and I couldn't bear to let you go." Georgie brushed Kenneth's hair from his eyes; sometimes he really did look so vulnerable so she tried to reassure him.

"Where you are concerned, dearest Kenneth, my heart is pure and true but everything else is an act and I am so tired because it makes me weary. Sometimes I forget who I am and am in grave danger of losing sight of Georgie, the person in here." Georgie touched her heart then took Kenneth's hand.

"When I am with you I relax, you calm me. Do you know that my favourite thing of all is when we are alone, doing anything or nothing at all? Like eating chestnuts from the bag, or walking in the park while you tell me stories of ancient Egypt, or how bees reproduce in the wild. Fancy that. Silly Georgie doing normal things."

Georgie winked and nudged Kenneth who looked brighter, less worried. "But don't get me wrong, I still *love* to dress up and go out on the town and yes, our friends are fun. Laurie is a cad and totally sweet, and I wouldn't have survived this far without him, but that's not going to be forever. He'll be off to America soon and I'll be left in Whiteley's. In fact I had almost forgotten what real is, apart from when I'm with you and dear sweet Dolly downstairs." Georgie held Kenneth's hand tightly and waited for him to speak, knowing he was full to the brim with questions.

"I understand all that, and I really don't care about any of the things you told me in the past although I am still curious as to why you behaved like a little monster. And don't look at me that way, you know it's true." It was Kenneth's turn to tease although he still needed answers and when Georgie sighed in a rather dramatic and exasperated way, he wasn't that surprised by the answer.

"Because I could and I liked it. They gave me the tools and training, good genes and opportunity so I took it. There, it's as simple as that. I have these uncontrollable moments when I get the urge to be wild, take off my shoes and dance on tables, drink whisky and swim naked in a lake. And I want to have sex, lots of it but nothing deep and meaningful, so I choose the most unsuitable men. I'm actually not too fussy but I'm not a snob or a gold digger either. Money means nothing because it just buys you things, even people, and it can make you a slave."

Georgie had to stop and catch her breath because it had all come out in such a rush, a torrent of truth but it felt marvellous, like she was almost clean.

"Goodness, well… I did ask. But I do think you should stay away from the married men, Georgie. The last thing you want is to be sued in the divorce courts and what if there are children in the family, perhaps some caution might be called for in future, choose a little more wisely." Kenneth raised his eyebrows and tried to look stern.

Seeing Kenneth's expression made Georgie smile. He had reverted back to type and was no longer a lost little boy but her knight, and she liked that, having someone to look out for her.

"Alright, I'll try. But I swear I'm not evil or cruel. I can be kind and loving and I know I should stop and think about morality and wedding vows but I don't, but I will, if it would make you feel better about me."

"I think it will make you feel better about yourself and that is far more important. I accept you just as you are, I promise I do." Kenneth placed his arm around her shoulders then kissed the top of her head, both were smiling, content and perfectly in tune.

In fact Kenneth proved exactly how much he accepted Georgie because the following day he suggested she moved into the

Kensington House and brought Dolly along too. The place was huge and had a very cosy nanny flat at the back, overlooking a small garden that Dolly could enjoy in the warmer months. He gave Georgie a cheque so she could spruce the place up and drag it into the present century and although he missed her dreadfully when he was at Tenley, felt comforted that she and his more homely abode would be waiting when he returned.

In the meantime, Georgie was free to do as she wished and with whom, and during his trips to London if Kenneth found a gentleman to spend the night with, and there were plenty to choose from amongst their circle, they had each other's blessing. They were young and free and for almost a year lived life as they wished, until it all came crashing down.

A fervent inquisition by his mother had sent Kenneth scurrying back to London, quite panic stricken that their love nest was about to be ripped apart by The Cuckoo who had heard rumours and was threatening an intervention, a royal visit at the very least.

While Kenneth related the tale, Georgie seemed far more engrossed admiring the lovely maxi dress she'd picked up earlier, only succumbing to his pleas that she took the situation seriously when he stormed off and took refuge in his room. Lighting a cigarette, Georgie followed and sat on the end of his bed, lounging against the bedpost as she observed him. He was deep in thought and staring on to the street below, arms crossed while his right hand covered his mouth, like he was holding in a scream. Not in fear; temper and frustration more like.

"Darling, come and sit by me." Georgie patted the bed but Kenneth remained by the window.

His resistance caused her to smile. She liked it when he was manly so allowed him his stubborn moment. After all, she had no clue of what to say or do so when Kenneth finally turned and began pacing, his hands placed in his pockets, forehead furrowed in concentration Georgie remained silent and let him think. He stopped mid-pace, inhaling deeply, savouring the second-hand smoke and Georgie's uncharacteristic silence. It had allowed him to work things out in his head, all alone, and his next words were a shock to them both.

"Do you know something? I'll be damned if that woman is allowed to ruin what we have. I have lived under her thumb for too long and it is time I stood up to her."

"I couldn't agree more, darling."

Kenneth frowned. "Please don't interrupt, Georgie."

"Sorry, dearest, do continue." Georgie chuckled at Kenneth's frown.

"I have you to thank for giving me both courage and a new life therefore I want you to be part of it, always. Mother can go to hell for all I care."

"Hear, hear." Georgie raised her hands as if to apologise for the interruption then smiled sweetly before Kenneth continued.

"I will not bow to her demands ever again and if she doesn't approve of you I really don't care, not a jot. How wonderful and downright liberating is that?" And as if to prove his point, Kenneth threw his head back and laughed loudly, causing Georgie to start.

"I must say I like this new determination but what exactly had you in mind? Are you going to present me at court as your muse… I'm sure Phyllis will have me hung drawn and quartered by dawn." Georgie wasn't convinced but had allowed Kenneth his moment in the spotlight, quite confident that by evening he would return to his senses.

"Oh my darling, I have a much better idea than that, not having you chopped up. I mean about Mother."

Georgie clapped her hands excitedly. "Are we going to chop your mother up?" On hearing Kenneth sigh she curbed her sarcasm and tried to be serious. "Go on then, spit it out, I'm all ears."

Kenneth came over to the bed, his long legs made it in two strides and before she knew it, he was on one knee, holding her hand in his. A clearing of the throat preceded his unrehearsed speech.

"Dearest Georgie, would you do me the immense honour of becoming my wife and remaining by my side through thick and thin, loving life and having as much fun as we can jam into it, so long as we both shall live?" Kenneth had never been so sure of anything in his whole life and gripped Georgie's hand, willing her to say yes.

In the ensuing silence, as Georgie held her cigarette in the air, astounded by Kenneth's proposal, in that moment she felt such utter love and deep admiration for the soppy looking chap on bended knee in front of her, there could only be one answer.

Pulling his hand upwards towards her lips, she kissed it gently, smiled and said yes. Of course she would marry him. It would be a pleasure.

Chapter 10

Sandy

Sandy shrugged on her jacket and picked up her handbag before heading for the back door of the retirement home where she worked. Her shift was over and as she stepped into the spring sunshine, inhaled deeply, sucking in the air, cleansing her body of the odour of death that prevailed inside the council-run facility. For most of the residents it was the final stage of their journey through life and Sandy's job as housekeeper was to ensure they had clean sheets on which to depart the herein. Whether they had an efficient household in the hereafter was for them to discover.

It was Sunday and owing to her six–two shift, Sandy had missed morning service at church but would be there for evensong. She actually preferred this as sometimes she struggled in the mornings, but that was her business, hers and the Lord's. He forgave Sandy anything, she knew that now.

After months of worry and scouring the newspapers for information and keeping her ears open for any hint of gossip, the perpetual feeling of fear that had gripped her heart since that morning by the swimming pool had vanished. It had been eased away by the love of God who saw everything. The Almighty would have known it was an accident and for that reason he had seen to it all, made things right and shown her the way once again.

Sandy's unexpected return to the church had occurred one week before New Year's Eve, 1965, when in a fit of despair, she had given God just one more chance to redeem himself, show her the way and prove he hadn't forsaken her. Sandy's epiphany was timely and took place after she carelessly knocked over her bottle of gin, the contents soaking into the rug, dissolving the pills she was about to consume.

On wet and bended knees, she had sobbed and begged God over and over for a sign, to reach out his hand and smile kindly, just like he did in the books she'd read in Sunday school. As she wiped her eyes and gulped back the last dregs of gin from her glass and bottle, Sandy staggered over to her bed and threw herself onto the mattress. Pulling the blankets over her body, she was grateful at least for the oblivion the alcohol afforded her, free from the dreaded nightmares.

As Sandy slept, she was unaware that God had in fact been listening and within days her prayers would be answered. Perhaps he'd been there all along, invisible footsteps in the sand, or along carpeted corridors and as she waited in turn at the off-licence, walking by her side, guiding her along a path since the day she left home, one which would lead to her daughter.

***

On that cold February morning, the day she denounced her family forever, Ivy headed to Bournemouth for no other reason than it was advertised on a poster that she'd spotted on the bus depot wall. She took a pleasant enough room in a boarding house on the seafront and then set about pawning or selling her stolen goods. Not in the same shop, but scattered here and there so as not to arouse suspicion. Ivy had amassed quite a nest egg so next, set about changing her identity. After a morning at the salon and despite the protestations of the hairdresser who would've died for a head of lustrous auburn hair, Sandy had it dyed the darkest brown and then kept her appointment with a solicitor. There, without too much fuss she changed her name by deed poll.

Once Ivy Emsworth became Sandy Taylor, her new name inspired by the wholesome teenage actress Sandra Dee, she went in search of a job. Sandy was taken on as a live-in chambermaid at The Northumberland Hotel, one of the most prestigious in

Bournemouth with its art deco styling and East Cliff position, looking out across sandy beaches and the English Channel beyond.

On the whole, she found the work easy but the people, both staff and guests, irritating and tiresome and for one reason or another soon began to despise most of them. Her colleagues were common and shallow who focused on skiving and pay day, then how to spend their wages in the most frivolous manner possible. Sandy had nothing in common with any of them and preferred her own company, that and a bottle of gin. The drinking was purely medicinal and aided a good night's sleep because it was imperative she kept the nightmares at bay, replaying every bad memory, haunting her. The doctor had given her pills but they made her lethargic and unable to do her job properly so after too many sleepless nights, Sandy had turned to alcohol. It worked, helped her to relax and forget for a while. It didn't cure the pain in her heart though, that never went away.

For the most part, Sandy tolerated the ungrateful snobbish guests and avenged their rude indifference and slovenly ways by stealing from them. She took items that wouldn't be noticed immediately and could have been lost anywhere in Bournemouth, like coins from a discarded trouser pocket, lighters, a silver compact, or an item of clothing that would go unnoticed and flung into her laundry cart then sold at the dress agency in Poole. Cutlery and porcelain were particularly easy because nobody noticed when a room service tray came back lighter than it went out. The cups and saucers, teapots and sugar bowls were easily passed off as her dead granny's bits and bobs. It was easy and the only thing that made Sandy feel fulfilled because in all aspects of her life, Sandy was hollow.

Nothing, not one single thing could fill the void her baby had left. Sometimes Sandy thought this and the memory of her baby girl being taken from her arms would finally kill her. It would have been so easy to die. The one and only thing that had prevented Sandy from flinging herself off the cliffs was the tiniest glimmer of hope that the fervent wish, one she made frequently, would come true; to be reunited with her daughter. Sandy was prepared to wait a lifetime and had she known where to look would have set off in search without delay, but there was no way of tracking her baby down so instead she marked time, it was all she could do.

And so life went on, endless toil that consisted of soiled sheets, cleaning away the detritus of others, and solitary hours in her tiny room at the top of the hotel while below, those more fortunate laughed and dined and fornicated. While Sandy took most of it on the chin, sometimes the unfairness of it all gnawed away, scratching, irritating, making her bitter.

In need of some release from constant angst, an outlet, a way to redress the balance, Sandy set her mind on punishment. If God didn't care who did what and with whom, then she would take matters into her own hands. This was why Mrs Gilmore received an anonymous telephone call one sunny afternoon, advising her that Mr Gilmore was currently spending the afternoon in Room 261 with a blonde lady called Cheryl. And why the very rude woman in Room 280 came out in an angry rash after spraying what she thought was Chanel No5 all over her scrawny neck. Urine can be quite astringent.

But on the day Sandy saw the mother slapping her little girl's hand in temper and afterwards, hearing the child sob when she was left with the nanny, the word punishment took on a new meaning. Some people didn't deserve children, like those who stayed out for hours while the listening service took over, and Sandy couldn't even contemplate those women who she spotted in town, who bred like rabbits yet were unable to feed and clothe their offspring. It was so unfair because they would be better off with her, she would love them properly and in return they would fill that big gaping hole in her heart.

That evening, Sandy was almost fevered in her excitement, fuelled mainly by drink but encouraged by the images in her head as she made wild plans. During her annual leave she had taken two short breaks to France after obtaining an excursion document from the post office. It was all incredibly simple, one had only to give proof of identity and hey presto, you could board a ferry to Le Touquet. What was stopping her doing it again but this time with a baby? They could be across the channel and on their way to a new life before anybody could raise the alarm. But she would have to be prepared and as soon as she spotted an opportunity, take it. All she would need were documents for the child and although the idea at first seemed unfeasible, Sandy couldn't let it go, she wouldn't.

Much to Sandy's annoyance the maids at the hotel gossiped about everyone and everything and that morning as she stripped a bed with her colleague, a simple and very irritating girl named Tracey was no exception. She was telling Sandy all about the latest family of ten-pound Poms who were staying in the next room on their list. Apparently they were staying over in Bournemouth, visiting family before heading for Tilbury Docks where they would sail to the other side of the world and begin a new life in Australia.

Sandy listened with interest. She'd spotted the family of five as they headed down for breakfast. The parents were accompanied by two little girls; the mother carried a babe in arms. Sandy's mind raced, her thoughts on what treasures their room would hold: vital papers needed for travel, passports and visas and no doubt, birth certificates. All she had to do was get her hands on them. As usual, Tracey felt the desperate need for a cigarette part way through their shift which was why Sandy less begrudgingly than usual said she'd carry on alone while her counterpart nipped outside.

Sure that Tracey was racing down the service stairs, Sandy opened the door abandoning any notion of methodically cleaning the ten-pound Poms' room. Beads of sweat formed on her forehead as her heart pumped, the search of all the obvious places had proved fruitless and then she saw the suitcases. Time was running out.

Dragging the chair over to the large double wardrobe, Sandy stood on top and reached above, pulling the first one down and then flinging it onto the bed before clicking open the catches. Nothing, it was empty so she ran back and dragged down the larger heavier one which she placed on the floor and with no time to waste, cursing under her breath, grappled with the buckles then flicked open the catches only to find this too was empty. Tears pricked her eyes as fury coursed through her veins, her breathing heavy as she pushed her dreams aside and snapped back to the present, swiftly fastening the locks then replacing both cases.

With seconds to spare, Tracey returned, stinking of cigarettes but ready to get on with work. Sandy, however, had no intention of cleaning the room and as she shoved past her colleague, glaring as she did so, left her cleaning cart at the door and marched off towards the stairs, in search of the head housekeeper.

An hour later, locked in her room and feigning illness, from her small grimy window, Sandy watched the holidaymakers below. She hated them all – every single one of them. Not the children though. It wasn't their fault that they had been lumbered with inferior parents. But it was the thought that one of them might need her, and that her baby was out there somewhere and might need her too, was like a crippling disease that festered in her blood and bones. It was killing her, Sandy could feel it.

Taking the gin bottle from the drawer, Sandy unscrewed the top and gulped a mouthful of the bitter liquid, bitter just like her. Tears rolled down her face which she defiantly swiped away, furious with herself for showing weakness. But Sandy was tired of it all – the loneliness, the anger, the loss. It was breaking her down bit by bit and she truly didn't think she had the energy or the willpower to go on. She also feared the tinge of madness because after all, she had pushed the boundaries and had she succeeded and continued with her plan she could so easily have been caught and arrested and then what? Spend her life in a prison worse than this, or the empty cell of her own mind, incarcerated and going quietly crazy.

Sandy opened the drawer and took out the bottle of sleeping tablets and by its side she saw the aspirin. Would that be enough to finish her off, along with the gin? Tipping them all into her hand, Sandy reached for the bottle of gin, staring at the pills in her palm, blurring quickly as tears spilled from her eyes. When a mixture of gin and fatigue caused a momentary lapse in hand to eye coordination, Sandy misjudged and sent the bottle toppling off the side of the cabinet and in her haste to prevent spillage, she also dropped the tablets which scattered and soon softened in a pool of alcohol, seeping into the swirling red and yellow patterns, sucking her chance of escape deep into the woollen fibres below.

It was then that she prayed. Sandy was overcome, so she begged and beseeched God to show her mercy, light the way, take her in his arms and right the wrong, prove his love for her when she needed it the most. Her wretchedness at the moment was akin to losing her baby and it was all she could do to heave herself onto the bed and cover her trembling body with the blanket. In the last pathetic moments before she collapsed in a heap, she drained the remnants of her glass and bottle, just a few drops and recognised in herself a pitiful sight. She was gripped by the demon drink, unable to escape its clutches.

Six days later during her afternoon off, physically recovered yet still mentally shaken by her dalliance with death and subsequent prostration before the Lord, Sandy had ventured outside. Hell bent on averting her eyes from babies in prams and doing her damnedest to resist the lure of the off-licence, she had sought the mindless distraction of having her roots done. Her usual salon had been fully booked so Sandy sought out another, much pricier and frequented by a higher class than she but following an earlier trip to the pawnshop she could afford it.

Sandy had no idea that the Lord frequented salons but that day he had walked by her side. He steered her in the right direction then made sure a copy of *The Lady* lay on top of the pile that the junior placed on Sandy's knee. While she waited for her cup of tea and flicked through the dog-eared pages of the magazine, her eyes settled on an article about some toffs and their wonderful day out at a county polo match. Sandy was about to turn the page when something caught her eye and her heart stopped, then beat rapidly as her cheeks burned hot, the same way her eyes burned into the image of a car and the two people sitting just to the side of it. That photo of the mind, the one she'd taken five years earlier of a car that sped into the distance taking her baby, its registration plate, KT 129 etched into her brain, flashed before her.

Her eyes looked upon the smiling man, his arm casually resting on his knee and then the woman, holding a little girl with dark curly hair. In that explosive second of realisation, Sandy's world flipped and the pages of the magazine blurred. Feeling faint, Sandy sucked in a lungful of air through pursed lips, willing herself to stay conscious as her trembling hands held on tight to the magazine. Feeling the panic ebb and her heart rate return to normal, she allowed her brain to regain order and sort through the jumbled messages that swam inside her head. Casting her eyes from one side to the other, seeing that she was unobserved, Sandy quickly folded the magazine and stuffed it inside her handbag. The photograph was precious, as was the information contained within the article. This was what she had been waiting for, the miracle she had so desperately prayed for. He had listened, she was not forsaken.

One month later, after buying herself a solid gold crucifix and serving her notice, obtaining in return a spotless and glowing reference, Sandy left Bournemouth and headed north, direction Frosham in Hampshire. The home of her baby girl.

***

Sandy was seated right at the back of the congregation, alone in her contemplation, soaking up the vicar's words and energy but most of all, God's love. Even though she was a regular, for the most part Sandy kept herself to herself, still friendly and affable, neither drawing attention nor standing out as being weird or a loner. She steadfastly refused offers to join the church committee, fearful it might encourage interactions and curiosity about her personal life although she did help out at church events as it was a means to an end. The tentacles of the good Christian community spread wide and it was useful to remain in the loop, privy to rumours and gossip camouflaged as chit-chat and concern. Preferring her communion with God to remain the focus of her devotion, Sandy resolutely resisted any offers of friendship and continued on her mission. The reason she had come to Frosham.

***

After her arrival in 1969, Sandy had been prepared to play the long game, taking employment when and where she could, watching and waiting. The unfortunate incident at the swimming pool had rocked her to the core but once the fuss died down and the gossip mill turned to other matters, she relaxed. Sandy also curbed her desire to get up close to her daughter and refrained from walking along the public footpaths close to the house. It wasn't worth the risk and anyway, there was no point. She'd heard via the gardener's wife who visited her old mum at the home, that the pool had been closed off since Mrs Tenley's sad death and that the little girl, Vanessa, was terrified of water and refused to go anywhere near.

Instead, Sandy focused on her child's school, a lovely private establishment in its own grounds, quite impenetrable and sadly not requiring any staff but still, she kept an eye on situations vacant in the newspaper. She also attended the Christmas and summer fairs, lingering by the stalls, hoping for a glimpse. It was like torture, knowing that her precious child walked the corridors and attended assembly in the polished halls. Sandy felt her imprint, her presence, everywhere. But despite such vigilance, Vanessa never appeared at the fetes with her father or one of the nannies employed to care for her. It was as though they were purposely keeping her out of sight, taunting Sandy.

Instead of giving up, she placed all her faith in prayers, and lo and behold, after hours on bended knee he had finally responded, just as she knew he would. Of this, Sandy was accepting but not grateful, why should she be? The Lord had chosen this path for her after *he* had made mistakes, taking away her father, placing her in the care of an unloving mother, in sight of a rapist and then given away her baby. No, the Lord owed her this, which was why when she asked, eventually, her prayers were answered.

Sandy made her way to the door of the church where she exchanged pleasantries with the vicar before heading towards her car, feeling cleansed and joyous, hopeful even. The next day was to be very important, and everything had to go just as she planned.

***

From the moment Sandy had clapped eyes on the photograph in the Parish magazine, she knew it was God's will. Everything that had happened from the moment she accepted him into her life was his way of making things right. There on the front cover was a photograph of the new Lady Tenley, and Sandy recognised her instantly. They had met twice before: once on the platform of Paddington Station then years later, again by chance, during Sandy's very lonely holiday in the capital.

It had seemed like a good idea at the time to broaden her horizons and visit London's landmarks but she had hated every moment. Even the B&B in Bayswater was smelly and shabby so along with the noise and the crowds, it helped Sandy decide to cut short her stay and head back to Bournemouth. The only positive experience was her visit to Whitley's department store where she purchased some undergarments and a new blouse for church, and it was there that she had a brief encounter with the floozy from the station.

Of course she didn't recognise Sandy, why would she? But there was no mistaking the blonde bombshell who laughed and joked with the lady before her in the queue. Whilst she folded and packed Sandy's garments with the same care and degree of politeness, there was not a flicker of recognition as the floozy handed over her change. This only served to depress Sandy more and left her feeling insignificant and strangely hurt as she battled her way through the crowds, holding on tightly to her suitcase and carrier bag, and her dignity, as she held in tears.

At the time, Sandy had put the meeting down to pure coincidence and forgot all about it but now, she knew it was a sign. God was throwing them together.

***

During visits to the nursing home to see her unresponsive mum, the gardener's wife was easily bored and seemed grateful when Sandy popped by with fresh towels, and spent a few minutes chatting about this and that. It was here that Sandy learned as much as she could about the new Mrs Tenley who by all accounts was the complete opposite of the previous lady of the manor. She had brought the house alive and everyone adored her, especially little Miss Tenley who was a changed child since the arrival of her stepmother. Somehow managing not to bristle at this news, instead Sandy extracted every single scrap of information on offer, and more besides. The latest nanny had been dispensed with, however, Mrs Tenley was finding step-motherhood a strain and with the imminent departure of Cookie the housekeeper, her job was about to get even harder.

It was common knowledge that Lady Tenley sought to ingratiate herself with the villagers and even insisted on ordering the meat in person and every other Saturday would take her place in the queue where, by coincidence, she would chat to a lovely lady named Sandy. This very same woman would also be helping out at the charity fair in the village hall where Lady Tenley was due to cut the ribbon and judge the Victoria sponge competition. At some point during the day and, quite by chance, the acquaintances would bump into each other. If everything went according to plan and the rumours were true, when Sandy offered her services as the next housekeeper and part-time nanny to Vanessa, Lady Tenley would at least give her an interview, or fall at her feet in gratitude. If it were God's will, then so be it.

Chapter 11

Vanessa

The clock on her bedside table said 4pm which meant Georgie would be back very soon, although Vanessa wished there was a way to make the hands spin faster, not just by twisting the wheel at the back, but actually make time go quicker and then she'd be home again. It had been such bad luck that the day before she had woken with a terrible cold which meant she wasn't allowed to the charity fete in the village. She had so wanted to go and hold Georgie's hand and show her off to everyone, especially the horrid girls from school.

One or two of them had actually been quite nice to Vanessa recently but only because they hoped to be invited for tea so they could meet Georgie and perhaps one of her famous friends, Vanessa knew that. She didn't care because it was a relief to finally be accepted and allowed to join in. The girls at school had always been mean, whispering behind her back, saying Tenley was haunted by Daphne's ghost and calling Vanessa cruel names, like Nessie after the Loch Ness monster. They never invited her to parties because they said she'd eat all the food and Jemima sometimes pulled her hair and laughed at her when they did ballet. Vanessa hated Jemima more than anyone and there was no way she would ever invite her to tea, or the party Georgie was arranging for Vanessa's birthday.

Vanessa had never had a proper party. Daddy and the nannies had said she could have one but nobody would have come so instead they went out for tea. This year things would be different, everything was different. From the moment Vanessa opened the front door and saw Georgie get out of the car and smooth down her dress, then smile the most beautiful smile, Vanessa's whole life had changed. Resting her head on the pillow, Vanessa closed her eyes and remembered 'Georgie Day.' It was like magic. A curse had been lifted from Tenley and a beautiful fairy stepmother had cast a spell of happiness over everyone.

***

When Vanessa spotted the stranger, a blonde-haired lady alighting from her father's car, for one dreadful moment she presumed it would be another nanny. After all the grumpy guts upstairs had already told Granny she was leaving at the end of the week. Stepping forward, Vanessa made her way down the steps towards her father who looked rather shifty, or was he nervous, yes that was it because he was red in the face like when he was called to Granny's room. The pretty lady had moved to the front of the car and smoothed down her skirt, then flicked back her blonde silky hair and smiled at Vanessa who was feeling awkward and shy. The cat seemed to have taken everybody's tongues until the lady spoke.

"So, you must be Vanessa. Your daddy has told me all about you. My, aren't you a little smasher. And I do love your dress. My name's Georgie, by the way." Again, a smile. Kind and encouraging as she held out her gloved hand, treating Vanessa like a grown-up.

Vanessa smiled back and stepped forward. "Pleased to meet you too, Georgie."

And then the strangest thing happened. When they shook hands, Georgie held on, she didn't drop Vanessa's but instead guided her towards Kenneth who appeared to be holding his breath.

Kenneth, looking and feeling relieved, took the other hand of his bemused daughter and realising that the cat had kindly returned his tongue, managed to speak.

"That's the tricky bit over with. Shall we go inside and find Granny? I want to tell you about our surprise, come along, and then we can all have tea." As the three of them climbed the steps and entered the shadowy hall of Tenley, Vanessa was less concerned about the arrival of the pretty lady and more perplexed about her father's comment. He had definitely said *'our surprise'* when she was sure it was supposed to be just for her.

"Married?"

"Yes, Mother. Georgie and I are married and I apologise for springing it on you like this but we are so very much in love and just decided to throw caution to the wind and as they say these days, get hitched." Kenneth was sticking to the script he'd rehearsed with Georgie and as much as his legs were desperate to pace the floor and release pent up anxiety, he remained by her side.

Vanessa in the meantime found she was still holding on to Georgie's hand and as her head flipped from one person to the other, noticed that her new friend was the only person who looked like she was enjoying herself. The sides of her blue eyes were crinkled and Vanessa could tell she was trying hard not to smile because her lips twitched slightly. Granny on the other hand looked like she had been frozen. Her face and body were so stiff Vanessa thought she might shatter, which would be marvellous because they could scrape her into a dustpan and throw her in the bin.

After the silence, Phyllis, drawing on years of experience, gathered herself enough to speak. "I must say this is all rather unconventional and has come as a great shock but what's done is done, so all that remains is for me to welcome you to my family… Georgie. Is that your actual name by the way, it is rather masculine?" Phyllis had resorted to condescension, her least-destructive weapon. Remaining seated, she imperiously held out her hand and waited for Georgie to approach, which meant letting go of Vanessa's hand.

Georgie walked confidently across the room to shake Phyllis's hand, watched intently by Vanessa who felt rather abandoned, which was odd really, but it was only for a few moments while introductions were made.

When she addressed Phyllis, Georgie's voice wasn't simpering or enthusiastic either, however, when she mentioned Vanessa it changed, sounding full of kindness and excitement. "Very pleased to meet you Phyllis and whilst I was christened dreary old Georgina, I much prefer Georgie, it's fun and far easier to say. Now, I must get to know this adorable little girl who I am sure is going to be my new best friend. Come over here and sit next to me so we can chat while Daddy brings us some tea. I'm parched, aren't you?" Georgie had turned her back on Phyllis and without being asked had taken a seat on the sofa which she patted, speaking directly to Vanessa. Kenneth on the other hand scooted over to the bell and rang for refreshments.

And that was how it began. Phyllis managed to control her temper for almost a week until her anger bubbled over and all hell broke loose, that was until the angel stepped in and calmed everyone down.

Vanessa knew a storm was coming and there was no way Granny would put up with someone like Georgie being part of the family, not after she found out she used to be an actress and had recently been working in a shop selling undergarments. Honestly, Vanessa thought Granny was going to die of shock. Her cup actually wobbled before she replaced it on the saucer, sloshing tea over her dress. Most unladylike.

Over dinner that night, Georgie told Vanessa all about her actor friends, one of them had been on television and would soon be making a film in Hollywood. And then there were the musicians and writers, and once, Princess Margaret had offered her a cigarette in a nightclub. Somewhere amongst her bits and bobs, Georgie had a photo of them seated together at a party, fancy that? Vanessa was in awe and while she tucked into her chicken, Georgie smoked and picked at her food and made Daddy laugh out loud while they both drank lots of wine. Granny didn't speak a word and looked like she'd swallowed a lemon and then to everyone's relief, retired early.

Later that evening, after Nanny had gone to her room to pack, Georgie came to say goodnight to Vanessa who was exhausted but unable to sleep after the thrill of it all. She was just about to climb out of bed and creep to the top of the stairs so she could listen to the music playing downstairs when she heard a gentle tapping on the door and a voice asking if she could enter. It was her.

When Georgie popped her head around the door, she made a funny face and then smiled before coming to sit on the bed, gently swiping a stray curl from the shy girl's forehead and then taking her hand.

"I just wanted to say goodnight and thank you for being such a darling today. I do realise this has been a huge shock for you but I really do hope we can be friends once we get to know each other. Would you like that too?"

Vanessa nodded. She wanted to be friends with Georgie more than anything in the world.

"And there's to be none of this evil stepmother nonsense. It is so tiresome when people don't get along and I have no intention of stealing your lovely daddy, we can share him, half each. Is that a deal?" Georgie made a chopping motion then tickled the back of Vanessa's hand, making her giggle.

"Yes it's a deal and I don't mind sharing, not at all. Today has been so much fun and the best surprise, truly it has." Vanessa meant every single word.

"That has made me extremely happy and rather pleased with myself. Right, now you snuggle down and then tomorrow the three of us can have some fun. Daddy's going to show me around Tenley but afterwards perhaps we can go for a picnic, would you like that?"

"I'd like that very much."

"Marvellous, I will look forward to it." Georgie pulled the covers up around Vanessa's shoulders and then gave her a peck on the cheek as she stood.

Before she had reached the door, Georgie was halted by a question from Vanessa.

"Georgie, can I ask you something?"

"Of course, dearest, you may ask me anything."

"What shall I call you… now you are married to Daddy?" Vanessa could feel her cheeks burning, quite shocked by her own forthrightness.

Georgie smiled that smile, like honey and sunshine and the good witch in *The Wizard of Oz*, before asking a question in return.

"You can call me whatever you like, as long as it's lovely and nice… I know, what about GT, short for Georgie Tenley but oh no, that sounds like a drink so perhaps we should wait a while and think of something fun. How about that?"

"Yes that's fine, I just want everyone to know who you are, like when we are out. I wouldn't want there to be any confusion." Vanessa had lost her nerve and desperately hoped that she didn't sound foolish or eager. But she had so longed to call someone Mummy again.

There was a silence and in it, Vanessa could hear the clock ticking and her heart thumping and then Georgie spoke.

"Oh, don't you worry your head about that, dearest. I assure you that soon everyone will know who I am and that you're my little girl. Now go to sleep otherwise that beastly looking nanny will tear a strip off me and feed it to your granny." That smile again and then a wink before a kiss was blown in Vanessa's direction and the door closed shut.

Wiggling further beneath the covers as she closed her eyes, Vanessa smiled, allowing in the lovely visions of golden-haired Georgie. Vanessa's heart was full of a strange feeling and her tummy swirled. It was as though she was fizzy inside. Like when Cookie made éclairs or Nanny took her to the sweet shop. Happiness, that's what it was and after waiting for so long for it, Vanessa was going to make sure it never went away. Those horrible pictures in her head, the ones of Daphne, and the blood, and that dreadful screaming and the sound of wailing sirens, all of it began to fade.

By the following week, shades of darkness were returning to Tenley, and as Vanessa listened on the stairs, she feared the worst – that she didn't deserve to be happy and just seven days of it was all she'd have. Vanessa remembered every single day of her happiness, imaginary hearts written in red, marked on a calendar in her head.

Day one began after waiting for Georgie to appear at breakfast. She finally surfaced just before eleven and after lots of cups of coffee and another lie down on the sofa, felt well enough to take a tour of Tenley. Vanessa trailed behind like a puppy, listening to her father desperately attempting to make their dreary home sound wonderful. She had waited in the kitchen as they explored the old orangery and pool, instead watching Cookie preparing their picnic. When the tour resumed, Daddy looked a bit pale but Georgie soon cheered him up. Despite shaking her head at the faded wallpaper and tatty carpets, she made Kenneth and Vanessa laugh, especially as they passed the private sitting room that belonged to Phyllis, the one that nobody apart from Cookie was allowed into.

"Kenneth darling, what is that dreadful smell? It's like something beastly is rotting away." Georgie sniffed the air and twisted her face in disgust.

On the wall where they stopped, hung a tapestry. The writing and figures woven into it were barely distinguishable and its only useful purpose was to soak up dust and provide a home for moths.

"Oh, it's this, the Tenley Tapestry. Been in the family forever, since they used carpets to warm the halls, but you're correct, it is rather smelly." Kenneth flicked it with his finger and peered behind as if expecting something odiferous to crawl out.

Hearing Georgie exhale rather dramatically interrupted his examination as she replied in a very relieved manner. "Oh, thank heavens for that. For one frightful moment I thought it might be your mother. Perhaps you should pop your head in and check she's still with us… but on second thoughts, leave her be."

As they made to leave, they heard the tinkling of a bell from behind the door.

"Oh well, at least we know that noisy budgie is alive and kicking even if Phyllis has croaked. Now come along both of you.

Let's go outside and get some fresh air before we are infected by the plague or whatever else lurks beneath all of this dust." Taking Vanessa's hand Georgie led the way, all three of them giggling as they went.

What fun Vanessa had that week even though her school days were interminably long and worse, nobody believed her about Georgie and it made her so cross. Daddy was in a flap most days because he had to get up early and run Vanessa to school, even when his head thumped because he'd stayed up rather late listening to music. But he still smiled much more than he used to.

It was on the Thursday evening that all hell broke loose, and Vanessa was already feeling particularly glum because she'd hoped to have a word with Georgie and ask if she could possibly come to school one day so all the girls could see her. But she was in bed with a dicky tummy and Daddy said she wasn't to be disturbed so after eating tea alone, Vanessa went in search of her father.

As she neared the bottom of the stairs, Vanessa heard a terrible row going on in the sitting room so edged closer and perched on the stiff chair outside. There was no need to put her ear against the door, not this time. She knew her granny could be mean but she was being especially horrid and shouting at the top of her voice. It was as though she'd gone mad.

"Kenneth. Have you lost your mind? I will not stand for it one moment longer. I mean it. She is meddling in matters that do not concern her and I would thank you both to remember whose house this is." Phyllis banged her stick in temper as Kenneth rolled his eyes, knowing only too well where this was going and also, that his mother was well aware the house and title now belonged to him.

She was exerting her authority; holding on to her last shred of control and could not cope with another woman, a damn strong one at that, daring to challenge her.

"For heaven's sake, Mother, Georgie wants to redecorate, not knock the house down and start again, and be honest, just look at this place, it's decaying around our ears and you know it."

"Utter nonsense. I will not have my memories erased, do you hear me, Kenneth?"

"Yes, Mother, I hear you but on this occasion I am standing by Georgie because I am sick and tired of living in a mausoleum so you will have to get used to the changes we intend to make, it's as simple as that. If you're that concerned, I can arrange for all of your memories to be removed from the walls along with every stick of furniture and have it stored here in your private sitting room or perhaps your bedroom. Then you can enjoy them at your leisure."

"You wouldn't dare. I don't know what has come over you, Kenneth. You are being flippant and impertinent and it's getting you nowhere. And what on earth possessed you to bring that shop girl home, let alone marry the common hussy? She may have you fooled with her fake accent but I can spot breeding a mile away and she has none, not one single drop."

"Mother, please. I will not have you speaking this way about my wife and I really don't care where she's from or how she speaks… It's irrelevant to how I feel about her and that's the end of the matter. We haven't deceived you, in fact we have been transparent with regards to her background which for your information is quite respectable."

"Poppycock. She has slut written all over her and you know it. But as with all men, I'm sure that is where the true attraction lies although I must say you have once again surprised me on that count. I suppose this means we can expect another breeding session once she has her feet under the table. Let's hope she's more fertile than your last wife, God rest her soul." Phyllis presumed that piety was always required when mentioning the dead unfavourably, especially if one hoped to go upwards rather than downstairs.

"Mother, stop. How dare you speak of Daphne like that. I won't have it. Think of Vanessa, what if she hears?"

"Pah, don't irritate me with mention of that interloper. I rue the day you brought the bastard child through the door. Still, all is not lost and the shop girl might serve one useful purpose and finally pack Vanessa off to boarding school. Your *wife* clearly has no interest in the child; she can't even drag herself out of her morning stupor let alone be a mother figure. You mark my words, if she manages to reproduce, it will settle the matter and Vanessa can pack her trunk and be out of sight and mind at last. Good riddance."

Frozen to the spot, Vanessa listened to every damning word as tears rolled down her flushed cheeks and it was only when she heard her father make a strange guttural sound before storming from the room that the spell was broken.

When he saw his daughter sitting by the door, he made to speak, apologise and soothe, but sufficient words evaded him so when Vanessa fled, all he could do was chase after her, taking the stairs two at a time, calling her name.

The noise of Kenneth pleading with Vanessa and a terrible wailing sound woke Georgie from her slumber and realising the gin she'd drunk that afternoon had finally worn off, she raised herself from the bed and went to investigate. Finding Kenneth on bended knees trying to placate Vanessa who was prostrate and hysterical, hiding her face in the pillows, Georgie placed her hand on his shoulder and signalled that he should leave them alone.

Settling herself on the bed, she waited a moment and once the door closed, she spoke.

"Dearest one. Please stop crying and tell me what's wrong, come on. I can't possibly help if I can't see your face or hear what you are saying. Would you like a hug? Hugs always make me feel so much better." Georgie stroked Vanessa's hair, waiting for the sobbing to ease.

After a while, Vanessa turned her red and blotchy face to Georgie and when she saw that smile and outstretched arms, slowly pushed herself upright and nodded, a hug would be lovely.

"There, that's better, isn't it? Now, blow your nose and then you can explain who has upset you. I'm sure it can't be your lovely daddy. Was it Granny?" Georgie passed Vanessa the handkerchief that was tucked inside her cardigan sleeve.

"Yes, it was Granny. She said the most awful things about you and me, and that you are going to have a baby and then send me away, and that I'm a bastard and she has always hated me." Vanessa cried and hiccupped at the same time so while Georgie fumed inside, she allowed the sobbing child in her arms to get it all out. As she had learned since her arrival, information was power.

"Granny has always hated me because I'm not really Daddy's little girl. I know she's ashamed of me but it's not my fault my real mother didn't want me and gave me away. I've tried so hard to make her like me but she's just like the horrid girls at school. Everyone hates me, Georgie, just everyone. Granny said you're not interested in me because you can't get out of bed and if you have a baby it will be yours and Daddy's. A real Tenley, not a pretend one like me."

As Vanessa cried, Georgie hugged her tight, the child's tears falling freely onto her new dress making the front all soggy and gooey. Ignoring the mess whilst making shushing noises, she wondered at the irony of the present situation and the foolishness of a spiteful old woman. There would be no babies for Georgie, of that she was certain because the Kenneth situation aside, she had no inclination towards motherhood, none at all. Yet in that moment, as Vanessa clung on tightly and her chubby little hand rested in hers, Georgie felt a swell of sadness and then to her own wonderment something akin to affection, not quite love, maybe protectiveness.

But whatever it was, it had ignited a fire in Georgie as memories of her rejection festered within. She knew what it was like to feel abandoned, packed off without a second thought and to yearn a mother's love, even one who had herself been pushed aside. In that instant she knew exactly what she should do and once Vanessa was calm, told the sweaty and confused bundle in her arms exactly how it was going to be.

"Now listen to me, Vanessa. We will have no more of this, do you hear me? I'm going to explain exactly why you shouldn't spend one more second worrying about Granny or those hateful girls at school. I'm here to protect you and I won't let anybody send you away, do you understand?"

Vanessa nodded, her eyes wide.

"For a start, I have no intention of having a baby. Babies stop you having fun and I've heard that you aren't allowed to smoke or drink when you are pregnant and I couldn't possibly survive without my cigarettes or a cheeky gin and tonic. Your father and I are quite content with just one dearest girl in our lives, and that's you." Georgie kissed the top of Vanessa's head then continued.

"And as far as I know, being a mother is about more than getting up in the morning and burning toast, which I am very good at by the way." Seeing Vanessa smile urged Georgie on. "It is about what I feel inside here." Georgie touched her heart.

"So I want you to remember something very, very important. I knew all about you before your daddy asked me to marry him and when I said yes it was to both of you. I chose to be your mother and that makes us special, not whatever name you call me, or if I make boiled eggs, which I'm terrible at by the way. I am going to be your friend, the best mother I can be and sometimes I'll get it wrong, just like you will get things wrong too. But we will forgive each other and try to do better, is that a deal?" Georgie smiled when Vanessa nodded again, her red-rimmed eyes crinkling at the sides, happier now.

"And as for your granny, I don't care a jot what she says about you, me, anything or anyone. She's a nasty, bitter old lady who will soon be dead and gone, and then we will all be free of her sour looks and acid tongue. You just leave her to me. I'm not frightened of her. In fact she should be very frightened of me."

Vanessa gasped, her eyes full of admiration and respect.

"Now I want you to wash your face and get ready for bed while I go downstairs to speak with Granny. And then I shall get Daddy to make us some supper and hot chocolate which we will eat in the kitchen by the fire. Doesn't that sound cosy?"

Vanessa had brightened already. Georgie was going to make everything alright and they were going to have supper together, away from Granny.

"Yes, it sounds lovely. Thank you, Georgie."

"My pleasure. So get a wiggle on and wait up here until I call you. I'm off to find the wicked witch of Tenley." Georgie winked and kissed the top of Vanessa's head again before striding from the room.

***

Almost four months had passed since that evening, one where everything had changed and just thinking of how Georgie had spoken to Granny made Vanessa smile. She felt bad for her disobedience when she crept back down the stairs and listened, her face pushed against the spindles, memorising every word. Vanessa understood the threats, heard the promises, swooned slightly at the thought of being possessed, and remained to that day in awe of how someone so beautiful and petite could tame a vicious creature like Granny. But Georgie had, and Vanessa was eternally grateful.

Hearing the sound of an engine then car doors close, footsteps on gravel and then the front door slam shut, a swell of happiness overcame Vanessa. Her parents were home and all was well, and as she heard high heels tapping on the stairs, waited for their heads or just one in particular to appear.

Sure enough the face of an angel popped around the door and on seeing Vanessa wide awake, Georgie entered the room.

"Hello, dearest. My, you do look much better. Daddy is bringing up a tray while I tell you all about the fair and how well I cut the ribbon and made a little speech but first, I have some important news. Now, before I begin, you must promise to be a sensible girl and although you may not be happy about it straight away, I just know it's going to be wonderful for all of us." Georgie looked very pleased as she straightened the counterpane and smiled brightly at Vanessa who despite having a sinking feeling in her tummy was trying hard not to worry.

Nodding vigorously, causing the dark curls to bounce against her cheek she forced out her bravest reply, desperate to make Georgie happy. "Yes I promise to be sensible and I will try very hard, whatever the surprise is."

As she said the words, Vanessa prayed silently that she wasn't being sent away or another baby was on the way because apart from anything else, it would mean that Georgie was a fibber and couldn't keep her promises.

Minutes later, Vanessa learned the truth.

Chapter 12

Georgie

Knowledge, they say, is power, and from the moment Georgie stepped through the door of Tenley, she gathered information to store in her arsenal of weapons, along with being observant and sensitive, a new and rather useful personality trait that had the potential to turn her soft. It amused Georgie to think of herself in this way, like an out-of-body experience but one that had its benefits and drawbacks. Her Achilles heel had turned out to be the child, in fact, she had two Grecian weaknesses, the other was Kenneth.

His proposal had come as a huge shock, more so because he came up with it all by himself and hadn't been coerced by his mother. But that was where Kenneth's streak of independence ended because from then on, Georgie had taken control. It was mainly borne from necessity after pre-empting resistance from Tenley's matriarch. They began with ground rules.

Top of the list was their relationship which was to remain purely platonic and private. Although their friends might joke and presume as to the true nature of the marriage, outside of their circle everyone would perceive them as a happily married loving couple. After all, they were naturally affectionate towards one another, Kenneth loved hugging and kissing Georgie on the cheek, and they always held hands and linked arms wherever they went. Nobody would ever guess.

Whilst being happily married they would still be free to pursue relationships outside it, but privately and discreetly, avoiding gossip or scandal, as if they were conducting illicit affairs. Georgie thought this sounded most exciting but agreed with Kenneth that extramarital liaisons were only allowed in London. Tenley was sacred ground and there they had to toe the line.

They both loved to spend time at the Kensington house and Georgie knew she would miss Dolly and vice versa so they settled on a timetable of visits that would satisfy all of their needs. Dolly would remain in Kensington as caretaker but was welcome at Tenley whenever she wished, an invitation that was welcomed but politely turned down. For now, Dolly was happy in her posh flat and had no desire to rub shoulders with country toffs.

While she was quite happy to give up her job at Whiteley's, Georgie wasn't too keen on losing her independence. Gaining new employment would be frowned upon so Kenneth suggested an allowance, a generous one at that. All that he asked in return was that she curbed her shoplifting tendencies as it would be the biggest scandal the county had ever seen if the lady of Tenley was arrested for theft. With fingers crossed behind her back Georgie promised she would do her best.

After discussing the reaction of both Vanessa and Phyllis, Georgie suggested a solution which would appease the old crone and prevent her from denouncing Kenneth and changing her will, the child she would handle herself. They had the most fun when they visited the solicitor to arrange the pre-nuptial agreement, something Georgie insisted upon as she would not be labelled a gold-digger – any other derogatory tags would wash off like rain. It still made Georgie giggle when she recalled the appointment and the look on the solicitor's pompous face when she mentioned her special stipulations. They had agreed the financial element which consisted of Georgie's allowance and a one-off payment should they divorce. Kenneth's will was his own business and anyway, death was a long way off. But Georgie wanted more; actually she wanted a little bit of fun.

"Now we've got the dreary part out of the way, I'd like to run through a few items of my own, just bits and bobs really. I've been so inspired by the wonderful Jackie Onassis and the very strict demands in her pre-nup with Aristotle. I do hope you don't mind me springing them on you like this, darling." Georgie looked over to Kenneth, her big blues eyes giving him her best puppy-dog look.

He saw the mischief in them immediately. "Not at all, my love, fire away. I'm sure it won't be a problem." Kenneth was trying to remain calm yet he was rattled, giving the game away when he uncrossed and crossed his twitchy legs, then twiddled his fingers.

"Marvellous. Here goes. Item number one is sex. Rumour has it that Jackie has limited poor Aristotle to once a month which is quite ridiculous so I am willing to compromise and settle for twice a week, minimum, is that acceptable, darling?" Georgie forced herself not to laugh as she watched Kenneth blush crimson whilst also hiding a smile, and when she turned to the solicitor, noticed he was a lovely shade of puce.

Kenneth coughed and gathered himself before agreeing. "Yes, my darling, I'm sure that will be fine… Is there anything else?" He looked at his fiancée with a quizzical look, rather curious as to what she might say next, rather enjoying her game. She was so much fun which was why he loved her.

After agreeing to fresh flowers every Friday, driving lessons and a sporty runabout when she passed her test, first-class travel, her portrait painted and hung at Tenley and a cat, like the one in *Breakfast at Tiffany's*, they stepped onto the pavement and dissolved into hysterics. Then went to the pub and got disgracefully drunk.

Georgie didn't invite any of her family to the nuptials although she did send a letter to the Butchers, telling them all about the Right Honourable Kenneth Tenley, his home and estate and the fact that she would be the new Lady Tenley. Adding that they were most welcome to visit once she was settled and after promising to always keep in touch, Georgie left it there. The news would filter through the rest of the family and she hoped it irked the Nibleys to be excluded from her wonderful new life.

The registry office wedding was attended by any of their circle who didn't have a crushing hangover from Kenneth and Georgie's joint hen and stag night. Photographs were taken of the happy couple who looked just as much in love, if not more, than any of the other brides and grooms who posed on the steps of the town hall. Afterwards they headed to the Ritz for lunch and stayed until dawn, walking home hand in hand, Georgie in bare feet after she lost her shoes. The following day, after leaving their separate beds and kissing Dolly goodbye, the newlyweds set off for Tenley House.

From the moment Georgie set eyes on Vanessa, a chubby dark-haired version of Shirley Temple who reminded her of an over-decorated gateau in a patisserie window, there was something about the child that touched her heart. It was most disconcerting.

And in the days that followed, during her induction to the dreariest house on the planet, Georgie found her mind straying to her own childhood, one smothered in fake love that prevented her from having a true relationship with her own mother. It was clear that the child lacked emotional support and had existed on scraps from her father, other than that she made do with the nannies who came and went. And as for the monstrous Phyllis, Georgie had decided to deal with her swiftly, long before she even set off from London.

Since that very first day when they sat on the sofa and Georgie held Vanessa's squidgy hand in hers, she had sensed nervousness in the shy child with flushed cheeks along with the admiration in her eyes, the same ones that averted their gaze away from Phyllis. And with her own baby-blues, Georgie noticed the lack of family photographs, the absence of Daphne in spirit, name or replica, and very quickly the snippets she'd had from Kenneth made sense.

Vanessa was tormented by the sight of her dead mother and would become hysterical if she was reminded, hence the lack of photographs. The pool had been closed and was a place the child was petrified of, along with deep water and the sight of blood. Kenneth had mentioned some of his mother's cruelty and nature especially with regards to Vanessa.

Long before she clapped eyes on the child, Georgie had vowed to curtail such behaviour which was why in those first few days she set about befriending the staff, dear Cookie, the grumpy nanny and the cleaner, Mrs Coombs.

Within days she had the mark of Phyllis, and after collating her evidence quite quickly reached five, no need to put two and two together. Georgie had intended to bide her time but the sight of Vanessa sobbing into her pillow and on hearing the second-hand account of such vitriol, she decided that it was time for the axe to fall, swiftly and brutally, better for all of them.

Nanny said that Phyllis forgot her name and had often called her Daphne and during the night could hear the old crone crying out against the demons that she swore invaded her room. Phyllis got days mixed up, even night and day, and once Georgie had found her in her undergarments on the landing, saying she was off to the theatre. Cookie had been sworn at many times for serving food Phyllis hated, even though it had previously been her favourite and Mrs Coombs was worn out from changing the soiled sheets.

When Georgie marched into the private sitting room without knocking, causing Horace to flutter from his perch in a panic, Phyllis ordered her to leave immediately. But finding herself being gripped tightly around the throat, a slender hand squeezing as the other pinned her to the back of the chair, the terrified old woman soon became silent, just as she was ordered to, and then listened to how it was going to be.

In the voice of an East End barmaid, a gravelly, mean, take no prisoners Georgie asked Phyllis a question. "So you fink I'm a slut do you? Let me tell you somefink, lady fuckin' muck... I seen what them upper class ladies get up to when there ain't nobody lookin' and I'm tellin' you now, don't you ever look darn yer nose at me... got it?" Georgie jerked her hand, forcing the shocked woman's head backwards and then she squeezed a little tighter before assuming a more ladylike tone.

"And a few little birdies, not dear little Horace by the way, have explained just how loopy old Granny Phyllis has become.

Like how she can't remember who she is or where she's going and dear oh dear, what about all those dirty linens, so very sad and embarrassing. What on earth shall we do about such an irritating and distressing problem… now let me think?" Georgie relaxed her grip and then stood before she paced the room, tapping her lip with one finger, a theatrical look upon her face, amateur dramatics at its best.

She fully expected Phyllis to cry out and when she did, calling for Kenneth, it came out as a panicked croak and before her second attempt, Georgie had sprung forwards, this time one hand hovering above the terrified woman's lips as the other held her against the back of the chair.

"Now you listen to me, Syphilis, and listen well." Georgie's voice had a sinister tone, just like Betty Davies in *Whatever Happened to Baby Jane*. "This is how it is going to be. From this moment onwards you will remember that *I* am lady of Tenley and *I* am in control, not you. In future, wherever possible, you will remain in this room, well away from Kenneth and me. You will be served your meals here and attended to by the staff who you will treat with respect and civility. I do not wish to dine with you or be in your company, ever. With regards to Tenley, you will not hinder my plans, interfere in any way with my running of this house, or for that matter, Kenneth's management of the estate, is that clear?" Georgie waited and admired the last ditch attempt of a doomed woman who whispered her venomous reply.

"How dare you treat me this way. I will not abide by your rules and Kenneth will not allow it. I am his mother and I *will* be respected." There was steel in Phyllis's voice but within seconds it would be silenced as Georgie brought down the axe.

"I have no respect for you and neither has Kenneth, who, if you haven't noticed yet, is besotted by me and under my spell so I doubt he will want to forgo any of the pleasures or magic I bestow upon him. And as for the staff, they despise your treatment of them so I think it's high time you learnt some self-control and humility because let's face it, Syphilis, soon those you treat badly and speak down to will be washing you down and spoon-feeding mashed up food, like a pathetic baby, incapable and needy. Diddums."

Phyllis raged inside, her fury leaked from her lips and spittle flicked on Georgie's face that was inches away. "There is nothing wrong with me, I am totally capable of caring for myself and I will *not* take orders from the likes of you, or anybody, now leave this room immediately." But the resolve that Georgie had heard moments earlier was waning; a tremble in the voice told her Phyllis was rattled, so it was time to put her out of her misery.

"Oh but you will take orders from me, Syphilis, because if you don't I shall get straight on the phone and summon one of my dear friends, a rather lovely chap from Harley Street who specialises in locking up batty old fruit cakes like you. All he requires is a big fat cheque. Now, add this to the testimony from the staff and poor sweet Vanessa who is traumatised by nasty Granny, and I'm confident that you will be carted off in a straightjacket well before teatime tomorrow. Do I make myself clear?"

"You wouldn't dare." Phyllis felt the blood run cold in her bones and sweat prick her brow as any words of defence dried up in her mouth. She had lost her power, replaced by fear.

"I would… in fact I am tempted to ring him anyway, just for fun. And mark my words, should you choose to disobey me I will make sure that when they pull the strings on the jacket, I'll make sure they are nice and tight and you never return to Tenley, unless it's in a coffin, do you understand?" Georgie saw the fear in the old woman's eyes and an almost unperceivable nod so she straightened and smoothed down her dress.

"Is that all?" Phyllis was determined to salvage some dignity from the situation but soon regretted it.

"No, actually I have one more warning for you and it is with regards to Vanessa. From this day forward she is in my care. Do you see this ring?" Georgie held up her wedding band. "It means that Vanessa is now mine, my daughter, all legal and above board, and unlike you, I accept her into this family, my family. For that reason, should you ever upset her in any way, ever again, you will suffer. Is that clear?" Georgie took one step forward and glared at Phyllis who nodded twice then averted her gaze.

"I think that's everything. I have so enjoyed our little chat, Syphilis, and remember, I'll be listening out for any hint of bad behaviour, oh, and do take care on those stairs. You hear about old folks taking a tumble and I wouldn't want you to make a mess of my new carpets. Now, I'm going to find my husband and daughter. We are dining together this evening. I'll find somebody to bring you a tray. Goodnight, Mother dearest."

Georgie waved, wiggling her fingers in the direction of Phyllis as she passed Horace who chose that moment to chirp a question from his birdcage. "Who's a pretty boy?"

Raising her hand, Georgie slammed it hard against the cage and as the budgie fluttered and squawked, she replied, "Not you, Horace, not you."

Within days, a fresh breath of life entered Tenley. A team of decorators were hired after Georgie and Vanessa perused huge books containing samples of bright and colourful wallpaper and a lady from town came with swatches of fabric that she would make into new drapes and furnishings. Georgie began with Vanessa's room which was fit for a princess then began her rampage through the rest of the house. In the spring, the orangery was to be refurbished and the pool cleaned and prepared for a summer season of parties and although Vanessa still refused to go anywhere near, Georgie hoped that with time she might at least dip her toe in the water and rid herself of bad memories.

Georgie learned to drive and Kenneth had presented her with a darling little sports car, a convertible MGB that was perfect for shooting around the lanes with Vanessa by her side, shrieking with laughter as their hair blew in the wind. Because Kenneth was such a darling and took Vanessa to school each day, Georgie made much of roaring into the car park each afternoon where she waited in her very best outfits, Jackie O sunglasses adding an air of mystique, studiously reapplying her lipstick in the rear mirror and bestowing delightful smiles to the other whispering mothers. Once a week, she drove to the village and placed the Tenley order at the butcher's. She preferred to choose the cuts herself and get to know the locals. That's what she told Kenneth.

The house was beginning to look superb, shiny and new, and smelling heavenly thanks to the flowers Kenneth sent every Friday. In the new year one of their artist friends had been commissioned to paint Georgie's portrait so all that was left was to get a bloody cat, she wasn't really too fussed so decided to give it to Vanessa instead. The child would welcome something to cuddle and care for and now they had been brought into line by Georgie, she could tell all of those beastly girls about it at school too.

Lady Tenley was a hot topic amongst the mothers from Vanessa's school and rumours of the socialite with friends in high places were rife, although not necessarily believed which was why Georgie decided to bash two birds with one big stone and invite the stuck-up nosey parkers to tea. The house was now adorned with the photographs that Georgie had hoarded over the years. Happy memories, famous friends, a couple of Beatles, roguish members of parliament, a royal dining companion, a happy couple on their wedding day beside lots of Georgie and her new daughter, Vanessa. It only took a platter of Cookie's sandwiches and a Victoria sponge, along with the photographic proof that Georgie was in fact well connected. It soon became imperative for their little darlings to become firm friends with the dumpy girl they referred to as Nessie.

Everyone in Vanessa's class soon wanted an invitation to her birthday party and a look at the handsome Laurie Lambert who was a star of stage and screen, and a DJ from Radio Caroline who would be playing music. Georgie loved making Vanessa happy, in fact it had occurred to her that the little monkey really was getting under her skin and for the most part, their relationship was both mutual and adoring. That said, Georgie would soon need to lay down some ground rules as she was beginning to hanker after London and all it had to offer. Kenneth felt the same way but owing to the departure of the previous nanny, escaping to Kensington was going to be a bit of a problem.

Amongst the gadding about and dining with their affluent neighbours who were eager to meet the new Lady Tenley, Georgie set time aside after school and at weekends for Vanessa who on the whole was undemanding and quite happy to sit and read while they all listened to music or watched the brand new television. It was just the mornings that Georgie found difficult because late nights and motherhood didn't go well together and apart from doing fun things such as choosing wallpaper and the like, running the house was fast becoming tedious. The problem was further complicated by Cookie's retirement after she tearfully handed in her notice to an equally tearful Georgie. It was becoming clear that a solution had to be found and the position would have to be advertised, meaning an even more tedious task fell on her shoulders.

Dilemmas often have a strange way of sorting themselves out and it came as a huge relief when, during the charity fete at the village hall, the young woman who Georgie often chatted to in the butcher's and was now serving tea and biscuits, enquired after a job at Tenley. Suggesting they took a seat to discuss the matter privately, Sandy, as she introduced herself, admitted she had heard rumours that the cook was leaving and a position might soon become vacant. Whilst Sandy appeared confident and eager, Georgie sensed shyness and a hint of sadness in her eyes so now being of a benevolent nature and quite desperate to avoid endless interviews, enquired after Sandy's qualifications.

Sandy it seemed had trained as a teacher but later pursued a career in hospitality and was more than capable of running a hotel, let alone a home. She currently worked in the retirement home in the next town and even better, could drive and had her own car. As she listened, Georgie's mind ticked over because there in front of her eyes, sipping tea and waiting nervously, was the answer to their prayers. Sandy was educated and could act as chaperone and governess to Vanessa whilst Georgie and Kenneth were in London. Sandy could run Tenley and keep an eye on the mad old crone who was becoming a daily nuisance, tempting Georgie to act on her threats and ring Giles in Harley Street. Still, with Phyllis she could bide her time.

"I must say you are just what we are looking for but may I ask, why on earth did you give up teaching? I am sure it is preferable to hotel work and attending the elderly." Georgie stirred her tea and watched as Sandy blushed and cast her eyes downwards.

The answer began with a whisper. "It was a private matter that I'd rather not discuss except to say that I decided to cut my training short and start a new life elsewhere, although I have excellent references from my previous employer." Sandy replaced her cup before looking upwards, dreading further interrogation.

Georgie had wanted to bite off her own tongue the moment she asked the question and had already surmised the cause of Sandy's embarrassment, so placed a gentle hand over the one fiddling with a napkin and sought to reassure her.

"My dear, it's fine, please forget I asked… I suspect you have had unhappy dealings with a man and for whatever reason chose to leave. That is your business and of no concern to me, believe me, I understand. Now, if you would be so good as to pop your references in the post and provide a telephone number I will discuss the matter with my husband immediately. How does that sound?" Georgie smiled kindly and saw that Sandy had brightened and was reaching for her handbag.

"Thank you so much, Lady Tenley. And there's no need to post them, I have them here. I hope you don't think me presumptuous but I like to be organised and thought it might save time." Sandy passed Georgie the envelope.

"Why thank you, Sandy, that is most efficient of you. And it's such a shame that Vanessa has come down with a dreadful cold because you could have said hello, but never mind, I'm sure you'll meet very soon." Georgie winked and was glad to see Sandy took the hint.

They said their goodbyes and Georgie promised to be in touch within the next few days when in truth she'd already made up her mind. Kenneth would be on board, she knew that, but would discuss it on the way home and with any luck they would be in London by the end of the month.

Vanessa had taken the news well, about everything really, but that was because Georgie had a way of putting things, laying out pros and cons, and how life was all about give and take and showing each other love and respect.

Georgie explained that she and Kenneth would need to spend time in London now and again which would mean finding someone to care for Vanessa in their absence, a nice person who could step in as a governess because nannies were for babies. It would be the perfect solution if they were busy or in Georgie's case, asleep or inebriated. When Vanessa asked if she could go to London with them, Georgie said that Kenneth had business to attend to and she wanted to see her friends so Vanessa would be bored. Instead she was promised a special trip before Christmas where they could do lots of shopping, and buy a new dress for her birthday, and go to the theatre and a pantomime, her choice.

Vanessa brightened at this but then became concerned about the new governess – what if she didn't like her or they didn't get on. At this, Georgie was quite firm and pointed out that she expected Vanessa to be sensible and grown up about it and not to cause trouble, after all it was the best way and would avoid any mention of boarding schools. Not only that, according to Georgie, adults deserved to have fun too so children should understand and not be selfish, reminding Vanessa that she had done everything she could to make school life better and protect her from Phyllis so it was her turn to be selfless and kind.

After assuring Vanessa that the appointment of a governess and housekeeper would be wonderful for all of them and give Georgie lots of free time when she was in Tenley, the tension in the room receded and a storm was averted. And to make it all even better, Georgie had brought home a delicious basket of jellied fruits and handmade chocolates from the fete and if she was good, promised to bring Vanessa back a gift from Fortnum and Mason, whatever she fancied.

Before Georgie headed off downstairs she remembered something else and after giving Vanessa another dose of the syrupy cough medicine, told her about the new addition to the family.

"And I have one more question, how would you like our little family to become four?" Georgie saw Vanessa's face cloud over a moment before she replied.

"What do you mean… are you having a baby?" Vanessa had tears in her eyes as Georgie dramatically flung her hand to her breast.

"Oh my goodness, no. Whatever gave you that idea? I wondered if you would like a kitten, something to keep you company while I'm away. I have told you before, dearest, I have no intention of having children, you're my one and only, always and forever. So, what do you say?" Georgie waited, eager to get downstairs for a G&T, she was drowning in tea.

"I would love a kitten, thank you so much, Georgie, and I promise with all my heart I will be good for the governess. Honest I will."

The transformation of Tenley was complete. What had once been a house whose dark eyes glowered across the tended lawns as shadows crept along corridors, and the greyest clouds seemed to always hover above its roof was now unrecognisable, inside and out. Lights would burn all night long, the windows glowing yellow as the halls and rooms were filled with laughter and music.

As winter approached, even the house seemed to hold its breath in anticipation for a Christmas of merriment and a summer of love, while its inhabitants settled into their new lives. The master and mistress of Tenley and their delightful daughter, Vanessa.

Part III

Chapter 13

Tenley House

Georgie is in her rightful place, embracing the applause in full glare of the spotlight, lapping up the adoration and admiration that washes over her perfectly made-up face in waves. She lives life to full and can be whoever she wants to be, to whomever she chooses. A mother and lady of the manor, a wife and a slut, a wonderful hostess and a gin soaked lush. Roles she enjoys in equal measure. And thanks to the good grace of her husband, she now has the one thing she craved most, no not money, respectability. The stain of shame and the pain of rejection have been erased. She belongs.

Kenneth is living the life he was born to, in deed and spirit, free from scrutiny and unburdened by prejudice, avoiding social stigma and humiliation. He has risen from the ashes of a shabby life in the shadows and behind toilet doors. He is a good father, an excellent husband and master of his home and more importantly his mother, thanks entirely to the strength and good grace of his wife. At Tenley, he is the epitome of an alpha male and has gained the respect of the estate, and in London he is free to love and be loved in the way he always desired. He has gained respect for himself. He belongs.

Vanessa is growing; much quicker and larger than most but this does not concern her, or her doting parents whose only concern is her happiness, and theirs. She misses them dreadfully when they are away but keeps her side of the bargain, following the rules and her wonderful Georgie's examples. But despite the separations, she believes she is loved, wanted and accepted as part of the family, never to be sent or given away again. She belongs.

Phyllis is fast losing her grip on life, her body and her mind. It is all slipping away, memories, names, faces, all turning to sand and slush. But she will cling on, the fear of incarceration, and ending her days like the womenfolk gone before her, left to wander halls in soiled gowns, abandoned by their family, strikes terror in her heart. This is why she obeys the rules laid down by the blonde temptress. Phyllis is left with no choice and remains closeted in her rooms, hidden away, dreading the night, tiptoeing through her day, being polite, as quiet as possible so as not to cause a fuss or give herself away. And as much as it rankles she knows it is the only way she can remain, clinging on. For now she belongs.

Sandy will shortly be in her rightful place, by her child's side. From here she will keep her safe from harm and contamination by those not fit or suitable, within sight of the good Lord who has reunited mother and baby. And she is prepared to wait and watch until the time is right to reveal herself and take back what is hers, regardless of any obstacles placed in her way. She has worked hard for this, shown great patience and trust so all she has to do is watch for the signs and let him lead the way. God has delivered her to Tenley. This is where she belongs.

Chapter 14

Bonfire Night

The crackles and whizzing of the fireworks that zipped overhead were eclipsed only by the sound of children's voices as they oohed and shrieked with every mini explosion. Amongst the villagers and estate families were the Tenleys and their watchful governess who hovered a few steps behind the group not seeming to enjoy the spectacle or the hustle of the crowd. Vanessa was enthralled as was Georgie who, whilst wrapped in fur, had just finished handing out toffee apples to the children. Georgie and Kenneth had recently returned from London where Georgie had been to see the new West End Show *Evita*, twice, and along with knowing every word of the soundtrack, that night saw herself as Tenley's very own Eva Peron. While Georgie played her part to the full, Kenneth dealt with more manly things like lighting sparklers.

As always, Sandy had insisted that despite being fifteen and well able to dress herself, Vanessa wore gloves and a hat to ensure that she didn't burn her fingers or allow a stray ember or spark to land on her hair. The governess watched from the sidelines, at the edge of the crowd, the eternal non-family member. But that was more from choice than circumstance because Georgie went out of her way to include her in every occasion: holidays, excursions, mealtimes. However, Sandy thought it best to remain detached and avoid forming relationships because after all, one day the quiet governess hoped to walk away, and take Vanessa with her.

Patricia Dixon

Until then, Sandy would bide her time and wait for the right moment, for the Lord to give her a sign which despite fervent prayers had not arrived, but it would, she trusted in him. For now she was grateful for being delivered to Tenley and able to spend every day with her daughter. Vanessa was a teenager, surrounded by friends, mere sycophants in Sandy's opinion along with a doting stepmother whose hold was strong, the genuine fondness and loyalty between them proved most difficult to sever.

Out of everything, it wasn't the momentous reunification of natural mother and child or the bond with the stepmother that had caused Sandy the greatest distress. It was the set of Vanessa's jaw, the shape of her head, her ungainly gait and those curly raven locks that had brought Sandy up short, right from the moment she first laid eyes on her daughter.

***

The day she pulled up outside Tenley, Sandy's heart was pumping so hard she thought she might die before she set eyes on her stolen baby. Her car contained only meagre possessions held inside two small suitcases and nothing that would expose her true identity. After a trip into Bristol to offload anything of value that she'd collected from the retirement home, Sandy's life didn't take long to pack up and carry to her car.

During the short journey, one in which she was held in suspended animation, travelling along a flat line not a tarmac road, adrenalin had a numbing effect. It was strange because in her many imaginings of this day, Sandy had been wild with joy and anticipation at meeting her child whereas now, reality had a sobering influence on emotion. As she drove through the gates of Tenley, the spell was broken and the anaesthetic wore off. The sight of the majestic house in the distance in which her child awaited, kick started her heart. Not only was she nervous but petrified of giving herself away and utterly terrified of one thing in particular – rejection. What if Vanessa hated her? Sandy hated that name and was hurt beyond words that the Tenleys had changed it from that on her birth certificate. Sandy's baby was named Rachel and that was how she would always think of her. Pushing away any anger Sandy focused on the road and the momentous meeting ahead. They had to get along, they just had to.

Vanessa had been waiting in the sitting room that smelt of fresh paint, lilies and new carpet, her mother by her side. Sandy hated that word because it belonged to her, not the blonde-haired clothes horse who poisoned the room the moment she lit a cigarette, seconds after she introduced her daughter, their daughter.

It was awkward at first. Vanessa stared and Sandy did the same and in that instant she imagined that her child's eyes, so similar to her own and the only visible connecting attribute held a hint of recognition. The precious moment that was supposed to be so special was rudely broken by Georgie stepping in.

"Now, Vanessa, remember your manners and say hello to Sandy. I'm sure you two are going to get on famously and will have lots of fun together. Come along, don't be shy."

Obediently, Vanessa stood and approached, holding out her hand, wary but not unfriendly, possibly more concerned about not letting her mother down than offending the new woman.

"Very pleased to meet you, Sandy, and welcome to Tenley." Then she smiled and contact was made.

How she was able to control her emotions remained a mystery to Sandy and all she could surmise was that the fear of discovery and after coming so far, she could not give the game away, not now. As she touched the soft plump hand of her beautiful baby girl, the one she had longed for since the day, no, the second she was taken away, Sandy felt a rush of blood to the head. Fearing she would faint whilst fighting the urge to drop to her knees and pull Vanessa to her chest, hold on tight and never let go, Sandy sucked in air and steeled herself. With every ounce of strength God gave her, she smiled, her lips quivering, forcing back the tears that pricked her eyes she somehow replied.

"I'm very pleased to meet you, Vanessa, and thank you for your kind welcome." It was all she could manage so left Georgie to take the lead. It seemed her role of preference.

***

Sandy quickly got used to it, that reminder of him, the flawed genes that swam through Vanessa's blood and linked her to an ogre. She had so hoped her child would be dainty and have auburn hair but apart from her eyes which were deepest brown, it was not to be. In fact, everything about Vanessa leant more towards her natural father, the cumbersome, large-boned rapist. But all was not lost because at least she didn't limp and apart from her size, Vanessa was physically perfect and with the help of a strict regime and exercise, Sandy had been confident that she could transform her daughter and remodel her in another image.

It had proved to be an uphill struggle because Georgie, as Mrs Tenley insisted on being referred to, spoiled and indulged the child at every opportunity. In fact she soon became Sandy's worst but most unlikely of enemies, simply because Georgie was kind and sweet and very hard to dislike. Her biggest mistake of all was being adored, by Vanessa.

Their bond was like an impenetrable fort and try as she might, Sandy could not break through. Yes, Vanessa was polite and obedient and never made a fuss even when her parents went up to London for days on end. Although it was clear the child fretted, Georgie quite openly explained to Sandy about her agreement with Vanessa who despite being a bit sad, understood that her parents needed alone time.

Then there was the cat, Miss Mittens. It had been some kind of consolation prize for Vanessa, bought by Georgie to paper over her absences and salve her conscience. Sandy hated the bloody thing, a stupid hair-ball that insisted on rubbing itself all over everything. It was nasty too and had given Vanessa a deep scratch on her cheek. The hoo-ha that followed made Sandy's own hair stand on end because Vanessa became hysterical at the sight of blood and refused to be comforted by Sandy and as usual, only mother superior would do. It was always the same.

Sandy judged the relationship between Vanessa and her stepmother as rather contrived and cleverly manipulated by Georgie, who in her own and seemingly guileless way, steered the whole family in whatever direction she chose, for her own self-serving reasons. The thing was she made everyone happy, apart from Phyllis, and her number one fan was Vanessa.

It irked Sandy greatly to admit that because of this, she frequently committed yet another sin and was riddled with envy, but compared to the rest of the household, hers were tiny and forgivable in comparison. And then there were the commandments. Dear Lord the things that went on under the roof of Tenley and no doubt in London broke almost every single one of them, not that Sandy could prove it but she had her suspicions.

During the summer months the house was invaded by all manner of visitors who slithered down from London and outstayed their welcome. Not in Georgie and Kenneth's eyes, who were consummate hosts and thrived on company. As far as Sandy was concerned the guests polluted the atmosphere while their contaminated and drug-fogged minds were unsuitable company for Vanessa. Again it was like banging Sandy's head against the wall because the child adored her ragtag band of faux aunts and uncles who draped themselves over the sofas and lounged in the garden, smoking magic cigarettes and drinking themselves into a stupor. During the night, floorboards would creak as footsteps stole along the corridor, doors opening and closing, betraying secret assignations.

Thank heaven Vanessa remained terrified of the pool otherwise she would have witnessed the goings on; naked swimmers frolicking in the moonlight. Oh yes, Sandy had watched it all from the shadows, telling herself that such voyeurism was necessary in order to keep Vanessa safe and out of harm's way.

As for the Tenleys, Sandy couldn't fathom them and often listened at their bedroom door, intimate conversations drowned out by the sound of records playing late into the night. If not, Kenneth would read in his study while Georgie watched television and drank too much gin before falling asleep on the sofa, woken only by the beep at the end of service. In public they were affectionate and Georgie would perch on Kenneth's knee, gazing lovingly into his eyes, or with their heads close together whispering, sharing a private joke before pealing with laughter. For all intents they were the perfect couple and from her observations, Sandy had no reason to assume otherwise as unlike their amoral guests, during the night they remained in their bedroom, albeit not in the traditional sense.

Sandy's role of housekeeper made her privy to most things, she had access to all areas and their bedroom posed the greatest conundrum. The suite of rooms consisted of a small sitting area along with a large and lavishly furnished bedroom with dressing room and en suite. What stood out and drew raised eyebrows when Sandy first spotted them were the separate beds.

According to Georgie, it was all the rage in America and considered to be both hygienic and the essence of a happy marriage, adding with a wink that it made naughtiness much more exciting. Sandy didn't believe her. She had spent too many hours at the hotel removing sheets soiled by lust or littered with its rubber remains and there was evidence of neither, although after rummaging through her bedside drawer, Sandy had ascertained that Georgie took the pill. This alone was telling. But it was the whispered telephone conversations, giggling like a schoolgirl and Georgie's flushed face and smug smile once the receiver was replaced that gave the game away.

Not only did the lady of Tenley commit the sin of lust, she broke the commandments too. Along with the graven images of Hindu gods and fat Buddhas that littered the house, lying to her husband, dishonouring her parents, coveting the child of another, regularly taking the Lord's name in vain and presumed adulterous behaviour were added to the list of Georgie's failings.

They were all sinners, each and every Tenley. During Sunday service, while Sandy paid penance for her own deviances, it pained her to admit that even Vanessa was guilty of greed and gluttony. It was another trait which harked back to her true origins and one that Sandy had attempted to curtail but as with all things relating to Vanessa, was thwarted at every turn by Georgie.

The conversation regarding Vanessa's size occurred while she was at school and had been much rehearsed by Sandy who had fully expected resistance from both mother and child. They had been here before, not long after Sandy took up her post at Tenley but in the six years since their first discussion, Vanessa had grown even bigger, both in stature and weight.

"But, Georgie, it isn't healthy for Vanessa to eat so much and I'm convinced some sort or regime would only be beneficial, both medically and socially. You know she is still bullied and ridiculed and soon the other young ladies will attract admirers. I'm sure you wouldn't want her to feel left out." The latter point was of no real concern to Sandy as she hoped that Vanessa might avoid all that nonsense but thought it might appeal to Georgie's romantic nature and secure her help.

"Yes, yes. I completely understand your concerns, Sandy, but Vanessa is an intelligent young lady and once it occurs to her that she might need to lose a few pounds then we shall help in any way but until then leave her be. I believe that children must be allowed to go their own way and not be moulded by their parents. She has her own mind and free will so let's wait and see."

"But what about the bullying and spiteful comments? Surely it must hurt Vanessa, and as for her friends, both you and I know they are fake and after their own interests. I'm convinced they only come here in the hope of bumping into Laurie or one of your other friends, and their mothers are no better."

"So what would you prefer… that I banish them all and leave Vanessa friendless? I have to endure those dreary stuck-up women in order to secure companions for Vanessa so I don't think it's too much to expect that you turn a blind eye to their envious offspring. I do admire your loyalty and respect your concerns but you will have to trust me on this. I know what's best for Vanessa and a diet would just make her grumpy and worse of all, think we are criticising or ashamed of her. That little girl felt rejected all her life until I came into it and I won't have her upset." Georgie folded the copy of Vogue that rested on her knee.

"Now, I think I will collect her from school today and give you a few hours off… it's the least I can do. You are such a good egg, Sandy, you really are, and I don't know what we would do without you." Bringing the conversation to a close, Georgie stubbed out her cigarette and rose from the sofa.

Unable to speak due to the rage swimming through every vein and sinew in her body, Sandy merely nodded as Georgie picked up her handbag and headed for the door. It had been the word rejected that stung the most. Vanessa hadn't been rejected, she had been stolen. That Georgie presumed to know best and credited herself for Vanessa's happiness paled in significance compared to that statement. How Sandy wished that the Lord would hurry up and give her a sign, show her how to be rid of Georgie and every single hurdle that stood in the way of her and Vanessa being together, just the two of them, as it should be.

***

Months had passed since the conversation and once the smoke of Bonfire Night had dissipated, Tenley would gear up for another period of indulgence and frivolity where no doubt Vanessa would eat her way through her birthday and the Christmas holidays, devouring every treat in sight. It wouldn't end there either because shortly after they'd see in the New Year and say hello to 1979 with another wild party, more or less par for the course at Tenley.

As Sandy followed the gaggle of villagers who were heading home, slightly ahead of Georgie and Kenneth but just behind Vanessa and her friends, she shivered, the drizzle seemed to seep though her overcoat and the cold penetrated the rubber soles of her wellingtons. But it wasn't just the weather that made her shudder, it was the reminder of Christmas past, her very first at

Tenley, the night she foolishly let down her guard and could have lost everything.

***

Georgie had arranged a Christmas party in the village hall to thank the tenants and farmers of Tenley Estate for their hard work, along with a rather large handful of hangers-on and useful notaries. Vanessa was too young to attend and was to be watched over by Dolly who was staying for all of Christmas and New Year. At Georgie's insistence, Sandy was to join them at the party. No matter how hard she tried to get out of it, she was eventually cajoled into going along and was even given a frantic make-over by Georgie whom she suspected of match-making or at least hoped to pair her up for the dancing.

Despite Georgie's best efforts, Sandy managed to avoid being dragged onto the dance floor preferring instead to remain seated in the corner with her tonic water which she surreptitiously topped up with gin from the hipflask hidden in her handbag. It was only when she attempted to go to the toilets that she realised she was drunk and before she lost control of her limbs or tongue, excused herself and asked the barman to order her a taxi. Georgie and Kenneth were far too occupied with dancing and socialising to protest and within minutes, Sandy was back at Tenley.

The house was silent when she let herself in apart from the hum from the television accompanied by Dolly's gentle snores. Creeping past and up the stairs, fearful of wakening the Phyllis-monster, Sandy continued to the end of the corridor and Vanessa's bedroom. After entering the almost pitch-black room, a streak of light cast from the small crack in the door she'd left ajar guiding her way, Sandy crept over to the bed and gently lowered herself onto the mattress. As she listened to her daughter's soft breathing, Sandy bent closer and whispered in her ear.

"Sleep well, my darling, and know that I am always here to watch over you, and keep you safe from harm. I missed you so much while I was away but I never gave up and always knew that one day I'd find you. I wish I could tell the world that you are mine, my precious girl, but they would send me away so for now it's a secret, our secret. Just remember Mummy is here and I will never leave you again." Sandy was about to bend and kiss Vanessa on the forehead when the door creaked and moved just slightly, a dark shadow blocking the light from the hallway.

Standing and moving swiftly from the bed, Sandy rushed to the door and pulled it open to find Phyllis on the other side, staring, her beady eyes inquisitive. Pulling the door closed behind her, Sandy held her breath before calmly guiding the silent naked woman whose face was smeared with red lipstick and smudged eye shadow, strings of necklaces hanging around her neck, back to her room. As Phyllis asked over and over again what time the party started, Sandy's heart raced as did her mind, terrified that the old woman had overheard.

As she lay in bed that night, Sandy comforted herself that it was impossible, there was no way Phyllis could have overheard her whisperings. But she was so angry with herself for once again succumbing to the demon drink and for laying herself bare. It couldn't happen again and Sandy resolved never to visit Vanessa's room when drunk or speak of her secret. Next time she might not be so lucky and find Georgie or Kenneth eavesdropping at the door, not a naked senile old woman.

For days, Sandy was on tenterhooks but gradually felt the fear of exposure ebb, and life carried on as normal at Tenley. Since that day, she had remained steadfast and tried hard to limit her alcohol consumption to her days off or when a helping hand was required to see her through the night.

***

Back inside the house after waving off their guests, Kenneth and Georgie retired to the lounge while Vanessa went upstairs, saying she needed to remove her smoky clothes. Her true mission was to hide the toffee apples and treacle sweets she'd stuffed inside her pockets when she thought nobody was watching. But Sandy saw everything and sighed as she watched her daughter waddle up the stairs, her angst aggravated further by the sound of a bell ringing, requesting her presence. Inhaling deeply, she sought to regain her composure. It was necessary when faced with Phyllis, her other responsibility and one that was fast becoming a burden, an irritating and dislikeable one at that.

In the beginning, Sandy had found Phyllis easy to manage and treated her like the retirement home residents, firmly and taking no nonsense, despite her lofty heritage. Sadly though, in the years that followed as the old woman descended into senility, her moods had worsened, her tongue became more acid and vengeful whilst her nature erred on violent. As Sandy's patience wore thin, Phyllis soon became one chore too many. Not only that, it had become increasingly hard to ignore some of the cruel and deeply offensive comments that Phyllis made about every member of the household, the worst she reserved for Vanessa. At first, Sandy rose above it, she had to in order to remain in her post but inevitably it became too much and she raised the issue with Georgie and action was taken.

According to the doctor, the only sensible solution would have been to send her to a home where they could care for her properly. It wasn't as though Kenneth couldn't afford it. However, when faced with the decision he was reluctant and to Sandy's surprise, Georgie sided with her husband. It was common knowledge there was no love lost between the former and present lady of Tenley but for some reason, Georgie didn't push her husband or seem keen on the banishment of Phyllis. After all, Georgie rarely saw the old woman and had no hand in caring for her so for all intents, Phyllis didn't exist.

Georgie's reticence had puzzled Sandy. In the end, a nurse was hired to come in three times a day, alleviating her of the more nauseating and troublesome tasks and Sandy's only duty had been to feed Horace and serve meals. When the budgie dropped dead, Sandy was sure that she wasn't the only one to wish that its owner would do them all a favour and follow suit.

Making her way to the kitchen, Sandy sighed and checked the clock, dreading the confrontation with Phyllis and the potential of having biscuits thrown at her again. The nurse was forever complaining about the state of the room when she arrived in the morning and whatever state she found Phyllis in. Thankfully the mess wasn't Sandy's problem and only proved the necessity for a trained professional.

As she prepared a tray, Sandy thanked the Lord for her lot, despite its trials. While waiting for the kettle to boil, she resolved to spend the evening in contemplation where she would ask him once again for forgiveness of her sins and strength to resist the demon she knew lay at the bottom of a gin bottle. But Sandy would pray hardest of all for him to show her the way, and rid her of those who sought to hinder or affront, especially the bitter old crone who regularly maligned her precious child. As she carried the tray upstairs, little did Sandy know that it was her lucky day because as a reward for her patience, the benevolent Lord was about to answer one of her prayers and without haste, eliminate a Tenley.

Chapter 15

Phyllis

The demon had come again the previous night. Phyllis saw it with her own eyes, a dark shadow closing in, hell bent on torment and terror. Poor Horace, he too had endured cruel behaviour at the hands of the demon that in the end snuffed out her dear birdie's life with its bare hands. Had she been able to remember its name or cling on to more than a moment's lucidity, then she could have pointed it out. She knew her grasp on the present was diminishing and for the rest of the time she had no idea where she had been, or was, never mind how many hours had passed between day and night.

When the wily demon came, it always began by removing her silver bell thus preventing the summoning of assistance or salvation, and then it would silently pull the covers from her bed, slowly, slowly, leaving her old bones exposed and cold. Poor Horace would flutter and cheep, sensing danger before it arrived at his cage that was shaken and banged, the steel bars vibrating as her little friend was knocked from his perch. The night Horace met his end, the demon was at its worse and while Phyllis could only lie there and beg for mercy, it had thrown cold water over her nightdress then set about smearing the remains of her uneaten supper across the sheets.

While she lay there, bedridden and humiliated, the demon opened the cage where despite poor Horace's attempts at escape, he was unable to avoid capture. The end was thankfully swift. The hand that broke his tiny neck then tossed him back into the cage and locked the door before leaving the room as silently as it had entered.

Once, the demon sat on the bed and whispered such vile things, telling Phyllis that after she had rotted in her maggot-infested coffin she would go straight to hell where sinners far more wicked than she would torment her for all eternity. The demon said it was a price she had to pay for being cruel and cold-hearted and even if she repented; her poisonous words could not be forgotten or forgiven.

The previous night she had been given a reprieve and even though the demon had stayed away it had been replaced by the Nazi bombs and as much as she'd called out, warning them to hide or die in the hell fire of the blitz. Nobody listened, nobody ever listened. But there was something else that troubled Phyllis. The thought came and went yet a voice lingered, warning her of great danger, urging her to look closely. Could she not see? It was there, right in front of her.

Twisting her fingers into knots, Phyllis tried hard to remember but her eyes were tired and her mind so very weary and now all she longed for was sleep and the fear to recede. A moment of relief washed over her frail body when, as she turned her head to the window a shaft of grey morning light penetrated a gap in the curtains. She had made it through another night, demon free. It never came during the day, or perhaps it did and she just didn't notice. Heavy eyes began to close as exhaustion finally claimed her and it was then, when she least expected it, Phyllis remembered. She could hear the voice so clearly and see the face of her tormentor in vivid colour.

As the door handle turned, the sound of crockery rattling on her breakfast tray failed to wake her and Phyllis drifted into sleep, her lips muttering barely intelligible words. The nurse placed the tray on the bedside table and removed the one from supper, rolling her eyes, ignoring the confused ramblings of a senile old woman who was trying to tell anyone who would listen that they should beware, because the demon lived amongst them. The demon was one of them.

Chapter 16

Vanessa

No matter how hard she clasped her hands over her ears, Vanessa could not drown out the sound of Granny screaming. It was dreadful and her shrill hysterical voice rang around the house while panicked footsteps ran for help, the nurse calling for Sandy, who then called for Georgie who then told Daddy to ring the bloody doctor.

Vanessa was supposed to stay in her room with the door shut but as much as Granny was causing a terrible fuss and her screeching went through Vanessa, grating on her nerves and causing her to wince, it was also quite fascinating and in some parts rather funny. Granny had called Daddy a raving poofter which of course he wasn't but it still made Vanessa giggle, especially when she accused the nurse of witchcraft and refused to see the doctor. Granny said he was an emissary of death and a practitioner of alchemy. Had she not hated Granny so much, Vanessa would have admired her use of the English language despite being a raving lunatic.

It had all begun with the fireworks because Granny thought that they were being bombed by Germans and wanted everyone to go down to the shelter. She had kept them awake all night and now Georgie was in a foul mood and told Daddy that she wished they'd had her committed, which Vanessa actually agreed with. And Granny was creating another huge fuss. The doctor was in there sorting her out and Georgie had gone for a smoke to calm her nerves so Vanessa remained crouched in the hall, hidden behind the armoire, listening intently.

***

The latest episode, that's what they called them, began just after Sandy went in with fresh linens and according to the nurse who was currently in the kitchen holding a lump of ice over her bruised cheek, Phyllis screamed and said they were all going to be murdered in their beds and then demanded to see Kenneth at once. It went totally bonkers from there because now she was talking of demons and Nazis and before Georgie stormed off she said that if the doctor didn't sedate Phyllis, then she'd bloody well do it herself.

Vanessa didn't doubt it for one moment as Georgie could be a kitten but quite fearsome too and wasn't a bit bothered by anyone or anything. Georgie knew the best ways to get revenge and make sure everyone did exactly as she wished. Vanessa thought she was amazing and wanted nothing more than to be just like her and if she could have one wish come true, it would be for Georgie to be her real mother.

Sometimes, when the girls at school were mean and said she was a fat bastard and it was no wonder she was given away, Vanessa would obsess over it, desperate to know why she was abandoned and rejected. The only thing that cheered her was remembering the dream she had one Christmas, it was the most beautiful dream ever and in the morning, for a moment, she wasn't sure if it was real or not.

Ever since then she had wished it would come true and that Georgie really had come to find her, like a magical fairy hovering by her side. Then she had remembered the little blue bottle of Babycham that Georgie had allowed her to drink as a special treat. It was to make up for not being allowed to the party and it had made her feel a bit squiffy and maybe gave her funny dreams too. At lunch the next day, Georgie had whispered she wasn't to tell Sandy or Kenneth about the Babycham or the chocolates she'd left under her pillow otherwise they would both get into trouble. It had to be their secret. Just like the whisperer in the dream had said.

Vanessa and Georgie had a special bond too. Vanessa's birthday was the same day as JFK was assassinated, and Georgie adored Jackie O, so that must mean something, it was like a sign. Then there were their secrets, lots of them. Like their special song, 'Summertime'. It was their private joke and Georgie had thought of it to cheer Vanessa up when the girls at school had been mean and told her that nobody could love the Loch Ness monster so she would die a fat old spinster. Georgie had played the record and the words had stopped Vanessa's tears and made them both smile. Because it was true, her daddy was rich and her mummy was good looking and with them both in her world, Vanessa had no need to cry.

Then there was all that trouble on the school trip to France. The horrible new girl Raihana was pretty and popular and, just because her father was a Saudi prince or whatnot, she had instantly become top dog. Raihana had mostly ignored Vanessa who didn't mind because for once she wasn't a target, this time it was nasty Jemima's turn. There was such a catfight when Raihana stole Jemima's best friend, Penny, and by lights out, the dorm had been split into two camps. Vanessa and her few friends had tried to stay neutral but plumped for the clear winner, who fought like a boy and made Jemima look like a tongue-tied amateur. The nastiest girl in school had finally been defeated and knew the meaning of the word dejected. The next morning, Jemima's life got a whole lot worse.

Vanessa had never heard someone scream and cry and swear in another language. But that's exactly what Raihana did when she woke up to find her two-foot long ebony plait had been lobbed off during the night and lay forlornly on her pillow, like a decapitated black mamba. Jemima was the instant suspect and when the teachers ordered a thorough search of the dorm and found a pair of scissors under the foot of her mattress, justice had to be seen to be done. Nasty Jemima was no more.

Vanessa had repeated the story to Georgie on the way home from school. The trip had been cut short so the teachers could bow and scrape to the Saudi prince who was en route from his palace in the desert. The panic-stricken form teacher had taken Raihana to London to buy a wig. Vanessa didn't mind that the trip was curtailed as she'd been terribly homesick and was looking forward to next term minus Jemima.

Georgie found it all fascinating although she did think that Jemima had been rather stupid to chop off Raihana's hair after a row, and wondered if instead, a really clever person had decided to take their own revenge, like she always advised, served ice cold. They had stopped at the traffic lights so Vanessa glanced at Georgie and spotted the twitch of her lips and those pencilled, raised eyebrows above knowing eyes, looking quizzically in her direction. Nothing was said but when they both began to giggle, Georgie placed her fingers over her lips, winked and seeing the lights had changed to green, drove on.

It was also a secret that Vanessa and Georgie sometimes snuck off to the teashop in the next town and treated themselves to yummy cakes and even though she wasn't old enough, they had seen *Saturday Night Fever* at the cinema. They'd actually gone to see *Pete's Dragon* but when nobody was watching Georgie grabbed Vanessa's hand and they slipped into the darkened theatre and spent the afternoon ducked down out of sight, watching John Travolta.

And Vanessa knew that Georgie's special water was Gordon's gin but she would never tell, and her magic cigarettes weren't really capable of casting spells although they did send everyone rather funny. Nice Uncle Clement, who painted Georgie in the nuddy as well as in her best dress for the portrait that hung in the lounge, wasn't really her uncle. Or that Aunt Joy and Aunt Lottie weren't really sisters who preferred to share a room when they stayed. In fact none of the nutty guests who frequented Tenley were her relatives but Vanessa didn't care. She would do anything for Georgie, just anything, because she had made everyone's life so happy and perfect.

What mattered most was that Georgie had kept her promises, maybe even a secret one too, and in return Vanessa had kept hers. She never ever kicked up a fuss when they left her with Sandy who, whilst being very kind and devoted, was rather boring and a bit too strict – and churchy too. Vanessa didn't mind all that hymn singing at school but no way was she being dragged along on Sunday. And even though her parents had been to Morocco and India, and the south of France and Italy with their group of friends, Vanessa had understood it would be far too hot and boring being stuck with grown-ups for two weeks. Instead they had all gone down to Cornwall and stayed in a gorgeous house by the sea.

Just like she had promised, Georgie was 'all hers' for three glorious weeks and they enjoyed it so much they went back each year. Even Sandy was invited because Georgie was so kind and never left anyone out. It had certainly cheered boring old Sandy up although she wouldn't go in the sea, she just paddled because she couldn't swim but neither could Vanessa. Doddery old Dolly came along too. Dolly made everyone laugh with her swear words and East End stories and big knickers that hung on the line, until they blew off and everyone had to search for them in the dunes. Georgie said Dolly was her surrogate mother and loved her to pieces, so Vanessa did too. That was the rule, Vanessa's rule. Whatever Georgie liked, she liked too, whatever Georgie loathed, Vanessa loathed too. It was simple.

***

It was realising that the shouting and swearing coming from Granny's room had stopped that dragged Vanessa back to the present. The silence was heavenly and after ten or fifteen minutes she saw the doctor leave the room, calling back to Sandy that he would check in on the nurse before he left. After listening to voices downstairs, Georgie announcing that they all needed a stiff drink and then Daddy offering the doctor some whisky, the clinking of the decanter told Vanessa the coast was clear and she could take a peep at Granny. Maybe they'd put tape over her mouth or bashed her on the head to shut her up. Whatever the doctor had done it worked, and curiosity was killing Vanessa as she crept along the hallway.

She could hear Sandy inside, stoking the fire and then the rattle of more coal as it toppled onto the flames. It was as Vanessa peered around the door, only allowing one eye to take in the scene, her gaze fell upon her grandmother who looked to be sleeping yet restless, her hands twitching as her head moved side to side. Then Sandy appeared, causing Vanessa to jump backwards, out of sight, and then look again when she heard Phyllis begin to mumble, the sound drawing Sandy to the bedside. Vanessa leant forward, exposing both eyes in order to strain her neck and listen.

"Where's Kenneth? Bring him to me, I must speak with him. Please. I beg you, fetch Kenneth."

"Shush now, Phyllis, and try to rest. Kenneth will come tomorrow."

"No, he must come now. I need to tell him my secret, a terrible secret. I heard it all, every word. We are all in danger because the demon is here, come for the child I hope, that bastard child who has stained our name... She is evil, they all are, bring the priest before it kills us in our beds. There is such wickedness in this house and it must be banished... That woman is evil, a common whore who kept me prisoner... and she is a fraud and a liar. I know everyone's secrets, so many secrets. Please believe me... please bring Kenneth... or a priest..." Phyllis gasped for air and was becoming anxious again.

Vanessa held her own breath. What did Granny mean, what demon, what secret, and what child... did she mean her? She was transfixed, terrified, half believing in murderous demons while trying to imagine what secret Granny might have overheard. Surely it was all nonsense but then again perhaps they should find a priest, just in case Granny had seen something scary.

"Now, now, Phyllis, there's no such thing as demons so close your eyes. That's right, try to sleep."

But Phyllis was having none of it. "Of course there are demons, you imbecile, one comes here to steal my jewellery and it tore up Winnie the Pooh and killed Horace, with its bare hands… I saw it, standing right there." Phyllis pointed into thin air at nothing in particular, her bony liver-spotted hands shaking as she spoke. As Sandy followed the direction of the finger, something caught her eye and she turned, saw Vanessa peeping around the doorframe.

"Vanessa. Go to your room at once. This is no place for a child. Hurry along, do as you are told." Sandy's cheeks held two spots of red. Anger and fatigue caused her to sound harsher than necessary or intended.

Shocked by Sandy's tone, Vanessa turned immediately and fled to the sanctuary of her bedroom where she flung herself onto the mattress, just as exhausted as the other members of the household yet intrigued and rather scared by her grandmother's words. She didn't want to go downstairs as the doctor would still be there, smoking cigars with Daddy and talking about dreary illnesses and nasty Granny.

Instead, Vanessa dragged the eiderdown over her body and closed her eyes, thinking it best to sleep for a while in case the resident lunatic had them up all night again. Until fatigue claimed her, Vanessa fumed at being called a child when she was almost sixteen for goodness sake, and then pored over the rambling of Phyllis and as her eyes drooped, tried to make sense of it all and piece together the clues, worry filling her heart.

Meanwhile, down the hall another storm was brewing and unbeknown to Vanessa, scary Granny was gearing up for her final hurrah, quite determined not to go without a fight.

Chapter 17

The Demon

The grandfather clock in the hall chimed three, each booming strike resounding along the darkened corridors of Tenley. Well used to the sound by now, the residents were not woken from their slumbers apart from two – Phyllis and the demon. The latter had waited until it knew everyone was sound asleep and the nurse had finally retired to her room, then an hour later it deftly opened the bedroom door and stepped barefoot into the hall. The shadows held no fear for the demon. It had walked these corridors for years during the night, listening at doors, restlessly wandering the rooms, unable to sleep and in need of entertainment. That night though, it had a job to do.

Ear to the wood, listen and wait, turn the handle slowly then push the door quickly otherwise it creaks, repeat and then watch. There she was, sleeping soundly, her vicious tongue silent for once. The demon considered waking its prey because perhaps it would be more fun, if the old woman were to look into the eyes of her tormentor for the last time. But this wasn't a place for theatrics, or regrets, it had to be done before she had a chance to speak out, cast doubt or even make them believe.

The demon, stealth like, took the spare pillow that lay at the side of the old woman's head and clutching it tightly moved around the bed. Tilting its head to the side, the demon took one last look at Phyllis in her breathing state because the next time it saw her, the bitter old bag would be dead and they would all be free of her presence, secrets safe. Taking a breath, the demon bore down, squashing the pillow over the sleeping woman's face who, despite her fragility and years, struggled somewhat, but not for long. Once her limbs ceased kicking and flaying and the twitching stopped, the pillow was removed.

Sighing deeply, waiting a moment to ensure that the job was done, the demon allowed itself a moment of congratulations and a satisfied smile before calmly walking back around the bed and replacing the pillow. After straightening the deceased's hair and nightdress that had become disorderly during the struggle, smoothing the bed covers and resisting the urge to linger and savour its act of revenge, the demon retraced its steps.

Ear to the wood, listen and wait, turn the handle slowly then pull the door quickly. Stepping back into the shadowed hallway, the demon made its way back to bed and there it waited until morning, knowing the danger had been averted. Phyllis was gone.

Chapter 18

Sandy

Something was afoot. The atmosphere at Tenley had shifted. It had been a slow creep, nothing dramatic or particularly noticeable but there was definitely trouble brewing, Sandy could feel it. Since the timely death of Phyllis and once the very short period of mourning was over, everyone just carried on as normal... as normal as one could in a house riddled with depravity and debauchery. But at least for a while it felt like they could all breathe, no more treading on shells or sleepless nights.

Sandy unscrewed the lid of a new bottle of gin and settled on her bed, pouring a generous shot then taking a gulp before resting her head on the pillow where she dissembled the past, looking for clues. The previous four years hadn't all been plain sailing and the days shortly after the nurse found Phyllis dead had been rather fraught. Vanessa obsessed about the funeral, and then there was Georgie, pretending to give a stuff about lilies and coffins and the wake while Kenneth hid himself away in his study, faking grief. Sandy, on the other hand, was torn between rejoicing and the fear of discovery.

In the midst of making plans to flee should her thievery be uncovered, she found herself praising the Lord who once again had come through, just when she needed him. Sighing contentedly, Sandy took another swig and then poured some more gin, the alcohol was beginning to numb her tense body, allowing her to relax, think clearly.

***

It happened so quickly, those last few minutes with Phyllis were a blur and how Sandy had berated herself later, first for losing her temper with Vanessa and then not staying put when the doctor and nurse came rushing back into the room.

Sandy had seen it before at the retirement home when those on death's door found their second wind and for a few minutes, became lucid, spoke coherently and made themselves understood for the first time in ages. When Sandy turned to face Phyllis, a second after ordering Vanessa to her room, the old woman gasped then shrunk back into her pillow, button eyes filled with horror and realisation, recognition even. As Phyllis began to speak then screech, Sandy's blood ran cold with every word, unable to silence or calm the hysterical woman.

"It's you." Phyllis once again raised a pointed finger at Sandy, her hand trembled as she spoke yet her eyes never left that of her victim. "I know who you are. I see it now… it's in the eyes. How could I have not noticed before, how could we all have missed it?"

"Missed what, Phyllis? Please don't alarm yourself again otherwise I will have to bring the doctor, just rest, close your eyes." The calmness of Sandy's voice belied the panic that was mounting inside as she pulled the covers over Phyllis, trying hard to remain in control.

"The eyes, they are the same as the brat's, sly and devious, and the smile… Yes, in some ways you are so similar, like mother and daughter. Dear God, that's exactly what you are."

"Phyllis, you must stop this nonsense right now. What if Vanessa hears you? The child will be distressed so please, hold your tongue. You're confused by your medication and tired so I beg you, sleep."

"I will do no such thing… not when there is an imposter in our midst, devils and demons everywhere hiding in plain sight, waiting to strike and kill us all. What do you want from us, what do you want…?" Phyllis was trying to sit and her voice whilst weak was raised in pitch and determined to be heard, silencing Sandy before she could protest. "And I've seen you, oh yes… I recognise you now, you're the thief who takes my jewels, the demon who creeps in here to steal my belongings. Dear God, Tenley is riddled with evil. Kenneth, Kenneth, help me, Kenneth…" Phyllis sagged onto the pillows, consumed by anger and fear, the confusion that swirled through her brain fought hard, desperate to hold on to her senses, making one last attempt at untangling a jumble of thoughts and images.

Hearing footsteps and voices drawing close, Sandy had no other option than to run to the door and feign concern, praying with every step that Phyllis would descend into total delirium and that way, the doctor would sedate her, properly this time.

Sandy found herself dismissed from the room, allowing the doctor and nurse to deal with Phyllis and in the meantime, Georgie went to check on Vanessa who she found in tears, woken from sleep once again by her monstrous grandmother. As Sandy listened at the door, she could hear Vanessa recounting the wicked words she'd heard Phyllis utter.

No doubt Georgie hadn't been amused to hear herself described as an evil whore who'd taken Phyllis prisoner, more so that Vanessa was terrified because a demon had come to Tenley to kill her because she was a bastard who'd stained the family name. While Georgie soothed Vanessa who sobbed and hiccupped about secrets and lies, fraudsters and priests, Sandy felt so weary, of everything. How she longed to comfort her child but as usual, Georgie was the one Vanessa turned to, and it hurt, a real physical pain.

Sighing, Sandy gave up and submitted to fatigue, not caring if anyone had eaten or her duties had been fulfilled. She'd had enough of the Tenleys for one day and they could look after themselves, or starve and drink themselves into oblivion for all she cared.

Hours later, Sandy knelt by her bed, praying so hard that her fingers ached from clasping them together, her eyes screwed and brows furrowed in concentration, lips twitching as she begged the Lord to help her, show her the way, or silence Phyllis. From behind closed eyelids, Sandy saw her life falling apart and the facade she'd created crumbling. It was only a matter of time and her secrets would be revealed by that poisonous old woman, she would be branded a thief and Georgie, who was sharp as a knife, would put two and two together.

In the darkness, Sandy continued to pray that the Lord would forgive her for stealing from Phyllis but she had so much old tat lying about that it was impossible for anyone to keep track of it, especially if it disappeared in dribs and drabs. God knew that the theft was in aid of a good cause because Sandy had to be prepared for the day she could reveal herself to Vanessa, who she was convinced would fall into her arms once the truth was told. The much-anticipated revelation was scheduled in Sandy's mind for Vanessa's coming of age at twenty-one, Vanessa would be able to make her own mind up about her future. It was entirely possible that if she chose her real mother, Kenneth might disown or disinherit and without a doubt, Sandy would be instantly dismissed from service. That was why she needed a nest egg, to provide for her and Vanessa, come the day.

***

The mere thought of yet another birthday caused the wound in Sandy's heart to ache because with every year, even before she arrived at Tenley, the 22nd November brought with it such bittersweet memories. In truth, watching Vanessa rip open her presents every year had been harder than the six years they'd spent apart. Sandy would relive the day of her birth and imagine what she was doing and who with. Now she knew. At Tenley, Sandy managed to hold back the tears, saving them for bedtime but she did at least get a hug.

Physical contact was kept to a minimum between Sandy and Vanessa after all, what reason did the chief-cook-and-bottle-washer have to embrace the mistress of the house. On birthdays it was different. Sandy left giving Vanessa her gift until bedtime when the hullaballoo had died down. It had become their special tradition. Vanessa always appreciated one last present which she rewarded with a hug. Sandy waited all year for it.

The stumbling block in her master plan, the thing that ruined the images of the momentous day when Sandy would reveal all, was the genuine love Vanessa had for Georgie. Surprisingly and much to Sandy's annoyance, the feeling was mutual so somewhere along the line, the Lord would need to rid the world of Georgie. She was the one thing that truly stood in Sandy's way. It was unfathomable how one so shallow and vain, and deeply flawed as Georgie could love an ugly duckling like Vanessa, because that's what she was.

Despite all Sandy's attempts to restrict the child's calorific intake, she was thwarted at every turn by Georgie and as she grew, taller and widthways, Vanessa resembled more and more the rapist. Sandy knew that a mother should love her child no matter what, but she just couldn't, not in the way Georgie did.

Vanessa was becoming more spoilt, was without aim, lacking in moral guidance and as far as Sandy was concerned an ignorant atheist. Had she been brought up correctly, in a God-fearing home, Sandy was convinced that Vanessa would be unrecognisable to the one who waddled around the house, growing more conceited and lazy by the day. The blame for this lay firmly at the feet of Kenneth who was weak and Georgie who was unfit to look after herself, never mind a child.

Sometimes, just watching them together brought on such terrible rage that it caused Sandy's body to tremble. How often had she spied on Georgie and Vanessa who were so free with hugs and caresses? The heart-warming tableau still rankled, that of a child who yearned for a mother's love and the unlikely stranger who just walked right in and claimed that role, her role, Sandy's.

When she was younger, Vanessa would lie on the sofa next to Georgie who, too idle to read for herself would enlist the child. While the love-thief smoked and rested her bloodshot eyes, Vanessa would recite poetry from one of Kenneth's first editions or read fairy stories. Their favourite past-time, one where Georgie made a bit of effort, was spent re-enacting plays. They would spend hours with *Pygmalion* and *The Rivals*, Eliza Doolittle and Mrs Malaprop being Georgie's characters of choice.

Nowadays, Vanessa was far too fat to snuggle in the crook of Georgie's arm like when she was young, so instead, took a position on the floor. Georgie would listen and stroke Vanessa's raven curls as she read from the newspaper, or they would share a joke about the gossip columns and listen to music. They even had a special song.

But that was by the by, and as much as Vanessa's personality and physical appearance pained Sandy, she was resolute in her mission and would, one day take back what was hers. The list of commandments Sandy had broken and the sins she committed did not cause concern. The good Lord was on her side and he always forgave sinners, even if they coveted and stole, were riddled with envy, succumbed to greed and wished people dead.

Having faith absolved Sandy of many things, like the fact she had collated an album by removing photographs from the leather-bound book in the library, then rearranging those that remained. Nobody looked at them anyway, especially those of Daphne and Vanessa's early years. Now, Sandy had a photographic history of her own, from the day they stole her baby girl. Pride of place was the grainy black and white image, Sandy's most precious possession, of her and Vanessa at the home just days after her birth. The photograph, whilst being something to cling to was another element of the torture she and the other girls had endured. It was a dangling carrot, a taste of happiness that was always beyond your reach like the soft wool of your baby's going away outfit. Since her arrival at Tenley, Sandy had taken snapshots of her own and added them to the pilfered ones so to anyone who looked, the album would appear to be that of a single mother who had brought up her child alone.

***

Tired from praying and wandering aimlessly in the boggy past, and with sore and aching knees, slowly and stiffly, Sandy crawled into bed where despite her exhaustion, found she was unable to sleep. She was too wired by worry yet too weary to listen on the landing for hints that Kenneth and Georgie were aware of her indiscretions, or check on Phyllis who Sandy hoped was sedated and silent.

Instead she would wait in the darkness for the Lord to reach out; he always came through in the end. After all, amongst her many failings, patience remained her strongest virtue. The clock ticked and the house fell silent. Wispy clouds skimmed a silvery moon that was suspended in an onyx sky that shrouded Tenley in darkness and under its roof, Sandy waited for divine intervention.

The next morning, as she filled the kettle with water and then lifted the copper frying pan off the hook, Sandy was startled by the nurse who bounded into the kitchen, her face ashen as she trembled and told of her grim discovery. It was so hard for Sandy not to smile and feign surprise. She certainly didn't feel sorrow, none at all. The only emotion that registered in Sandy, as the nurse shot off to ring the doctor and wake the living Tenleys, was gratitude.

During the night, the Lord had answered just as she knew he would, she had been saved. Placing the pan back on the hook, realising she wouldn't have to cook breakfast, instead taking cups and saucers from the shelf, Sandy whispered to herself, "Praise the Lord, God is good."

Next came the farce that was the funeral, where Vanessa refused to attend and was, in Sandy's opinion, pandered to by Georgie who put the tears and recurring nightmares down to the trauma of Daphne's death. Sandy had it on good authority from Cookie who came in to help with the wake, that on the morning of Daphne's funeral when six-year-old Vanessa spotted her grandmother and the other leading women mourners in dark veils, all hell broke loose because the child thought they were black ghosts. Vanessa became hysterical, Phyllis slapped her legs and according to Cookie, Kenneth looked like he wanted to slap Phyllis.

Georgie, as always was made aware of the past by faithful Cookie and then insisted Vanessa be spared the ordeal once again, and as with most things, got her way. With Phyllis six feet under, Kenneth's title and inheritance secured, Georgie was left to rule the roost in any manner she saw fit.

When Vanessa turned sixteen and decisions had to be made regarding her education, Georgie's grip on her stepdaughter tightened even further. In all areas of Vanessa's life Sandy felt impotent and was resigned, however reluctantly, to being her loyal servant. It therefore came as a shock when for once she and Georgie actually agreed on something.

Sandy's role at Tenley was to maintain the smooth running of the house and step into the breach when Georgie and Kenneth nipped up to London. It was therefore imperative that Vanessa remained at Tenley until she was at least eighteen otherwise Sandy's services might be dispensed with.

When she wasn't at school or with her small circle of false friends, Vanessa had no hobbies and similarly, no idea what she wanted to do with her life. She wasn't very bright, which irked Sandy greatly, despite her genes and one-to-one extra schooling. Kenneth had suggested a spell abroad at a finishing school which was met with tears from Vanessa and a scowl from Georgie. Eventually they settled on her becoming an assistant in the estate office where from ten till four on weekdays she answered the phone and typed letters, very, very slowly.

Once that conundrum was solved, life at Tenley continued as it always had done with a stream of guests, foreign holidays and jollies in Cornwall. The only blip was Dolly's tragic death which knocked Georgie for six and exposed her fragility and in some ways, set off a chain of events that reverberated through the halls and walls at Tenley.

Dolly had been dead for five days before she was discovered in her flat at their Kensington house, and this fact alone distressed Georgie as much as her demise. Whilst they were up in Scotland having a ball, quite literally, at the castle of one of Kenneth's old school chums, dearest Dolly had taken a fall and unable to reach the telephone, had suffered a lonely and painful end. Grief stricken and riddled with guilt at not ringing Dolly more often, Georgie insisted she was brought to Tenley and buried in the village churchyard.

After the funeral, Georgie didn't bounce back, and her swift descent into depression rocked the household who were used to a tour de force, not a damp squib who remained in her room for over a month, smoking and drinking herself into oblivion. During this time, Sandy savoured the opportunity to sail the ship, becoming everything to everyone, especially Vanessa who, after a time, became rather impatient and irritated by Georgie's behaviour. After being turned away from her stepmother's room, a gloomy place that stank of cigarette smoke, Vanessa sought solace in Sandy who for once was able to bask. Not in adoration, but at least she had her child's full attention.

They had little in common with regards to music or film so when Vanessa, bored by her own company in the evenings, showed interest in Sandy's knitting, a thin woollen bond was formed as a mother taught her child how to cast on, each stitch a lost minute returned. For the next few evenings after dinner, Vanessa would sit next to Sandy on the sofa in the lounge, the closest she had ever been in body and mind and there, as they knitted one, purled one, they chatted about this and that until one evening, the past paid an unexpected visit.

"Sandy, I don't mean to pry but why do you never speak of your parents? You said your mother taught you to knit so I presume you must have been close once. Do you not miss her, or your father?" Vanessa had dropped a stitch and as her clumsy fingers attempted to pick it up, she was unaware of the effect her question had on her instructor.

Of all the conversations Sandy had hoped to have with Vanessa, this was not one of them but there was no way around it, so as she schooled her voice to remain calm, stuck to the story she had told Georgie years before.

"No, I don't miss my mother. She wasn't the most loving of women but perhaps this stood me in good stead because I was able to manage without her. As for my father, I never knew him because he died in the war. Mother remarried and I didn't take to her husband so struck out on my own. I am glad I did because the path led me here, to Tenley. Now concentrate otherwise you'll have another hole in your scarf." Sandy silently sucked in air through pursed lips, praying the conversation would turn. It did but not in the direction she had expected.

"Oh I see. I'm glad that you're happy and I shan't ask any more, although I do know what you mean about our paths because I am so happy that mine brought me here, so on that we are very similar."

Sandy was unable to speak. Her throat was tight just like her heart which constricted with sadness. Vanessa, who was lost in her knitting and in a chatty mood for once had more to say on the matter.

"Had my mother not given me up I would have missed out on my life here at Tenley so I am rather thankful that she was perhaps of the same ilk as your mother, you know, not the most loving of women. We should both thank heavens for small mercies, don't you think?"

Vanessa paused and glanced at Sandy who was fiddling in her sleeve for a handkerchief and had become rather flustered. "I say, Sandy, are you alright? I hope I haven't spoken out of turn. I'm sure your mother was very decent and all that. Please say I haven't offended you." Laying down her knitting, Vanessa took Sandy's hand and was rewarded with a small smile and a short reply.

"Of course you haven't offended me, the fire is rather smoky tonight, it must be the peat that Ernest brought in. It's made my eyes sting. Now, shall I make us some cocoa and perhaps some toast before bed? You finish a few more rows while I'm away." With that, Sandy patted Vanessa's hand and hastened from the room, knowing that Vanessa would never refuse supper but most importantly, Sandy needed to escape and gather herself in private.

When she returned carrying a tray and two steaming mugs of cocoa, the aroma of toasted bread filled the room. Sandy hoped that the matter would be closed but unfortunately, it seemed that Vanessa was set on righting her perceived wrong. Sandy's heart was about to be tugged in two directions, in one lay the truth, in the other a box full of secrets.

Food always quietened Vanessa and it wasn't until she'd wiped the butter from her lips and fingers that, in between sips of cocoa, she told Sandy she had remembered a snippet about her natural mother.

"You know how I said we were similar, you know, with our mothers? I have thought of another coincidence. I remember when I was very small and Daphne and Daddy explained to me that I was adopted, they gave me a box. I can't remember it exactly but it had small flowers on the lid and inside, wrapped in tissue paper was an outfit. Daphne said it had been knitted for me by my real mother. It was what they brought me home in. Fancy that. My mother knitted too, like yours. I've only just recalled it but like I said I was very little at the time. Would you like the last piece of toast or can I have it?" Vanessa reached over and allowed her hand to hover, snatching up the triangle the second she saw Sandy nod.

While Vanessa chewed and sipped, Sandy was waging a battle between her heart and her head. She remembered every stitch of the pale lemon cardigan, with its matching bootees and hat. Now, only inches away sat her daughter, her own flesh and blood on whose lap laid a half-knitted scarf, a vital clue to her true identity. It would only take a few words to explain the truth, right there and then while the two of them were alone enjoying a moment of harmony, a common bond made of wool. Once Sandy had forged peace and her brain had accepted her decision, allowing her heart to settle its beat, her lips managed to speak coherently.

"Do you still have the box, Vanessa? I'm sure it's a precious keepsake and your mother would be so pleased to know that

Daphne was kind enough to give it to you. I would very much like to see it, if you didn't mind."

"I have no idea where it is... perhaps in the attic. I haven't seen it since and have no desire to. All that is in the past, just like my real mother who didn't want me, and Daphne who decided to have another baby when she already had me. Georgie is my mother now and for that I am so grateful. Even when she's in a terrible fug, I still adore her to pieces."

"Oh Vanessa, that is such a harsh thing to say. You have no idea why your mother gave you up so perhaps you should show some humility and understanding in your ignorance of the facts." Sandy could not hide the hurt and annoyance in her tone which she regretted instantly because Vanessa picked up on it and rounded, never taking criticism well.

"I do know the facts. She didn't want me and that's that so I would prefer it if we didn't speak of this again, Sandy. You have seen fit to consign your unloving mother to the past so why can't I? And I do not appreciate being called ignorant. I am the injured party here not the woman who abandoned me. Now, if you don't mind, I will say goodnight and check on Georgie before I turn in. I will see you in the morning." And with that Vanessa flung her knitting in the basket and left the room.

Remaining by the fire, fighting back the tears, Sandy leant across and removed the half-finished scarf from the basket and with her free hand, dragged the stitches from the needles then began pulling each row undone. As the wool unravelled and fell into a heap on the floor, Sandy knew it represented the bricks of the bridge she had spent the past few weeks building with Vanessa. There would be no more knitting by the fire. Vanessa was offended and rarely forgave, and at the same time, Sandy hadn't the patience or the inclination to continue. All she could do was move on, bide her time and be patient. Just like always.

***

Sandy screwed the lid tightly onto the bottle. There would be no more drinking that night as she needed a clear head for the next day. There was to be a gathering for Vanessa's twenty-first birthday. The lady of Tenley had emerged from her state of gloom just in time to celebrate but if Sandy's suspicions were correct, the party atmosphere wouldn't last, not for long anyway.

Chapter 19

Kenneth and Georgie

In some ways, Dolly's death had ushered in the end of an era, not that the Tenley household were immediately aware of it but privately, within Georgie and Kenneth's relationship, things were about to change and their once-harmonious existence would come under threat.

During Georgie's period of mourning, all of Kenneth's best suggestions were batted away. His wife had no intention of coming downstairs to watch Lady Diana marry her prince, just like she'd refused to go up to London and join in with the street celebrations. The Kensington house was the scene of Dolly's hideous death and ultimately such a crass suggestion resulted in Kenneth's great grandmother's Wedgewood vase meeting a smashing end. Similarly, when the idea of a week in the sun or a shopping trip to Paris was met with derision, Kenneth was told to bugger off – so he did exactly that, literally.

As they all expected, Georgie recovered in good time for their wedding anniversary bash and for a while, all seemed tickety-boo, as Kenneth was prone to say. Then after a terrible bout of bronchitis and then a dreadful spell where pneumonia wiped Georgie out, leaving Kenneth once again to his own devices, a hairline crack appeared in their relationship.

At first, glad that her husband had benefited from her social tutelage and wide circle of friends, Georgie encouraged Kenneth to get up to London and have some fun while she convalesced or as Vanessa pointed out to her father, visited Dolly's grave far more often than was healthy. Not wanting to miss out on all the fun and with appearances to uphold, a weak and skinny Georgie dragged herself out of bed for a shooting weekend at a neighbouring estate. It was here that she sensed a shift. Her eyes, while slightly dulled and tinged with a hint of jaundice, were perfectly capable of spotting danger. In this case it came in the form of a young and beautiful young man named Simon.

It didn't take long for Georgie to work it out; by the time they served dessert to be precise. After watching the exquisite and softly spoken Oxford graduate flirt discreetly with her husband, she decided to swap places with the old toad seated beside him. From there, Georgie undertook a mild and discreet interrogation of the enemy. It soon transpired the furtive lovers had know each other for a while, Simon's green eyes looking straight into hers as he confirmed this fact, the challenge in them unmistakable. He was cool, confident to the point of arrogance, and enjoying every minute of regaling his friendship with her husband.

While Georgie plastered on a smile and held on to Kenneth's hand which prevented hers from trembling, beetles crawled across her skin and a green monster writhed inside her stomach, its tail whipping her heart. Simon was infatuated with Kenneth and by the time they brought the brandy, Georgie suspected that unless she stepped in soon, the sentiment would be reciprocated.

Like any sensible wife, Georgie remained silent whilst gathering evidence and in the meantime, embarked on a revenge affair which she accepted was a ludicrous notion because really, Kenneth would not care. But she did, deeply. And contrary to what she imagined would be common opinion, it wasn't all about Tenley and Vanessa, or their gorgeous house in Kensington and their jollies in Cornwall and Europe. Georgie loved Kenneth so very much. With Kenneth she belonged.

With him, when it was just the two of them, she didn't have to act and although he loved her funny voices and parodies, with dear darling Kenneth, she was his Georgie, just like old times in the damp smelly attic apartment. In their private moments, away from Vanessa and prying eyes of socialites and gossip columnists, they would lie on his bed, her head on his chest, the scent of tobacco and the tweed of his waistcoat tickling her nostrils. He would explain why on some nights they could see the sun and the moon in the sky or tell her about the planting of rapeseed in the far field and why the damn Argies had invaded the Falklands. They would make plans for the summer and Kenneth would suggest some far-flung destination that Georgie would imagine in her head, planning her wardrobe and picturing her handsome husband in his panama hat and linen suit. For a few precious hours and minutes she was home, in heaven, with her husband.

Still, a deal was a deal and she may have been a thief and a part-time prima donna but Georgie knew she would keep her end of their bargain, even if it killed her. With every made-up reason to nip off or unavoidable overnight stay at a friend's, she was convinced that losing Kenneth was inevitable and worse, it would be her undoing. The drinking didn't help and it was this that caused their first row. He had arrived home after a weekend of polo to find Georgie in a bad way physically but still in control of her mind and tongue, just.

When Kenneth opened the door to the gloomy lounge, the curtains closed and music blaring from the record player, the room enveloped in cigarette smoke that he could almost part with his hands, for the very first time he lost his temper with Georgie.

"What the hell do you think you're playing at? Dear God, Georgie, are you purposely trying to kill yourself?" Kenneth was shouting as he marched over to the sideboard and lifted the needle from the record, plunging the room into silence. "Georgie, answer me. I mean it. This has to stop at once."

Georgie was lying on the sofa with a large cushion over her face and when she finally removed it, revealed two panda eyes, the tracks of her tears evident on deathly white skin. After regarding Kenneth for what seemed like an age, she deigned to reply, her voice hoarse and laced with sarcasm.

"Why, it's my darling husband. So very kind of you to make an appearance… Did you enjoy all that *riding*?" Georgie smirked while Kenneth ignored her comment and simply tutted which served to rile her even more.

"So, has Simple Simon allowed you to come home to wifey or is this just a duty call? Don't let me stop you. I'll be fine by myself, all alone in this fucking museum going slowly mad, just like all the Tenley women do in the end." Georgie attempted to sit up but the room began to spin so she flopped back down again.

"Georgie, that's uncalled for."

"Really. You don't know what it's like, being left to run a house singlehanded while your husband is off gallivanting."

Kenneth rolled his eyes and tried not to smile but Georgie had replaced the cushion over her face and couldn't see. It didn't stop her from talking though.

"Oh and by the way, Miss Mittens is dead. Ernest thinks she fell out of the window on the top floor. Apparently bloody Sandy left it open so on top of everything else, I've had a huge drama to deal with."

"Good Lord, how very tragic. But I thought cats were supposed to bounce."

"Clearly not."

Kenneth ignored Georgie's sarcasm. "Have you told Vanessa? She must be dreadfully upset."

"Yes, of course I've told her and ever since she's been in her bedroom. She says she's fine but perhaps you might drag yourself up there and make yourself useful for once."

"Do you think we should buy her another?" Kenneth felt sad for Vanessa and the cat.

"Not if it's like Miss Mittens, that thing was feral. I'm sure of it. Anyway, back to pretty boy Simon. How is the queer little chap?"

Kenneth sighed and shook his head, refusing to rise to the bait. He hated to see Georgie like this. Her bouts of drunkenness were becoming a regular occurrence but this time, instead of being rather wild and abandoned, she sounded bitter, belligerent in fact. He felt under attack and it unnerved him so as he was prone to do, Kenneth decided to placate rather than defend himself.

"Darling, please, keep your voice down, someone might hear. I'll pop up and see Vanessa then make you some coffee and perhaps we can talk this through. I hate leaving you here all alone and I do keep asking you to come with me but you can be such a stubborn old thing. I don't know what to do with you sometimes." Kenneth feigned a jolly laugh, hoping to diffuse the atmosphere but instead he'd wound Georgie up.

"Old thing! Did you just call me an old thing? If that's what you think of me why don't you have me stuffed like those hideous beasts that are hung in your study? Old, am I? So that's why you trot off with your rent-boy… How dare you, how dare you patronise me."

"Georgie stop! Stop at once. I insist." Kenneth leapt towards where she was laid, terrified that Vanessa would hear and in a desperate attempt to silence Georgie, seated himself on the sofa, taking her hand in his. Her next words cut him to the quick.

"What are you doing? Don't think you can soft soap me. Oh and do be careful, darling. I'm sure your arse is rather sore after a weekend with Simon. Would you like me to bring you some cold cream or a soft cushion?" As Georgie smirked Kenneth gasped, withdrawing his hand sharply, and in that instant she knew she'd gone too far.

"Kenneth I'm sorry, I'm so sorry. That was unforgiveable, please forgive me. I'm just drunk and tired and yes, old and jealous. I miss you so much… I miss the old days and the fun we had. I can feel it all slipping away and I don't know what to do. Please help me, Kenneth, please don't leave me." And with that Georgie broke down, sobbing uncontrollably into the pillow and it was only when Kenneth took her in his arms that she began to calm and listen as he soothed away her troubles.

"Oh you are a silly old thing, but your my silly old thing and I promise I am not going to leave you, do you hear me? But you have to stop all this nonsense and I won't have my beautiful Georgie behaving like a fishwife. Good Lord, you'll be throwing my underwear out of the window and into the hydrangeas next, and we can't have that. What would Ernest say and worse, Sandy?" He rocked Georgie in his arms and waited as the sobs subsided.

"Now come on, pull yourself together and let's make a little plan. I think you and I need some time together, just the two of us somewhere special, like the old days. How does that sound?" Kenneth kissed the top of Georgie's hair that he could tell hadn't been washed, ignoring the odour of sweat and stale booze and cigarettes.

He also ignored the pang of doubt because despite her present state, maybe Georgie was right. What they had, their fantasy world, was slipping away and their bubble of love could be in danger and about to be popped. There was something else too, that twisted his gut as Georgie accepted a handkerchief and blew her nose, already perkier at the thought of some alone time.

Kenneth knew things were moving fast with Simon and their torrid affair was turning into something much more and whilst he remained loyal to Georgie, his heart was being tugged in two directions. Much worse, was that his wife was formidable when faced with a challenge but he feared in Simon, she might meet her match. When his young lover found out about whatever plans they were about to make he wouldn't take kindly to them, not at all.

By some miracle, whether it was down to Kenneth's conciliatory prowess or the patient guile of his wife and lover, a truce was negotiated and for a while he managed to keep both happy. Simon vowed to respect Kenneth's arrangement with Georgie and agreed that Vanessa's happiness was paramount, while Georgie vowed to uphold her side of their original bargain and allow her husband certain freedoms. Unbeknown to Kenneth, both Georgie and Simon made identical vows of their own, swearing silent oaths to be victorious and keep the man they loved just for themselves.

Peace and harmony reigned for over a year but as Georgie always feared, the desires of man were destined to win out and despite her best efforts, which entailed being less reliant on the pills and laying off the booze, her hold on Kenneth loosened. She had tried to be jolly and fun but it was becoming harder to fake it, fake everything really. Georgie knew she was turning into the bitter has-been actress who ironically had never actually been one in the first place. Her love life was a tacky sitcom, always the bit-part actress who was happy to take the throw away lines and cast of jokes that the real stars had no use for. Just like philandering husbands and fickle gigolos who moved on to the next amoral or sad candidate, leaving Georgie to straighten her skirt and laugh off the shame she felt inside.

Oh how she tried to ignore the loneliness that crept about inside her head as one by one, her group settled down or moved away, or grew up. Georgie was almost forty and felt every single year of it. Whilst their friends were always on hand for a gossipy chat on the blower or a party at Tenley or Kensington, and never said no to a free holiday, the shallow existence that had once seemed a riot was wearing thin. It left Georgie unsettled and for the first time, out of control and on the edge of her marriage and if she wasn't careful, her mind.

By 1984, the year of Vanessa's twenty-first birthday, the little crack in Georgie and Kenneth's marriage was turning into a chasm. Georgie knew it was time. They couldn't live a lie any longer and before she lost her sanity or her liver, because as Doctor Humphrey had suggested, the pills of paradise and special water were not helping one jot, something had to give. Georgie knew it had to be her.

After losing the best part of a week to a bottle of vodka and her husband to his Oxford pretty boy, Georgie had managed to pull herself together just in time to throw Vanessa the most fabulous birthday party the county had ever seen. Her daughter, on the other hand had insisted on a sensible do with the usual suspects from London and a few of her own friends, those who Vanessa joked were desperate enough to attend.

Over the years, mainly due to Georgie's lack of patience where pandering to silly women was concerned, the local in-crowd had petered off. Nowadays, Vanessa was left with what could only be described as the rejects from school, those who were also left on the shelf. Sometimes, Georgie wondered if Sandy had been right after all and an attempt to take Vanessa in hand should have been made, but then again she seemed happy enough with her lot. She was a big girl, in more ways than one and eating habits aside, Georgie felt she had done her best to ease Vanessa through a difficult childhood so it was high time she took control of her own destiny. Anyway, Georgie had enough on her plate with the Simon problem and unfortunately, since her dalliance with a regiment officer from Kew, in her belly.

As she dressed for Vanessa's birthday bash, Georgie took a gulp of brandy. It helped with her chest which was prone to flare ups and always resulted in a tiresome period of malaise that dragged her down. That was the last thing she needed, what with bloody Christmas just weeks away and the looming anniversary of dear Dolly's death. It was all frying Georgie's brain. Something had to give and unfortunately, it was the birthday guest list that did it.

Kenneth came darting into the dressing room, fiddling with his shirt buttons and asked Georgie to fasten his bow tie. "Darling, could you do the honours?"

Smiling at the sight of her husband in his dinner suit, Georgie left fastening her earrings and set about tying the knot, and as she did so, Kenneth asked her a question, a statement really, and one that flipped her world on its axis. He had broken the rules.

"By the way, I've invited Simon to the party. He's staying with the Squires so I thought it would be rude not to include him, one more won't matter, will it?" When Kenneth caught the look in Georgie's eyes he could tell instantly that it would.

The silence was unnerving as his wife thought long and hard before replying, never taking her eyes from his while her hands deftly tied the bow, just as she'd done hundreds of times before.

"Yes, it does matter, Kenneth, because you're breaking the rules."

"B… but it's just a party, darling. He won't be staying over. I wouldn't even consider–" Kenneth was cut off by Georgie who refused to listen to another word on the matter, pulling hard on the tie, causing his neck to jerk before she spoke.

"No. It's not just a party. It's our daughter's twenty-first and a very special occasion, one I wish to remember always as perfect. Therefore I *will not* allow the presence of your lover to taint it in any way so I would be grateful if you could telephone him immediately and revoke the invitation. Now, Kenneth." Georgie glared.

Her lips felt numb and her face she knew would be white with anger. Georgie ignored the fear in her heart, terrified that it would rise up and consume her if she acknowledged its existence or the ramifications of Kenneth's refusal.

Knowing when to back down, Kenneth nodded curtly but even though he acquiesced for the sake of Vanessa's special birthday, this time it rankled and it showed in his face, just before he nodded, turned sharply and left the room.

Georgie spotted it too.

To the untrained eye and champagne soaked guest, the party was a resounding success. The band played all their favourite songs, Laurie arrived from Los Angeles looking suntanned yet ravaged by some strange disease that was eating the gay community alive. He assured Georgie he would be fine and just needed rest but there was something about his eyes that told her he was lying. There was a lot of it about.

Kenneth made a wonderful speech about his darling daughter, and Georgie got her photograph for the top of the piano. It would take pride of place next to the one of the Princess. But as soon as the flashlights pointed in other directions, Georgie's guard came down and Kenneth sloped off to a corner with the estate manager, the cool manner he'd adopted all evening turning slowly to ice.

Vanessa was happily giggling with her friends as they waited for the hot buffet supper to be laid out so Georgie reverted to type and took solace in a bottle of champagne. The London set just didn't do it for her anymore.

As she made her way upstairs, Georgie stopped and took in the scene. Sandy was asking Vanessa if they could have a photograph, how sweet, especially as the dear dowdy woman looked so out of place and uncomfortable in a room full of black liquorice sticks and brightly coloured lollipops. Shaking away the phantasmal image, Georgie knew that the pills she downed in the bathroom were playing havoc with her brain and the champagne wasn't helping either. Still, she wouldn't be missed so it would be nice to escape to oblivion, away from the chill of her husband's stare.

When she reached the first landing, instead of heading to her bedroom, Georgie continued higher, to the top floor where Sandy slept. After passing her closed bedroom door, Georgie carried on to the end of the thin dimly lit corridor and the long sash window that opened onto the parapet that ran around the roof. Feeling the need for air and to spread her wings, a strange notion seeing as though it was November and bloody freezing, Georgie ignored sound advice from the unpickled cortex of her brain and pulled up the sash, gasping slightly as the ice-cold wind whipped at her hair and froze her skin. Regardless, she ducked under the frame and dragged her legs and evening gown through the gap before standing and walking the couple of feet to the edge.

"Gosh," said Georgie. "What a long way down."

The Rollers and Jags parked on the drive below looked like toy cars. It made Georgie feel slightly dizzy so instead she looked straight ahead, over the tops of the trees and beyond the Tenley estate, with its sweeping fields and cosy cottages where lights blazed and happy families sat by their fires. That image was bloody depressing so Georgie tipped back her head and gazed at the sky above. The heavens were velvet black and dotted with stars, like the ones that should have hung on her dressing room door in the West End and every theatre across the land, even Times Square.

Staggering slightly on her heels, Georgie praised herself for having the common sense to kick them off and as one flipped over the edge, it made her laugh. Bending slowly, so as not to follow suit, she picked up the other shoe and hurled it as far as she could. Down below she heard a thud causing her to smile contentedly, hoping it had landed on Kenneth's precious Bentley and left a dent in the roof.

"Lordy, it's cold!" Georgie shouted to the moon. The wind was getting up as she took a long swig from the bottle, the fizzy liquid escaping down her chin and neck, disappearing into her cleavage and staining her dress. Spreading her arms out wide, Georgie closed her eyes and allowed the cold northerly to ruffle her Balenciaga dress as strands of hair came loose from its clasp. She was lost in a frozen world, a bird ready for flight perched on the edge of a cliff and perhaps just one more sip would give her the courage to leap and fly, soar across the tree-tops and up to heaven. Dolly would be there waiting with a fish supper and strong sweet tea, how wonderful that would be.

Placing the bottle to her lips, Georgie drank and took a step forward. Her feet were stinging from the cold of the parapet roof, the felt was harsh under her skin. One more step, dare she? Just as the thought penetrated the fuzz in her head, it was interrupted by the sound of a voice, sharp and familiar, somewhere behind her. Turning slowly, Georgie swayed and tried to focus, the light from the hall casting the body at the window into shadow. As the voice called out again, this time Georgie recognised it; Sandy.

"Madam, Georgie, please come inside at once. It's very dangerous out there and you will catch your death. Here, take my hand, that's it. Step forward, nice and slow." Sandy held out her hand.

"Sandy, how lovely to see you… Why aren't you at the party getting sloshed like everyone else? Off you go. I'll be fine out here, although I must say you're right. It's brass monkeys. My nipples are like torpedoes but don't tell anyone, it can be our secret… Sssh." Georgie was beginning to giggle as she placed her fingers over her lips and soon her mirth turned to mild hysteria, building by the second.

"Georgie. I insist you come inside otherwise I will have to fetch Kenneth and we don't want to ruin Vanessa's party now, do we?" Sandy held out both hands and watched as Georgie swayed on the edge of the parapet, her rival's close proximity to death evident.

Georgie took another drink but most of it she spat out as angry words mixed with champagne. "Ha… he won't come and save me. Kenneth doesn't care a jot about me, not anymore."

"I'm sure that's not true, Georgie. Mr Tenley loves you very much and would be horrified to see you out here so please, come inside."

Sandy's voice served only to irritate Georgie. "Aren't you listening? I said he doesn't love me anymore, in fact he never has, not properly, like a real man should. I bet you didn't know that, did you?" Another emboldening swig and a slight sway preceded her next tirade.

"My Kenneth can't get it up, not up me, anyway, but he has no trouble when he's shafting darling pretty boy Simon, who wants to take everything and ruin my life." Georgie pointed at Sandy.

"You just mark my words, I'm going to ring pretty boy Simon tomorrow and tell him he can have good old Kenneth. He can have the lot. Just like fucking China can have fucking Hong Kong. They can both go to hell… Isn't that where sodomites go, Sandy, to burn in hell's fire?"

For a moment, Sandy said nothing and her silence gave Georgie the opportunity to continue, thoroughly enjoying her role as the injured party who had pushed the self-destruct button and was going for broke. Georgie basked in the spotlight before a captive audience of one.

"Well? I'm waiting Mrs Churchy-Pants. And what about me, what'll happen to me because I'm no saint either? Where do dirty whores go? Is there a special hell for an adulterer, and what about a murderer? They definitely go downstairs, surely they do." Georgie was angry but on the verge of tears, her voice catching in the wind.

"Georgie, enough of this! I do not wish to hear another word of your sordid confession or such foul unladylike language and I can only hope it is the drink talking. Now for the last time, come inside or I shall call for Kenneth."

Sandy leaned forward, her body hanging out of the window, touching the silk of Georgie's flowing gown as she waited, her stern look practised on Vanessa as a young and obstinate child. Maybe it was her tone or the bitter wind, or the talk of death that had a sobering effect on Georgie but something broke the spell and made her see sense. Grasping the outstretched hand, Georgie stumbled towards Sandy and fell to her knees, the top half of her body at the window's edge, face to face with her rescuer who held on tight from the corridor. But Georgie wasn't finished.

"You have been so kind to me, Sandy. All these years you have been such a good friend and helped me so much with the house and Vanessa, everything really. Which is why I owe you the truth, you deserve to know that I am a bad person, the very worst because each and every word I said is true. I *have* behaved like a whore. You would be shocked at what I would do for a bottle of scent or a handbag, and I am an adulterer and worse, a murderer." Georgie knelt before Sandy, dropping the bottle then grasping her hands tightly as tears flowed from stinging eyes, pinching her skin as they fell.

"If you can forgive me, Sandy, perhaps I have a chance... You understand about God and his rules so maybe you can put a word in for me, he will listen to you, I know he will." Georgie was becoming hysterical, rambling and almost incoherent, sobbing and gasping as Sandy asked a question, her voice incredulous.

"What do you mean a murderer? You're confused and very drunk, Georgie. Please tell me you are."

"I will be a murderer. I am going to kill, very soon. Don't you see I have made a terrible mistake and my wicked behaviour has left me no alternative."

Sandy gasped, then in a hushed tone asked the most obvious question. "Who are you going to kill, Georgie, and why, what have you done?"

"The baby, the one inside me… I have to get rid of it. I can't be a mother, not like this. I'm a useless wretch, a stinking alcoholic who can't get through the day without a happy pill. What type of mother would I be? No, it has to go, the sooner the better." Georgie's face was awash with tears which she wiped from her eyes and in doing so was able to see Sandy more clearly, and the dark look that had crossed her face.

It was as though a shadow was sweeping downwards and the eyes that once implored her to come inside, and seemed kind and understanding were hard and cold, just like her face which was set in stone. Georgie's teeth chattered and her lips trembled and whereas before she was insistent on remaining outside, she sensed danger and animosity and the parapet edge seemed far too close. Sandy simply stared, her immobility and silence unnerving Georgie further, prompting her to speak.

"Let me inside now, Sandy, and go and find Kenneth. I need to speak to Kenneth so move aside. I'm cold, please move, I want to come in. Sandy!" Georgie was forced to raise her voice that held a hint of panic because for a split second, she feared that Sandy wasn't going to move, she looked so hateful and angry. Then a voice from along the corridor cut through the hush, it was Vanessa and the sound of her calling for Georgie prompted Sandy into action. As she stood and held out her hand, Georgie saw Vanessa appear in the corridor and called out to her for help.

Vanessa took in the scene, catching her breath after the climb, her shocked face turning to panic as she ran to Georgie's aid and along with Sandy, helped the trembling, frozen wreck inside.

"Thank you, Sandy. I will take it from here. Could you go and tell Daddy I need him. I'll look after Georgie until he arrives. Thank you so much for looking after her, you've been an angel." Vanessa guided Georgie towards the stairs, rubbing her skin as they walked, trying to get some warmth into her.

"Yes of course. I'll go ahead and do take care on the stairs. I wouldn't want either of you to fall." With that, Sandy went in search of Kenneth while behind her, Georgie sobbed and apologised, for what was anyone's guess. Her words were unintelligible, garbled and lost amongst Vanessa's assurances and shushing sounds.

By the time Vanessa had manoeuvred Georgie to her bedroom, Kenneth arrived and at the sight of his wife, he sighed and felt so desperately sad. Taking her from Vanessa and then into his arms, he let Georgie cry it out. Over her head, he spoke softly to Vanessa.

"You go and have some fun, my darling. I'll take care of things here, go on. Enjoy what's left of your birthday."

Nodding silently, Vanessa backed out of the room, closing the door then made her way forlornly downstairs.

As the band played and the guests danced the night away, Kenneth ran a bath for his wife and helped her undress. While pouring warm water over her frozen skin and shaking bones, he too shed tears, speaking softly to his incoherent wife.

"Oh I do love you, darling girl, I really do, but we can't go on like this, can we? What am I to do with you?"

Kenneth washed Georgie's hair and then helped her stand, towelling her dry before wrapping her in a blanket and helping her beneath the sheets. Once she was comfy, he flicked off his shoes and lay beside her, holding her close as he listened to her shallow breaths. Had she been conscious, Georgie could have held on to the memory forever. She would have heard his words of love and the promises that Kenneth made, but as it was, their last night huddled together was lost forever in a haze, confused by pills diluted in a sea of bubbles.

While Kenneth's tears mingled with Georgie's damp hair, he lamented the end, one that heralded the beginning of his future. It was something he had tried to resist but now longed for – a new life with Simon, far away from Tenley.

Chapter 20

Sandy

Outside, the rain continued to pour as Sandy stirred the soup pan and waited for the kettle to boil. It was approaching lunchtime and she had decided to serve something simple, the last of the cold meats from Christmas and whatever lingering leftovers she could lay her hands on. Georgie had bought so much produce from the butcher's that Sandy had been forced to freeze the majority of it, confirming her worries that the lady of Tenley was slowly losing her mind. The day before, she had cancelled their usual New Year celebrations and instructed Kenneth to ring round and tell everyone to bugger off. As a consequence, they would be eating beasts of every description well into 1985, as long as they all still lived there.

Two days had passed since Sandy had stumbled on Kenneth and his visitor… not quite stumbled, she had crept up on them and listened to their conversation and now knew all she needed to about her employer and his dirty secret. Oh yes, she had considered blackmail and even telling Georgie what she had heard but both courses of action might have led to her dismissal. The thought of being parted from Vanessa far outweighed the pleasure she would get from outing him, or how much money she could extract in return for her continued silence.

Once common sense prevailed and she had spoken with the Lord, Sandy knew that the end was in sight and all that she had craved might soon be hers. She prayed so hard for a sign or an answer and eventually, with God's help and the calming influence of one of Kenneth's finest malts, Sandy worked it out.

To her shame and for which she had prayed forgiveness, Sandy wished that Georgie had done everyone a huge favour and fallen from the parapet, one less Tenley to deal with. It had even crossed her mind as the drunken slattern knelt before her and confessed to such wicked sins, that with one quick push it would all be over and her rival for Vanessa's affections would be gone forever. It had been mention of the baby that saved Georgie because when it came down to it, Sandy just couldn't take the life of an innocent unborn. If the slattern wished to kill her child that was her business, and the good Lord's.

When it came to sinners, there was nobody more abhorrent than Kenneth and to think she had lived under his roof for over twelve years with no clue about the depths of his depravity. It was there in the Bible, written in black and white; Leviticus 20:13, irrefutable proof he was a sinner and it was quite clear how he should be punished. Sandy assured herself over and over that she wasn't a hypocrite or an accessory because while she had witnessed and frowned upon their bohemian lifestyle, she had never condoned it. To think she had skivvied after him and their ragtag group of wasters from all walks of life, who came and went, all the time turning a blind eye to their lascivious behaviour. But to realise Kenneth was everything Phyllis had said he was, came as a great shock.

What pained Sandy most was that her precious child had been ripped from her arms and given to a man like Kenneth and then, through no fault of her own was left motherless. To add insult to Sandy's injury, akin to an open wound or loss of a limb, Vanessa had been brought up by Georgie. What cruel fate had sentenced her to this? Forced to look on, impotent and sidelined. It made Sandy shudder.

She had finished laying the table, another whim of Georgie's that only served to irritate Sandy, this insistence on eating in the kitchen whenever the fancy took her. She was a hypocrite that's for sure. Georgie once told Sandy, as they peeled potatoes for chips, that it reminded her of her childhood and mealtimes in the kitchen at her grandparents' house. Sweet as the notion appeared, Sandy couldn't equate this rosy image with the scrunched-up letters she'd found in the bin, the ones from a Mr and Mrs Nibley. None of her family came to visit yet the maternal side exchanged cards, but only on birthdays and Christmas. It was all very awkward for Sandy when Georgie refused to take the call from her mother, saying her grandmother had passed. Flowers were sent but apart from that it seemed as though Georgie had cut her family out of her life. It was all very odd.

Anyway, the kitchen was Sandy's domain and she resented the intrusion even though it was something that Vanessa enjoyed, but then again she loved *everything* that Georgie did or suggested. At least eating in the kitchen saved the walk to the dining room which was in a rather sorry state after the ceiling collapsed. The never-ending rain and the sight of a sloppy mess on the polished parquet had sent Georgie into meltdown.

Lately it only took the slightest thing and Georgie would crumble, her nerves were shattered. Despite Sandy's criticisms, she did have a heart and it was pitiful to see the woman in such a state and all because of him, Kenneth. Trouble was brewing. Sandy could sense it from the moment she woke until she retired in the evening. It was like static in the air. Despite them having a decent and peaceful enough Christmas, it was clear that something had to give, it was like waiting for the bomb to go up and it was grating on Sandy's nerves.

Her little nest egg had grown to a substantial pot, topped up nicely by Kenneth's hush money she was ready for any eventuality. Georgie was going quietly mad and if all went as Sandy hoped, Kenneth would soon be history which meant Vanessa, in the absence of a father and sane mother, would be in need of a shoulder to cry on and a steadying influence.

So as long as she timed it right, Sandy was convinced that her patience would be justly rewarded. Her precious daughter, on hearing of her real mother's devotion and sacrifice, and after realising everything Sandy had done on her child's behalf was for the greater good, Vanessa would fall into her arms, reunited forever.

Straightening her aching back, Sandy walked to the utility room and unhooked her raincoat. It was time to look for Kenneth who had reluctantly acted on her suggestion that the overflowing gutter had backed-up and needed clearing. Looking back at the table, she wondered if her efforts had been for nothing, then again no matter what, Vanessa was unlikely to refuse food, a crisis mild or major never seemed to affect her appetite.

Lifting the catch, Sandy stepped outside and looked upwards and as she did, the sun burst through, causing her spirits to lift, knowing it was God's way of smiling down on her, letting her know He was watching and on her side. Closing the door behind her, Sandy went in search of Kenneth.

Chapter 21

Kenneth

The wind howled and torrential rain pounded Kenneth's sodden raincoat. The hood tied fast around his head still left his face exposed and drenched as he hauled the ladder from the gardener's shed and carried it back towards the house. Trust the blasted gutters to block while Ernest was away for the New Year, but then again the old chap really shouldn't be going up ladders at his age. It was about time they took on someone younger and able-bodied. But that was a task he would save for another time as there were more pressing matters to attend to, like the waterfall cascading from the blocked gutter that had caused the roof above the dining room to leak. Currently there were strategically placed buckets lining the parquet floor and above, a rather gaping hole had been left by soggy plaster. That was another job on his list, to get the builders in to repair the ceiling. At least it wasn't urgent, not since Georgie had cancelled their usual New Year celebrations, a decision which had left Kenneth hugely relieved.

After the incident on Vanessa's birthday, things had really gone from bad to worse and it had taken all Kenneth's strength and mettle not to run away to London and hide from everything. Although the idea was tempting, as was spending time with Simon, Kenneth owed it to Georgie and Vanessa to stay and sort out his affairs and do the right thing by them both. It was a chore he dreaded and his fraught situation had not been helped one bit by the surprise visit from his angry lover and then, what could only be described as a similarly frank inquisition by the pious bloody housekeeper.

Kenneth sighed as he placed the ladders against the wall and pulled on the thick rubber gloves he'd found in the shed, not looking forward to scraping out the gutters or the climb. He hadn't a head for heights and the stomach for whatever gunge he was about to dislodge. Still, he actually preferred being outside even if it was in such dire weather because the atmosphere inside was simply awful.

After a protracted conversation with the family solicitor where they discussed minor alterations to his will along with his obligations and options, Kenneth decided to ponder a while. He was adamant that if he divorced Georgie, she was to get a much larger settlement than their pre-nup stated, and that Vanessa was to take control of the estate. She was of age and it was her right. He would not sell it from under her feet, everything would go to her.

Steeling himself for the climb, he looked down at his hands, unsure whether the gloves were a good idea as they lessened his grip. Hearing the rumble of thunder in the distance, he decided to plough on, the task ahead firmly on his mind, as was his wife and daughter and the troublesome events over Christmas. Shaking his head as a flash of lightning streaked overhead, Kenneth began his ascent, determined to get it over with, just like everything else.

***

The morning after Vanessa's party, Kenneth entered their suite to find Georgie sitting by the window, gazing into nowhere as she listened to music, her choice of song quite apt and her way of broaching a most painful subject. Placing the tea tray on the table, Kenneth took the chair beside Georgie and listened to a song from *Evita*, such a sad lament, 'Another Suitcase in Another Hall'. It summed up the situation and Georgie played her role perfectly, holding out her hand to Kenneth who enfolded it in his before she asked the question.

"So what happens now?" Keeping her eyes fixed firmly ahead, Georgie sounded resigned. There was no fight left in her and while he knew she was being melodramatic, Kenneth didn't deny her the moment as it gave him time to think.

Kenneth was at a loss, so used to her taking the lead in everything, but this time it was down to him, he had to sort it out. The thing was, he had no clue how to go about it. Instead he focused on his wife and the more pressing issue of her physical and mental health.

"All I care about right now is getting you well. I mean that, Georgie. We can't even contemplate the future until you are fit and strong so I suggest we take a trip up to London and consult Dr Humphrey. He's very understanding, and I'm sure between us we will have you right as rain in no time."

"What, so you can be rid of me once and for all, the second your conscience is clear?" Georgie refused to look at Kenneth who was hurt by her accusation and unnerved by her calm deliverance of every sentence.

"Georgie, that's not the case, far from it. You are my wife in both the law and my heart and therefore I will not abandon you. I don't know how many times I have to say it for you to believe me." Kenneth was becoming exasperated and on the precipice of anger.

Perhaps it was his tone that flared a more spirited response from Georgie, her voice sarcastic. "I'm so sorry if I've misjudged you but really, do you blame me? My whole existence is falling apart and you expect me not to worry, to fear for my future. But you are right about one thing and I have already made arrangements to see the doctor after Christmas, but I won't require your presence, it wouldn't be appropriate."

"Why not, and when did you arrange this? Is it your chest? I've told you to cut down on the cigarettes, darling, you really must try harder." Kenneth was worried and also felt shut out.

When Georgie finally turned to face him, Kenneth presumed he was going to get a ticking off for lecturing her and as she held his stare, waited for an ear bashing.

"It's nothing to do with my chest. I'm pregnant and I need to get rid of it, the sooner the better. There, now you know. Judge away." Georgie turned from Kenneth, satisfied by the look of utter shock on his face. The record had ended and the quiet of the room was suffocating.

Over the years, Kenneth had learned from experience that if one had nothing sensible to say, it was often best to remain silent, thus avoiding putting one's size nines in it. This was one of these situations. He had no quarrel with her decision. It was definitely for the best under the circumstances but then again, this might be her last chance of becoming a mother. Kenneth felt he owed her the opportunity so would do the honourable thing if required.

"Do you want to get rid of it? Are you sure? I would stand by you if you decided to keep it. We could say the child is mine… for propriety's sake and all that. In any case I wouldn't want you to make a hasty decision." Whilst Kenneth meant every word, he desperately hoped for all their sakes Georgie would decline.

Turning once more, Georgie swiped away a tear then addressed Kenneth matter-of-factly, laying the subject to rest in her unusually calm manner. "I'm positive. I would be a dreadful mother even if I wanted to keep it, which I don't. And I have never yearned for a baby of my own so the day after Boxing Day, I will head up to London and some clinic or other. Dr Humphrey has taken care of all the details. I'll be back a couple of days later and that will be the end of the matter. But I thank you for your kind offer, it means a great deal. Now, let's move on to other arrangements." Georgie straightened in her seat and pulled the blanket over her knees.

Kenneth saw her lips tremble and he could tell she was trying so hard not to cry. When she was composed and after a sip of cold tea, Georgie continued.

"Laurie would like to stay for Christmas and then he'll be heading back over the pond soon after. I expect it's the last we'll see of him because from the looks of it he's rather ill, no matter how much he tries to convince me otherwise. Is it alright for him to stay?"

Kenneth cleared his throat and shuffled, disturbed by Georgie's acceptance of her own fate and that of Laurie. It was as though she was emotionally disconnected and on autopilot.

"Of course, Laurie is always welcome here but surely you are wrong, he was having a ball last night and he hasn't mentioned a word to me about his health. Perhaps you could get him to see a doctor here, have him checked out by one of our quacks."

"I've already suggested it and he refused so we must respect his wishes, just as I expect you to respect mine."

Kenneth's heart pounded and he could feel the blush rise from his neck to his cheeks, silenced by the firmness in Georgie's tone, reminded now of his mother and how she would imperiously lay down the law.

"I want us to have one last Christmas together and for Vanessa to remain oblivious to my predicament and the situation between you and I. I'd like to hang on to the dream for a while longer if we can."

It was at this point, Kenneth heard the catch in Georgie's throat and when he looked, saw the tears escaping freely from her eyes. A lump formed in his own throat which he cleared with a cough. "Of course, Georgie, whatever you suggest. I will be happy to comply."

Kenneth could've kicked himself, angry at his own impotence at such a vital time. Her heart was breaking and as always she was stepping into the breach, rescuing him from himself. Just as he was feeling less threatened, the tone changed with Georgie's next question.

"Now, tell me about you and Simon, what are your plans? I presume he has made some for you." Georgie was slowly reverting to type, a hint of sarcasm in her voice which had lost its softness, there was an edge to it.

Kenneth sucked in air and willed himself not to stammer and waffle. This was his opportunity to get it over and done with, repeat the words Simon had been subtly drumming into him for months. It was now or never.

"He's going to live in America and wants me to go with him, to San Francisco. He's been offered a job there at a research facility. He believes we can start a new life and not have to hide away from who we are. I told him I had to think it over, that it's not as easy for me. I can't just pack a case and hop on a plane. I have responsibilities here, to you, Vanessa, the estate. I don't know if I can leave it all behind so I asked him to give me some time, to speak to you and perhaps come to an arrangement."

"And how did he take it, your dithering?"

Kenneth ignored the slight even though it was on the money. "He was upset and angry but I think he understands, although he didn't take kindly to being told he wasn't welcome here and was rather bolshy when I ended the call last night." Kenneth recalled the conversation with Simon where for the first time he experienced the petulant side of the young man he was considering leaving his life for.

"Diddums, poor Simon. I'm sure there's a lot more where that came from. He sounds like a spoilt brat. How delightful for you. Anyhow, back to our situation. What do you intend to do with Tenley and more to the point, me? Is Simon demanding a divorce or will he make do with your body and bank balance? I need to know where I stand and if I will have a roof over my head because I can't see lover boy settling for second best. I imagine he wants it all. Am I right?"

Georgie's tone had moved up a notch, she sounded bitter but knowing her so well, Kenneth could hear fear too. But she was right, as always, and there was no point lying, she would see right through him.

"I don't think there's any need for divorce or selling up although it is what Simon would prefer. I could just go to America with him and leave the running of the estate in Vanessa's hands then the two of you could continue to live here. That way the busybodies would be in the dark and I will concoct some story about taking a sabbatical, whatever works best for all of us." When Georgie laughed out loud, shaking her head in a derisory manner, Kenneth was both astounded and offended. After all, he was doing his best to find a solution for everyone.

"My dear, darling Kenneth. You have no idea what you are getting yourself into, do you? If you think for one moment that Simon will agree to that you are sadly mistaken. He wants me gone for good and I doubt if his ambitions are all for love. I suspect it's more to do with power and getting his way. You have to understand that he's insanely jealous of us and what we have, or had. He will not allow me to remain here and he doesn't want to share. If he did he wouldn't continually push the boundaries, expecting more than you can give. The mere fact he wants you to throw away your life and relocate thousands of miles away tells me that. And I fear the drip-drip effect will soon intensify to ultimatums so please tread carefully, Kenneth, because you are out of your depth."

Kenneth was stunned into silence. Surely Georgie was wrong, how could she know what made Simon tick or second guess his motives? And then the light dawned and he knew she was right, a realisation that scared and depressed him equally. Georgie was an excellent reader of people and could play anyone like a fiddle which was why she saw through Simon, or thought she did. He had to think this through because it was huge, too huge to mess up.

In the midst of the silence came a knock at the door and from the other side, Vanessa's voice asking if she could enter. Before either of them answered, Georgie leant over and took Kenneth's hand in hers. She had one more thing to say.

"Please, darling, remember I love you very much and I will honour and respect our agreement and your wishes. Whatever you decide, I will stand by you always and if I have to let you go, I will. Let's get Christmas over and then you must make up your mind, for all our sakes." She smiled kindly at Kenneth whose eyes were misted with tears, then called for Vanessa to enter.

Christmas went as planned with the actress taking the starring role and in between fending off phone calls from Simon, Kenneth played his part well and Vanessa was none the wiser. When Georgie headed up to London to see the doctor about her troublesome chest, Vanessa begged to tag along and sulked for a whole day when she was fobbed off. Instead Laurie accompanied Georgie on the train and back at the Kensington house, and then held her hand after the deed was done.

Kenneth had literally replaced the receiver after enquiring over Georgie's state when Vanessa appeared at his office door. He could see her through the frosted glass and as she entered, he was rubbing his temples with his forefingers, hoping that the magic circles would ease away tension. Her next words almost caused his head to explode.

"Daddy, Sandy has just telephoned from the house and says there's a young man to see you. She said his name is Simon. Should I ask him to come down here or will you go up? I did try to connect you but you were on the phone to Georgie."

Kenneth was stunned and quite stiff from shock as he stared at Vanessa, his fingers glued to his temples. Somehow he spat out an answer.

"No. I'll go up there. Ring Sandy and tell her I'm on my way. You hold the fort here." With that, he stood and grabbed his coat from the hook and barged past Vanessa who closed his door and went back to her desk looking somewhat baffled by her father's behaviour.

They were in the garden, out of sight of the house and shrouded by a circle of trees, seated under the pagoda that was littered with dried brown leaves being tossed around by the gentle breeze. It was cold but not bitter for the time of year yet Simon had already taken umbrage at not being offered refreshments or a seat by the fireplace. Instead he was herded from the house the moment Kenneth arrived.

There was no question of talking inside as lately, Simon was prone to flying off the handle whenever a discussion didn't go his way and the minute Kenneth had laid eyes on him, knew a confrontation was on the cards. They had walked through the grounds at the back of the house in silence, through the flower beds until they reached the pagoda where Kenneth sat first, gesturing for Simon to do likewise.

"Why are you here, Simon? We had a pact and I've already agreed to meet you next week. You should have waited. What if Georgie had been here or Vanessa?"

"See, there you go again, pushing me aside and putting them first like always. I've spent Christmas alone, and New Year is going to be a God-awful bore with you stuck here in the back of beyond. I just wanted to see you. Is that such a bloody crime?" Simon was raising his voice and Kenneth told him to be quiet.

"No, I'll not be silenced any longer. Have you told her that we're leaving and you want a divorce?" Simon stood and faced Kenneth, the fury in the young man's face clear to see.

"Simon, please, keep your voice down, I insist. And for the record we have discussed certain matters but not made firm plans. Georgie is unwell and I cannot risk her health. I still have a responsibility to her; she is my wife." In hindsight it was a stupid thing to say and Kenneth regretted it the moment the words came out and he heard Simon's anguished cry.

"Oh my God… what's wrong with you? Can you not see she is playing for time? We discussed this, all of it. You were supposed to demand a divorce and say that you want her out, is that so difficult? And what about Vanessa, have you told her about finishing school yet… no of course you haven't, or put the estate up for sale? How can we fund our new life and do all the things we planned in the States if everything is tied up here… Don't you want us to be together and live as a couple? It's our right to be happy and we can have it all if you'd just grow a spine and tell them you are leaving." Simon was pacing, white with anger and flicking spittle as he spoke.

"Simon, I agreed to nothing. These were just ideas, flights of fancy that sound wonderful but they will take time and what's more, don't you think we need to take things slowly, build trust between us before I throw away my life, never mind Tenley and the estate. This should all go to Vanessa and I can't just sell it from under her feet. She's my daughter and I must do the right thing by her and Georgie."

Simon placed his hands on his head and stared at Kenneth in mock horror before spewing forth a torrent of bitter words, the sum total of his pent-up frustration aimed solely at his apathetic lover.

"She's not even yours, you stupid man, she's someone else's bastard child and as for Georgie, she doesn't even warrant the title of mistress let alone wife. What use is she to you? She serves no purpose, not anymore. You don't need a shield or a safety blanket and anyway who cares what society says, fuck them, fuck the lot of them and their bigotry."

Kenneth stood, similarly angered, and about to object but he was interrupted, the palm of a hand shoved in his face preventing him from speaking.

"No, I swear I will not listen to another of your weak excuses. I have had enough so just listen to what I came here to say. I'm leaving for America on the tenth of January with or without you, but hear this, Kenneth, if you want to spend the rest of your life with me then think long and hard about my terms because I will not share you. It's all or nothing otherwise I will go alone and you will never see me again. It's up to you now. That's all I have to say." And with that Simon turned and marched away, his blond hair blowing in the wind as Kenneth raced after him, imploring him to wait and not be hasty, desperate to talk it through and state his case.

As they burst through the circle of trees, Kenneth grabbed the cuff of Simon's jacket which was angrily pulled free before he continued along the path, refusing to stop, hell bent on having the last word. Kenneth would have pursued him had something not caught his eye. The sight froze him to the spot and before she could duck further from view he called out Sandy's name, forcing her to reveal herself. Rather than appear ashamed that her snooping had been discovered, she looked indignant and waited for Kenneth to speak first. When he did, he was surprised by the anger in his own voice.

"I don't take kindly to eavesdroppers, Sandy, and I'm most disappointed by your behaviour. I would like to speak to you in my study. Please wait for me there while I see our visitor off the property." Kenneth glared, especially when Sandy merely nodded and walked away.

By the time he had reached the drive, out of breath and panting, Kenneth was just in time to see Simon slam his car door before driving off at speed, gravel flicking everywhere as he went. Turning despondently, ignoring the sound of stone as it pebble-dashed the Bentley, Kenneth headed indoors to have it out with Sandy or more pointedly, find out exactly what she had heard.

Kenneth was furious and stormed straight past her as she stood outside his office, subservience etched on her face. After summoning her inside, he began by asking why she was listening to a private conversation. Instead of her usual civility, Kenneth was shocked when Sandy's whole demeanour changed. It appeared as though the worm was enjoying turning.

"I didn't intend to, I was on an errand for Vanessa. She telephoned to ask when you were coming back as she wanted to lock up. She has completed her work for the day and said she was bored. I merely came to find you and pass on the message. When I heard you arguing, I wasn't sure what to do, in fact I was rather concerned owing to the young man's temper but then you both came bolting through the trees and spotted me. I did nothing wrong, nothing at all." Sandy held his gaze, her cupped hands resting in front of her apron, relaxed and seemingly unperturbed by Kenneth's accusations.

Kenneth puffed out air and squinted, the anger in his voice receding slightly. "That's as may be but whatever you did hear I would ask that you keep it to yourself as the matters discussed were private and I wouldn't want Georgie or Vanessa to be upset in any way. If one word of this gets out, I will have no alternative than to dismiss you immediately. Do I make myself clear?"

"Yes, crystal clear. But at the same time, I'm in a very awkward position myself and my loyalties are torn. Poor Georgie is about to be evicted and divorced and as far as I am aware lives in ignorance of your adultery. Not only that, Vanessa is to be banished to a finishing school, I imagine overseas, all on the whim of your young lover. Is that correct?"

Kenneth was rather nonplussed by Sandy's forthright retort and thoroughly exhausted by his dash through the gardens and the strain of the day's events so decided to sit. It was a schoolboy error because Sandy looked down on him, a belligerent child being scolded by his nanny.

"Excuse me, Sandy, I would remind you to know your place and not speak out of turn on matters regarding my private life. However, for your information, nobody is being evicted, divorced or otherwise. It is complete conjecture at this moment in time."

"Ah, I see. So, on the one hand you regard me as a valued member of staff and I am to behave accordingly but when the occasion suits you, encouraged to feel like part of the family whereas now I need to know my place. It all seems rather confusing and may I say, unfair. I have dedicated twelve years of my life to you and your family and have become very attached to Vanessa and this house. I would thank you to remember that it is also my home and I too stand to lose it *and* my livelihood should you acquiesce to your lover. There are many people to consider in this situation, Mr Tenley, and I hope you appreciate the ramifications of running away to America."

Kenneth could not believe he was being spoken to like this, in his own home. Jumping to his feet, he raised his voice yet Sandy stood firm, fixing him with her best school-ma'am glare. "That's enough, Sandy. I do not wish to hurt or displace anybody. As I said, I have not come to any decisions and therefore respectfully ask that you keep your counsel and avoid unnecessary hurt to my family while I put my affairs in order."

"And I respectfully suggest that you should have thought about that before you embarked on an affair and jeopardised all you hold dear. However, under the circumstances I will do as you wish but only to protect the feelings of Vanessa and your wife." Sandy's omission of Kenneth spoke volumes.

Ignoring the slight which had hit home, Kenneth simply nodded. "Thank you, Sandy, and if it makes you feel any better I will ensure that you are compensated for your loyalty and service, perhaps by way of a New Year bonus and if the situation arises, provided with a fair and generous settlement should your employment be terminated. In any event I will endeavour to ensure that alternative arrangements can be made to prevent that. Are you agreeable to these terms?"

With a curt nod, Sandy signalled that she did and watched as Kenneth opened his desk drawer and withdrew his cheque book. In the uncomfortable moments that followed in which he paid for Sandy's silence, Kenneth's pen scratched the paper as he filled in the box, each zero a mark of shame, scribbling his signature before tearing at the seam. After folding the cheque in half, he passed it across the desk without making eye contact.

It was clear that Sandy was determined not to bow or scrape or let him off lightly and instead, asked Kenneth a question, just like nothing had happened. "Will that be all? I need to prepare tea for Vanessa and tend to the fires."

"Yes, that will be all."

With that, Sandy popped the cheque into the pocket of her apron, turned and left the room, leaving Kenneth alone to ponder his own fate and foolishness.

***

Kenneth had reached the blocked gutter and downpipe so held on tight to the top rung of the ladder, telling himself not to look down and if possible, not to look at the sludge he was scraping out of the gutter that felt like mashed up leaves and twigs, even through his gloves. He really hoped that was all it was because in the past, Ernest had fished out maggoty birds and mounds of pigeon shit, and Kenneth was rather hungry and didn't want putting off his lunch.

Determined to concentrate on the task, Kenneth forced thoughts of his confrontation with Simon and then Sandy from his mind. He still hadn't decided what to do about Simon but at least he'd been able to get it off his chest with Georgie when she returned from the clinic. Whilst livid at the intrusion, she respected Kenneth's honesty and after giving erudite advice, left him to make his choice. She really was an amazing woman and despite her introspective opinion, Kenneth admired her in so many ways, not least for giving him the chance to be free should he so wish.

He knew it was cruel, dangling her on a string and her nerves were shot, but he had to be sure and as much as he yearned for the delights of Simon, after his behaviour in the garden and the callous denunciation of Georgie and Vanessa, Kenneth was getting cold feet. Maybe Georgie was right in her summation of Simon's ambitions and motives. If this were the case he would be foolish to throw away everything away and for what, lust? There were hundreds of Simons in London and as Georgie pointed out, the odd dalliance here and there had sufficed before. She had even suggested a test, to let Simon go, quoting the oft-used bird analogy and the *Wisdom of Solomon*. Come to think of it, Georgie came out best in both scenarios because she loved Kenneth so much she was prepared to let him go while Simon just made demands and gave ultimatums.

In his head, Kenneth had almost made up his mind to stay with Georgie, if only his heart weren't so divided because as he'd told her time and time again, that very morning in fact, despite her moods and histrionics, he loved her very much. He loved Simon too and that was the problem.

The rain was easing off slightly and Kenneth thought it was sod's law that as he was reaching the end of his task the clouds were thinning and a speck of winter sun looked about to peep through. The bloody idiot weather forecasters had said it would rain all day, causing Kenneth to tut as he continued to scrape and flick, glad that after a good rummage it seemed to be clear and he could finally descend.

It was as he took his first step down that he felt the ladder move and in a panic, grabbed the gutter in order to steady himself, but then it moved again which was impossible because he was standing still. When the rung beneath his feet slipped downwards, Kenneth knew he was going to fall as the slippery gloves, covered in rainwater and slime, grappled for a hold on the gutter as he desperately tried to secure the wobbly ladder. It took only seconds before he was dislodged completely, toppling sideways, leaving his legs dangling, fingers slipping, terrified heart pounding.

As Kenneth flew through the air, dropping downwards, screaming in fear, his final sight was that of the sun breaking through the clouds, casting a bright white light, perhaps a glimpse of heaven, before his skull smashed onto the concrete balustrade below.

Thankfully his brains and blood remained contained within his hood that was still tied firmly around his head, saving his watchful murderer from a grizzly sight. The thud and strange crunching sound was gruesome enough without being splattered by organs and bone fragments. Satisfied the job had been done and life was definitely extinct, a silent figure smiled and began to retrace its steps, eager to escape the heavy drops that began to fall once again.

Demons hate the rain.

Chapter 22

Georgie

It hurt so much. Deep inside her chest there was a real physical pain, a dull ache that stayed with her every minute of the day, right from the second she opened her eyes up to the moment the sleeping tablets forced them to close. Georgie liked it and never wanted it to go because it reminded her of Kenneth, of how much she loved him. She would never see him again so the pain that was etching itself onto her heart was all she had left.

The room was in darkness, silent. She couldn't bear noise, the sound of a voice, a ticking clock, china teacups clinking, even her own breathing made her want to scream. How she hadn't done so at the church, Georgie would never know. The urge to cover her ears and run was overwhelming, more so when the bells chimed and the organ struck up, the singing of the choir almost sent her over the edge, too loud, too mournful. The only thing that got her through was the pills and having Vanessa by her side. And on the other had been Sandy, both of them holding her up and guiding her through the day until they arrived back at Tenley and she could escape to the sanctuary of her bedroom, where she intended to stay.

Vanessa had really come into her own since the day Kenneth died, one Georgie couldn't even bear to think of although it would be carved into her brain always, preventing her eyes from unseeing the horror of her beloved husband's body. Georgie would never forget the scene and then being questioned by the police when all she wanted to do was hold him in her arms and shake him back to life. Ever since, Vanessa had taken control of Tenley and the funeral arrangements, even Georgie, and for this she was glad. For the first time in her life, she had no idea what to do next, apart from putting one foot in front of the other, taking her pills and praying for sleep.

Downstairs, the mourners were attending the wake. Georgie was glad she couldn't hear the gentle murmuring of respectful conversation or see their pitying faces and drab clothing. It was all so depressing, reality. It soaked into her skin and weighed her down. Nevertheless, she had promised Vanessa and Sandy that once everyone had gone she would come downstairs and eat something. They said she might waste away which Georgie thought would be just perfect, then she could be with Kenneth.

It seemed Vanessa had made some plans for the future and wished to discuss them, and if only to reward her for being so brave of late, Georgie had agreed. Until then she covered her head with the pillow and closed her eyes, then opened them when the image returned.

It was always the same one, that of Kenneth lying in a pool a watery blood, unseeing eyes staring heavenwards, his gloved hands covered in black slime while his body looked distorted, arms and legs twisted out of place, like a rag doll. Georgie began to cry and gave in to the tears knowing that soon her eyes would be too weary to remain open and sleep would follow, until then she sobbed in the darkness, her only thoughts were of Kenneth and the day he finally left her.

***

Georgie had been in her bedroom, flicking through the Christmas edition of *Vogue*, not really concentrating and mildly irritated by the loud music playing in Vanessa's room. If Georgie heard that bloody song one more time, asking everyone if they knew it was Christmas, she would scream. She also had a pathological desire to smash the record into smithereens along with Bob Geldof's smug face.

She had considered asking Vanessa to turn it down but couldn't be bothered and anyway, Georgie would only be taking her temper and frustration out on someone else when the person she really wanted to punish was Simon, and if he didn't stop dithering, Kenneth. The rain was also getting her down. It hadn't let up for days and had ruined the dining room ceiling. The sight of it made Georgie think of her own brain, all mushy, and then her heart, broken into pieces.

Georgie was going to skip lunch, she had no appetite so decided to have a nap instead, anything was better than going mad with worry over Simon. Pulling the curtains closed, she noticed the sun was finally out and the sight of it cheered her, then the feeling went and she dragged them shut. It was as she pulled back the covers that the doorbell rang, incessantly, long bursts followed by short intermittent ones then back to a long, shrill uninterrupted period just before the banging started. It wasn't the pleasant ringing that one associated with the delivery of a nice parcel or the arrival of guests. It was the panicked portent of doom. Georgie's heart stopped, she was sure it did, then a feeling of dread rushed through her body aiding the swift movement of her legs as she flung open her bedroom door and raced down the stairs in stocking feet.

The whereabouts of Sandy crossed her mind fleetingly along with the thought that she might have gone deaf because it was impossible not to hear the racket or the sound of a male voice calling through the letterbox. Gasping for breath, Georgie's nicotine-lined lungs struggling to keep up, she pulled open the door to find the postman, his bag on the floor, its contents strewn and soggy on the steps while his bicycle looked to have toppled over, squashing the perennials in the border. The man's face was ashen and he appeared dumbstruck when faced with Georgie who demanded to know what all the fuss was about. Even as she spoke, she knew, just by the way he looked at her, casting wide eyes to his left and then back to Georgie. When she stepped forward to follow the line of his eye, the postman grabbed her upper arms and tried to block her path.

"No, Lady Tenley, please stay there... I need to use your phone, there's been a terrible accident. Where's Sandy, could you go and get her? Please, madam, stay indoors."

Georgie was having none of it and shoved the postie out of the way and moved onto the stone steps, not feeling the cold, too wired to care. It was as she looked along the pathway that ran around the house she saw him, lying on the floor beneath the dining room window. While her voice called out his name her legs ran, petrified eyes locked on the inert body that was surrounded by pale watery blood. She fell on him the moment she reached him, her knees scraping the ground as she covered her body with his, begging him to wake up, screaming for someone to call an ambulance, desperately hoping there was still a chance.

Touching his face, tracing his features with her fingers, tears dropped onto his eyes but there was no fairy-tale magic that day, her sorrow couldn't wake him and neither could the kisses she placed on his cheeks. While his beautiful face remained intact, the back of his skull was flat, crushed, and when she looked at her hands saw they were covered in blood that was seeping through the hood of his jacket, merging with the pools of rainwater on the ground.

As Georgie stared at her palms in disbelief, the truth filtered through and hysteria swept her body and found its escape through her lips as she began to wail. The noise of her own voice was just as terrifying as the sight before her so she placed her hands over her mouth, hoping to hold in the horror. It was as she rocked to and fro, Georgie heard a recognisable voice and then felt arms around her shoulders, close by, holding her tight. It was Sandy, who was sobbing too, and then Vanessa appeared and lowered herself to her knees, resting her head against Georgie's, repeating the same word over and over, 'Daddy'.

Then the sirens came, such a dreadful noise, confirming their urgency to attend a futile situation. Within moments there were footsteps and doors slamming, voices saying she should move away but she couldn't, she wouldn't. Kenneth was hers, her husband, so she should stay with him, hold his hand and make sure he was looked after at the hospital. Was that where they were taking him, to make him better? For as long as she lived she would never forget the next words she heard, or forgive the man who spoke them for taking away her dream, her life, her love. Fourteen very precise words were all it took to steal a piece of her heart.

"I'm very sorry, madam, but there's nothing we can do. Your husband is dead."

Silence. Georgie remembered everything went so very still as those gathered around the body took it all in, waiting respectfully, heads bowed. In the quiet, she looked at Sandy who was now composed and motioned for her to stand. Georgie followed the command and on the other side Vanessa helped her to her feet. What a state Georgie must have looked, in torn sodden tights that exposed grazed knees, and her feet stung as she limped away, passing the ambulance driver and police and the postie.

The police questioned each of them, as a matter of procedure, a formality they said. It was clearly a terrible accident, a combination of appalling weather and the ladder not being secured correctly. The gutter, which hung like a broken tree trunk, told them Kenneth had tried to cling on but the weight of his body and the cold caused his hands to slip.

Through glassy eyes that were veiled in sorrow, set in a blood smeared face with hollowed-out cheeks, Georgie told them where she was, had been all morning, and at the time of the accident. Vanessa sobbed and hiccupped, wiping her eyes and blowing her nose as she explained that she was in her room listening to music and it was only when she decided to come down for lunch and turned off her cassette player that she heard the commotion downstairs. Sandy confirmed that she'd been in the kitchen and was on her way to inform Kenneth that lunch was ready when she spotted him and Georgie under the dining room window.

From that day, life had descended into a black hole where the three women went through the motions. Sandy was on hand to assist Vanessa who made all the arrangements and shielded Georgie from anything and anyone unnecessary. Kenneth would have been so proud of his daughter, and how lucky they were to have Sandy who was a rock, stoically keeping order, watchful and attentive in their hour of need.

There was only one task which Georgie personally undertook the very next morning, placing a call to Simon where she informed him of her husband's death. Leaving her crumpled bed at first light, Georgie went downstairs to Kenneth's study and searched his desk drawers and when she found his leather address book, flicked through the pages until her eyes fell on the number she was looking for. Her hands shook as she dialled, her whole body consumed by rage the like of which she had never experienced before.

Simon answered after the fourth ring, sounding half-asleep and hungover. Georgie wasted no time and delivered her message in the manner of perhaps a doctor, or a police officer, but whichever suited, she did a damn fine job.

In the moments after Simon heard the words 'Kenneth' and 'dead', an audible intake of breath preceded a prolonged period of silence during which Georgie fought hard to swallow down hate. She had spent hours lying awake, going over what she would say to the man who had tormented the last weeks and months of her marriage. When it came down to it, instead of scathing accusations and condemnation, Georgie seized the opportunity to take control and save face.

"Once the funeral arrangements have been made, I will place a notice in *The Times* so please watch out for it. Only close family and friends will be invited back to Tenley, however. Should you choose to attend the church service you will be welcome." Georgie held her nerve and waited for him to protest or take offence. He did neither.

"Unfortunately I am leaving for America on the tenth of this month so unless the funeral is before, I will be unable to attend."

Simon sounded unaffected by anything Georgie had said which fuelled her disgust of him.

"I'm sure you appreciate these things take time to organise and as I wish to give my husband a fitting send off, I can be certain the funeral will take place after the tenth."

"Then there is no more to say on the matter. Please accept my condolences. Will that be all?"

"Yes, that will be all. Good luck in America. Perhaps you will find fortune there. Your luck seems to have run out here." Georgie hoped her words hit home.

"Goodbye, Georgie."

Yes, they'd hit home.

"Goodbye, Simon."

It took two attempts to replace the receiver in its cradle. Her hands were trembling so badly, as was her body that had stiffened the instant she heard his smooth soulless voice. Georgie knew she had been right about Simon all along and he would never have made Kenneth happy. But she would rather her beloved had flown across the Atlantic, even if it meant leaving her alone because at least then he could have come back, once he realised his mistake.

Climbing back into bed, Georgie pulled the covers over her head and blocked out the world which just kept on bloody turning while hers had stopped. From then on, she marked time, leaving Vanessa and Sandy to soldier on. A glimmer of her old self returned on the day of the funeral when she descended from her bedroom, resplendent in her mourning attire and although she had maligned them in the past, she yearned for the days when Jackie Kennedy donned her dark veil and shrouded her face from the eyes of ghouls, a black gossamer sheath separating her from the harshness of death. Before they left, Georgie paused in the hallway and closed her eyes, remembering the happy day when she stepped inside Tenley for the first time, holding hands with a nervous little girl and her handsome, equally nervous husband, the love of her life, dear darling Kenneth.

***

Georgie watched as the mourners left one by one, their cars making their way down the drive, fleeing misery and no doubt shrugging off the day's events as soon as they turned onto the lane. Knowing she had made Vanessa a promise, Georgie brushed her hair, wiping away smudged mascara with her finger before heading downstairs.

It was warm as she descended, Sandy had obviously turned up the heating so that their guests wouldn't shiver and there was a fire in the hall grate. This and the glow from the wall lamps presented a cosy image, and the sound of the television in the lounge gave the impression of normality. Georgie thought she would never feel normal again. Following the mumbled voices, she found Vanessa seated on the sofa, watching the news, a plate of food resting on her lap, presumably left over from the wake. The sight of her caused Georgie to brush away a sense of irritation, after all what did she expect? Taking a deep breath and reminding herself to devote some moments of her day to her daughter, Georgie gritted her teeth and forced a hint of concern into her voice.

"Hello, darling, how did it go?" Not that she cared but it was all that came to mind.

"Oh Georgie, you're up. Come and sit by the fire. I'll go and make a pot of tea, would you like some food? There are lots of leftovers but I could ask Sandy to make you something warm if you prefer."

Georgie's heart melted at the eagerness and relief in Vanessa, and Georgie felt bad for her earlier pique and leaving one so young to host the wake all alone.

"Perhaps some tea, and some toast. I really couldn't stomach much else."

"Excellent. It's probably best to eat something light but we need to build up your strength. Here, cover yourself up and I'll be back shortly. You look dreadfully pale so the fire should put some colour in your cheeks." Vanessa pulled the blanket from the back of the sofa and laid it over Georgie's knees.

"And then I can tell you what I've decided and the plans I've made for us. You're going to be so pleased when you hear. I think it's just what we both need."

"What plans?" Georgie was worried. What on earth had Vanessa done? Georgie was in no mood for hints and secrets.

Looking pleased with herself, Vanessa batted away Georgie's questions and set off towards the kitchen, promising to reveal all when she returned.

While she waited, Georgie gazed into the fire, fatigue consuming her body and brain, the latter having no intention of second guessing Vanessa so instead she waited, enjoying the silence.

When Sandy came in later to collect the tray and say goodnight to Georgie and Vanessa, she found them huddled on the sofa, deep in conversation, so much so that at first neither noticed she had entered the room. Lifting her head from what she was reading, Georgie smiled before asking Sandy to join them for a while, they had something to discuss with her.

It took only a few moments for Vanessa to inform Sandy of her plans and then ask if there were any questions. Georgie had remained silent throughout, allowing Vanessa to lead the conversation who against the odds was turning into an extremely organised and confident young woman, something that bade well for the future of Tenley.

During the conversation, Georgie observed Sandy who it had to be said took the news well yet looked rather crestfallen, which was to be expected. Nevertheless, Georgie was sure she would soon get used to living without them and it was for the best. When Sandy finally spoke, excusing herself for the evening, there was an audible wobble to her voice but she recovered well, still it prompted Georgie to offer some words of comfort and encouragement.

"We really can't thank you enough, Sandy, and I know you will miss us but please be assured we will miss you too. You're like family and it won't be easy to say goodbye."

"That's very kind of you, Georgie, and means a great deal, and the feeling is mutual. But if you don't mind it's been a long day and I'm very tired so perhaps we could talk again tomorrow and make firm arrangements."

"Of course. You have worked extremely hard today and thank you once again for your support at church. I wouldn't have got through it had you not been there with Vanessa and I. Now you get off to bed and leave everything else until morning. Sleep well, Sandy." Georgie smiled. It was something she had almost forgotten how to do and it was met with a curt nod before Sandy left the room, the tray of supper things remaining on the nest of tables.

They waited until she had disappeared from sight before turning back to the brochure on Georgie's lap and continued to flick through the pages. Vanessa chatted on about the cruise she had booked for them both and how wonderful it was going to be, travelling the globe together and leaving all the misery behind them. It was going to be perfect. The agent had arranged everything, their passage aboard the QE2 to New York, then they would fly to the Caribbean and for the rest of the year, he had rented villas and apartments in major cities and resorts around Europe.

They would depart at the end of the month when Vanessa would leave the estate manager in charge of the office and Sandy would be the guardian of Tenley, making sure the house and grounds were cared for. Georgie had insisted that while they were off holidaying, Sandy was given a bonus so that she too could have some fun. They both admitted to feeling bad that she would be left alone in the house but then again Vanessa insisted that Sandy should treat Tenley as her own while they were gone.

Conscience appeased and embracing the spark of excitement that had ignited inside, Georgie concentrated on Vanessa who was currently looking at the ships brochure and marvelling at the photo of the restaurant and the idea of dining with the captain. For some strange reason Georgie felt tears well in her eyes and flicked one away before it had chance to escape onto her cheek. It wasn't sadness she was feeling, it was love and gratitude for her daughter and the man she had met all those years earlier, a forlorn chap sitting on a park bench. She had gathered him up and saved him, and in return he had rescued her. Kenneth had given her a home and a family and this funny creature by her side, her daughter.

There had been enough tears shed, too many deaths in this house so a year away from Tenley was just what the doctor would have ordered had they asked him, but on this occasion they didn't need to pay an extortionate amount for the advice. Instead, Vanessa had come up trumps, and soon Georgie would be lapping up the luxury of a beautiful ship, surrounded by sun and sea, bustling cities and desert plains. Leaning over, Georgie wrapped her arm around Vanessa's shoulder and pulled her in for a hug, placing a firm kiss on her cheek.

"What was that for?" Vanessa turned and laughed at Georgie.

"It was for being simply perfect and wonderful and the best daughter anyone could wish for." Georgie smiled and winked, then grabbed the cruise brochure from Vanessa. As she flicked through the pages, a thought occurred. Perhaps the future might just be bearable, mother and daughter together, the two of them against the world.

Chapter 23

Sandy

While Georgie and Vanessa made plans to head up to London and buy whatever they needed for their trip, outside in the hall someone listened. Sandy leant against the wall, her eyes closed, holding in the tears caused by the rage which flooded every cell of her body. How dare they cast her aside, leaving her behind like a discarded toy while they went off together. Once again, Sandy berated herself for missing an opportunity, for not shoving Georgie off the ledge when she had the chance because then her prayers would have been answered. All the Tenleys would be gone, save Vanessa.

She knew God would understand her anger and forgive such wicked thoughts but that didn't make her feel better, nothing would. Tired of listening to them laughing, all thoughts of a dead father and husband seemingly set aside, Sandy pushed her body from the wall and made her way upstairs, silently vowing not to make the same mistake again. If she had to wait a year, then so be it. The twelve months that lay ahead would be painful, parted once again from her child, taken away by another woman. But on their return, Sandy would be ready and this time there would be no reprieve. Georgie was the only thing that lay in her path and somehow, she had to go. For now, all Sandy could do was paint a smile on her face and wave them off, then wait. She was good at that.

Part IV

Chapter 24

Vanessa and Sandy

After saying goodbye to the doctor who had kindly promised to have the prescription sent straight over once it had been dispensed, Vanessa closed the door and rested her head on the oak panels before sighing and making her way back upstairs. She was tired but thankful. The hours she'd devoted to caring for Georgie were paying off. The doctor was pleased with his patient's progress and after giving Georgie a thorough examination, confirmed that she was well enough to get out of bed.

She had been diagnosed with another bout of acute bronchitis and a serious dose of viral pneumonia but as long as she took baby steps, Georgie could return to the land of the living. It had been such a shame that their world tour that had culminated in Sydney, watching a spectacular display of New Year's Day fireworks, would end with Georgie falling ill once they arrived home. The doctor suggested she might have contracted the bug during the cruise from Australia, a long but luxurious trip and one Georgie enjoyed every minute of. Vanessa did too, there were seven restaurants on-board.

She was fine when they docked at Southampton but Georgie became unwell just days after they arrived and was convinced that Tenley was cursed and as a result, wanted to leave as soon as possible. Vanessa and the doctor had assured Georgie that it was nothing of the kind and she should avoid getting into a state. Her mood had dipped the minute they drove through the gates so being bedridden hadn't helped one bit.

Neither had Sandy who seemed to be in a queer mood ever since they stepped foot inside Tenley and Vanessa had no idea why, perhaps she felt usurped or neglected. After having the run of the place for a year it must have been strange to return to staff status even though they'd tried to make her feel valued. Georgie had bought Sandy some lovely gifts and Vanessa sent postcards throughout the year, telephoning once a month to make sure everything was okay. Vanessa was at a loss as to what more Sandy expected but if she continued with her rather stilted and almost belligerent attitude, they would be having words.

Vanessa felt she too had changed since the death of her father. His passing had in some ways allowed her to step up and take her rightful place at Tenley. How it would have infuriated Phyllis, to see the interloper take control of the estate and find herself sole heir, extremely rich and rather powerful. Vanessa loved it. To be fair, it was something she had cultivated over the years after observing Georgie who was the master of getting what she wanted. Without knowing it, Vanessa had been her willing pupil and now it was time to put everything she had learned into practice.

Apart from Georgie's wobble, the atmosphere at Tenley was a thousand times happier and stress free. Vanessa vowed to do whatever it took to maintain it. No more aged tyrants or strange male visitors upsetting the apple cart, sending Georgie into meltdown and ruining everyone's fun. This was why Sandy had better watch her step. Nothing would be allowed to affect their newfound equilibrium.

It was a shame about Georgie though because her pre-nuptial arrangement left her almost penniless, not that it mattered because Vanessa had sworn to look after her for the rest of her life, in the manner she was accustomed to. In fact they were going to have a ball, just the two of them, exactly how it should be. But first things first, she needed to get Georgie back on form. They had made so many plans on the journey home it would be sad not to fulfil them. There would be another royal wedding in the summer when Prince Andrew would marry Sarah. The idea of a commoner marrying up had tickled Georgie no end so they intended to join in the celebrations and remain in London to attend the opening night of *The Phantom of the Opera* and *Les Misérables* that had taken the West End by storm while they were away. Yes, spring was definitely in the air.

Pushing open the bedroom door, Vanessa stepped inside and went over to check on Georgie who looked pale, even under her tanned skin and her eyes were set in dark hollow sockets. Thinking that some fresh air would do Georgie good, maybe a trip down to Cornwall to the cottage they used to rent, Vanessa took her book from the bedside stand and lowered herself into the chair, feeling the arms dig into her sides, flattening her flesh. Ignoring the pounds she had piled on during their trip, not caring that she hadn't turned heads or garnered the attention of young men, she began to read, determined to keep vigil and focus on Georgie. Vanessa needed nobody else.

Downstairs in the kitchen, Sandy had abandoned her cooking. Leaving the unrolled lump of pastry on the table, she tucked a lock of her unwashed hair behind her ears, wiped floury hands on her dress then poured a glass of malt. It had become her favourite tipple over the past year and along with the selection of fine wines she had made good use of, Kenneth's stash of whisky had helped her through many a long and lonely night. What a strange time it had been, left alone in a huge house that, despite being almost deserted, still gathered dust, the stairs and corridors creaked during the night and woodland noises from beyond the windows seemed far louder than before.

***

During her isolation, Sandy had experienced such incredibly diverse emotions. Sometimes she was sad, bitter, frightened and at times jumpy as she wandered Tenley with all the lights blazing. Other times she had felt slightly manic, dancing in her nightdress in front of the telly or creeping down to the pool, dangling her legs in the cold water, going over the past, talking to ghosts.

Sandy had found great solace in alcohol and her church where on sober days she'd make twice-daily visits, praying long and hard in the draughty pews. During her intense communion, Sandy asked for very little, just the return of her daughter and on her lowest days, for another worshipper to offer the hand of friendship, a chat and a cup of tea would do. Accepting that her situation was of her own making, revolving life around Vanessa and Tenley, her fellow churchgoers had become wary of the stand-offish woman who lived in the big house. In desperation, Sandy made excuses for Mrs Coombs to come in and help her clean. They had rearranged linen cupboards, cleaned windows and polished brass together and Sandy had felt such a blessed relief to hear footsteps and tuneless singing, or eat lunch with another human being.

When left to her own devices and with too much time on her hands, Sandy mulled over the past and her current abandonment, sinking into periods of deep depression and barely controllable rages. Her life resembled scales; up and down, frequently unbalanced. What had surprised her most was that resentment had crept up and was making its presence felt on a regular basis, and worse, it diluted the love Sandy felt towards her child, being slowly replaced by scorn and disappointment. How could this have happened? Instead of loving Vanessa unconditionally, as Georgie seemed to do, Sandy couldn't hide the disappointment she felt whenever she thought about her or looked upon the photos that lined the lounge.

Vanessa was the image of her father the rapist and bore no resemblance to Sandy other than in her eyes, two dark currants which burned right inside you. Phyllis had been right about that. That wasn't all that irritated Sandy so. It was the raven ringlets that were childish and bobbed upon her head as she walked and talked, reminding Sandy of a dark-haired Shirley Temple, blown out of all proportion. Vanessa wasn't obese, far from it, but her saving grace was the daily walk to the office and maybe the flights of stairs at Tenley because otherwise, the comfort eating and love affair with food would be the death of her.

Vanessa's size and gait was a constant reminder of *him* and hard to wipe from her mind, but the bone structure was genetic and this inherent attribute pained Sandy so. But it wasn't just physical, it went deeper than that. While Vanessa was a pleasant enough young woman, her shallow outlook on life, lack of ambition and self-pride was most frustrating. Her enjoyment of trivial pursuits such as listening to pop music, reading trashy novels and watching television shows as she lounged in her bedroom drove Sandy to distraction. The one thing that eclipsed all of these was Vanessa's refusal to accept God into her life and over the years it had become a moot point and sometimes, Sandy saw it as an open challenge to her authority. Then she remembered she had none, not where her daughter was concerned.

In between her growing disdain and despair, frequent drunkenness and the saving grace of Mrs Coombs, Sandy occupied herself in a more constructive manner, adding to her nest egg and obsessively looking for something that she now realised had been thrown away long ago, Vanessa's knitted layette. The huge attic was an untapped treasure trove which Sandy methodically pillaged and then embarked on a spot of sightseeing, offloading her haul on unsuspecting, far flung antique dealers.

Still, no matter how many hours she spent looking through dusty boxes and chests, Sandy couldn't find the box she pictured in her head, the one scattered in flowers that contained the pale lemon layette. At the mother and baby home they'd allowed Sandy to write a few words to her daughter and promised that the carefully penned letter would one day go to her daughter. Sandy wondered if it could be in the box. But maybe it was just another lie and they'd simply left it in a dusty file with Sandy's details, clues and a paper trail to Vanessa's real mother. Sandy had trusted them all, the social worker, her mother and even for a while the rapist. She knew she had been a fool on all counts.

In her bitter moments, she imagined Daphne crinkling her nose as she carried Vanessa from the home, desperate to get back to Tenley where she would have removed the knitted outfit and replaced it an outfit bought from a fine store in London, chucking Sandy's offering straight in the bin. How she hated them, every single person who had a hand in stealing her baby, and Georgie was no better because she stole Vanessa's heart when she didn't deserve it. None of them did.

In her more positive moments, Sandy considered the possibility of coming clean and presenting the truth to Vanessa and Georgie in a calm and rational manner, explaining her motives and simple desire to have a relationship with her child. Sandy loved this scenario, it was the most agreeable solution and one in which the three women lived together in harmony and friendship as equals, if only in the relative sense. Sandy would always be the poor relation, the hired help, the shameful teenage mother who had tempted a rapist, a young girl whose own cold-hearted mother had treated her so cruelly. It was no wonder that by the end of a very long year, a ball of negative emotions was festering inside Sandy, ready to explode.

When Vanessa rang to confirm their arrival date, Sandy almost wept with joy, swiftly replaced by disdain as she realised her temporary reign of Tenley was over. To be fair, Georgie insisted that Sandy should remain in the sumptuous guest bedroom she had occupied in their absence, unhappy at the thought of their loyal housekeeper being banished to the top floor. After graciously accepting, for a moment Sandy felt peevish for seething at the thought of returning to her poky room. Then it passed.

Apart from this concession nothing else had changed and Sandy was now expected to resume her previous role and basically, know her place. It was ironic that after missing Vanessa for so long, she had hardly seen her since the homecoming. Bloody Georgie had fallen ill again and Sandy suspected her lifestyle was finally catching up and it was no more than she deserved. But while Georgie festered in her sick bed, Vanessa had taken it upon herself to play nursemaid and spent every available hour upstairs, by her beloved stepmother's side.

***

Sandy had had enough, of everything. Pouring another glass, she felt the honey-coloured liquid warm her blood and that familiar rage stir inside. She had money of her own. There was enough to buy a small place in the village and live independently. It would be easy to find another job and she didn't need much to survive on so something menial would do. Why should she hide in plain sight and in the meantime, cook and skivvy for her own daughter and a woman she thoroughly despised for so many reasons?

Vanessa didn't need Sandy and she certainly didn't need the nest egg that was resting in a high interest savings account, which was why it had been left to the church and religious charities. It was Sandy's way of thanking God for his abiding support. Not only that, the missionaries in Peru or even the cats' home would appreciate it more than Vanessa.

Sighing, Sandy resigned herself to the truth. She might as well throw in the towel, reveal all and take the consequences. Either way she would probably lose, stay or go, so if she was going to get the boot it would be with dignity. Draining the glass of whisky, Sandy poured another, her courage building as an alternative outcome formed in her mind. Yes, she should chance her luck and roll the dice, what had she to lose?

Hearing the doorbell ring, Sandy tutted and seeing that her bottle was almost empty, decided to fetch another from the cellar and on the way, if she could be bothered, would answer the door. Getting to her feet, she swayed slightly and took a moment to balance herself, kicking off her shoes to make walking easier before heading for the hallway and the sound of the bloody bell.

Flinging open the door, she found the delivery lad from the village shivering on the step. Sandy knew Tommy well and had always treated him kindly so was rather offended when he took a step backwards. Realising the fumes from the whisky and her slightly dishevelled state might have surprised him, Sandy attempted to save face, failing miserably as her words came out slurred.

"Yes, young man, can I help you?" Sandy leant against the doorframe, feeling groggy and impatient.

"I've brought this for Lady Tenley, could I leave it with you?" Tommy stretched out his arm, unwilling to go closer.

Sandy snatched the paper bag containing the medicine and answered sarcastically, leaving Tommy wideeyed as he backed off.

"Oh it will be my pleasure. Don't you know that's why I'm here? To serve the gracious lady Tenley and bow to her every whim... So you leave this with me, young man. I'll be sure her royal bloody highness gets it. Now you run along... go on, sod off." Sandy was about to slam the door when she heard an angry voice behind her.

"Sandy! That's enough." Stepping out from nowhere, Vanessa snatched the bag of medicine and apologised to Tommy who no doubt couldn't wait to get back to the shop and tell everyone about the drunken housekeeper.

Vanessa watched him cycle up the drive into the mist, calling after him to take care before closing the door. When she turned, Sandy was nowhere to be seen. About to go in search, a figure at the top of the stairs caught Vanessa's eye, it was Georgie, holding on to the banister as she pulled her gown around her frail body.

"Vanessa what's going on? Is Sandy alright? I heard raised voices."

"It's fine, Georgie, now go back to bed and I'll bring your medicine up shortly, please don't concern yourself. I'll deal with Sandy."

Georgie nodded wearily and Vanessa waited until she turned and headed back to her room, doing as she was told. Shaking with anger, she set off to find Sandy, determined to give her a ticking off, torn between administering Georgie's medication and sacking the grumpy housekeeper.

Hearing footsteps on the corridor, Sandy recognised them as Vanessa's and looking up at the clock, was able to focus on the time, causing her to smirk. The mistress of Tenley never missed mealtimes and was right on cue. She'd be disappointed because Sandy wasn't going to prepare dinner so she would have to make do with a sandwich, or three. When Vanessa entered the room it was clear that she was unhappy, both with Sandy's state and the absence of cooking aromas.

"Is dinner ready, Sandy? Georgie is awake and she needs something light, perhaps scrambled eggs." When Sandy didn't answer Vanessa's eyebrows furrowed, her voice stern.

"Sandy, answer me. Have you been drinking? You look rather odd. Your behaviour at the door was most disappointing and I will expect you to apologise to Tommy next time you see him. Do I make myself clear?" Spotting the almost-empty bottle of whisky on the table Vanessa realised the stupidity of her question and was angered further by the response from Sandy.

Picking up the bottle and waving it in the air, squinting as if to examine its contents, Sandy replied, not even caring that her words were slurred.

"Sorry, I forgot to make dinner… but you know where the cooker is, it's that big shiny thing over there and you're no stranger to the fridge so be my guest. Oops, I must remember my place, silly me." Taking another drink, Sandy regarded Vanessa closely and waited to be scolded.

"Sandy. Stop this immediately. I won't have you speaking to me in this way. What on earth has come over you? Now give me that bottle and sober yourself up. It's clear you're no use to anybody in this state. We will say no more on the matter but in the morning perhaps you and I should have a chat. Your attitude has been rather tiresome these past few weeks and I'd like to get to the bottom of what's bothering you because something clearly is."

Once again, Vanessa had surprised herself in her handling of the situation until Sandy laughed in her face, shaking her head as she stood, swaying slightly before placing her hands on the tabletop for support.

"I think that would be a fine idea, Vanessa, and I agree, it's time you and I had a little chat because you're quite right, there is something bothering me. In fact there has been a very important matter on my mind for a long time now and I'd like to get it off my chest... I know, let's do it now, right here in the bloody kitchen."

Sandy could no longer control the swell of rage that was washing over her entire body and while she knew now was not the time, in this state, something inside, wild and abandoned was urging her on.

"That's fine by me, Sandy, but I'd prefer to have a discussion when you are sober. Drink some coffee and once you are in a better frame of mind we can talk." Vanessa was astounded by Sandy's attitude and shook her head before turning to leave the room.

Sandy, however, wasn't finished. "Don't you dare turn your back on me, young lady. I demand you stay here and listen. You will damn well show me some respect for once in your life... Vanessa, Vanessa, come here at once." Sandy was incandescent, literally shaking with rage as her daughter ignored every word and walked away.

Pushing the chair backwards, the wood scraping on the clay floor tiles, making Sandy wince, she stood quickly and went to follow Vanessa, determined to make her listen but as she stepped forward, tripped on her discarded shoes causing her to tumble and land in a heap on the floor. Once down, it was hard to stand in her inebriated state so instead Sandy muttered expletives as she crawled on hands and knees to the cupboard and opened the door. Reaching inside, she moved the vases and from inside the tallest she pulled an unopened bottle of Napoleon brandy, laughing as she complimented her own guile and began to unfasten the foil.

Why should she chase after Vanessa? She would return soon enough because there was no way she'd get through the evening without food. Instead, Sandy resolved to wait patiently and in the meantime enjoy a perk of the job, one she would no doubt soon be out of.

Upstairs, Vanessa related the scene in the kitchen to Georgie who was feeling weak after even a short walk to and from the hallway. Both women were shocked at Sandy's outburst and curious as to what could be the cause. After settling Georgie and making sure she was warm and her medicine administered, Vanessa waited for a while until her patient began to doze, promising a light meal when she awoke.

It was clear to Vanessa that she would have to make their dinner but first, Sandy had to be dealt with. The situation had become untenable and despite her long service, it appeared that for whatever reason Sandy was unhappy with her role and life at Tenley. Unless she was prepared to explain her strange behaviour and apologise, dismissal was inevitable.

Vanessa felt quite sad at the thought because despite her odd ways and obvious faults, Sandy had played a huge role in her growing up, providing stability and comfort albeit at arm's length. Vanessa reminded herself to mention this and perhaps provide some kind of severance payment should the need arise, after all they wouldn't want Sandy to be destitute. As far as everyone knew she had no family to speak of and few friends apart from the church brigade so Vanessa decided that in the event of letting Sandy go, it might be kind and prudent to check she had somewhere to live. That's what Georgie would want no matter how rude and obnoxious Sandy had been.

When her tummy rumbled and Georgie was snoring, Vanessa slowly crept from the room, hoping that Sandy had taken herself off to bed and there would be no more confrontations. Once again, it looked like she was going to have to take control of the situation and restore order to Tenley but for the moment all that she cared about as she descended the stairs was looking after Georgie and finding something decent in the fridge.

Chapter 25

Vanessa

Sandy was nowhere to be seen as Vanessa entered the kitchen, all that remained were her shoes and the empty bottle of whisky and glass she'd left on the table. Picking up a cork, she was just about to call Sandy's name when she heard a door bang, the noise coming from further down the hall. Vanessa knew exactly what it was and it made her blood run cold.

The long corridor that led to the rear of the house was in darkness but a shaft of white light stretched across the floor in the distance, illuminating Vanessa's path as her heart thumped. When she reached the door of the orangery, she paused, placing her trembling hand on the handle, steeling herself to go inside. More than seventeen years had passed since Vanessa had entered the room. The memories of that day had been banished, surfacing occasionally in times of deep anxiety when her brain was overloaded and she was forced to remember. Over the years she had learned to take control and focus on the present but now and then the past had a way of catching up with her.

Vanessa considered doing just that, turning around and leaving Sandy to whatever was troubling her but then again, perhaps it was time to face her demons. Taking a deep breath, Vanessa pushed down on the handle and opened the door. A flashback of a little girl in her nightdress jumping for the handle was banished before she stepped into the bright light, her eyes taking time to adjust then search for Sandy.

The scummy water was rippling slightly, it hadn't been used for such a long time and the room smelled musty, of mildew and chlorine. Flies and insects bobbed on the surface along with the odd bird feather. Grimacing at the sight and stench, Vanessa wished it had been drained a long time ago. During their travels, she had suggested to Georgie that on their return they convert the orangery into a sunroom, somewhere they could read and listen to music, making the most of winter sun and summer days. Georgie couldn't risk getting a chill and Vanessa hated the place so they had agreed to get the builders in and begin work in the spring. The sooner the pool was filled in the better. The sight of Sandy, standing at the edge of the deep end, staring mournfully into the water only served to harden her resolve.

Walking slowly towards the silent woman, Vanessa waited for Sandy to acknowledge her arrival and when she finally looked up, there were tears streaming down her face. When both women were just feet apart, the quiet calm of the room was made more eerie by the windows as the deep black of night peered in.

Sandy spoke first. "It's cold, the water. I come here sometimes to think and remember, going over things in my head. It helps, you know, talking it through, asking for forgiveness." Sandy's voice had lost its bitter edge and she sounded sad but at least talking sensibly.

"You really shouldn't come here alone, Sandy. You can't swim so what would you do if you fell in, and why do ask for forgiveness, what have you done?" Vanessa was rather cross to find that Sandy had been coming here, there were plenty of places in the huge house to find solace for heaven's sake, but that was by-the-by. It was the mention of forgiveness that made her curious.

"Oh Vanessa, there's so much I need to explain, why I came here. I have to make you understand but I don't know where to begin. It's been so hard for me but now, after all this time waiting I'm scared of how you will react when you hear the truth."

"What do you mean, why you came here, what truth?" Vanessa couldn't believe what she was hearing and presumed it was the drink talking but then again, there was something in the way

Sandy spoke. She wasn't rambling or angry, just thoughtful and yes, scared. Vanessa could see it in her eyes.

"Do you ever think some things are meant to be? I know you have no time for God but he has been my saviour, guiding my path, showing me the way and in his wisdom he brought me here, all those years ago and ever since he has helped me in so many ways. He is my saviour and as a reward for my faith and prayers he gave me everything I asked for. One by one, all my problems were solved, it was like a miracle." Sandy grasped the gold cross that lay on her blouse, twiddling it nervously.

The hairs on Vanessa's neck stood on end and she had goosebumps. Sandy was giving her the creeps and the fear she'd spotted was now replaced by a glazed, rather manic, look.

"Let's go upstairs, this is no place to talk and it's cold in here. Come along, I'll make you some coffee and we can get you warm. How does that sound?" Vanessa was freaking out and desperate to get away from the pool and, if she was honest, Sandy.

"No, I have kept too many secrets for too long. It's time you heard everything, this is about you as much as me and you need to listen. Let me get it all in the open and then we can move on."

Vanessa remained silent but was aware of a thudding, the sound of her heart reaching her ears, fear prickling her skin as she stepped backwards, not sure if she wanted to stay and listen or run. As Sandy turned away, briefly looking down at the water before lifting her free hand, a bottle of brandy dangling from the other, she pointed towards the windows.

"This is where it all began, in this room and over there. It was God's will that sent me here so I know he will forgive me. It wasn't my fault, you have to remember that but in the end I know it was for a reason, she had to die. It was all part of his plan."

Vanessa couldn't make her lips move but her brain was ticking furiously working it out, the terrible truth starting to dawn. Finally able to force out some words, she managed a sentence, she had to be sure she was right.

"Do you mean Daphne? Is that who you are talking about? Were you here the night she died?" Visibly shaking, Vanessa clasped her hands together, desperately trying to stay calm so when Sandy nodded, Vanessa's gasp rang around the pool.

"I was watching, through the window and as she climbed out Daphne saw me. My face pushed against the glass must have frightened her so she ran, along there and then tripped. Her head hit the frame. Oh God, it was awful, and then she fell to the ground and the blood, it was everywhere. I didn't know what to do, I was in shock, you have to believe me I was terrified." Sandy sobbed, her hands covered her mouth as hysteria built and all the time, Vanessa just stared while she processed the information, fear rising with every heartbeat.

"So it was your fault she fell, you caused Daphne to slip and then you stayed to watch her die..."

"Yes, yes it was me. But we need to talk about what happened next, and why God sent me here. There are too many secrets, Vanessa..." Sandy's voice had reached a high pitch as she implored her daughter to listen yet she could see from the look on her face she was angry, pale and trembling, riddled with shock and no doubt hate.

"No! Stop. I don't want to hear another word. Do you hear me, Sandy? Be quiet, be quiet, be quiet."

Vanessa was screaming and her balled fists reminded Sandy of her childhood tantrums, her ashen face turning red, such was her anger and determination get her own way. But Sandy had come too far, it was now or never.

"Vanessa, please, trust me, trust in God, he has a plan and it is time everyone knew... I have kept our secret for so long and it is time we told the world the truth." Sandy held out her arms, beseeching her child.

In that moment, when she heard the word 'truth', Vanessa screamed, her mouth open wide, teeth bared in anger, eyes wide, crazed and glaring as she ran forward with arms and fingers spread wide. When the palms of Vanessa's hands made contact with Sandy's chest, the thud knocked the wind from her lungs as she hurtled backwards, arms flaying and legs kicking as panic etched her shocked face. The brandy bottle dropped and landed in the water with Sandy who hit the surface with force, going straight under and disappearing in a slimy whirlpool of bubbles before fighting her way to the top, gasping for air as she flapped and thrashed, begging for Vanessa to help before going back under.

Vanessa watched transfixed from the edge of the pool. Sandy came up for the second time, coughing and spluttering as water filled her throat and nose, making its way to lungs which pumped and sucked, then began to fill. The brief flickering of a fluorescent light about her head snapped Vanessa from her trance and alerted her to the need for action. Turning, she spotted the large pole which hung from the wall, the one Ernest used to scrape leaves from the surface of the water in summer. She had watched him many times through the window, from the safe zone of the patio, skimming and scooping, so she ran and unhooked it then raced back to the pool edge as Sandy came up for the third time, weaker, losing the fight for life.

Stretching forward, Vanessa saw the look of relief in Sandy's eyes who, with her last ounce of strength, tried to move closer, her fingertips inches away from the wire. Vanessa waited, just a little closer was all she needed and then suddenly Sandy was within reach so she lowered the net quickly, like when she caught fish or tadpoles in the stream, this time covering the head of the panic stricken women before her, pushing downwards, twisting the net tighter, forcing her back under, holding her in place. It was hard, remaining on the side of the pool and keeping hold of the pole and as she watched Sandy writhe. Vanessa imagined this was just how it felt to be a fisherman hauling in giant tuna, or battling a shark to its death on the open sea. It didn't take long for the tension to ease and Sandy's body to become still.

When she knew it was all over, Vanessa wiggled the pole and untangled the net from around Sandy's head. Hauling it in back to the poolside, Vanessa banged it dry before replacing it on the hook and as she did spotted some stray hair caught in the mesh so pulled it free and flicked it into the pool. She watched for a moment as the hair bobbed on the ripples, along with the brandy bottle and Sandy's body. Feeling her tummy rumble, Vanessa made her way around the pool and exited, closing the door firmly behind her.

In the kitchen, Vanessa hummed as she skirted around the discarded shoes. Leaving the unused pastry, glass and whisky bottle where they were, Vanessa set about making dinner for her and Georgie, searching the cupboards for something delicious to salve her appetite. She was famished.

Smiling as she cracked eggs into a bowl and fried some bacon, Vanessa felt so pleased with herself for taking control and silencing Sandy who had become far too bothersome and really didn't deserve severance pay or kindness, not after her dreadful behaviour and what she'd done. It would all look like a terrible accident. A drunkard had toppled into the pool and drowned in a place that was cursed, a ridiculous notion but one which suited Vanessa, just like the idea of demons stalking Tenley.

Chapter 26

Georgie and Vanessa

Georgie opened her eyes and waited for the fog in her head to clear. Her lips were dry and her tongue felt enormous and was stuck to the roof of her mouth, a sure sign she'd been out for a while. She had to hand it to Dr Humphrey. The old quack didn't scrimp on the dosage when he was dishing out sedatives but then again that was what his Harley Street patients expected. A cure for all manner of ills and psychosis, rid them of whatever seemed troublesome or unsightly, a big nose, floppy jowls, the odd foetus here and there. He wasn't so good at scraping away guilt or heartache; instead he had tablets for that, little pills of paradise.

A voice and clinking cutlery, breaking through the safety of her cocoon, made Georgie start before turning her head and following the sound. Her eyes rested on Vanessa.

The dedicated daughter smiled. "Awake at last. I saw you were stirring. Here, would you like some water?" Vanessa held out the glass, holding on until Georgie had it in her grasp, her hand betraying a slight tremor as she sipped slowly.

After loosening her tongue and wetting her lips, Georgie settled back on the pillows, exhausted by such a slight movement. Never had she felt so weak and depleted, even after Kenneth. Maybe she should cut down on the medication otherwise she would spend the rest of her life wandering in a haze but it was so nice, her fluffy synthetic cloud.

Focusing on Vanessa who had been such a darling and rather neglected of late, Georgie noticed that she was deathly pale, more so than usual, perhaps a result of too many hours indoors. Her unhealthy pallor was extenuated by a film of perspiration on her brow, causing her to look slightly feverish and somewhat agitated.

It was such a drag to have to talk and even though Georgie could hear her own voice, it sounded like that of a stranger, gravelly and weary, and so bloody old. This thought depressed her, educing a large sigh before she spoke.

"Vanessa darling, are you feeling unwell? You seem terribly pale, is everything alright?"

"I'm fine, Georgie. Don't exert yourself. Now, would you like something to eat? I've made you some soup." Vanessa smoothed the covers on the bed, allowing another faint smile.

"That would be lovely, darling, but not too much." Pushing herself upwards, Georgie watched as Vanessa brought the over-bed table and placed it in front of her.

Taking her seat by the bedside, Vanessa watched as Georgie sipped her soup. At the same time, Georgie observed Vanessa whose demeanour always gave her away. She was being shifty and coy. Something was up so Georgie played the game of old, circumventing the issue to give Vanessa time to show her hand.

"Has Sandy calmed down now? What on earth was the matter with her earlier? I've never seen her that way, not in all these years. Really, her behaviour is most out of character. I shan't have her speaking to people like that so she will have to apologise, when she's sober. Have you dealt with her for now?"

It was then that Vanessa let out a slight chuckle which she corrected quickly, but she was definitely amused by something, excitable even. Her voice confirmed any suspicions Georgie had.

"Oh yes, Georgie, I've dealt with her, and Sandy won't ever speak to anyone like that again, not ever." Vanessa was becoming bolder and looked Georgie straight in the eye.

"What do you mean you've dealt with her, have you dismissed her?" Georgie was beginning to worry because even though Sandy had been drunk and out of order, after years of loyal service, she deserved another chance. Not only that, they needed her to run the house.

Vanessa didn't answer straight away and instead she went over to the window and drew the curtains, shutting out the early evening, closing them inside. In that precise moment, Georgie knew Vanessa was hiding something, working out an excuse, just like when she was a child. What had she done this time?

When she turned, Vanessa's smile sent a slight chill through Georgie's weakened bones. The girl looked rather odd, there was a strange look in her eye, like she had a secret to tell and one she was bursting to share and get Georgie on side. Like the time she put bleach in the fish pond after she tumbled in and got covered in green slime. Poor fish, even though Georgie had mentioned they were smelly and the water attracted midges, there had been no need to kill them. Yes, that was how she had looked that day, as though she wanted praise for her actions.

Of course, Georgie had kept the secret and was rather glad when the pond was filled with soil and planted with lovely flowers, but still, it was rather cruel and she cautioned Vanessa against causing pain to any living thing, making her promise never to do it again. Something about the way Vanessa stood tall and walked slowly over to the bed, confident and yes, amused, reminded Georgie of that day, and a prickle of unease accompanied the chilling of bones.

Vanessa picked up her chair and moved it closer to the bed so that when she sat, her body was right by Georgie's side, much too near, oppressive even. "Now I don't want you upsetting yourself but I have something to tell you and you must listen very carefully to what I have to say."

"Oh dear, it's about Sandy isn't it. What's happened? Has she been rude again?" Georgie placed the spoon in her bowl and looked perplexed.

"Yes, it's about Sandy."

It was there again, that look. Georgie rested back against her pillows, for some reason wishing to create distance between her and Vanessa. Her manner was very unnerving.

Vanessa broke eye contact as she pushed the table nearer to Georgie, indicating that she should eat before Vanessa answered the question.

"There's no need for you to worry about anything. I have made sure Sandy won't cause any more trouble or go sharing secrets. We will manage quite well without her and from now on it will be just the two of us, you and I against the world." Vanessa took hold of Georgie's hand, stroking the back of it with her free clammy palm.

"What do you mean? What have you done?" Georgie tried to pull her hand away but it was held in a firm grip while the stroking was making her skin crawl.

"Now please don't panic or distress yourself but Sandy is dead. She drowned in the swimming pool."

"Dead? Sandy's dead?"

"Yes. I found her in the orangery, staggering about with a bottle of brandy in her hand, talking rubbish and going on about God and miracles. It was like she'd lost her mind."

Georgie could not speak at first. Her lips felt numb and a cool liquid was swirling around in her stomach while a maelstrom of fear and disbelief confused and fogged her brain. During the enforced silence, Vanessa chose to continue with her confessional.

"She was there, you see, the day Daphne died. Sandy told me it was her fault that Daphne tripped and banged her head. That odious woman was peering through the window of the swimming pool like a creepy snooper and startled Daphne, Sandy admitted it to me."

Somehow managing to form words through the haze of confusion, Georgie spoke in a hushed, incredulous tone.

"Sandy was responsible for Daphne's death…? Oh dear God, all this time she's lived under our roof and kept such a dreadful secret. I can't take it in, or believe she would do such a wicked thing. You should have called the police and had her locked up."

"No! I can't call the police not yet. I'll ring them in the morning and tell them I found her there. It will look like an accident but we have to get our stories straight otherwise they might suspect foul play. Do you understand?"

"Yes… I think so. But what do you want me to say? I'm confused, Vanessa. What's going on, why can't we just tell the truth?" Georgie's heart was racing and that uneasy feeling was spreading through every part of her body and she so wished Vanessa would let go of her hand.

"All you have to do is say that Sandy brought our food upstairs, she was very drunk and we were cross so dismissed her for the evening and that's the last we saw of her. I will discover her body in the morning and make the necessary phone calls."

"But why do we have to lie?"

"Because if I tell them what she said about Daphne, I have a motive for killing her and it's not worth the risk. This way is best, you have to trust me."

"Yes, I see that now, I understand." Georgie felt relieved when finally, on hearing what she wanted, Vanessa let go of her hand and released her from a trap.

"But that doesn't explain why she was there in the first place. What was she doing? Did she try to hurt you, Vanessa? And how did she fall in? Did you try to save her? It must have been terrifying."

"Georgie! You need to keep up… Sandy didn't fall in, I pushed her. It was my fault she drowned. She knew too much and had been telling lies. All this time she had been keeping a secret so she had to be punished and silenced." Vanessa's spoke quickly and not in a gentle way like earlier. "Now do you understand?"

The sharpness of Vanessa's voice betrayed anger and impatience, causing Georgie to start and shrink back slightly. Vanessa's face was awash with irritation and it was there again, that hint of amusement, an eagerness to share. Despite her growing sense of unease and with a certain amount of dread, Georgie asked her to continue.

"I'm sorry, Vanessa, I am listening, I truly am, so why don't you explain."

Vanessa smiled, glad to have Georgie's full attention and this time, in a soothing tone, eerie even, she answered as if talking to a fool, or an innocent child who believed in the tooth fairy and Father Christmas, and it was time for them to grow up and leave such nonsense behind. Cruel to be kind.

"I told you, she saw what happened, she was there. She knows I killed Daphne."

As the words fell on Georgie's ears, it was as though they were being sucked through a vortex, a swirling spinning cyclone of disbelief and horror, the ferocity of which made her swoon, only just able to cling on to consciousness. Tears swam before her eyes and as Georgie's pill-soaked brain grappled with whatever erudite thoughts remained, the only thing it came up with was that Vanessa was disturbed, perhaps by the sight of another floating body or the loss of her father and some psychotic episode had taken hold, haggling her brain.

"What do you mean you killed Daphne? Please, Vanessa, stop this nonsense at once. I don't believe you would do such a wicked thing, you were just a little girl at the time."

"It's not nonsense, it's true and I'm not wicked, I'm not. You just don't understand. It wasn't my fault, it was all their doing... Daddy and Granny and that nosey parker Sandy. They made me do it and Daphne deserved it; she was going to have a baby and I didn't want one, then she slapped my legs so I made her a picture to say sorry..." Vanessa was in a rage, her face puce, forehead dripping with sweat while her eyes burned, full of anger. And the voice, it was that of a petulant child, speaking from the lips of a grown woman.

Tears spilled onto Georgie's cheeks that were frozen by horror while her ears rang with the voice of triumph, unable to block out the sound of Vanessa's eager confession. All Georgie could do was listen, the truth of the past bearing down, crushing her chest and paralysing her body with fear.

Chapter 27

Vanessa

It was cold sitting by Daphne who was motionless, lying on her side on the swimming pool floor. Vanessa had been mesmerised for a time by the rivulets of blood that leaked from the cut in her mother's head. It ran along the tiles and over the edge before trickling down the side and into the water which turned a misty pink, clouds of blood spreading across the surface. It was a bit creepy in the poolroom. Vanessa's voice echoed when she spoke and outside in the grey gloomy morning light, a mini gale was blowing. The summer storm had blown in overnight, breaking through the humidity of a sweltering July. As the rain lashed down, it sounded like fingers tapping on the windows of the orangery and it was beginning to scare Vanessa.

"Please, Mummy, wake up, wake up now so I can show you my drawing… stop being a big baby and wake up." Vanessa implored Daphne; after all it was just a bit of blood, like when she cut her knee on the terrace. That's what everyone told her when she had cried, so Mummy was no different.

Vanessa prodded her mother, a firm poke, temper and impatience at the fore. From deep within her unconscious state, Daphne responded just slightly, barely opening her eyes before groaning in pain then slipping back into blackness.

"Mummy. Wake up, wake up now!" Vanessa shouted and pushed Daphne hard which caused her to roll onto her back, her right arm slipping from her hip and hanging limply over the side of the pool, fingertips skimming the water.

Exasperated, Vanessa sat back onto her bottom, her bent legs were stiff and her knees hurt from the hard tiles. Tilting her head to the side, she observed her stupid mummy who was sleeping like a big baby. Perhaps Mummy needed a plaster for her cut, but they didn't give Vanessa one when she hurt her knee. Instead they cleaned it with stingy antiseptic and said the air would make it better.

Stretching out her legs, Vanessa placed her feet against Daphne's left arm and kicked out in temper. "Mummy, Mummy, Mummy." Nothing.

Vanessa kicked harder, really angry. She was cold and hungry too. On the last kick, she saw Daphne's shoulder tip downwards, tilting into the water below. Vanessa giggled, thinking how funny it would be if Mummy went in. That'd teach her. Resting her wet feet against Daphne's midriff, Vanessa pushed hard against her mother's cold damp skin and instantly the weight of the overhanging body caused enough momentum for her to tip and as she entered the water, making a small splash, a delicate plop.

Nudging across the tiles on her bottom, Vanessa watched from the side of the pool as Daphne's submerged body was enveloped in pink swirls, her arms flapping gently like a swan, hair swishing gracefully outwards as bubbles popped to the surface. Sitting cross-legged Vanessa was transfixed by Daphne who, while still sleeping, began rising to the surface. When her body emerged at the edge of the pool just close enough for Vanessa to touch her, she slid her feet over the side and rested them on Daphne's shoulders, pushing downwards, sending the body back below the surface. This time it moved further away and bobbed up out of reach so Vanessa watched in silence as Daphne floated face down across the pool on a pale pink tide.

A flash of lightning streaked across the grey sky, making Vanessa jump and become fearful of what she knew would come next, thunder. She hated it more than the lightning and as she heard the slow rumble and the tapping fingers on the window, she scrambled to her feet, covering her ears as she made for the door. Standing on her tiptoes, she tried to grab the handle and pull open the door but it was too heavy so she thumped and kicked instead, crying out in terror. While lightning crashed behind her and thunder rumbled overhead, Daphne's body glided serenely across the pool, bathed in pink, illuminated by bright flashes of silver.

The rest was history and had been reported in the press, local and national, and everyone grieved for the tragic family who had lost a wife, mother and unborn baby. The star of the story was the poor little girl who had found her mother drowned in the pool and then, to add to the horror, had become trapped.

Traumatised by her ordeal she was absented from the funeral and ever since treated with kid gloves, indulged and forgiven many transgressions, not least by Georgie. Vanessa had thrived on the drama, took advantage of her father's grief and capitalised on her grandmother's spite, suffering a stream of incompetent nannies and just about tolerating Sandy. The only person she truly loved and admired was Georgie and for her she would do anything, absolutely anything.

Chapter 28

Georgie and Vanessa

Vanessa was illuminated, quite clearly energised by the telling of her tale and finally unburdening herself of such a thrilling and well-kept secret. Georgie was, however, horrified and as she swallowed down bile and begged her hammering heart to be calm and not burst through her chest, waited for Vanessa to continue as right at that moment, words failed her.

"You look shocked, Georgie, but you have to understand that Sandy was there, she told me she was looking through the window and saw everything. It was only a matter of time before she started blabbing to anyone who would listen… The woman was a drunken liability who I fear was about to expose me. She was unhinged. I had to do it, you do understand, don't you?"

Unhinged, the word sounded hollow but came with warning lights and flags that were flashing and waving in Georgie's face because the true mad person was sitting by her side, smiling like a deranged angel, convinced of her own saintly mission. Shock was beginning to perform its own sobering miracle and perhaps the desire for survival aided her brain which began assembling its thoughts, grappling amongst a mound of information.

When she needed it the most, Georgie remembered she was an actress, always had been, always would be and now was the time to put on her very best performance and earn herself an academy award.

"Yes, of course I do, Vanessa. You were so little I'm sure you didn't understand the consequences of your actions and nobody would blame you, I certainly don't. But what about Sandy? We have to ring the police or the doctor tonight. It's not right that we leave her down there. Perhaps once you've explained she was drunk they'd understand that it was an accident, I'm sure they would."

"No! Pay attention, Georgie, have you not been listening? None of it was an accident, not Daphne or Sandy… Don't you see I did it on purpose, it's quite easy. Actually I'm rather good at it. I can kill anything and anybody just like that." A click of the fingers, a slow smile, then she continued.

"I've always had to protect myself, you see, and us. I'd do anything to keep you close to me, just anything. So I kept my ears and eyes open and believe me, in this house it was necessary, you can't trust anybody."

Whatever bravado Georgie had felt moments earlier was fast escaping her and like a starlet caught in the footlights waiting for a prompt from the wings, she strained her ears and waited. When it came, her voice was barely audible, gripped by stage fright.

"What do you mean, you did it on purpose, and why did we need protection? Dear God, Vanessa, what have you done?" Georgie swallowed down her terror and placed a trembling hand to her throat. Her lips could barely move, fear was seeping into her bones but she forced out a question, spoken in a whispered voice, full of dread. And as she waited, Georgie knew the next words would haunt her forever.

Vanessa inhaled deeply, then let out a deep sigh and rolled her eyes as though she were addressing a fool. She was enjoying the drama of the moment. Tilting her head to one side, Vanessa observed Georgie who had no idea how instrumental she had been in all of this and how hard she had worked to secure a wonderful future for them both. It was time she came clean. How proud Georgie would be of her clever, willing devotee who had watched and learned from the very moment they met.

"Shush now, Georgie. Don't distress yourself because I have it all under control. I will leave Sandy where she is and tomorrow, when Mrs Coombs comes in to clean she will find the empty bottle of whisky in the kitchen and another one floating in the pool with Sandy. I will explain that after dinner, which we ate in here, we both went to bed and at some point afterwards, she must have drunk herself into a stupor and toppled into the pool. We will be bereft at the loss of a loyal member of staff although it might be prudent to mention that her drinking was becoming a worry of late. The delivery boy will back us up. After all, he saw what a state she was in earlier. I promise, it will be fine, trust me."

"Vanessa, Sandy was our friend. She looked after you all these years. How can you hope to get away with it and lie to the police... What if you're found out? You'll go to prison, we both will."

"Georgie please, shush, shush... I told you I'm good at this, I always get away with things, like when I strangled Horace, and threw Miss Mittens out of the window... I hated that bird and the scratchy cat. See, I still have the scar." Vanessa pointed to an almost invisible mark on her cheek and pulled a glum face.

"All I wanted to do was feed Horace but Granny wouldn't let me so one day I sneaked in and he pecked me. That's when I decided to punish him and Granny because the only person she was kind to was that stupid bird. You didn't like him either. I saw you bash his cage that day, remember, when you told Granny you'd send her to a home if she didn't behave. I was listening at the door. You were incredible and I knew then I wanted to be just like you."

"Vanessa, what's got into you? I can't believe what I'm hearing. I didn't want you to emulate me. And I would never kill an animal, not even a bird, and Miss Mittens didn't mean to scratch you so you shouldn't have killed her."

"It wasn't because of the scratch although it did hurt at the time. No, it was because of the sandwich."

"The sandwich?" Georgie thought she was losing grip on reality, Vanessa appeared to have already let go.

"Yes. Sandy made me salmon sandwiches for lunch and I was going to have them in my room but when I came back from the loo, Miss Mittens had eaten one of them and was licking the other. I simply lost my temper and grabbed her. I'm sure you can imagine the rest." Vanessa studied her nails and then glanced up at Georgie who had covered her mouth with her hands.

"I can't believe this is happening. I always thought you loved your cat and were such a good girl. How could I have not known you were capable of such things?" It was a simple statement but one that Georgie would regret as Vanessa seemed intent on confessing all, or was she showing off?

"Ha, you think that's bad. None of you guessed about Granny, did you?"

"What do you mean, about Granny?" Cold sweat was clinging to Georgie's entire body as she listened in horror, wide awake and living each second of a nightmare.

Vanessa leant forward and lowered her voice slightly, speaking as though to a fellow conspirator as she bragged about her evil past.

"You all thought she'd died in her sleep but I suffocated her with a pillow, trapping in all those horrid things she said about us that night. When she pointed at me from her bed, I thought she was going to tell you and Daddy about Horace or that I tormented her. That was great fun, by the way. I loved creeping into her room and being nasty to her, just like she was nasty to me. It served her right and in the end, I enjoyed getting rid of her. I didn't plan to do it, or what I did to Daddy it just happened."

Vanessa wasn't looking at Georgie anymore, instead she stared into the middle distance, her eyes fixed on the past where she became lost, her face quite serene.

Georgie was aghast, pinned to her pillow and riddled with panic but she had to ask, even though she dreaded the answer. "Vanessa, look at me. What did you do to Kenneth?"

Vanessa tutted and folded her arms, reverting more and more to a naughty, petulant child with every confession.

"Now, Georgie, you must remain calm and be brave because what I'm going to tell you next will be dreadfully hurtful and shocking but you need to know. I really wasn't going to tell you any of this, ever, but now, with this Sandy business it's probably best you hear the whole truth."

Georgie's mouth had gone dry but she managed to speak. "What truth? Tell me."

"Okay, as long as you're sure." Vanessa paused and when she saw Georgie nod slightly, carried on, leaning forward, her eyes wide, an incredulous look on her face.

"It seems that Granny was right about Daddy because he was a great big poofter after all and if that wasn't disgusting enough, he was betraying you, and me. He was planning to elope with that Simon chap, the one who called while you were in London. I came home early and heard Daddy and Sandy arguing in his study. I was so annoyed with him when I found out the truth and what he was going to do. We were both for the chop. How dare he send me away and divorce you? How could he do that to us? There was no way I could let him sell up and leave us behind. Tenley is my home and my inheritance. I deserve it, it's my right. And as for Sandy, she took money off Daddy to keep quiet, the sneak. But I let that go because she was more useful alive than dead, until now of course. Anyhow there was nothing for it, I had to protect us. He had to go."

The gasp and strange choking sound broke Vanessa's reverie, and on seeing Georgie's distress and tear-soaked face she reverted back to nursemaid and hurriedly held the glass to her lips.

Managing a sip, Georgie sunk back into the bed that was vibrating, no, that was her own body, trembling from head to toe with shock. Her voice, when she found it, betrayed every single terrible emotion that was consuming her body.

"You... you killed Kenneth? Dear God, Vanessa, how could you?"

Vanessa placed the glass back on the stand and grabbed Georgie's hand. "Oh I'm sorry, Georgie, that came out all wrong and I should've broken it to you gently but now you know the truth about Daddy so you must understand why he deserved to die. I was utterly disgusted but held my tongue, so he wouldn't cotton on while I had time to decide what to do. I just wanted revenge, so when Sandy asked him to clean the gutter I saw my chance."

"But you were in your room. I heard the music playing."

"I was, but I crept downstairs after I saw Daddy carrying the ladder. Sandy was in the kitchen preparing lunch so I went out the front way and there he was, asking for it."

Unable to take it all in, unwilling to believe that Vanessa had killed her father, Georgie tried to make sense of it all, desperate for it to be a wicked lie. "H... he fell off the ladder, Vanessa. It was an accident, a terrible accident."

There was a strange ringing sound in her ears and everything was going fuzzy. Georgie couldn't catch her breath and then realised it would be the best thing, to die, right there on the bed and end this nightmare.

"Yes, yes, he fell off the ladder but that's because I pushed it from under him. It was very quick though, not like Granny who was stronger than you'd imagine but she stopped struggling in the end." Vanessa waited for her words to sink in and watched Georgie closely, waiting for her congratulations.

Georgie inhaled deeply, forcing herself to look into Vanessa's eyes. That's when she saw it, what had always been there, the thing she had turned a blind eye to, possibly encouraged, nurtured even. Through eyes swimming with tears, Georgie managed to focus on the smiling face of a demon.

The bedroom was silent. Georgie had never been inside a courtroom but imagined that this was how it sounded in those seconds before the verdict was delivered and everyone held their breath, waiting for the words guilty or not guilty. For some insane reason, although she had committed no crime, not lately anyway, Georgie felt as though *she* was on trial and the jury was in.

"Are you not going to say anything, Georgie?" Vanessa was seated in the Queen Anne chair, not bolt upright and animated as before, she was now reclining, arm's spread in a relaxed manner, tapping her fingers, observing, inquisitive.

Georgie did not attempt to hide her tears, why should she? That would be unnatural. Anyone, apart from the psychopath seated before her, would be distressed by such a revelation so Georgie allowed the tears to flow. In the meantime, as she hid between sobs and blowing her nose, she was biding her time, getting her act together because if there was ever a moment she needed to perform, this was it.

"Seriously, Vanessa, what do you want me to say? You've just confessed to murdering four people, three of them members of your own family, not to mention countless defenceless animals whose only crime was to give you a nip and a scratch. How would you react if someone told you the same thing? Go on, answer that." Georgie could hear the fatigue in her own voice and it was becoming a strain to get words out, her chest was tight and she feared a panic attack was looming. But she had to hold it together. It was imperative to find out what Vanessa planned next and prayed it wasn't murder number five, the silencing of her confidante.

"That's an excellent question, Georgie dear, and one I already know the answer to. I'd be proud as punch. Yes, I admit I'd be slightly taken aback but glad at the same time. I would realise how much this person cared for me and wanted to protect me from being cast aside or maligned in any way. What greater demonstration of love and devotion could anyone ask for?" Vanessa smiled.

The angel of death looked smug in her response. Georgie felt her heart rate slow and the panic recede. Now she knew how to play it and what Vanessa wanted; praise and gratitude, a show of loyalty equal to that which she had given. As much as it pained her, Georgie played along.

"Darling, whilst I am grateful for your love and devotion, I would have preferred something a little less severe. Surely we could have shuffled Granny off to an asylum and as for Daddy, he was very naughty and I did suspect he was being unfaithful, not with a chap of course, but I think between us we could have found a suitable punishment, for him and that hateful Simon. All you had to do was tell me, not make it your personal mission to rid the world of Tenleys. Now we could both end up in jail and I for one don't fancy that, do you?" Again, Georgie threw the question back to Vanessa. It was the only way to get inside her head.

"I'm not concerned in the least. I won't be going to jail and neither will you. And why on earth would the police think I killed Sandy? She lived in the lap of luxury especially while we travelled, we brought her presents from all over the world and to top it off, I didn't even kick her out of bed and send her back to the servants' quarters when we returned. The police will think we are marvellous and Sandy was just a mad old lush."

Vanessa took a sip of water and then settled back into her chair and defence.

"As for Daddy and Granny, it was a spur of the moment thing. I had to act quickly, to prevent us being humiliated or in my case, exposed. I thought you'd be pleased that I used my initiative. I wanted to be like you; fiery and in control. You taught me to serve revenge cold and use a situation to my advantage, like at school with Jemima and her cronies. You can't blame me for following your lead and like I said, you should be grateful."

"I am, Vanessa, I am. Just rather shocked and disturbed by the thought of everything, not to mention a dead body floating in our pool, in fact it gives me the creeps."

"I don't care and to prove it, I'm going to go downstairs and make some supper. Would you like anything?"

"No, not for me, thank you, dear. I really couldn't eat a thing. I might be suffering from shock. All these revelations are playing havoc with my nerves. I'll just close my eyes and rest for a while. You go ahead."

Vanessa didn't need to be told twice and after pulling the covers over Georgie, who somehow resisted the urge to shrink away, Vanessa left the room, eager to get to the kitchen. Once the door closed, Georgie did in fact close her eyes in an attempt to shut out the horror. No matter how shell-shocked she was, now was the time to gather her wits and form a plan of action, weigh up her options and most of all, stay alive.

She began with Vanessa. How it crucified Georgie to realise the truth about the little girl she had loved unconditionally and saved from bullying at the hands of her grandmother and school friends. Georgie had accepted her and never judged her humble beginnings or attempted to change how she looked. Nevertheless she had turned out to be a monster. To have killed Daphne, even if it was just in temper, not premeditated or out of pure malice, must have damaged her in some way. Or had she always been evil and some genetic fault had fostered inherent wickedness. Maybe that was it. What if one of her natural parents had been bad, or mad, or both? Georgie shuddered.

Her next inclination was to pick up the phone and call the police but then what? If she told them that Vanessa had killed Sandy, it would open a huge can of worms, great monstrous things that would suck the life out of her marriage and bring shame on the man she loved. Would they believe that a little girl had killed her mother all those years earlier? Surely Vanessa would deny it. How could Georgie make them believe that Vanessa had killed Kenneth without exposing the reason why? The police would look for a motive and if they found out about Kenneth's plans, she might also be in the frame. That settled it. There was no way Georgie was going to tell them about Kenneth or be punished for Vanessa's crimes, both outcomes were unthinkable.

And what of her future? Georgie was virtually penniless. Vanessa had vowed to provide for her and at the first hint of betrayal would take revenge in the second-best way possible, eject her from Tenley then leave her to struggle alone. While Georgie considered this to be preferable to the first option, being murdered in her bed, the thought of life on the outside didn't appeal. To be without status and a home, having to start over or ask for favours from her impoverished band of friends was not something Georgie had imagined for the last years of her life, or how she would end it.

As the truth dawned on her predicament, Georgie was consumed by panic. She was trapped. It would all come down to Vanessa's word against hers and whilst she prided herself on her powers of persuasion and dramatic abilities, perhaps she was a mere understudy to the calculating she-devil who had fooled everyone for so long. It was the mention of satanic forces that reminded Georgie of something Phyllis used to say, that a demon visited her room and walked amongst them. And as much as she had despised the bitter old crone for much of the time, Georgie now felt some pity for Phyllis and accepted that she was right, there was a demon living inside Tenley. Her name was Vanessa.

It was 3am. Vanessa had returned after her feeding frenzy and refused to sleep. She insisted on keeping vigil beside Georgie who was unsure whether she was under observation or held prisoner. They were both counting down the hours until morning and a suitable time when the police could be called, and then the lies and fakery would begin. Until then, Georgie was trapped in a room with the demon who would not stop talking. Just when Georgie thought the nightmare could not get any worse, Vanessa decided to reminisce, talking of the good old days as though the bad ones had never existed.

After a while, Vanessa pulled her chair closer and nudged the bed, forcing Georgie to open her eyes from her pretend sleep. Focusing on Vanessa, whose piggy eyes were set in a face that resembled a lump of dough, Georgie thought it ironic to have never regarded her in this way, but she did now.

"Georgie, can I ask you a question? It's something I've always longed to know, say really."

"Yes of course, Vanessa, what is it?" From behind closed lids, Georgie had spent the last few hours turning everything over in her mind and didn't welcome the interruption but had no choice in the matter. This fact was becoming ever more clear.

"Why did you never ask me to call you Mummy?"

The question threw Georgie, more so because knowing the truth, it was the last thing she wanted to be called. "I've no idea, Vanessa. Perhaps because you never asked or indicated it was your wish."

"Oh it was. I so longed to call you Mummy. In fact for a long time I believed you truly were."

"Why on earth would you think that?"

"Because of my dream... Do you remember the Christmas party in the village when Dolly looked after me?"

"Yes, yes I do."

"You let me try Babycham and it was so lovely that once you left, I drank some more and got a bit tiddly and fell asleep. Later, I had the most wonderful dream that you came into my room and sat on the bed and spoke to me. I can remember every word of it. You said that you missed me and came to find me and that you would watch over me and keep me safe. You wanted to tell the world I was yours but they would send you away so it had to be our secret. You said, 'Mummy is here', and you'd never leave me again. When I woke up in the morning it felt so real and I was sure you'd been to see me in the night."

Georgie would have rolled her eyes had she not realised the danger in doing so and instead poured water on Vanessa's fanciful dream. "I'm sure it was a lovely dream but that's all it was. What on earth made you think it was me?"

"Because of the chocolates and the pretty dress. Don't you remember? I found some chocolate favours under my pillow and during breakfast you asked me if I'd found them and winked, then whispered it was a secret. I thought it was a special code, please tell me you remember."

Georgie didn't, then a faded memory returned, of her tiptoeing into Vanessa's room and slipping something under her pillow but she certainly hadn't whispered sweet nothings in her ear, why would she? Perhaps she'd told Vanessa to keep quiet to avoid a telling off from Sandy but that's all. "I'm sorry, Vanessa, but I really can't remember. Never mind, it's all in the past now."

"But what about the dress and the perfume? It had to be you." Vanessa was angry at her memory being dismissed and was determined to make her point.

"What dress, what perfume? I don't understand."

"You were wearing the pink dress, one of your favourites, with the organza overlay scattered with pearls and as you sat next to me, I could feel it scratching on my hand and the little pearls, and your perfume went up my nose, it was Chanel, you always wear it. Even though I was half asleep I remember every second." Vanessa was leaning forward, animated eager, desperate for Georgie to confirm her belief. It was never going to happen.

"Vanessa, dearest." How those words stuck in Georgie's throat. "Please stop this right now. I know you want to believe it was me but I assure it was just a dream, you were a little bit drunk and I was very naughty to give you Babycham but you need to put it out of your mind. Really, there are more pressing issues to think of." Georgie closed her eyes and blocked out the sullen dough ball who had slumped in her chair, bad temperedly tapping her foot.

How quickly though she bounced back and within seconds, Vanessa had resumed her position and asked yet another question.

"That might be by-the-by but my feelings remain the same and I still want to call you Mummy. There's no reason why I can't, you are my mother in name and everyone knows who you are so why not? From now on I'm going to call you Mummy, is that alright, would you mind?"

Georgie's eyes snapped open and looked into those of the demon. "Of course not, darling, why would I? You are my devoted daughter to whom I owe so much. It will be an honour. Now please, Vanessa, I need to sleep, remember what the doctor ordered. Tomorrow is going to be a trying day and we both should rest. Now I beg you, be quiet." Closing her eyes, Georgie tried hard not to scream.

Instead she focused her mind that was awash with memories of Christmas and Kenneth in his dinner jacket, and dear Dolly bringing her jellied eels that she couldn't do without, and Sandy attending her first Tenley bash. And then she remembered. She remembered it all so clearly. While her heart pounded in her chest and her head screamed the truth, one she was fighting hard not to hear or accept, Georgie travelled back to that evening, to her dressing room.

Sandy had knocked on the door and brought in Kenneth's shoes. He'd left them in the kitchen after giving them a quick polish and as Georgie turned, she surveyed their housekeeper and was dismayed by her appearance. Sandy was wearing a dowdy green dress and a gold cross and chain, her plain stockings and black shoes did nothing for her whatsoever and in that instant, Georgie flew into action, insisting she borrowed one of her dresses. The pink silk with overlaid organza and pearls had been hanging on the wardrobe door and admired earlier by Vanessa. Georgie had opted for the yellow full-length dress, it was sure to make a splash at the village hall. By the time she'd finished poo-poohing Sandy's protestations, Georgie was immensely pleased with the transformation and with a final flourish, sprayed a very liberal blast of Chanel all over the flustered housekeeper. Afterwards they all set off in a taxi but halfway through the night Sandy sloped off, she came home, probably to check on Vanessa.

Georgie lay motionless in her bed, regulating her breathing so that Vanessa would think she was sleeping and not be alerted to her distress. Inside, Georgie's body flowed with a noxious mixture of nausea and molten lava, fear hovering on the surface like a mist, her body going from hot to cold, panic to numbness. Dear God it was all so obvious, so hideously painfully clear.

From a distant buried memory had come clarity and truth. Sandy, poor, poor, Sandy, who lay floating in the pool downstairs, was Vanessa's mother. Somehow she had found her child and lived side by side, watching over her, keeping her safe, yet always on the outside. A sob hurtled up from Georgie's throat and almost escaped her mouth which she masked with a cough, then gathered herself and forced the next one down.

Peeping through tired, burning eyes, Georgie saw that Vanessa had finally gone to sleep in the chair, and it crossed Georgie's mind that had she the energy and the guts she would have taken a pillow and given the demon a taste of its own medicine. But there had been enough death under this roof and she might be many things, but Georgie wasn't a murderer... not in the biblical sense. Instead, using her wiles and whatever gumption remained, she would have to think of another way to punish Vanessa, fight fire with fire, just as something that crawled up from hell might expect.

Georgie needed to think and as the clock ticked and the demon snored she spent the rest of the night deep in thought.

By the time the clock struck seven and a shaft of light could be seen through the crack in the curtains, Georgie had her answer and knew exactly what she must do.

Chapter 29

Georgie

Once Georgie worked it out, or more to the point how to punish Vanessa, the rest was easy. It had been a living purgatory but she endured. The end game was her only goal in which she was determined to be the victor. All it took was a little planning and fortitude along with latent acting skills, but she was able to pull the wool over Vanessa's eyes and hide her true intentions in plain sight. Vanessa may have been a willing and devoted student who thought she had graduated from the school of deception with honour but Georgie was the master, and had a final lesson to teach. She began the very next morning.

Leaving Georgie with firm instructions to remain upstairs and feign illness, Vanessa had gone downstairs to prepare for her charades. She had waited until Mrs Coombs arrived and the plan was simple – they would fall upon the debris in the kitchen and then the body, together. It was such a blessed relief to be left alone for the first time in hours, but Georgie had no time to languish so dragged herself from her sick bed and hurried to Sandy's bedroom. Apart from the opulent furnishings there wasn't much to see, or search through, because Sandy's belongings, whilst orderly, were meagre and uncovered nothing of use. This led Georgie upstairs, an arduous task thanks to her drug-soaked body held up by weak legs, all the time listening out for footsteps, confident that Vanessa would be occupied elsewhere.

It didn't take long for Georgie to find what she was looking for. It was hidden at the bottom of Sandy's old wardrobe under a pile of neatly folded blankets but Georgie knew it would be there somewhere. Instinct told her that if Sandy had prevailed for so many years there would be some clue, even a tiny shred of proof to confirm Georgie's suspicions. After removing the small rather tatty suitcase, Georgie opened it briefly and after casting her eyes over the contents and sure there were no other hiding places secreting treasure, she descended as quickly as possible. With a pounding heart, she paused at the top of the stairs, catching her breath before scurrying back to her room, desperate to investigate the contents of the case but wary of being discovered.

Instead, Georgie waited for the wail of sirens and the inevitable commotion downstairs, to be questioned by the police who were told a story identical to the one concocted and repeated verbatim by Vanessa. They searched Sandy's bedroom along the corridor for a suicide note and also her old room on the top floor but found nothing of interest. Poor Mrs Coombs was distraught and after speaking to the police handed in her notice on the spot. It had all been too much, decades of death at Tenley, so she picked up her handbag and marched off down the drive, never to return.

The Coroner's report recorded death by misadventure. Poor Sandy was labelled as a troubled drunk which was inevitable after Vanessa's tearful but damning evidence. Once the delivery boy and the village policeman's wife spread their own version of events, the rumour mill consigned the whole affair to the Tenley Curse. And just as Georgie suspected, everyone felt so sorry for poor Vanessa who was left all alone in the big house with her sickly stepmother to care for, and with such selfless dedication. It made Georgie so angry, to think of Vanessa being painted as a sad but saintly figure. Nevertheless, once the dust died down and the floating housekeeper was chip paper, Georgie got on with the task of living life, honouring the memory of her dear darling Kenneth and punishing a wicked demon.

Her health never really recovered and a more fragile person would have been devoured by their nerves and conscience but not Georgie. Instead she rose to the challenge and whilst her body didn't always play ball, her mind was more than ready for a game of mental cricket and her favourite opponent was an unsuspecting Vanessa.

To begin with they struck a bargain. They would never ever talk again of the secret, it was too risky and one slip could have landed them both in jail. In reality, Georgie could not bear to hear of it or listen to the demon as she gloated. Yet despite her solid conviction that she'd got away with it, Vanessa feared arrest and imprisonment most of all. Perhaps it was a result of Georgie's inference that she would starve to death on prison food and that some of the inmates would have her for dinner, in more ways than one. This acerbic notion was then sweetened by Georgie's tearful lapses where she would speak of her terror at the idea of Vanessa's incarceration or being left alone in the world, unable to countenance an existence without Vanessa by her side. In truth, what Georgie actually feared was the notion of being in an adjoining cell or worse, sharing one with a demon. Nevertheless, each ghastly scenario ensured Vanessa's silence and compliance.

Georgie knew that Vanessa was quite mad and had she been so inclined would have sought information to confirm her status as a psychopath. Preferring to sleep at night, she chose to spare herself the details but bearing the possibility in mind, Georgie handled Vanessa carefully. It wasn't difficult and meant nothing more than treating her as she did during childhood, indulging, cosseting and making her the focus of attention but this time, to the exclusion of all others.

It was easy to convince Vanessa that apart from new staff to maintain the house, they were a team, just the two of them, and she loved it. Soon Vanessa sought no other counsel than Georgie's and slowly abandoned her hanger-on friends. And while Georgie thought she'd sometimes go silently mad, she endured. It was easy to lose oneself in a book, film or play, become immersed in music and memories while marking time, waiting to be reunited with loved ones.

During her period of living with a lunatic, it was also important to maintain the upper hand which Georgie did by reinforcing her position as mother. Vanessa absolutely loved this, along with calling her Mummy. To begin with Georgie's heart lurched each time she uttered the word but after time got used to it. It was just a six-letter title that meant nothing at all, not to her. Georgie took the lead in everything, subtly, by means of a hint or suggestion, hence Vanessa believed she was pleasing her beloved mother. On other occasions, she was downright demanding, playing the drama queen, the crazy pragmatic Georgie of old that Vanessa remembered from her rose-tinted childhood. Apart from holding the reins, it was imperative to not anger the demon – thus being murdered in her bed.

At the beginning, Georgie didn't have a firm plan, it built slowly. The only thing she did know for sure was that she had to find out as much as she could about Sandy. Georgie had felt such despair when she opened Sandy's suitcase. The contents broke her heart. After waiting until she knew Vanessa was gone for the day, on an errand into town that Georgie was too weak to run herself, she took the case from the wardrobe and placed it on her bed. Her hands shook terribly as she unzipped the lid and removed the photo album from the top. The moment she turned the first page, Georgie knew she was vindicated in her intrusion because there it was, a faded black and white photograph of Vanessa and her very young mother, Sandy. The snaps that followed, of Vanessa's first few years had obviously been taken from the Tenley album but later, after the arrival of Sandy, Georgie realised she had lovingly collated her own history, taking photos of her child and here and there were some of them together.

At the back of the album, she found a number of items placed under the plastic protector. Bus and rail tickets from a town in Yorkshire, destination Bournemouth, and postcards showing a large cliff top hotel. Georgie suspected these were part of a trail, the provenance of Sandy's life and her journey to Tenley. There was also a large brown envelope and inside a birth certificate belonging to an Ivy Emsworth and a change of name deed. From these Georgie gleaned that not only had Sandy created a new identity, she must have been around eighteen when she had Vanessa. Next, Georgie found the jewel in the crown, the clue that led Sandy to her child, an article torn from a magazine showing Daphne and Kenneth with their adopted baby girl.

Without haste and with utmost secrecy, Georgie enlisted the services of a private detective who earned his fee well. It didn't take him too long to retrace Sandy's steps to her hometown where he managed to unearth the saddest story, the reason why she left everything behind. There were plenty of old souls who were around at the time of a great scandal and eager to relate the tale which he noted and reported back to Georgie.

Sent first to a mother and baby home, Sandy returned briefly and once she had punished those responsible, ran away and never went back. News got out of the headmaster's dismissal after the Board of Governors and the Parish Council received a handwritten letter, exposing how he raped his stepdaughter and impregnated her with a child she was forced to give up. His wife went into rapid decline after reading her own truth and reeling under their public shame and vilification, all of which ended in divorce. He was never prosecuted since Ivy had disappeared, leaving both mother and stepfather to see their days out in council care homes. Georgie was horrified by Sandy's story which made her even more determined to ensure Vanessa suffered a similar or worse fate to her wicked grandparents.

In the meantime, Georgie suffered Vanessa's lapses when the she-devil could not be subdued. It was as though a switch flicked inside her brain whenever she felt denied or obstructed, threatened or patronised. There had been some terrible moments in restaurants and stores when her rage at being served the wrong change, or a dish that was too cold, too spicy or too paltry had erupted into a tsunami. Such shameful behaviour always reminded Georgie to beware because inside Vanessa lurked something manifestly evil. Georgie had no desire to die at the hands of the demon which was why, for as long as it was feasible, she slept with the light on and her door locked.

Life wasn't without its trials and rather frightening moments when the floorboards creaked outside her bedroom door and keeping such a tight grip on Vanessa was trying, as was living such a lie, but it was worth it. While their peers still walked the earth, Georgie vowed to protect Kenneth's name and good character, just as he had done hers. It was to remain her secret, that the marriage she held so dear was a sham and nor would anyone look down their noses, or with pity. Not in her lifetime. However, once she was gone Georgie would care not of gossip and pride and this notion spurred her on.

Georgie made it her mission to live the life that Kenneth promised, either with or without him. She would not be ejected from her home, die in poverty or shame. She was Lady Georgina Tenley and would be so until the day she died. To this end and another, Georgie set about spending as much of Vanessa's fortune as she could. Whether it was living a wonderfully luxurious life to encouraging one of philanthropy, becoming the patron of local charities and donating to whatever disaster fund they advertised on television, Georgie led the way.

There was always some function or other the merry widow and her spinster daughter could attend and there Georgie danced and laughed, smoked and drank to excess. But when she fell into bed, alone, her tears would be for Kenneth. There had been admirers along the way but none of them tempted Georgie, nobody could, not while she still held a torch for a ghost and there was something else, a portent of doom that held her back. Even if after all that time she did meet a suitable chap, Georgie was loathe to place him in danger, in the glare of a jealous demon.

Still, her perseverance began to pay off and it was shocking how much money one could get through if you set your mind to it. In recent years and months, dear Mr Harcourt had been a frequent visitor, becoming more agitated and exasperated at each appointment. Vanessa's accountant had done his best to reign in her spending but to no avail and as much as Georgie suggested she took heed, it seemed her high-rolling ways had rubbed off on her daughter. Vanessa's desire to emulate and please Georgie knew no bounds. Land had to be sold off and owing to the state of the economy, her stocks and shares soon dwindled, as did the size of her bank balance. Without the means or staff at their disposal, Tenley fell into a state of disrepair, as did Georgie.

The Harley Street quack did a sterling job of not saying 'I told you so' but inevitably fifty cigarettes a day and living life to the full soon took their toll. Once the cancer in her chest took hold, it rampaged through Georgie's body and soon she was firmly within its grasp. Vanessa refused to believe the prognosis and as a consequence, they spent almost four years visiting American and Swiss clinics being sold futile alternative cures. While the patient allowed the infusions of vitamin C and spent hours in oxygen tanks, and as Vanessa wrote another fat cheque, Georgie smiled and looked forward to the end game.

While she would have preferred never to return to Tenley again and take her last breath in some private hospice, Georgie had to be close to her hidden treasure. It was blatantly obvious to everyone except Vanessa that even a trip to Lourdes wasn't going to do the trick so after pleading to be allowed to die in her own home, they headed back, medical entourage in tow.

The time had almost come for Georgie to depart the world, she knew that, but before slipping into a semi-conscious state controlled by diamorphine and due to incapacity, the whims and delusional mind of Vanessa, Georgie had put her affairs in order. With the help of her solicitor, Georgie was ready to serve her revenge, stone bloody cold.

If by virtue of her own testimony, Vanessa managed to stay out of jail, an outcome that would depend entirely on lack of evidence and her ability to appear sane, Georgie had a final hand to play. Imagining Vanessa under intense interrogation and suspicion, drinking water from a plastic cup as she lied her way out of trouble, gave Georgie a small amount of pleasure. The secondary outcome, of her living in a ruin of a house, penniless and alone with only ghosts and her conscience for company, was eclipsed by one single notion. If all else failed, the truth about Sandy was to be Vanessa's final punishment. More than anything, Georgie hoped and wished that murdering her very own mother and being betrayed by her beloved stepmother would send the demon of Tenley completely and utterly mad.

Chapter 30

Tenley House

Present Day

It is time. I cannot wait any longer and the nurse has given me what I know will be my last infusion of the elixir of death, or freedom, whichever way you wish to look at it. The doctor has placed his stethoscope on my chest and listened to the death knell of my slowing heart, and I don't need to hear the words. I can see the truth in his manner, that shake of the head as he gives the nurse one of those looks. They forget, don't they, that I am an actress and can read them like a script.

I am alone. The nurse has gone to summon Vanessa. My hand rests upon the suitcase which the nurse fetched from the wardrobe and placed beside me on the bed. On top sits a letter. I wrote it before the chemotherapy burned away my nerve endings and prevented me from feeling my fingertips. I am pleased with its contents, confident that my words will convey my true feelings. It would be impossible to explain everything to Vanessa out loud. I am far too weak and have not the energy for speaking or interruptions and this way, I can sit in the stalls and watch the performance where tonight, my stepdaughter, the little demon of Tenley, has a starring role.

My breath is shallow and for a moment I feel the swell of panic, not at the notion of death but of missing out on playing my final part, just a small cameo really but one I shall enjoy, as will my guests who as expected have arrived for the show. I move my head slowly and see them so clearly. There he is, my husband, waiting patiently. But it is not him I seek so I cast my eyes along the row, past Daphne and the Crone until Sandy steps forward holding the baby who is thankfully asleep. I do not want interruptions during my swan song. Our eyes meet briefly but our clairvoyant communication is interrupted by the sound of the door handle turning slowly and footsteps, heavy on the wooden floor before they are absorbed into the wool of the rug.

Here she is, my bête noire, rushing around the bed to take a seat by my side, her eyes awash with tears which she dabs with her handkerchief. It is clear the doctor has told her the news and she is here to say goodbye. For some reason, I have the urge to laugh as the strangest idea has just popped into this drug-drenched brain. It is one of Vanessa having me preserved in a glass case, the haggard Sleeping Beauty, or maybe stuffed like one of Kenneth's wild beasts that hang in his study. He would find that amusing, as do I. How odd, to conjure mirth from such a dire situation so I force myself into civility and focus on my final task. Coughing slightly, I clear my throat and taking a very shallow breath, step out from the wings and onto the stage.

"Vanessa… there is something I need to give you before I go. Here, take this letter and read it."

"Please, Mummy. Don't say that… you're going to be fine, just rest. That's all you need."

"No, Vanessa, it's time so please, do… as… I… ask."

It exhausts me to speak and I so wish she would hurry as the light is fading, the edges of the room swirl and I feel as though I am looking down a tunnel and all I can see is Vanessa who is thankfully opening the letter. She is starting to read. Good. I know every word that is written and while I watch her eyes move upon each of them, I recite the message in my head.

Vanessa,

Before you read on, I want you to know that despite what is to follow, that in the beginning I did love you, I truly did, unconditionally and with all of my heart. I never judged or attempted to change you and tried so hard to shield you from the pain of the past.

I did my best to be a good mother and your friend. But I was ignorant of the truth, with not the slightest inclination of the monster within or that you were capable of such wicked acts. This knowledge not only broke my heart but killed any love I ever felt for you. I was left with nothing more than the desire to seek revenge. You see, Vanessa, you took away the one thing I treasured most in this world, you murdered my husband. When you snuffed out his life, you did the same to my soul because even if Kenneth had left me, I would have had him in my life, he would have still been my friend, my one true love.

I knew all about his nature, of course I did, and had he wanted to be free I would have let him go. It was a promise we made to each other at the beginning. So while you thought you were saving me, us, all you did was exterminate our relationship, you severed our bond. In that swift act of revenge, you lost both father and mother because I never forgave you and never will.

To this end I have spent the last years of my life trapped in a lie, one in which every moment with you has been torment. I vowed to avenge Kenneth's death and take from you everything you held dear, your money and home – even your happy memories.

This illness which eats me alive has been my ally and will release me from the hell of life on earth with you.

A letter resides with my solicitor which documents your confession and heinous acts and will be given to the police on my death. It will be my word against yours but I hope it is enough to cast suspicion. Maybe they will presume they are the ramblings of a bitter old woman and you will remain free. Or maybe they will see you for what you are, a deranged, cruel murderer.

I have told them everything because the exposure of your father's nature and our marital arrangement is of little consequence to me anymore, I preserved it whilst I lived but the only thing I care about now is serving you a very cold portion of revenge.

Do you remember I used to tell you it was the best way? Well, Vanessa, I have had this on ice for a while and it is my parting gift to you.

Inside the suitcase lies the truth, of who you are and what you have done, the demon you have become. It's all there in black and white, everything you need to confirm that your father was a perverted rapist who defiled his stepdaughter. The rest of the tale is quite tragic.

From somewhere deep within, this poor young woman, whose mother sent her away, who never sought to comfort or seek her out, to apologise or make things right, found the strength to search for her baby girl. She never stopped loving her, she never gave in.

But do you know what the saddest part is, Vanessa? That after everything she suffered and even after finding her little girl, watching on as another woman took all the glory and love, in the end, she was let down, betrayed once again by the person she cherished most in the world.

Have you worked it out yet, Vanessa, have you realised who sat on your bed and whispered in your ear?

It was Sandy.

Dear sweet Sandy was your mother and you killed her. You pushed her into the cold water, held her down and watched her drown .For this and so many other things, I hope you are punished, in this world or the next but until then, I want your soul to torment your mind, day and night, every second of every day. It is all that you deserve.

Open the case and cast your eyes on the truth, the proof you need, your shame.

It is my parting gift to you.

There is nothing more to say, I have served my revenge and now I can go.

Goodbye, Vanessa,
Georgie.

Her hands are shaking. In between reading the words, she glances up at me, those beady eyes of coal, Satan's fuel, boring right inside my head. I do not fear her anymore and even if she pounces and as I have feared for so long, covers my face with the pillow, I will not fight it.

She has reached the end and flings my letter to the floor then stands and grabs the case, grappling with the zip. I feel the lid hit my hip as it is flung open. I watch intently although I can barely focus. I am drifting into sleep or death but I cling on. She is opening the album and turning the page.

There is silence, just for a second, and then she screams, pulling at her hair and now she is dragging out the contents of the large brown envelope. The screaming intensifies as the truth, the provenance of Sandy's life drops to the floor, like scattered pages of retribution.

I close my eyes. Now I can rest. It is done.

Epilogue

I open my eyes slowly as if from the deepest dream and for the first time in an age, I feel happy. The weight that rested in my heart for so long has gone. I am lying on the top of my bed, I must have had a nap, and as I take in the room I see it is bathed in a warm glow. The swirling patterns on the wallpaper, reds and golds, are bright and vibrant and mimic how I feel, alive.

Rising, I notice that my body and bones are no longer weary and stiff. I am light as a feather, almost gliding, gracefully towards the mirror where I gaze upon my image and smile. I look marvellous. My hair is set and my make-up is perfect even though I say so myself, and my darling heels match perfectly my gown, Dior if I'm not mistaken. In the midst of my self-appreciation, I am aware of being observed and turn slowly and there she is, dear Sandy holding the baby.

She smiles nervously and gestures that I should come and look, which I do. He is a darling little cherub, snug in his knitted blue layette, sleeping peacefully. Sandy holds out her arms, offering me my child and I see nervousness in her eyes, a trace of sadness and a hint of love. I place my hand on her arm to decline and in that moment she knows. He is a gift, mine to give, from one mother to another. He will be safe with Sandy. Of this I have no doubt.

I am distracted once again by a sound, a gentle humming and a bright white light that shines from within the dressing room. I follow the tune and push open the door, my giddy heart on fire as I search him out. There he is, trying to fasten his bow tie in the mirror but when he sees me he stops and turns. I walk over to him, and our eyes and lips smile as I fold the silk into place. Once he is smart I stand back and admire my handsome husband who holds out his hand.

It is a moment I have longed for, waiting an eternity to feel the warmth of his skin and see such love in his eyes. He places a gentle kiss on my cheek before offering his arm which I take.

Stepping forward into the light, I am aglow, my soul at peace and my heart has never known such happiness because tonight I am going dancing, with my one true love, my dear darling Kenneth.

The End

Acknowledgements

Thank you for reading Death's Dark Veil and I hope you enjoyed the story as much as I loved writing it. I would also like to thank a few more people who helped along the way to produce the book.

First is Alexina whose insightful suggestions were invaluable in the early stages as was her belief and encouragement. To Heather, Mandy, Susan and Angela who read early copies and patiently listened to my questions and gave great feedback. Thank you to Morgen for her superb editing skills plus the smiley faces and ticks in the margin. Thanks to Abbie for proofreading and the wonderful Bloodhound team Sumaira, Betsy, Fred and Tara who do their magic behind the scenes and support me every step of the way. A special mention has to go to my ARC group of readers who have been brilliant and given their time and support, you are truly wonderful. To all the loyal readers who buy my books, write reviews, get in touch and become friends, I appreciate each and every one of you.

Finally and as always I want to thank my family for being the best cheerleaders, who love, support and encourage me. You are my world.

Lightning Source UK Ltd.
Milton Keynes UK
UKHW041837070319
338688UK00001B/2/P